A YOUNG MAN DREAMED OF SUCCESS...
AND A BEAUTIFUL WOMAN TAUGHT HIM
THE MEANING OF THAT WORD...

Lucille Morgan looked down, then walked slowly to the window. The words of L.J. Hays had hurt her and he knew it. His remark was spurred by envy, he knew. It was mean. He regretted it immediately.

"Please forgive me," he whispered to her. "I'm discouraged and running out of money."

"Tell me what you think it is like to be rich," she demanded. "Tell me about wealth."

"You're making fun of me," L.J. responded, irritated.

"No, I'm not. Come here."

L.J. stood and moved slowly toward her.

"Being rich means having the sting removed, L.J. It means having things . . . no, *assuming* things will, ultimately, be just fine. Being rich turns life into a game, since, after all, nothing very important can really happen."

He thought he heard a sadness in her voice, a weary regret. He looked at her. Tears fell from her eyes.

"When I win, I will let you know." It was a feeble attempt at humor, his best attempt to end the conversation that had clearly upset her.

"Hush," she sighed, tears still glistening on her cheeks. She took his hand in hers and brought it to her lips. Lucille kissed his fingertips gently. "Now, before the sun sets," she whispered, and led him to her bed. . . .

# RAILROAD KING

**PAUL ROTHWEILER**

A Dell/Banbury Book

Published by
Banbury Books, Inc.
37 West Avenue
Wayne, Pennsylvania 19087

Copyright © 1981 by Paul Rothweiler

All rights reserved. No part of this book may be
reproduced in any form or by any means without the
prior written permission of the Publisher,
excepting brief quotes used in connection
with reviews written specifically for inclusion
in a magazine or newspaper.

Dell ® TM 681510, Dell Publishing Co., Inc.
ISBN: 0-440-07392-8
Printed in the United States of America
First printing—September 1981

# PART I
# BEGINNINGS

# Chapter 1

*St. Paul, Minnesota Territory, 1857*

L.J. Hays watched broad shoulders wade through the frigid night air as the banker marched ahead of him. He felt like a skiff in tow, hustling behind his massive host, afraid to lose him in the crowds on the city's main street. Snowflakes sifted past lights from the few illuminated windows along their route and the wind blew straight at the pair. They plodded, leaning into the bitter-cold gusts coming off the northern plains. L.J. shivered, his slim frame stooped, bandy legs churning and thin coat useless in the cold. But, despite the icy air at his face, he kept his head up, straining through tearing eyes to keep the huge sable collar of Williams' coat in sight.

Hays was intimidated by Williams. The sheer size and ruddy good looks of the banker were enough to overwhelm the thin young man. But more important, Williams possessed an unabashed, outspoken arrogance that echoed in Hays' mind whenever he heard the banker speak. Williams seemed to have been blessed with absolute certainty: simple, clear, almost glib, self-confidence. Hays wondered to himself, as he fingered the hole in his coat pocket, how Williams managed it.

The banker seemed to honestly believe that his life was an irresistible force bound for untold wealth.

At last they arrived at the Riverboat Saloon, St. Paul's largest emporium for drinking and gambling. An old and rugged building, it had stood in the middle of town since the days when St. Paul was still known as "Pig's Eye." Hays glanced at Williams as the banker gestured him inside.

"Get in, L.J.," Williams ordered. "The knife in this February air is likely to cut that coat of yours to ribbons."

L.J. nodded and hurried into the saloon.

"Oughta get yourself some winterized-type protection, son," the banker chuckled, clapping his gloved hands together.

L.J. quickly fell in behind Williams once again as they made their way to the back of the saloon. Merchants and workmen waved to the banker and occasionally one would pump his arm in a vigorous handshake, as though congratulating him on his existence. Williams clearly enjoyed the attention and took his time working his way toward the table in the shadows beyond.

Hays, his hands still buried in his coat, felt sweat forming on his palms. He was about to play cards with rich poker players. It was a stupid thing to do, he knew. He could ill afford even modest losses. But the almost unearthly power that Williams exuded fascinated and terrified the young shipping clerk. The clamor in his veins, the sting of itching joints somehow set awry by the influence of those he would soon meet, compelled him.

Watch carefully, Reverend, Hays thought to himself. He wiped the sweat from his hands, preparing to greet his fellow players.

Hays was introduced, but no one paid much attention to him. The men sitting around the large table were as indifferent to him as they were oblivious to the cold whistling through cracks in the walls. Their interest was concentrated on the playing cards in their hands and the money anted in the center of the table.

L.J. Hays was a Scottish-Canadian who clerked for the St. Paul Shipping Company, a firm that operated a number of steamships on the Mississippi between St. Paul and New Orleans. While making his small but regular deposit in Williams' bank, L.J. had found himself invited to play cards. He had tried to decline the invitation but the banker had insisted. "Lord, boy," he'd chided, "everybody's got to play one kind of game or another." Hays, piqued by the banker's constant use of some diminutive—"boy," "son" or "young man"—had decided he would risk the encounter. But he informed Williams he could play for only a while.

Hays stuffed his hands back into his coat and stared at the money in the pot. He wondered to himself if he could stand one hand at such high stakes.

"I've never played for money like this before, Mr. Williams," L.J. muttered.

"Sit down, L.J.," the banker barked, a condescending order, ignoring Hays' remark.

Not wishing to appear a fool, Hays took the seat across the table from the banker and fumbled in his shirt pocket for the spending money he'd brought with him for the occasion. It had been some time since he'd played poker, but he was familiar enough with the game. And his mind, accustomed to the complex world of variable freight rates and schedules, manipulated figures with staggering speed. L.J. Hays could hold the most complicated numerical considerations in his mind, compare and alter them, discard and select from among them, almost by instinct. It was, in fact, an awesome kind of agility that he wasn't quite sure he understood.

After an hour of play Hays had begun to assemble a feeling for the game that made him comfortable. The relationships between the personal wealth of the men involved, the pattern of their bets and the cards they were dealt seemed consistent to him. Thus, the men began to appear predictable. He could see in their actions quantifiable trends, palpable indicators of what they held hidden in their hands and what they intended to do with their money.

Having deduced the ebb and flow of personality that was taking place inside the card game, L.J. began to win. Not long after, he had doubled, and then redoubled, his meager stake. Some of the other players then offered Williams their slightly drunken thanks for having brought the "young fella" along. And they needled the banker whenever L.J. managed to lighten the wealthy man's considerable load of silver and gold coin. Williams grew more and more annoyed as the evening wore on.

Across the game room from the poker table sat Tim Wolfe, Hays' fellow clerk at the shipping company. He was sitting with Hildy May Hawkins, the handsome sister of the saloon's owner. Wolfe was two years older than Hays, but looked much more mature. Tim was a native of the American Northwest, well over six feet tall, his hair yellow and shaggy. A good-humored sort, he had the gleaming eyes of a prankster and the quick laugh of a man who took life as it came. On this particular evening, life had delivered Tim the impressive figure of Hildy May and he was enjoying her flirtations to the fullest. Only when the girl left to serve drinks to a table of locals did Tim glance over to see how his friend Hays was doing. After two hours of play he was astonished to see a mountain of cash in front of the young clerk. Grinning, he picked up his mug of beer and sauntered over to watch the proceedings.

The game had grown deadly serious. While L.J. had given the players a laugh with his early, tentative betting, they had grown less and less amused with time. Only Hays was ahead of the game and two of the men, including Williams, had lost a lot of money to him.

It was cool in the room in spite of the heat generated by the large wood stove in the corner. But L.J. felt neither warmth nor chill. His body seemed numbed by the weight of concentration he applied to his hand. Silent, he was apparently unflinching, but inside he churned. In front of him sat a pile of cash that would add up to more than a month's pay. No small sum, even to Williams.

The banker dealt three cards to each player with the quick moves of a man made impatient by continued bad luck. Wagers circled the table and soon there was a stack of money in the pot. Since the game was seven-card stud, Williams' two aces showed, and betting heavily he forced a number of other players to fold their hands. L.J. showed a pair of kings.

Suddenly Williams raised twice before calling. He had a pair of nines tucked under. L.J. wondered if the banker had another ace concealed in his hand. The only beer that had been delivered to L.J. during the evening sat warm, flat and untouched on the table. Staring into it he recalled an ace that had been dealt to one of the players who had dropped out of the hand early. His mind rattled through the probability of Williams' holding all three remaining aces. There were three ways to look at the question, each mathematically more remote than the last.

Williams dealt the last face-down card to complete the hand. The only other man remaining in the game with Hays and the banker cursed as he looked at his last card. L.J. felt Williams' eyes on him as he fixed his expression as best he could and peeked at his own last card. A king. He held a full house. L.J. tilted his head, feigning a sort of perplexed curiosity about the quality of his own hand and looked at Williams. His ruddy face was furrowed and he had yet to even look at his seventh card.

The banker bet his aces—twenty dollars falling to the table—and the bet caused the third man to fold his cards and throw them into the pot. Williams, his gray eyes glinting in the light, watched Hays as though he were a bird of prey studying a stranded rodent.

"Up to you, boy," he challenged.

The onlookers chuckled, apparently certain Williams had at least three aces, perhaps backed by a pair. His calm demeanor and flamboyant betting seemed to indicate as much.

L.J. felt the room closing around him and heard his friend Tim Wolfe clear his throat, an obvious tip to fold and walk away. But though the young clerk was not as old as his rival, who was nine years and hundreds of poker games his senior, he felt impelled to see Williams' raise. The seventh card, the one the banker had not yet bothered to look at, stuck in his mind. Too confident, he thought to himself. A bluff.

"Your twenty dollars, Mr. Williams," Hays now said with a slight smile, "and fifty dollars more."

Even though he was aware of the clamminess of his palms, L.J. felt a certain satisfaction when the raise forced Williams to pick up his three hole cards, including the one he had been ignoring, and shuffle them slowly. Williams' eyes dropped and he scanned the cards one by one, looking for the stranger. When he saw it, a small smile touched his mouth for just a second.

The powerful man had either done the wrong thing at the right time or was trying to force Hays into withdrawing. He had bet without the hole card but was now happy to see it. L.J. watched as the banker made a show of pushing fifty dollars into the center to see the raise. Then the banker added a hundred more. Tim Wolfe coughed again. L.J. decided. He was being bought.

Still, the young clerk had a problem. He had only fifty dollars left on the table—all the money he had with him. And he had resolved not to invade his growing account at the bank in order to stay in the game. He looked at his hand, three kings and a pair of nines.

"Well, young fellow," the banker said, running his hand through his chestnut hair, "do what you want, but do it soon, for others are standing in line to use the outhouse."

The reference to either employing or releasing the pot wasn't lost on L.J. In response, he picked up his own hole cards and began shuffling them slowly, one by one as the banker had done. He felt a cool trickle of sweat run down his side. When at last he took his eyes from the cards, he could clearly see that the banker was a trifle angry. L.J. sighed, trying to mimic what he imagined to be the sound of a weary, experienced cardsharp proceeding toward the inevitable. He pushed his last fifty dollars into the center of the table. "I'm short fifty to call, Mr. Williams," he said, "but I've enough in your bank to cover the other fifty and the hundred I want to raise you."

The banker's head jerked in surprise. "Wait a damn minute!" he croaked. "If you don't have it on the table, Hays, you'll have to . . ."

"Come on now, Ben," broke in one of the other players. "You can't push this kid and then close the door on him. Especially if his marker is covered by an account in your own bank. And I gotta believe you know just what he's got in there, too." L.J. smiled at this not-so-playful kibitzing by Williams' friend.

Williams was fuming, but cornered. He shot the onlooker a nasty glare, but said to Hays, "Very well, boy. I ought to raise you back, but since I do know how much you have in my bank, I'd be taking unfair advantage of you, so I'll just call. Show your cards."

L.J. felt a rush of blood pouring through his veins. He had overstepped his limits; he was exhilarated. He barely managed, in a raspy voice, to say, "Full house, kings over nines." He turned over his hole cards.

Williams' thick eyebrows shot up in surprise. "Well, I'll be damned!" He was clearly stunned. "I didn't figure . . ." He looked at Hays and shook his head.

As L.J. gathered in his winnings, he couldn't resist. "You should have known, sir, that I had a strong hand. I don't have enough experience with the game of poker to actually bluff." Those in the room boomed with laughter, and a stormy stare knifed across the table from Williams. The banker rose, stuffed the remainder of his money into the pocket of his elegant blue business suit, dropped his overcoat over his arm and stalked away.

"Hey, L.J.," Tim Wolfe cried. "I don't believe

that banker appreciates the lesson you taught him." His voice was boisterous, slightly drunken, ready for celebration. Hays concealed his pleasure, quieting his friend with a stern look. With Williams out, the game broke up and L.J. made his way over to Tim and Hildy May.

"How much you win?" Tim asked, still too loud.

Hays shrugged, then smiled. "Six hundred fifty dollars."

"Say, that's a potful. A few more games like that and you'll own that boat you been dreamin' on."

L.J. grinned and then absent-mindedly sipped at his beer. It was warm, nearly rancid and brought a twisted grimace to the clerk's lips. Tim thought his expression hysterical, and said so. But Hays didn't care. His mind pictured a steamship, or even a small, shallow-draft mountain boat, with the name *Hays Forwarding* emblazoned across its bow.

"There's money to be made with boats, Tim. Lots of it."

"Yeah, well, the way you play cards you're likely to end up with a fleet of 'em."

"Mr. Williams pushed me too hard, Tim, that's all. He wanted to beat *me* more than he wanted to *win*. He has the money to do the job, and, all things considered, his cards were all right this evening. But he pushed too hard." L.J. seemed ready to elaborate, but didn't. Dark patches of perspiration showed below his armpits and he had the look of a tired man.

"Whatever the cause, L.J., you won. And I'll wager there'll be some boat of yours to ship out on sooner than not."

Hays brightened perceptibly at this remark. "Will you come to work for me when I get it?" he asked.

"You're a confident man, L.J. And I'm no fool.

When there's a thing that floats with your name on it, I'll sail it where you aim it." Tim grinned, his enthusiasm bubbly, infectious, delightful.

"All I need is a boat and a few freight contracts . . ." Hays was once again the serious, ruminating clerk. ". . . but I'll find them somehow."

Tim pulled Hildy May onto his lap. His chin dropped to his chest in a not-so-surreptitious effort to ogle the girl's cleavage. Noticing, she pushed him away. "You men," she muttered, flattered by his attentions. "There's only one thing you ever think about." Tim kissed her broadly, making his friend turn away, face reddening. L.J. had always been too busy studying to become very involved with women. His aunt and the teacher she had hired kept him busy with everything from Greek to *Pilgrim's Progress*. And neither his aunt nor academic pursuits had taught him much about the softer sex. His only dream, a shady fantasy shrouded in mist, was of an Oriental woman greeting his ship as it sailed into a Far Eastern port. But it was an illusion, an imagining based more on power and wealth, on travel and adventure, than on a fair lady's beauty. She was not so much a woman to be desired as the emblem of an ambition to be gone after. She was impossible, and so infinitely desirable to Hays.

Hays, in fact, had found his way to St. Paul as he was wandering across America on his way to the Orient. He was fascinated by the thought of the East, by its remoteness. He'd once idly considered hiring himself onto a ship bound from San Francisco to Japan, thinking his fortune lay beyond the sea. But the river trade that ebbed and flowed through the American Northwest and the great human migrations out of Canada west of the Great Lakes had caught his attention. Huge tracts of open land, multitudes of people and rivers that seemed to serve—all arrested him. What's more, by the time he arrived in St. Paul he had only ten dollars to his name. So he had taken up residence in a small rooming house near the river and had stayed nearly a year.

Joshua Laurence, a balding man who ran the St. Paul office of St. Paul Shipping, had taken one look at L.J.'s slight frame and had scoffed at the idea of employing the man. "There's not enough to you," he'd laughed.

"Not enough that you can see," L.J. had answered.

"Show me what I can't see."

Hays thought fast as he eyed a huge blond clerk moving a batch of crates off the dock and into the warehouse. "Well, sir," he answered, "I've a good head for figures and can help you greatly with keeping track of inventory and adjusting freight rates to a satisfactory level."

Laurence frowned. "Big words from such a scrawny boy. How are you at loading and packing?"

Hays had smiled and pointed to Tim Wolfe, who was moving crates around as if they were empty. "With a man as big as him, Mr. Laurence, I wouldn't think you need me for work of that kind. But I'll wager I can best any man in St. Paul at inventory control, rating and warehouse costing."

The manager had been impressed. "Aye, lad, you might win such a wager. But how do you come to know anything about such things?"

L.J. had spent the last three days poring over freight schedules and reading two stray texts he had found on warehousing. And he'd talked to three idle skippers in the busy port of St. Paul on the workings of steamship traffic. His astute mind had quickly constructed a working understanding of the business. At least he knew a score of essentials that could be offered to Laurence. His memory served him well and he recited what he knew about the setting and adjusting of freight rates. The manager shook his head in disbelief.

"If you understand even a tenth of that, boy, I can use you."

Over the next six months L.J. had become invaluable to the St. Paul Shipping Company. He assumed many of the routine tasks of the business that Laurence had earlier performed. What's more, he devised a system of warehouse management that shortened layovers under the company's roof and allowed St. Paul Shipping to both lower its general rate structure and increase profits. Yet the most important lesson Hays learned during the period was that his boss quickly left the company's main office, the one in St. Paul, as soon as L.J. could run it.

Laurence set himself up in New Orleans within weeks of L.J.'s arrival. Hays had pondered the gambit, puzzled for a time. But its purpose was quickly made clear to him. Once his employer had stationed himself in the South, business increased appreciably. Additional contracts for steamship journeys literally flowed into the offices and revenues skyrocketed. Laurence had been shrewd. Once the wonderful pipeline that was his company could be run efficiently, he had concentrated on pumping as much as possible through it. He'd gone where the traffic was and grabbed his share. L.J. Hays thought the move simple, logical and brilliant.

Tim Wolfe, though, was disgruntled. For it was he, after all, who was forced to tote much of the increased business. And so early on, he and L.J. were at odds with one another. The big Irishman was unhappy with the distribution of the "real work" of the business, the loading and unloading, and was furious with L.J.'s concentration on pace.

Inevitably, one day in late summer, the two had argued. But Hays had managed to convince his fellow worker that if they could move crates just a little more quickly and handle only one or two boats more a month, the company could afford, indeed would require, an assistant for Wolfe. L.J., determined to make a name for himself, had then taken to moving cargo in the warehouse during the night. It was backbreaking, slow work for him, but he knew he had to win Tim Wolfe over or he would never work St. Paul Shipping into a first-class operation.

Tim, of course, had noticed the work each morning. And, incredulous, had finally hung around the warehouse to watch his frail coworker one evening.

"What the hell do you think you're doing, little man?" he'd asked L.J. For all his desire, Hays was slow and clumsy at the work.

"Moving crates, hauling sacks."

"By all that's sane, why bother after hours?"

"Behind one of them I'm sure to find you a man to help lift crates and move sacks, that's why."

Tim had shaken his head, put down his beer and labored with Hays evenings for nearly a month thereafter. While a full-time assistant for Wolfe had never been forthcoming, a man was put on two days a week. So Wolfe had put aside his smoldering resentment and the two had become playfully belligerent to one another, criticizing each others' weaknesses with obvious affection. Tim constantly urged L.J. to "set down" his books and have some fun with the "belles" and "lookers" that flocked to him. Hays responded with pointed suggestions that Tim save a few dollars for the day he found himself "quite married."

As the two men left the Riverboat Saloon following the poker game, L.J. made a playful remark about Hildy May's interest in his substantial winnings as the game progressed. But Tim had not taken the bait. He was genuinely concerned about the huge wad of bills Hays had stuffed in his pocket.

Leaving the saloon he offered a low-voiced warning, "I'd be careful if I was you, lad. Ben Williams isn't the sort of man who likes to be shown up, 'specially in front of his friends. And he's not above . . . well, just watch yourself is all, and let's get those winnings home."

Hays wasn't sure if he understood, exactly. "I did nothing to embarrass Mr. Williams, Tim. It was a fair game."

The other man shrugged. "Ben's a money man, L.J. That's a different breed altogether. Unpredictable, don't you know. And dirty about it. So out here you gotta get along with the likes of him; you never know when he'll be the only one around who can bail you out of trouble. You know what I mean?"

L.J. could well imagine. If he were ever to go into business for himself, he'd need to borrow a lot of money for his first boat. But there were, he tried to tell himself, other sources of capital. When the time came, he'd find them.

"Fact is, L.J., I think we ought to go back to the saloon."

"What?" Hays had been thinking about steamships again, not paying much attention to Tim.

"I'm thinking we ought to go back."

"And drink?"

"No. I think we should ask Hildy May to put that money of yours in her safe for the evening."

"You're kidding," L.J. exclaimed. Standing in the

clean, fresh snow of midwinter, Hays couldn't imagine anything disrupting his successful evening. But Tim thought otherwise and led his friend back into the saloon. Wolfe then asked the favor of the girl and she quickly agreed.

"Course, we can't guarantee the money against a holdup," was her only hedge.

"We'll take the chance," L.J. said flatly.

Fifteen minutes later, L.J. and Tim found themselves plodding through the snow toward the boarding house where they both lived. The light from the town spread eerily through the falling snow, offering only the dim suggestion of buildings. The flat light of the sky turned the quiet waters of the river into a grey plain that seemed to swallow the snow in complete silence. Suddenly, two men appeared out of nowhere.

"That's far enough, you two," a man holding a pistol snapped. "Stop right there if you value your lives."

Tim and L.J. halted, mutually sensing it was useless to resist. The snow was drifting and was so deep that they could not reach cover even if they tried. And neither was armed. Tim never carried a gun, certain he'd lose in such a contest and equally confident he would win in a test of strength. L.J. simply hated the things.

As they stood in the snow, water seeping through the thin soles of Hays' boots, one of the outlaws approached the pair. He searched L.J. while the leader held his gun on the two. When he discovered that the bankroll Hays carried consisted of only ten dollars, the leader demanded to know where "the rest of it" was.

"If you're referring to my poker winnings," L.J. said, "I gave them to a friend to hold for the weekend."

"Search the other one," the man standing in the shadows ordered.

"I wouldn't give it to *him*!" L.J. almost laughed. Tim elbowed his friend in the ribs.

Still, the search continued. The moment the man got between Tim and his friend, Wolfe acted. He knocked the gun out of the outlaw's hand, then seized him in a strangle hold, swinging him around so that his body was shielded from the distant gunman. L.J. reacted to Tim's attack by diving to his right toward a well house. Before he could get behind it, however, a gun roared and he felt a searing pain in his left shoulder.

As L.J. crumpled in a heap and turned a snowdrift red with his blood, Tim let out a roar of anger and hurled his prisoner into the snow, picked up his fallen pistol and fired it randomly toward the outlaws. Panicked, they fled.

Tim carried L.J. to the nearby home of St. Paul's only doctor, woke the man and watched over his friend. Prompt care saved Hays from serious injury but on cold, wet nights for many years thereafter, a deep ache reminded L.J. of the incident. And whenever that pain came upon him, he thought of the great, bellowing anger that had come from Tim that night in the snow.

# Chapter 2

For L.J. Hays, three years passed in a blur of activity, timeless, filled with work. As the weeks turned into months, he became one of the most successful freight agents along the Mississippi. He managed the feat through industry and dedication, but was aided by the rising tide of river-borne trade to the north. The world, it seemed, was heading to the Northwest. And the St. Paul Shipping Company was willing to take it there.

L.J. profited more than most from this migration. He developed an almost paranoid compulsion to anticipate disaster and growth along the river. He peered into the dimly lit future and drew conclusions from it. He schemed and planned, studied and considered everything that was happening to the frontier. And in the end he lay awake at night, his imagination endlessly pondering the vagaries of commerce in a booming world. More than once he fell asleep with a ledger spread across his chest. The result of his almost desperate efforts was that L.J. found new markets to replace fading ones even before his rivals recognized the weakness of those he'd abandoned. With uncanny accuracy, he identified shrinking industries, selected those merchants in them that might survive the decline, and built solid contracts with the healthy members of each sickened market. Such foresight had developed a prosperous, diverse clientele for his company.

But Hays remained a long way from achieving the most important dream of his life—that of owning his own steamship. His bank balance, though healthy, was still far short of the amount required to make even a beginning payment on a small boat. For all his success, he was frustrated with his progress.

Had L.J. voiced his displeasure with the way things were going—or announced his determination to rise above those around him to become some sort of uncrowned king of freight on the great Mississippi River—those few people who knew him would have been shocked. For Hays did not often act audaciously, at least not in ways that others could perceive. Though his thoughts ranged well beyond his current restrictions, his behavior was always dutiful. Still, he hungered for success with a great and fearsome appetite. He starved for it. Though he appeared to most of his acquaintances as nothing more than a bright young man who was reliable and trustworthy, L.J. Hays was much more.

He was a caldron of drive. Dissatisfaction afoot. A man whose desire for power, or wealth, or whatever it was that success might bring, surpassed most mortal imaginings.

In the night, falling to sleep with a journal in his lap, Hays drifted off to the sound of Tim Wolfe entertaining a saucy young woman in the room next door. Their whispers and laughter invaded his financial reveries through thin walls, their moans washed over him like the waves of some endless river. He heard the cajoling voices and the cries of pleasure regularly, swearing to himself his allegiance to a triumph beyond women. And then, more times than he would ever admit, L.J. would awaken, the white-hot iron of some unspeakable nightmare prodding him to consciousness, reminding him of his solitary existence.

L.J. kept his passions to himself, though. Except for the banker Ben Williams, most people who knew or dealt with him merely liked and respected him. Many St. Paulers thought so much of his orderly ways, in fact, that they made special efforts to introduce their daughters to him. Painfully shy with girls, he put up with the attention, but tried wherever possible to dissuade all local matchmakers. As he had often told Tim privately, there was a time and place for him to get involved with women, a time and a place not yet discovered.

Beneath the polite façade he offered his customers, though, Hays harbored a great concern. A war was coming, he knew. In restaurants, over coffee, along the docks, everywhere, he heard the emotional reaction of his fellow Minnesotans to the slavery issue. But Hays knew that the question was a political one. He was certain that the conflict between the North and South was economically based, a disagreement over commerce and manufacturing. Though the argument might have been cloaked in debates over freedom, the bones of the issue, its frame and members, were built on simple greed.

L.J. Hays felt sure that there was a way to profit from such adversity. As with declining markets, fortunes could be made by those who saw the calamity in advance. So he sailed to St. Louis on the St. Paul Shipping Co. steamship *Lakeland* to pursue the question with J. Parnell Brown, the lawyer who represented the eastern interests that owned the company. Brown was surprised to see him, although not at all displeased. He wined and dined the young freight agent and showed him the sights of St. Louis as they discussed the potentially disastrous effect on company business of war between the states.

It took little for Hays to convince Brown that a war would restrict Mississippi River shipping almost from the start. From there it was only logical that the conflict would eventually close the port at New Orleans and so the entire Mississippi. The lawyer, though acknowledging that this would cost the company dearly, had no idea what to do about it.

But Hays had definite ideas and offered them. "Suppose," he whispered, "we make private arrangements to ship southern cotton from pickup points north of New Orleans, so as to avoid any blockade the North may lay down?"

"If New Orleans is blockaded," Brown pointed out, "chances are there'll also be picket ships up and down the river from here to New Orleans."

"Not right away, Mr. Brown. It takes time to build a navy and the United States has more than a little building to do. But when there are picket ships to contend with, we've still a chance. To put it simply, bribery will serve us well in a pinch. It's either that or go out of business. So I'm in favor of bribery. A few ship's captains and the Mississippi is ours."

"You think we can find skippers willing to risk their necks to get our ships through?"

"My belief in the influence money has on men, sir, is profound," L.J. observed.

Brown, a St. Louis politician of some repute, was neither shocked nor outraged by L.J.'s suggestion. He was, however, doubtful, and his expression showed it. L.J. tried to allay the man's doubts. "There have always been those who put riches above honor," he said, "and that is no less true in war than in peace."

The lawyer had studied the brash young man carefully before posing his question. "And you, L.J.? Do you put riches before honor?"

Hays had reached a juncture he had not anticipated. It seemed clear to him that the business of commerce had little if anything to do with war. He wondered if Brown felt some great allegiance to one side or the other.

"To be honest, sir," L.J. replied, "I see no conflict. Wars are the business of those powerful enough to engage in them. The cost of such madness, in terms of men and money and wasted effort, is colossal. So, while I understand the boundless importance of a war between the North and South, I see no honor in either side. Profit, but not honor."

"You are a hard young man, articulate, but hard," the lawyer had smiled. "There's a gap in your reasoning, a problem hidden in your solution to my question. But, if you can ignore that gap, you will, I think, grow rich." Brown chuckled, almost paternal, nearly callous. "But enough of that. Take a steamer to New Orleans immediately and spend whatever time you need there. I leave all the details to you and Joshua Laurence. He knows quite well the rules of trade down there."

Two days later Hays arrived in New Orleans. He was greeted warmly by his former superior, Josh Laurence.

The bald and fattened agent agreed that war was inevitable and took no issue with the probability that New Orleans would be closed to trade—"if the North is strong enough to do it."

Hays did not argue the point. "Can we get plantation owners to arrange private shipments with us, Mr. Laurence?"

Josh, a Southerner by birth, nodded. "Of course. But they'll be wanting arms and ammunition, lad."

Hays shook his head. "They'll not get them through us," he vowed. "Mr. Brown has already rejected the idea and I agree with him. If we ship goods, we're simply involved in honest commerce. If we lade guns and ammunition, we can be accused of treasonable acts."

"By which side, L.J.?" asked Laurence with a laugh.

"By the North, of course, though I suppose we'd be heroes by southern standards."

"We surely would..." Laurence began.

L.J. interrupted him. "And heroes we are not meant to be."

"Then it's cotton we must find."

"And not get caught doing so."

"True. The North might frown on even that coming out of the South."

"We will tread the line, Josh, between doom and risk. Mr. Brown is willing to chance it and so am I."

"Then I'm off to the work. But tell Mr. Brown when you get back that I'll be leaving him once the war starts. I'll be wearing a uniform for the duration and it won't be blue."

"He asked me to get your recommendation for a replacement—says you're the only man he knows who might know your equal." L.J. paused before continuing. "Brown says to tell you to look out for your skin if you're going to be fighting."

"Mighty nice of him, a Northerner after all. Yeah, I guess Brownie would know he's going to lose me when the war comes. We go back a long ways together."

In the end, Hays spent a month in New Orleans with Laurence and they put together enough private deals to keep St. Paul Shipping's steamers busy after the blockade of New Orleans was instituted by the Union Army. All shipments were unloaded well north of the Louisiana port. During the first year of the Civil War, the arrangements stood L.J.'s company in good stead. But then the Union commanders, learning that shipments were getting through the South, extended their blockade of the river all the way to St. Louis.

As soon as Hays learned the identities of the ship's captains involved in the enlarged blockade, he sent undercover emissaries to recruit the cooperation of a number of them—with funds supplied by Brown. The effort was only partially successful, yet resulted in a continuing flow of southern goods to the North and Canadian goods to the South throughout the war. St. Paul Shipping Co. steamers managed to keep busy and avoid attack by either side. Steamships of other stripes often were not so lucky.

One steamer, a side-wheeler named the *Cuyahoga,* was owned and operated by three southern plantation owners. Following the Union's blockade of New Orleans, it was commandeered by the Confederacy and sailed up and down the river carrying munitions secured in Canada in exchange for cargoes of southern cotton. Joshua Laurence was the ship's captain.

In November of 1863, two Union ships followed the *Cuyahoga* north from Memphis, almost caught her at St. Louis, but missed. The *Cuyahoga* fled north, but was overtaken as she stopped for cordwood to feed her fireboxes. Just south of St. Paul, Union gunboats opened fire on her.

The *Cuyahoga* was a magnificent ship. Its wedding-cake superstructure was built of the lightest poplar and pine for speed and its gingerbread pilothouse, perched atop the huge vessel, was adorned with scrolled friezes. Two great yellow suns, streaming crimson, decorated each side paddle. In all, the ship had six boilers feeding two great engines, and was both fast and maneuverable. But taken by surprise, the engineers barely got the *Cuyahoga* up to speed before cannonballs from the Union ships began whistling through the upper decks.

As Captain Laurence swung the ship into deep water, a shell skipped twice on the water, like a stone pitched by a boy. The iron shot ripped through the side of the hull. Then another found the same mark farther aft. The flat-bottomed, shallow-draft boat took water furiously on the port side and began listing badly. But still the brash engineers fueled the fireboxes. Within minutes, though, the *Cuyahoga* had tilted so badly that water from one of the boilers ran through a leveling pipe into its matching boiler on the port side.

Dry, or nearly dry, the huge wrought-iron cylinder quickly superheated, melted the gleaming brass dome of the boiler and exploded. Fifteen men were scalded to death in seconds. Three others were killed by shards of iron flying through the air. Those that were still alive and conscious dived into the river and swam for their lives.

With two boilers out, and listing badly, the *Cuyahoga* thrashed only one side paddle into the churning water. Its engineers were dead and so could not adjust for the helpless circling of the boat. The skipper, Josh Laurence, lay unconscious in the pilothouse. Like some great wounded animal, struggling in its death throes, the steamship spiraled in ever-wider circles as the Union gunboats looked on. Finally, the once-magnificent *Cuyahoga* ran aground, her stern sunk nearly to the second deck, her bow lifted onto the sandy shores of the Mississippi.

Josh Laurence somehow managed to make his way off the ship. He tossed the vessel's log overboard and clambered ashore, heading for St. Paul. It had been cold and snowy for days, and the captain was close to death when he reached the city. He lay unconscious for almost a day before regaining his senses. He peered, bewildered, into the face that hung above him as he did so, trying to blink himself awake.

"We thought we'd lost you, Josh," L.J. breathed softly as the older man stirred.

Laurence's eyes widened. He tried to speak, but found for a moment that he could not—his throat dry, his lips cracked from the cold.

When at last he'd gathered his strength, he croaked out a greeting to Hays, then told him what had happened to the *Cuyahoga* and how he came to be in St. Paul. As the import of Josh's news sank into L.J.'s imagination, a wave of excitement spread through him. As soon as he was certain that Josh would live, Hays began to think about the possibility of salvaging the *Cuyahoga*. Maritime law allowed anyone who could raise a sunken ship to claim the vessel and its cargo as well. Perhaps a brace of Union gunboats had delivered him his chance to enter the shipping business on his own.

Laurence began to drift into sleep again as Hays stood thinking above him.

"Josh, hey Josh! Wake up," L.J. demanded. "How much of her is out of the water?"

"Of the *Cuyahoga*?"

"Yes."

"Hard to say by now," Josh offered weakly. "When I left, though, it looked like the top deck would stay dry, though the better part of the stern was under. She took two or three balls at the water' line and God only knows how much damage from the boiler blowing."

"What were you carrying?"

Laurence hesitated. Even semiconscious he was wary of answering questions so far north. "Munitions," he finally reported. "We need them bad. You know, the war's not exactly goin' our way."

Hays nodded. He thought to himself that the outcome had been obvious from the beginning. The manufacturing capacity of the North so outstripped the South that the Confederacy could never have won. And, as if to seal the South's fate, the overwhelming superiority of the Union's railroads allowed the shipment of men and material to the battleground with a speed and efficiency never before known in war. The railroads were defeating the South. Great, steaming, rushing engines borne on gleaming rails were battering the Confederacy.

But L.J. offered none of this to his old benefactor. The lecture would be lost on the man. And soon enough Josh would find himself in a Union prison. Minnesota was, after all, a northern state and solidly in the corner of the Union.

The next day found Hays and Tim Wolfe riding south to the scene of the *Cuyahoga*'s destruction. The weather was cold, but clear, the sun reflecting dazzlingly off the hard-crusted snow covering the frozen Minnesota turf.

The two men rode silently, each with his own thoughts. Tim had been doubtful when L.J. related his idea about the *Cuyahoga*. "What the hell do you know about salvaging a ship?" he asked his friend.

"I know what the law is—it gives me the right to raise the boat and then own it. I know I can get Joseph Higgins and his boat builders to do the salvage work and refurbishing."

"That'll cost money—a lot of it, L.J."

"So would a brand-new boat, Tim. I've accumulated a fair-sized bank account, though it's a long way from being enough to buy a new boat. Maybe it'll be enough to raise and rehabilitate the *Cuyahoga*."

"And if it ain't, L.J.? Seems to me you're bettin' a damn long shot."

L.J. shrugged. "If I haven't enough, I'll raise more, Tim," he offered. "I'll get it somewhere." And Hays was sure he would, though at the same time certain it would not be easy in the trying times of the Civil War. Even if he raised the funds to repair the ship, he would have to pay an enormous rate of interest, for the war had caused interest rates to soar to two-digit levels, presently twelve to fourteen percent.

But when L.J. and Tim reached the *Cuyahoga*, L.J. saw that raising the ship might well be an impossible dream. As Josh Laurence had said, the upper deck of the two-tiered steamer was above water. But nearly all of the hull was below the surface. And, to make matters worse, much of the immense superstructure had been twisted in the grounding. L.J. gaped at the steamer, trying to imagine how really big it might be if high and dry. What he imagined was chilling, for he couldn't begin to think how such a large ship, once sunk, could be raised. She was at least a hundred and seventy-five feet long, he thought, and must be filled with tons of water.

"Well, L.J.," Tim grumbled, trying to control the

snicker that bubbled in his throat. "Do you still think you can salvage this boat? Looks to me like you've as much chance of walking across the Mississippi on stilts."

"I never thought it would be easy," L.J. replied.

"Easy? Hell, it's impossible! Before you could get this ship up, you'd have to figure out some way to pump her dry. And I don't see how you can do that unless you raise her first." Tim finally laughed out loud at the thought of two mutually exclusive chores holding the ship on the bottom.

But L.J. was not so easily discouraged. As he and Tim rode back to St. Paul, he tried to gain a perspective on the immense problem that faced him. Could he haul the *Cuyahoga* partly out of the water so that it could be patched and pumped out, then slide the steamer back into the river? What would it take to move it? Teams of horses? L.J. quickly discarded the idea. The *Cuyahoga* carried too many tons.

Just as that thought was completed, L.J.'s eyes gave him something new to ponder. The two men had come into sight of the roadbed of the St. Paul Railroad, which nearly touched the Mississippi about half a mile from where the *Cuyahoga* lay. A steam engine! L.J. thought. A locomotive might have the power needed to edge the *Cuyahoga* up on shore. If one locomotive couldn't do it, perhaps two could—the St. Paul had two, even though it had not as yet completed its roadbed all the way to Minneapolis from St. Paul.

When he explained his idea to Tim Wolfe, his friend once again regarded him as if he were daft. But then Tim frowned. "Well," he advised, "them railroad locomotives are pretty powerful, L.J., and two back to back ought to give you a chance. But would the railroad lend their equipment to you? I figure they'd

## Railroad King

laugh. Hauling muddy boats out of deep water ain't exactly the railroad's stock and trade."

But by the time they had returned to St. Paul, Hays could see in his mind's eye the wreck of the *Cuyahoga* rising slowly from the Mississippi at the end of cables hauled by locomotives, the ship's nose running with river water, dirty black water from the boat's interior rushing out of gaping shell holes in her hull. Whatever anyone else might think, Hays decided it was worth a try. The first thing he had to do was sound out the railroad on the possibility of renting their equipment.

Leaving Tim to mind the freight office, L.J. paid a visit to the railroad's small temporary office above the village feed store. Phil Crabtree, the general manager, was not in. According to the bearded young clerk who minded the office in Crabtree's absence, he would not be back until dark, as he was out with the crew laying track to the north.

"Try early, Mr. Hays," the clerk told him. "He usually spends a half hour here before heading out to the railhead—between five and five-thirty."

Hays was more than disappointed. The task ahead of him, almost imponderable, beckoned. It whispered in his ear like some teacher asking the same question over and over to a bewildered student. It appeared an impossible undertaking, a doomed endeavor that no sane man would attempt. But its proportions, and the pathetically limited resources that L.J. could bring to bear on the sunken ship, formed a dramatic confrontation in Hays' mind. The frail young clerk saw himself as beleaguered, overcome, apparently defeated. And it was this element of sublime risk that thrilled him.

As he stood outside the railroad office, he suddenly found himself face to face with the prettiest young woman he had ever seen. Surprised, he stepped aside to let her enter the building, his hand reflexively removing his hat as he did so.

"Good day," he managed to say, stunned by her. In an instant, she was gone. He turned and looked at the closed door. A first, he thought. I've never spoken to a girl before being spoken to. The back of his neck felt warm. A moment later she poked her head out of the door and smiled at L.J.

"It is a good day, isn't it Mr. . . ."

Hays, somewhat of a social hermit, was buffeted by the woman's pleasant, forward gesture. "Hays," he introduced himself. "L.J. Hays." The way her silver-blonde hair trailed across the dark velvet of her collar and the gleam in her blue eyes baffled his normally articulate mind.

"I'm Lucille, Mr. Hays. Lucille Morgan. I teach school here. I see that we are both disappointed that Mr. Crabtree isn't about." She stepped to Hays' side. "I came to see if he might be coerced into talking to the children about his railroad." It seemed to L.J. that she sparkled as she spoke.

There was a long, awkward silence as Hays wondered what was wrong with him. He was behaving like Tim Wolfe. Instantly, the thought relaxed him. He reached inside his coat and produced a cigar. It was windy and bitterly cold, but pausing to light it gave him a moment to think.

"Well, Mr. Hays, since I can't talk Mr. Crabtree into a short lecture, might I prevail upon you to offer us an hour of your time?"

"I'm sorry?"

"I understand you are in charge of the shipping company."

"I run the office here, yes."

## Railroad King

"Well, might you explain the steamboat business to my students one day?"

The directness of her manner beguiled L.J. and he was flattered by her invitation. But talk to a bunch of children?

"At the moment I'm afraid you've got the wrong man, Miss Morgan. I'm only an agent with my company and . . . right now I'm up to my neck in problems. Problems of my own." He seemed to hear himself talking, rambling, not wanting her to leave. "I'm trying to figure out a way to raise the Confederate steamer *Cuyahoga* that is half-beached downstream."

"That *is* exciting!" Lucille Morgan clapped her hands in glee. "Won't you consider paying us a visit after you've salvaged the boat? My children would love to hear about it."

Hays, surprised he'd brought the subject up, was alarmed she assumed success. "I'm not at all certain I can salvage her," he coughed, "but I suppose I'll consider a visit."

"Well, that would be great, Mr. Hays! What is your first name, by the way?"

He hesitated. "People call me just L.J., Miss Morgan," he replied. "I prefer it that way."

"Well I don't," she teased, her smile taking any sting out of her words. "How would you like to call me L.C. Morgan?"

Hays had to laugh. "I see what you mean," he admitted. "But . . . well, all right, I'll tell you if you'll promise not to laugh or pass it on to anyone else."

"Is it that bad?"

"Depends how you look at it, ma'am. I was named after my mother. Her maiden name was Lynne and she prevailed upon my father to give it to me as a first name. They were going to call me by my second name—Jerome—but it didn't work out that way. Everybody just called me L.J."

"Lynne Jerome?" Lucille repeated. "I love it, Mr. Hays. It's beautiful and you ought to use it. Do you mind if I call you L. Jerome?"

Hays shrugged. He found it difficult to say no to this irrepressible young lady. "Whatever you say, Miss Morgan. But, you'll have to excuse me. I must be getting back to my office." He seemed immobilized, not wishing to leave nor daring to stay.

"You won't forget us when you've raised that boat?"

Hays laughed. "If I succeed in raising the *Cuyahoga*," he bubbled, "I'll be glad to give all of your students a free ride aboard her, Miss Morgan. Until then, though, I'd appreciate it if you'd keep your own counsel on the matter. Salvages are open to anyone who wishes to attempt them, you know."

"I understand, Mr. Hays. I do wish you luck with it." And, as abruptly as she had appeared, she was gone.

Luck, L.J. thought. Luck was something he didn't believe in.

The next morning Hays was at the railroad office waiting for Phil Crabtree when the manager arrived. He was a pleasant sort, very businesslike, and made it quite clear to L.J. that he didn't have a great deal of time to allow him. So L.J. quickly outlined what he wanted to do and how—telling Crabtree that he wished to hire the St. Paul locomotives and a track construction crew.

Crabtree looked at him as though he were out of his mind. "You're not a well man, Mr. Hays," he said with a chuckle. "It's the middle of winter and I've a devil of a time getting my men out to lay track for the railroad. But even if I wasn't busy completing our line to Minneapolis and could lend you our locomotives and crew, the cost of laying the track you need is greater than the value of the boat you want to haul."

Hays was stunned. He had never imagined that a half mile of track might cost so much.

"So your enterprise sounds like a fool's mission to me, sir." For some reason, though, Crabtree studied the young man with a sympathetic eye, in spite of the harebrained idea. "I don't mean to discourage you, Mr. Hays, but I've seen that Rebel boat. She's mired in the mud and filled with holes. To be realistic, she's unsalvageable. A dozen river men have looked her over with an eye to claiming her and each of them has reached the same conclusion. The *Cuyahoga* is a lost cause."

L.J. liked the man. His tone was warm, almost paternal. "Mr. Crabtree, I appreciate your advice. But I think the boat can be salvaged if I can just get her out of the water a bit. I talked with Mr. Higgins at his yard yesterday and he thinks she can be patched and floated."

"Higgins actually believes you can drag that flimsy craft ashore with a pair of locomotives?"

Hays did not return Crabtree's smile. "Mr. Higgins believes me mad, but that is his privilege. Still, he has agreed to repair the ship if I can get her to him."

"Perhaps this is a task for your employers, St. Paul Shipping? It seems to me they've the money for such an undertaking."

"I want no partners, Mr. Crabtree. I aim to see my name on that ship. And one way or another, I'll manage it." For the first time, though, L.J. was beginning to doubt his own bravado. But he persisted in it, waiting for some crack to open in the dilemma so that he could slip through it.

Crabtree furrowed his brow, impressed with Hays' determination but perplexed by his absurd inflexibility. He wondered . . .

"Mr. Hays, I've a thought."

"Please, sir, share it with me."

"If you can acquire a length of cable, say a half mile long, perhaps we can haul your boat from the track that already exists."

Hays' deep-set eyes were transformed by the remark. The grim clerk suddenly became a delighted boy, captured by the image of a cable stretching out of sight to the railroad tracks, straining and stretching and finally bringing his boat ashore as though it were a fish at the end of a line.

"Wonderful!" he hooted.

"Wonderful if you can find such a cable, sir. And if we get some snow."

"Snow?"

"I'll not engage my crews in this madness of yours unless the weather tears them from the railhead. So find your cable and pray for snow, Mr. Hays." With that, Crabtree donned his thick fur cap and prepared to leave the office. L.J. barely noticed him. Lost in thought, he wondered where he might locate a cable of such dimension.

"There's one thing I should tell you, young fellow," the manager offered in parting. "River boats will not long reign supreme as freight carriers along the Mississippi or any other river. Today your steamers have a monopoly, but tomorrow you'll see railroads everywhere. They can and will carry freight cheaper and faster than it's ever been carried before. Already the Union Pacific is headed for the coast and soon it will bridge the country. And there are plans and grants for lines running into every corner of the continent."

L.J. paused in his reverie to consider this railroad man's smug prediction. But he knew that Crabtree wasn't bragging idly about his industry. Railroads ruled the East and would one day change the face of the West. Though steamships were only just entering their fourth decade on the country's major rivers, it was possible they would, indeed, be antiquated soon. And railroads might, in the end, perform the service he perceived a transportation system must accomplish better than anything afloat. For they could go anywhere.

Hays' vision of motion, of the interplay of need and fulfillment, receded in his mind as he stood in the office. For now, all he wished to do was drag a steamer from the mud. And all he needed to make this wish a reality was a bit of wire and a good snowstorm. Or so he thought.

L.J. Hays, much to the amusement of his friend Tim Wolfe, actually wired Pittsburgh to request a quote on a half mile of cable. But as he waited for a price and delivery date, it began to become clear he might never need it. As fate would have it, the winter of 1863–64 had been an unusual one for the frozen wilds of Minnesota. December and January had been snowy and cold, but February brought no snow. March proved even drier.

While waiting, L.J. Hays filled his hours with the only sort of work that consistently satisfied him: study. In fact, he labored like a man possessed to understand the great, swift and awkward creature known as the steamship. Should the beast *Cuyahoga* ever be raised, he decided, Hays would know what to do with it.

L.J. spent many hours along the waterfront in St.

Paul. He cajoled and harangued more captains, stevedores and lading clerks than he cared to recall. But, for all his understanding of the freight business, he didn't really know much about the ships that carried the freight. Since he hoped soon to own one of the things, he was sure he should become an expert.

So, on a cold, bright day in February, he wandered down to the docks and gazed at the remarkable creatures moored there.

A steamship, he quickly learned, was a flimsy, multitiered shell erected above a flat-bottomed hull. The base of the boat, its foundation, was designed to slide over the water rather than float in it. This peculiar characteristic was built into them so that they could pass through shallow waters, essentially skipping over sandbars, mud flats and hidden rocks. Many of the most modern boats, in fact, drew as little as thirty-six inches of water while transporting three hundred tons of freight.

These marvels were powered by huge, crude, immensely powerful engines that, with terrible regularity, exploded in the faces of their keepers. Their steam engines were inefficient, burning outrageous quantities of wood in order to propel themselves. And the ships were fragile: built for speed, they were light; built to make money before they sank, they were cheap.

Most extraordinary, though, was the attitude of those who owned, controlled and worked on these vessels. L.J. found the men at the river's edge almost impossible to understand. They were fatalists. They performed their tasks in the face of great danger, fully aware that their equipment teetered at the limits of effectiveness. None, of course, could have put it so succinctly, but all shared a sense of possible disaster as they regarded their crafts.

From a fireman about his boilers: "In the ollen days we stoked 'em to say forty pounds of pressure, till the heat would hit you even in a stiff wind. Was the feel of the fire and the girth of the iron that mattered. Now, great God knows it, we run 140, 150, 160 pounds in six sep'rate boilers. And then the captain'll call for a wad o' steam and we'll jury-rig the safety valve to give it to 'im. 'Sno wonder the boys'll drink, on shore and off."

From a carpenter at the shipyard: "The things are too light, too thin, too quick. There's not enough heft to a hull in one of them to build even a semblance of rigidity. I've seen boats rounding a turn at full steam twist like a string of jerky, the engines thrown out of line, their pistons akilter, steam belching everywhere. You can't keep building boats with no guts to 'em. They sink."

From a crewman: "Heard tell of a boiler going, for no good reason, just south of here. Went slow, though, and everyone got off. Swam for their lives to the shore and made it, so they tell. Won't none of us know, 'course. Indians scalped 'em all."

And so it went, wherever L.J. asked. The world of steamships was filled with risk. They were fragile things, fast and profitable, but required cunning control. They were perfect for him.

He thought as much while sitting astride his horse one day, looking down through the leafless trees lining the river's edge. Below sat the *Cuyahoga*, her pilothouse still majestic above the wreck. He saw himself in that windowed booth, churning toward some unimagined destiny, alert for the treachery of the river. And then, dreaming, he saw her name: the *Resurrection*. An appropriate enough tag for his ship, the sign of a miracle.

It was late March and the weeks of waiting had long since kept Tim from accompanying him on his regular journeys to the river. So he stood alone, looking at her. She seemed, he thought, different. Week after snowless week couldn't have changed the boat. And the air was only a bit warmer. What, he wondered, could it be? Then it hit him. The *Cuyahoga* was riding a bit higher out of the water than she had been. But, of course, she hadn't moved. It was the river that had changed. The dry winter had lowered the water nearly a foot.

Immediately a new hope sprang into L.J.'s mind and he rode back to St. Paul to consult his shipbuilder. When he told Higgins of his discovery, the old man had grinned. "Looks like you may be in luck, L.J.," he enthused. "The snowless winter seems to have sucked the life out of the Mississippi just so's you could float that steamer. If the water drops a bit more . . . who knows . . . we just might raise that carcass."

Hays began inspecting his ship almost daily, measuring the water level and surveying the holes that were slowly climbing out of the Mississippi. Inch by inch the river was shrinking. By the middle of April, one great ragged hole in the *Cuyahoga*'s side was completely above the surface and a second could be seen not far below it. Standing on the boat's hull, Hays decided it was time to make his move. For he knew that if he could see what was happening, so could others. As Crabtree had warned, other river men would covet the wreck and perhaps try to claim her before Hays could.

But there was nothing he could do about the threat of a competitor. He could only move quickly. Gamble before others felt secure, take his chance and hope he held the right cards. And, in spite of the receding river, there were still many risks involved in the salvage effort. There was no way of knowing how many holes the Union gunboats had put through the sides of the ship, no way of assessing the damage. From a practical standpoint, it was impossible to predict whether or not the ship could be refloated.

So the dry winter was both a blessing and a curse. The river would have to drop still lower before there could be an accurate estimate of the vessel's chances. So other interested river men could, and probably would, mark time for a few weeks longer. But at any moment one might begin work on the *Cuyahoga*, ending L.J.'s plan. Hays decided to ask Higgins about other inquiries concerning the ship in order to determine just how many men remained interested.

"I'm in a difficult business, L.J.," Higgins explained rather ponderously, puffing on his pipe. "I work with just about every shipper in the region and have to respect their wishes and retain their trust. So, I have to treat matters like this one with considerable care."

L.J. was perplexed. He'd asked a simple enough question.

"You see, inquiries into the condition of the *Cuyahoga* have been made by others than yourself. And, to protect all those involved, I've treated each with confidentiality. You, of course, are protected just as is everyone else."

That was, Hays thought, fair enough. But Higgins had managed to put him on notice. There were others, that was clear.

A few days after his conversation with the shipbuilder, Hays was in the town barbershop when he noticed an article in the *Gazette* that quoted Ben Williams as saying, "As good as the shipping business was before the war, it will be better once the conflict is over." The implications of the remark were not lost on L.J. Williams had his eye on the *Cuyahoga*.

That day, the young man rode to his boat only to find that more had inched above the water. The second jagged shell hole was now poking from just below the water line into the air. He wheeled his horse and headed back to St. Paul. He'd hesitated long enough.

While L.J. was riding furiously back to St. Paul, Ben Williams was talking to Joseph Higgins at his shipyard.

"Yeah, Ben," Higgins told the banker, "I know where that ship went down." The shipbuilder's expression revealed nothing of his involvement with Hays.

"You told me she couldn't be refloated, is that right?"

"I told you I doubted the effort would be worth the salvaged ship."

Williams grinned and shoved a finger into Higgins' bulging midsection. "That was then and this is now. She can be raised cheap, I bet. A good part of her is already above the water. Seems to me she just needs to be patched and pumped."

"If that's true, Ben, she might be worth bothering with."

"It's true enough, all right. River's dry this spring and her level's down. Boat's growing out of the water like a mushroom."

Higgins shrugged.

"How much will it cost me to have you bring her up?"

Joseph Higgins was a canny businessman. He enforced a simple but effective rule when it came to commercial inquiries: serious men were willing to pay for estimates and pay handsomely for firm quotations. If Williams wanted a price, it would cost him.

"Hard to say, Ben." Higgins puffed on his pipe, enjoying the banker's impatience. "I'd have to sail over there and do some looking, some poking around and some figuring. Have to calculate how long it'll take to pump her out, how much patching she'll need. The estimate will take some time and cost you some cash."

Williams nodded. "Anyone else interested?" he asked matter-of-factly.

Higgins did not reply. Williams knew better than to ask. "Can't tell you and you know it, Ben."

But Williams drew the wrong conclusion from Higgins' simple answer. "Well," he said, "I want you to estimate the job for me, Joseph. While you're at it, I'll get my financing together." He reached inside his coat pocket for a checkbook. "I'll pay for the estimate, of course—how much?"

"Can't tell you till it's done. Let you know then—all right?"

"Fine."

"Take two days."

"Fine." Williams was clearly thinking of the money required for the task. He wasn't listening to Higgins. Considering the ship as good as raised, he left the shipyard distracted. His mind churned with a number of ways to finance the ship. The banker was intent on controlling as much of the boat as possible, while using as little of his own money as he could. He was so involved in contemplating how to do so that he didn't notice L.J. Hays ride hard into Higgins' yard.

At the sight of Hays, Higgins allowed a smile to show on his face. L.J.'s thin frame clambered from the horse like a loose bundle of kindling wood. The young man was all elbows and knees, Higgins thought. And the older man noticed a ripple of affection for the perspiring, agitated youth as Hays marched into his office. He might be thin and brusque and impatient now and then, but L.J. was no fool. If Williams knew the *Cuyahoga* was high and nearly dry, then so must Hays.

"Still harboring that pipe dream about the *Cuyahoga*?" Higgins asked with a smile.

Among all those men a generation older than L.J., Higgins was the only one whose condescending jokes were a pleasure to Hays. There was something warm, even respectful about them. Before replying, L.J. smiled at the man.

"Pipe dream! You grisly old man. My pipe dream's going to keep you in work for months. And I don't need the railroad to haul my boat."

" 'My' boat?"

"Now listen, will ya? The river's way down! It ought to be a snap for you and your crew to patch and pump her. The holes in the boat's hull are partially out of the water. You can wade through the job!"

"Simple little job, you say, L.J.?" Higgins chuckled at Hays' enthusiasm.

L.J.'s answering smile turned a bit sheepish. What had to be done might be easier because of the receding river, but it couldn't be classified a simple job. "Not exactly, sir," L.J. retreated. "But a lot easier than it might be. I'll want whatever remains of her cargo offloaded at the dock, of course. I'll dispose of it to help pay for the repairs."

"Sounds like you're three steps ahead of yourself, young man." The shipbuilder's eyes bore down on him. "You commissioning me to raise that boat without so much as a quote on what it'll cost?"

Hays knew he couldn't wait for a formal estimate. He nodded firmly. "I am," he confirmed.

## Railroad King

"Can you afford the work?"

Hays pursed his lips and he considered the question. "Well, you won't cheat me, so the price will be fair. So I'll lay my cards face up on the table, Mr. Higgins. I have nine thousand, eight hundred and fifty dollars saved. I can raise more when I have to. But not until I have to. You won't need all the money right away and both of us know it."

Higgins was impressed by L.J.'s good business sense and his fair-sized bank account. The industrious young man had squirreled away a small fortune. Still, the shipbuilder figured it would cost twice as much to put the *Cuyahoga* back in business, even though the money wouldn't be needed right away.

"You'll certainly need more before we're through, L.J. And if you can't find it, I'll find myself stuck with your ship."

"You have my pledge, Mr. Higgins," Hays quickly responded, "that should I be unable to raise the balance of monies required, I will offer you a share of profits from the ship and pay you your fees in full as well, on a deferred basis, of course."

"Out of profits? What profits?"

"I'll draw no salary until there are profits, Mr. Higgins. You'll be paid before I am."

Flat-bottomed boats were a dangerous disease, Higgins thought. Men pledged what they didn't have in order to acquire them. Sacrificed what they couldn't afford for them. Lied and cheated and ran for the hills over them. But L.J.'s madness was not for ships, Higgins could see that. He simply loved the velocity of business and would be honest in this pursuit of ever greater speed. Higgins would trust him.

"You ought to be able to borrow the balance, L.J.

The steamer will give you a handsome piece of collateral to put up."

"Perhaps I *can* borrow it, sir. But, considering who controls the bank here in Minnesota, I won't count on it. I fear Ben Williams might refuse me a loan, no matter what collateral I have. He finds me . . . vexing, somehow. I wish, to be honest, I knew why."

Higgins' eyebrows skipped across his forehead. Vexing, indeed, he thought. "You are an odd one to him, L.J. Perhaps it's the cards. He hates to play cards with you. On any given evening he's a whiz at the table, a winner who's cool at the game. But when you sit across from him, your brow furrowed and your beer sitting warm by your side, he is unnerved. It seems he spends a lot of himself trying to figure what it is you're thinking."

L.J. smiled broadly. "I take it we have a deal?"

"We have a deal once you have visited the bank and transferred five thousand dollars to my account. Bring the receipt for the transfer here and I will have a contract waiting for our signatures. And we'll discuss your boat. There are chapters to her tale you do not know."

L.J. was puzzled by this remark, but didn't pursue it further. He turned immediately on his heels and made for the bank. Once there he saw his poker adversary, Ben Williams, talking to a group of prominent businessmen. Hays frowned when he noticed that one of them was Jay Calhoun, a power in the Hudson Bay Company. The huge firm controlled the fur trade along the Red River and into the Canadian provinces. And their monopoly made them few friends.

While waiting for the bank clerk to complete his transaction, L.J. heard a familiar voice greeting him

## Railroad King 47

and turned to see Lucille Morgan. She wore her perpetual smile. For all her loveliness, though, L.J. was unhappy to see her. He cautioned himself against being too open with the young lady about his project, and hoped she would keep her voice low.

"Good day to you, Miss Morgan," he said stiffly.

"I'm Lucille, if you don't mind," she answered, a twinkle in her clear blue eyes. "And how is your boat venture proceeding?" she bubbled. "I visited her not long ago, poor thing."

Hays grimaced. He had been a first-class fool to tell this woman of his undertaking. How could he change the subject?

"Still," she beamed up at him, "I'm hopeful that my students will one day churn the Mississippi on the *Cuyahoga*."

The girl's voice had risen when she mentioned the steamer's name and Hays winced. He couldn't help but notice that Williams froze at the sound of the ship's name.

"Miss Lucille," L.J. whispered, "I would appreciate it if you would not talk about my little folly. There are, you see, others hereabouts who are as interested in the ship as I."

Her eyes widened, genuinely intrigued. "Oh, L. Jerome, I am sorry!" She turned to scan the bank but L.J. stopped her with a gentle touch.

"Please, don't look around. The damage done is not quite complete. At least not yet."

Dismay crossed her face, the schoolteacher suddenly aware that her heartfelt interest in L.J. was causing him real difficulties. "Is there anything I can do to make up for any trouble I've caused?" she mumbled so breathlessly that he could barely hear her.

"You may pray, if you believe in God, Miss Morgan," he responded, turning to leave.

"It is done," he announced to Higgins. "Now tell me about Ben Williams' interest in my boat."

The boatman was surprised and didn't mind showing it. "Well now," he chortled, "I can neither confirm nor deny your suspicions. Let's simply leave it that there have been others, breathing down your neck where that boat is concerned. You have secured my services only by not requesting an estimate on the work."

"Hah!" L.J. was thrilled. In the nick of time. "The best of it is that old blowhard will know by now!"

Higgins cocked his head, an unspoken question.

"I would guess, sir, that Mr. Williams will be arriving here any moment now. Surely he knows of my bank transfer already."

Higgins, in spite of his age, cut an imposing figure. He worked with his hands and back and so, a brawny, calloused man, he hardly looked the sort to be easily intimidated. But for a moment, he blanched. The builder turned away from L.J. to stare blankly at the half-completed steamship occupying the other end of his yard. It sat, a skeleton at dry dock, because the St. Louis firm that had ordered it had been put out of business by the war. What work had been completed on the steamer had been paid for, but until the war ended, Higgins had little hope of finding someone to finance its completion. Even a half-finished steamer of the size of this one—more than two hundred feet—cost a pretty penny.

Ben Williams, as head of the state's largest bank, could help Higgins find a buyer for the vessel. He had, in fact, been talking about buying the steamer himself when he'd suddenly realized that the *Cuyahoga* was not the lost cause it had previously seemed.

"When can we get started on the *Cuyahoga*?" Hays asked, breaking into Higgins' thoughts.

"I've already made arrangements to have a crew sail my tug to the site tomorrow. If the hull's structurally sound, we'll have her patched, pumped out and ready to be towed back here within two to three days. Pray we don't get enough rain to swell the river in the meantime."

There was a silence between the two men that L.J. found uncomfortable. Still, he had nowhere to go until morning and absolutely nothing to say.

Higgins ended the pause. "If, as you say, Mr. Williams is headed here, you'd best be on your way."

"You admit he's the one?" Hays asked with a grin.

"I admit nothing," Higgins replied, "but if he is the one, I would guess you don't want to confront him."

"I'm sorry *you* have to do so, Mr. Higgins. You must be concerned. He's an important man in Minnesota."

The shipbuilder shrugged. "I have no choice, L.J. As for the other party—he won't be happy to find out that he can't employ me. No doubt he'll try to change my mind about working for you."

Hays' eyes widened with alarm, but he said nothing.

Higgins' right eyebrow arched skyward and a pleased smirk appeared on his ruddy face. "Don't worry, L.J. The man cannot tempt me. Nor can he intimidate me with threats. And here he comes now."

Hays had no desire to flee the confrontation. In

fact he had several reasons for witnessing it—to make certain Higgins did remain true to his promise and to hear firsthand what Ben Williams would say when he realized he'd lost. And so he stayed and watched as Williams strode up to Higgins and demanded to be told "where I stand."

Higgins puffed placidly on his pipe. "Near as I can tell, Ben, you stand right smack in front of me, if that's what you want. On the other hand . . ."

"Don't mince words with me, Joseph," the banker spat in a threatening voice.

"If you're referring to the matter you asked me about this morning, I'm afraid I've some bad news for you. Bad news, indeed! I've just accepted a contract to do that job for somebody else, so I won't hold you to that contract you gave me to estimate what it'd cost."

Williams' mouth dropped open in surprise at Higgins' simple, direct admission. The banker's always florid face became nearly crimson with anger. He glared at Higgins, his hands balling into fists. Hays wondered if the banker might actually send a roundhouse at the shipbuilder.

"So," Williams murmured. "It is true that you have betrayed me and gone to work for Hays! You, Joseph, who I have thought of as a friend ever since I came to St. Paul. I have broken bread with you, drunk with you, played poker with you, financed you in your undertakings."

Higgins regarded the banker calmly, a trace of a smile playing upon his lips. "I have betrayed no one, Ben. You had a chance to engage me to raise the *Cuyahoga*, but you did not. You only hired me to estimate its cost. The one with whom I have contracted had the same chance you had—and the same knowledge. But he chose to hire me and did. His sub-

## Railroad King    51

stantial down payment now lies in my account in your bank."

But Williams was not through. "I repeat, Joseph, you have betrayed me. There can be no other explanation for Hays' sudden interest in the wrecked boat on the very same morning I commissioned you to look into her salvage."

"On the contrary, Mr. Williams," L.J. broke in. "There is absolutely no connection between the two events. I have been interested in the *Cuyahoga* from the day I learned of her fate. On a number of occasions Mr. Higgins and I have discussed raising her."

"A likely tale!" Williams declared. "There's little doubt in my mind what happened. You're working together to keep me from acquiring title to that sunken steamer and I'll not have it. You'll soon learn you can't freeze me out this way!"

Williams turned and stalked away—almost knocking over one of Higgins' carpenters who happened to be coming out of the shipyard office as the banker stormed by.

"Does he mean it, Mr. Higgins?" Hays asked. "Can he keep us from salvaging the *Cuyahoga*?"

Higgins' eyes were still on the retreating figure of the banker. "He has many friends," the shipbuilder admitted. "So, if you want to play it safe, I'll gather a crew and sail the *Mighty Mite*—my tug—over there right now."

"How long will it take? I want to be there and I have to arrange with Tim to run the office for the rest of the day."

"With luck, I can be ready to sail by one-thirty."

"You'll have a passenger, Mr. Higgins," L.J. declared, then turned and strode out of the shipyard.

The *Cuyahoga* seemed a pathetic giant, a great and desperate animal that had struggled in vain to free itself of the murky Mississippi. The ship's bow edged ashore, riding unevenly on the muddy bottom. Its stern fell into the depths, submerged in the cold, grey waters of early spring. It gave the impression of being a monstrous creature whose last effort had failed just short of success. The beast, once graceful and powerful, lay broken, twisted and painfully alone along the shore of the river. Waves lapped at it in silent triumph. The wind blew through its railings, windows and open doors. Bits of lumber tilted in the breeze and a red shirt, long abandoned, clapped against an unused boom. Apparently exhausted, it had died within easy grasp of salvation, a swimmer who'd drowned in only inches of water.

One of its two towering chimneys leaned to port and its white paint and gleaming decorations were weathered to a dull glow. Scattered all over was glass from the small panes that once windowed the pilot's house, and a boiler lay askew on the deck.

L.J. considered this beast and a tear came to his eye. The *Cuyahoga* had once been proud, a marvel in an age of marvels. The glistening pine of its decks, the starched poplar doors and casements, the taut design of cabin and hoist had made it a thing to be reckoned with. But as the young shipping clerk gazed, he saw an aging empress, a remnant. And he knew the ship for what it was: a thing of the past. He would raise the *Cuyahoga*, sail it, build an empire propelled by its great, steaming engines. But he would never restore its greatness. Near-death had revealed an ultimate weakness, for steamships were, finally, fragile. And as he looked at his prize from the bluff above the river, L.J. Hays resolved to build an empire of sturdier stuff.

Hays watched with narrowed eyes as Higgins and his crew maneuvered around the *Cuyahoga* in their tug. Finally, they nosed up to her on the port side and moored their stout little craft to a pair of railing uprights that rose out of the water. As the shipbuilder directed his men to assess damage to the ship, Hays returned to the workmen's sides. He'd climbed the bluff so as to contemplate his enterprise before the work engulfed him. He wanted to savor his folly for a moment before it became a panicky rush to victory. Instead, though, the sight had saddened him. His extraordinary measures would leave the boat flawed, at least in his own mind, forever. She may well be beautiful once again, he thought, but she can never again be wonderful.

There were two sizable shell holes in the ship's bow—on the port side—and both were out of the water. It took Higgins' crew less than two hours to patch them. But, having completed these chores, the far more difficult problem of locating the underwater ruptures lay ahead. No attempt could be made to pump out the tons of water in the ship's belly until the hull was once again watertight.

Josh Laurence had said that all of the ship's damage was on the port side, and Hays had passed along this information to Higgins. The shipbuilder then had concentrated his search for damage on that side. Eventually, they found two more places where the *Cuyahoga*'s hull was torn open, one of them, according to Higgins, a "monstrous gash." Because of its size, Higgins wasn't sure it could be patched well enough to seal it off.

Higgins' men were patching the smaller of the underwater holes, one not far from the two they had previously repaired, when he told Hays about the big one.

Hays met the shipbuilder's eyes unblinkingly as he and Higgins stood on the *Mighty Mite*'s deck watching the proceedings. "You *will* try?" Hays asked.

"Of course. If that hole can be patched, my men will manage it."

"It must be patched," Hays replied grimly. He paced the tug's cluttered deck as the shipbuilder moved to the stern of the tug, where his men were working on a large wood-and-canvas patch. Seeing the size of it, Hays could understand Higgins' concern. Would they be able to jockey such a large patch in place and secure it against the river water? Would it hold? Would it keep the hull watertight long enough for the ship to be pumped out, raised and fitted with interior patches?

Hays agonized as he watched Higgins' crew finish preparing the large patch and carry it forward, where a rowboat awaited its delivery. Inside the tug two of Higgins' men waited, one of them a broad-shouldered black man called Jumbo. He had, Higgins told him, come up from the South in the early days of the war. He'd fled out of fear the Rebel army might overwhelm the Northeast. Jumbo was a good man, Higgins judged, who made up in strength and willingness to work what he lacked in experience.

The men took the patch into the skiff and oared over to the fully submerged stern of the *Cuyahoga*, where they stripped to the waist, discarded their boots and slipped into the stone-cold waters of the Mississippi. Hays shivered. Not until June were these waters warm enough to swim in.

Jumbo and the other man dragged a stout rope underwater, attached it to a submerged section of deck near the stern, then tossed the other end to the tug. Using it to guide them, they carried the patch down to the *Cuyahoga*'s hull some ten feet below.

## Railroad King

It took more than an hour and four different two-man teams before the last man crawled out of the water, onto the tug, and reported that the patch had been secured. Men shivered like terrified animals in the cold air, but none would go below. Each wrapped himself in a rough blanket and watched the work. And there was much concerned murmuring among them. But they waited, the extraordinary hope of hard-working men as thick as fog in the cold, still air.

The remainder of Higgins' men now strung out the long, flexible supply pipes from the tug to the midsection of the *Cuyahoga* and downward, like snakes, into the water-filled hold. Soon the discharge pipes had been attached to the steam-driven centrifugal pump and were extended out over the tug's other side, ready to carry river water out of the *Cuyahoga* and back into the Mississippi.

The fan at the core of the pump was already making raucous chugging noises as the supply pipes began drawing water from the depths of the submerged ship. Hays focused his attention on the discharge pipes—willing them to begin sending a spray of water out into the river.

Night was a short time away, but gas lamps already had been lit along the inland side of the tug, while others had been placed on the top of the sunken ship where the supply pipes were strung. A single lantern hung near the stern of the *Cuyahoga* above the place where the giant gash had been patched. Though it was not yet dark, Hays thought the scene looked like a cluster of fireflies was hovering over a pair of beached whales.

Just then the sound from the pump changed to indicate that water had reached its core and was being whirled about and sent up the discharge pipes. A moment later the first of the water keeping the *Cuyahoga* pinned to the bottom of the Mississippi was cascading out of the pipes. Cheers sounded from the crew. Then Higgins, who had stayed in the skiff, near the side of the sunken steamer, was heard to utter a string of curses—totally uncharacteristic of the shipbuilder!

"Slippery eels in the pastor's shoes, the damned patch has slipped!" was the mildest of them. A moment later the gruff old man had rowed his boat back to the tug and climbed aboard. Though his eyes betrayed a battered heart, his words were simple, even, professionally bland. "I told you that was a bad hole," he advised Hays.

"Can it be repaired?" Hays asked, looking at the side of the ship.

Higgins sighed. "It can be and must be, L.J.," he replied, "only it'll have to wait till tomorrow. It's almost dark and it's just too cold in there. I'll not send another man into that river tonight."

Hays thought for a moment, then met Higgins' eyes. "I can do it, Mr. Higgins," he blurted. "I'm young enough. Just tell me what to do and I'll do it."

"No, L.J.," was the shipbuilder's reply. "Not you. I won't allow it."

"What's the alternative?" Hays demanded angrily. "To shut down the pump until tomorrow?"

Higgins shrugged. "It can't be helped."

"Yes, it can." He began unlacing his boots.

"You don't know what you're doing," Higgins scolded. "Your body won't take that cold for more than a few minutes, L.J. Five—ten at the most. And the cost to you could be your life."

"My life? My life's tied up in that boat down there, Mr. Higgins. Now please tell me what to do once

I get my head wet." L.J. smiled, an unsuccessful effort to put Higgins at ease.

Hays was no Tim Wolfe, but he was, at one hundred seventy pounds, strong and capable. And if determination could aid a swimmer, L.J. would have nothing to worry about. But Higgins remained adamant. "It's not your job, L.J.," he argued. "I won't let you go down there."

"You've nothing to say in the matter, Mr. Higgins. You work for me and I'll make this decision, thank you. Now, don't get in my way, old man," L.J. growled, his voice hard and vicious. "There's no telling when Ben Williams may show up here, or what he may try to do to stop me from raising my boat. I won't be stopped, by him or by you."

Now Higgins drew closer to Hays. He lowered his voice against the ears of the men standing around on deck. "Please, L.J., don't try it. You could die." The aging carpenter, tough boss and rigid businessman heard his own voice crack with concern. It startled him and he fell silent.

Hays felt the sound of concern break over him but ignored it. He cast his boots aside.

It was barely light when L.J. Hays slipped into the icy waters of the Mississippi. The chill of the river ran across his skin and burst like a flower in his skull. For a moment, he was senseless. Black water and darkened skies surrounded him. A shudder racked him. He was numbed, lost. Not yet, Reverend, he thought.

But there was no time to consider, each motionless moment a moment lost. So he sucked into his lungs all the air they would accommodate and followed the rope down to the ship's stern. As Higgins had said, the patch had moved, nearly a foot. As fast as water could be pumped it would pour back into the *Cuyahoga*.

He shivered, his body feeling as if it were locked in a block of ice. Steeling himself, he shoved the patch with his left hand, trying to move it back into place against the damaged hull. It would not budge, held in place as it was by three large U-clamps anchored on the far edge of the hull.

Because the river's bottom dropped away sharply forty feet farther in, the *Cuyahoga*'s stern had water under it, so Hays now swam to the keel to loosen the clamps enough to move the patch. Although his fingers were numb with the cold, he managed to do so. But then he had to surface to catch his breath. His lungs were bursting when he broke the water, gasping.

"Are you all right?" came Higgins' worried voice.

For a moment Hays could not respond. He was too busy breathing again. Although the air above was cool—in the 50s—it felt warm as bathwater to him. The rest of his body felt numb.

"Aye, Mr. Higgins," Hays managed, "I . . . I had to loosen the clamps. The patch wouldn't budge."

"You'll need some help, then. One of my men, Jumbo Jones, has offered to come in to help you, L.J. He was down earlier and did his bit, but he's a strong young fellow and can take it."

Hays welcomed the help, knowing now that the task he'd taken on was not only difficult, but nearly impossible for one man. Jones joined him in the water moments later and Hays told him what they had to do. "Once the patch is back in place, Jumbo," Hays directed, "I'll swim over to the other side and tighten the clamps, then come back to tell you we're finished."

Jones, his teeth clamped together against the cold, nodded and murmured a terse "Whatever you say."

## Railroad King

Then they went down, Hays first. He tried to move the patch, but it continued to resist his ever-colder muscles. Jumbo joined him and added his strength, and slowly the reluctant assembly of wood and canvas slid back into place. Jones held the rope with one hand, his body and other hand against the patch as Hays dove under the hull to tighten the clamps. L.J.'s lungs were already tortured as he fought to turn clumsy hand screws without losing his bearings. His fingers were barely responsive to his command, his eyes wanting to close against the biting cold. But he managed it and soon could turn the screws no more. Quickly he dove under the hull, grabbed Jumbo's arm and headed upward. Both of them were gasping for breath when they surfaced, but Hays felt as if he were still underwater. He passed out just as Higgins' men grabbed him and began pulling him from the deathly cold Mississippi.

The sky had deepened to pitch black when Hays finally awakened. He felt warm air against his skin but was shivering nonetheless. For a moment he couldn't remember where he was, but then he heard the steady chug, chug, chug of the *Mighty Mite*'s pump and the hiss of water traveling through her pipes. He knew he was aboard Higgins' tug.

The pump! he thought. The patch must be holding!!! Hays tried to rise but his head reeled. He lay back.

"You jes' better take it easy, Mr. Hays," came a voice nearby. "You sure as hell got cold down there and it's gonna take some time before you can get up."

"Is that you, Jumbo?"

"The same. We're in the tug's cabin, case you care."

"Is the patch okay?"

The huge black man laughed. "If it ain't, Mr. Higgins is sure wastin' a lot of coal keeping steam up to run the pump!"

Hays fell back into an exhausted sleep.

Dawn was breaking before Hays again awakened. The cabin was toasty warm from the coal stove and Jumbo was sleeping soundly on blankets in the middle of the room. Hot, Hays shoved away the covering blankets, then pulled them back, realizing he was naked. He looked around the cabin for his clothes, didn't find them, and sat up. He managed it now without difficulty.

As his mind cleared, his eyes came upon a porthole across the way. Wrapping a blanket around his middle, he padded over to the embrasure. His legs were wobbly, but held him.

Through the dim morning light he saw the *Cuyahoga*. It was still underwater! The sky remained dark, but was lightening from a deep blue to a much lighter shade. He could still hear the steady throbbing of the pump. Behind him he heard the sound of the cabin door latch. He turned to see a smiling Joseph Higgins.

"And how are you feeling, my young friend?" Higgins asked.

"I'd feel better if I had something on besides a blanket—and if I hadn't just seen the *Cuyahoga* still underwater."

Higgins chuckled. "There are some work clothes in that footlocker. Put them on and you can come outside and be a witness to a grand show."

"A grand show? I don't understand."

"You'll see, L.J. Just dress and meet me on deck." Higgins was gone before Hays could protest.

## Railroad King

Jumbo Jones was snoring loudly as Hays, now wearing an old but comfortable pair of work trousers and a woolly plaid jacket, stepped across him and went out the door. It was six o'clock and the sky was brightening steadily as a well-rested but impatient Hays strode barefoot down the tug's deck and stopped next to Higgins.

"How much longer can this go on?" Hays asked, his eyes on the *Cuyahoga*. Though the steady throb meant Higgins' pump had been draining the great craft all night, the reluctant giant still sat, submerged. L.J. studied the pleased, relaxed faces on deck and peered at his ship. He wondered if some disaster had occurred that none of his fellow workers perceived. He was confused by the *Cuyahoga*'s apparent refusal to float.

"She'll surface soon," Higgins answered.

"Really?"

"Aye, she's buoyant enough to float now."

"Then, what's wrong?" Something was amiss, L.J. thought.

"Simple enough, she's stuck in the mud. Suction along her great flat bottom is holding her down. But it'll break up, you'll see." Higgins remained so calm that Hays had no alternative but to accept his prognosis.

Only moments later it began. A stream of bubbles, bursting at the surface along the port railing, sent ripples across the Mississippi. Then another vent opened and air hurried to the surface like a line of bubbles in a glass of champagne. Soon the starboard side rose with a rush of water, waves lapping the shore, and for a moment L.J. thought all was lost. The massive ship, listing to port, had raised its starboard side first and so tilted, nearly capsizing. The clap of doors and the clanging of metal could be heard on the deck.

Glass shattered. Barrels rolled like thunder in her hold. Suddenly the creak and twist of wood erupted in an ear-shattering song and the entire stern of the *Cuyahoga* rose like a whale leaping from the water.

As the *Cuyahoga* splashed to the surface and bobbed there, the bow broke loose from its muddy mooring and the ship floated, rocking gently in the wake of its own escape. Dirty water poured from the decks, driftwood snarled the superstructure like burrs, and the two, massive paddle wheels seemed clogged with silt.

"God, it's a mess," L.J. said breathlessly.

"Wait till you're aboard. It'll all look worse," Higgins smiled, but he was already on the move, headed with his men for the rowboats. Hays clambered after him, determined to be the first man on board. As they came alongside the *Cuyahoga*, Higgins deferred to L.J., who ducked under a shattered railing and rolled aboard. He was instantly mired in the muck of the river. It covered his back and hands, face and knees.

"Huzzah!" he bellowed, throwing a fist into the air. Higgins grinned so broadly he thought he'd die and the tough, tired, hard-working members of his crew clapped their oars against the sides of the boat in celebration. L.J. was a sight, filthy and smiling on a ship that looked a horror and could do nothing more than float.

Higgins and his crew quickly boarded and disappeared, some bound for the hold to patch the makeshift seals, the shipbuilder to inspect the *Cuyahoga*'s cargo. L.J., though, could do nothing but wander around. Until that moment he had not fully understood how truly immense his ship was. It took him fifteen minutes to make his way through its mazes.

Then Joseph Higgins appeared. "She'll need a lot

of work," he stated, almost blandly. "But she's a ship, not a wreck. Congratulations, Mr. Hays." Hays beamed as they shook hands.

Above the hammering and orders of men working below, L.J. heard a distant cry. A man screaming. And he turned to look up river only to see a Union gunboat, followed by a tug, bearing down on them.

"That'll be Ben Williams," Higgins offered, not a trace of speculation in his voice.

"And the Army," Hays added. "Got a hammer?"

The shipwright pulled an ancient tool from a loop in his belt and handed it to L.J. with a somewhat puzzled look. Then Hays produced a small, rectangular piece of wood from his coat and nailed it roughly into the water-logged wood of the lower deck. The homemade plaque read, RESURRECTION. Below the name of the ship were the words, "Property of Hays Forwarding Co., St. Paul, Minnesota."

A short time later the Union gunboat came alongside the *Resurrection*'s stern and cast out an anchor. Williams and two young Army officers paddled toward them in a small boat. Hays watched silently. When they arrived and tried to throw over a mooring line, he let it fall at his feet and slip back overboard.

"It's customary, gentlemen," he shouted to them, "to request permission to come aboard another man's ship."

"The hell you say!" snapped Williams. "I've as much right to that derelict as you!"

"You are entirely wrong, Mr. Williams," Hays rejoined calmly. "Under the maritime laws, this ship belongs to me, for I have raised her."

"Permission to come aboard, sir," called out the taller of the two Army men, a mustachioed, blue-uniformed officer who identified himself only as Captain Stevens.

"For what purpose?" Hays countered, suppressing a grin.

"To talk," returned Williams, "about your claim to the *Cuyahoga*—and the Union Army's."

Williams' gambit didn't surprise Hays. Nor was he lulled by it. He knew his situation was a difficult one. There was, after all, a war going on and his ship's hold was loaded with munitions. The Union had a natural interest in the boat, even if it weren't for Ben Williams' influence. Still, the issue of an Army claim on the vessel had to be resolved immediately and his most direct defense against any takeover effort was to keep the intruders off his boat. "Permission to board is not granted," L.J. announced.

Williams was about to reply when the tall Captain quieted him with a gesture and turned to Hays across the water that separated them. "Mr. Hays," he began, "I assure you we mean no harm. I have orders to look into this ship's cargo. It was our Navy which sank it and we want some guarantee that its contents won't wind up in Rebel hands. The matter is that simple."

"Do you know what the cargo is, Captain Stevens?" Hays asked.

"We believe you hold munitions, sir."

"I do, Captain. And they are mine. My question, sir, is whether the Union will pay me a fair price for them."

"Wait a damn minute!" Williams roared. "I didn't get you out here, Captain, to bargain with this young whippersnapper. He doesn't own what's aboard the *Cuyahoga*."

"The *Resurrection*," Hays corrected with a laugh.

Stevens shrugged. Williams had paid him a visit

late yesterday afternoon to persuade him that certain "friends" of his could do Captain Stevens a great deal of good if he cooperated in preventing Hays from salvaging the *Cuyahoga*. Stevens would have rejected the banker's request out of hand but for two factors—the man's reputation in Minnesota politics and the Army's interest in learning what the steamer had carried in her hold the night she was sunk.

Stevens pointed a warning finger at Williams. "You are not in charge of me, sir," he declared. "If it is in the Army's best interests to strike a bargain with Mr. Hays, we shall do so. I am certain he realizes that the store of munitions aboard this vessel, whatever her name is, has more importance to us than money or the possession of one derelict ship. The cargo, though it may not belong to the Union Army, cannot be allowed to be misused."

"Of course, Captain Stevens," Hays broke in. "I've no objection to returning the stores to your custody for the right price. It must be obvious to you that I am expending a great deal of money in order to salvage them along with the ship."

"We can certainly discuss the matter, Mr. Hays," Captain Stevens said. He picked up the mooring rope and held it up once more to toss over to Hays, but L.J. shook his head.

"I will discuss nothing with you as long as Mr. Williams is at your shoulder," he declared. "I will be glad to talk with you, however, as soon as my ship is in St. Paul. You have my personal assurance that I will do nothing with the cargo until I have paid you a visit and we have talked things out."

"You will take this ship nowhere, Hays!" declared Williams. "Captain Stevens, I demand that you order these people off this ship. If you will not, I'll have you demoted so fast your head will swim."

Stevens, an imposing young man, proud of his service and sure of his worth, bristled at this last remark. A silent, implied threat from the banker was one thing, but he'd seen too much death, had come too close to it himself, to be bullied by a greedy civilian.

"Mr. Williams, I am tired of the sound of your voice," he growled, silencing the banker. "Mr. Hays has a perfectly valid claim to this vessel. So long as its stores are kept from the South, I have no complaint." For a moment L.J. thought a mute but clear look of approval crossed the Union officer's face as he gazed up at Hays. It seemed for a moment as though the two young men, without ever having conferred with one another, had conspired to keep the blustering Williams in his place. One had beaten him to a ship, the other would not be threatened by him. Both forms of courage struck L.J. as remarkable. He waited for Stevens to speak again.

"If you don't mind, Mr. Hays, I will be sending a platoon of my men to keep an eye on your ship until we've met in St. Paul. They will stand ashore, with a boat, until you make your way out of here."

"Three of your men, if you think three sufficient, may come aboard to guard the hold, Captain Stevens. I have your word that the Army will not challenge my ownership of the *Resurrection* and your word is enough," Hays stated, his voice clear and ringing above the silence around him.

Captain Stevens doffed his cap with a tight-lipped smirk and ordered his skiff rowed back to the tug. As they moved away from Hays, L.J. could hear the fading sound of Williams' curses and see his broad, random gestures of infuriation. L.J. Hays thought to himself that this was but the first of many rounds with the banker. And knew there were encounters he was destined to lose.

# Chapter 3

The small, brown-and-white one-story house L.J. Hays shared with Tim Wolfe, a joint venture of the pair, was built of stone and timber and stood on the banks of the Mississippi. It stood little more than twenty-five feet above the river, to the east, on a twenty-five-acre tract just south of the docks. Tim's father had bought the land for fifty dollars from a prospector in need of a grubstake to prospect in the Dakota Territory. Shortly after having bought the land, though, Tim's mother ran off with a drummer hawking cutlery. Tim's father, disgusted, gave the property to his only child and headed back East. Hays had financed the materials used in building the house and, in return, received half interest in the entire property from Tim.

While it was not prime residential property—most of that was to the north and east, on the highest of the bluffs on which St. Paul was built—the house and grounds were ideal for the needs of Hays and Wolfe. A dirt road just outside its front door, narrow and winding, followed the river to other equally narrow roads.

From their house, L.J. and Tim could see the docks, the Riverboat Saloon adjacent to them and

Joseph Higgins' shipyard. There, being refurbished, the *Resurrection* loomed high over the river, in dry dock.

Hays thought this last a stirring sight and arose early enough each morning to watch his steamship appear out of the gloom and mist that burned away as the sun rose. The vessel seemed an eternal dream to him at this hour, a thing transforming itself from a wish into wood and iron. At times he wondered, watching the shrouded outlines materialize in the distance, if it were the heat of the day or the strength of his imagination that brought the *Resurrection* into sight.

The Civil War had recently become a part of history, but the country was still staggering with the confusion of its end. The Mississippi, just as L.J. had predicted, was slowly filling with ships and St. Paul was growing. While all this went on, the Hays/Wolfe house became the first general office of Hays Forwarding Company. In it, Hays waited impatiently for the day his firm would go into business with the relaunching of the *Resurrection* onto the river. As he bided his time, L.J. had little choice but to confine himself to the humble house. He could ill afford a more suitable office at the docks. Yet, he was far from discouraged. He had a start in the freight business even before he owned a seaworthy boat. As a result of the fair deal he had struck with Captain Stevens over the *Resurrection*'s munitions, the officer had arranged a contract for L.J. with the Army. His boat would have cargo the first day it floated.

Over a year had passed since the old steamer had been raised and towed to the Higgins shipyard. It proved a trouble-filled year for Hays, thanks in no small part to banker Ben Williams.

Joseph Higgins ran into an endless chain of problems in rehabilitating Hays' ship, and L.J. went through every dollar he could beg or borrow to keep the work moving forward. Not a dime came from traditional lending sources. Ben Williams, his reputation and outspoken disapproval of the *Resurrection* preceding L.J. everywhere, had managed to harass him at every turn.

At war's end, Hays had a ship, an incorporated shipping company, a contract to supply the Army with flour milled in Minnesota—and no money to hire a crew and actually begin operations.

Banker Williams' first action following his unsuccessful try at stalling Hays' salvage attempt was to contact J. Parnell Brown in St. Louis and inform him that his agent in St. Paul now owned a steamship and planned to go into business for himself. Brown did not immediately fire Hays, but did make it a point to investigate the matter personally. A month after the *Resurrection* was towed to St. Paul, Brown was an unexpected visitor in Hays' office. He fired Hays on the spot.

Brown did not fire Tim Wolfe, but L.J.'s friend, now the St. Paul agent, offered to quit if Hays asked it. L.J. told him to stay. "Why should we both suffer for my sins?" he told Tim.

There were few jobs in St. Paul, but Hays paid the railroad office a visit and asked Phil Crabtree for work. Crabtree already knew about the circumstances of Hays' firing from St. Paul Shipping. Crabtree also suggested that Ben Williams was "mentioning" to his bank's customers that L.J. Hays was not a man to be trusted.

"You won't give me a job, then, Mr. Crabtree?" asked Hays.

"The hell I won't!" Crabtree exclaimed. "Ben Williams and his bank need the railroad more than it needs him. I won't help him carry out his personal vendetta against you, young fellow. You can start tomorrow. It'll be hard work, but at least it's work."

And it was hard work.

The St. Paul Railroad had completed its main line to Minneapolis and now was moving farther west, toward the Red River, where the railroad expected to reap a bonanza by connecting with the Hudson Bay Company's steamers trading with Manitoba and the Canadian provinces.

It was backbreaking labor and the winter was brutal, its snowfall three times as heavy as normal. L.J. thought this was surely to make up for the extraordinarily dry winter of a year earlier. The construction gang was on the road six days a week and on the seventh, when Crabtree hauled the crew back to St. Paul, Hays slept all the way. But he did not go home until he had paid Joseph Higgins' shipyard a visit to check on the progress of the *Resurrection*.

The wages he earned from the railroad paid his bills and kept him afloat. But the experiences made a mark on the youth.

The smell and sound and power of the gargantuan machines thrilled him. Flames belched from fireboxes with an anger never found aboard a ship. And the lunge of rods, the clatter of valves and the clouds of vapor that accompanied a steam engine bespoke the power of its cylinders with an eloquence that awed L.J. The stench of sizzling oil and the rancid fumes of gas and steam confirmed in his mind the sense that progress was a grim, churning endeavor, beautiful only in its proportions. The vision made his heart pound. The machine age, with all its revolutionary implications, was upon them, he thought. And L.J. Hays' mind reeled with the possibilities of power, magnificent power.

Nothing so much as the track crew proved to him that railroads were the industry of the future. The laying of rails, a simple, direct process, was, it turned out, an extraordinary undertaking. Even a small line like the one for which he worked employed two hundred men in its crew. Piers and bridges rose before them, grading proceeded at a staggering pace, always just ahead. Mountains were leveled, valleys filled, and always the rails were carried forward, trains transporting them, men toting them, hammers securing them. It was an overwhelming logistical effort. But to L.J. it was a ballet propelled by power, moved by a vision few could understand. It was all at the heart of empires and the building of them. Each spike, each groan from every man, a bit of the whole, staggering mosaic.

But even as Hays watched the stupendous procession creeping across the land, he discerned a flaw in the endeavor. He quickly learned, from the ache in his own back and the grousing of his fellow workers, that railroads moved in mysterious ways. The waste he saw surprised him, for it was obvious that the most efficient route between the two points the St. Paul office wished to unite was not being followed. Logically, track should be laid as straight as possible and should avoid sharp grades. But whoever had done the planning for the St. Paul's road to the Red River had built all manner of detours into its path. Scuttlebutt had it that the engineers in charge, or else stockholders in the road, were trying to line their own pockets by touching land they owned. The road wandered everywhere, progressing only two miles for every three that were laid.

In the spring, when the snow was gone and the weather warmed, Hays explored the country north and south of the railroad beds and was surprised by the rich, black soil of the region. With the Indian uprisings of the past several years ended, the land would be ideal for farming, he thought. If the railroad could be extended north and west, Hays decided, wheat grown in Minnesota could be shipped to the West Coast and Canada. A bonanza for railroad and farmer alike would result.

Of course, neither the St. Paul, for whom he was toiling, nor its chief competitor, the Pacific Northern, which was planning to reach the coast, had plans to build a northern spur to Manitoba. But it was obvious to Hays that Canada must one day soon build a transcontinental railroad of its own. Trade and settlement demanded it.

Hays was also impressed with the potential of the Red River, which flowed north and served as the boundary between Minnesota and North Dakota. Unlike the long, deep Mississippi, the Red was narrow and shallow, and had few steamboats—all of them owned and operated by the Hudson Bay Company. And this was a jealously guarded monopoly. If one could buck that monopoly, he would do well, Hays thought.

As the summer of 1865 approached, Joseph Higgins' men were putting finishing touches on the refurbished *Resurrection* and Hays suddenly found himself in a financial bind. Try as he might, he was unable to obtain a line of credit from either of Ben Williams' two banking competitors in Minnesota. The two rejections were suspiciously similar, both banks refusing him because he had never borrowed before, and both ignoring the substantial collateral that Hays had in the *Resurrection*.

Hays was furious. He was certain Williams was

somehow behind his failure to obtain credit, but uncertain what to do about it. He needed capital and had to raise it soon. Even though he had managed to pay Higgins for all but the last of the repairs, L.J. could not operate the steamer without monies to pay the cost of fueling it, hiring a crew and advertising for passengers and freight.

L.J. decided there was only one place where he could obtain the financing he required—St. Louis. The Missouri port was a thriving center of commerce and had a number of national and even a few international financial institutions operating there. Williams, Hays was sure, could not plague him in such a city.

And so, he put on his best business suit—his only one—booked passage to St. Louis on the *Lakeland* and on a rainy, miserable day in early June strode slowly up the gangplank to the ship's main deck. Hays was almost out of money, for he hadn't worked in a month. The St. Paul Railroad had stopped laying track due to financial problems. Worse, if he could not obtain credit in St. Louis, he would be in desperate straits, personally and professionally. He still owed Higgins a small amount for the final painting on his ship, he had ordered advertising posters and owed for the new section of dock erected for his steamer last month.

Where once he had owned a bank account with nearly ten thousand dollars in it, he now had little more than the clothes on his back—and his as-yet-unlaunched steamer.

It was, he thought now, a sorry state of affairs and one which had to be rectified soon. Still, he supposed things could be worse. If he had not succeeded in raising the *Cuyahoga* in the first place, he would not have had this opportunity to fail so spectacularly. If the thought was less than funny, at least it entertained him. For if nothing else, L.J. Hays was a spectacle in the making, and he knew it.

Reaching into his pocket, he procured his last cigar and managed, after a few attempts in the light rain, to ignite it. Then he walked up to the first-class deck and stood watching as the steamer began backing out of berth at the St. Paul dock. As he smoked, Hays remembered a prayer his aunt once had taught him. A prayer that offered hope that God might grant a solemn wish. Hays did not know God very well, but closed his eyes and mouthed the words silently, hoping for the best. If he could not obtain his line of credit in St. Louis, his new shipping company would die aborning.

That idea was as repulsive as any he could imagine and the fact that he was only twenty-seven did nothing to make such an early bankruptcy palatable. At the moment, he was both the youngest steamship owner in America and the poorest. As he considered that strange condition, his reverie seemed a self-inflicted goad. As he contemplated the possibility that he had come so close only to fail, he felt revulsion, even disgust. To entertain defeat suggested surrender, he concluded. And only the weak gave in to adversity. He would not, could not, allow a trace of resignation in his mind. He could not be satisfied with anything but his goal. Any alternative was unacceptable.

Suddenly a voice from behind him startled Hays. "Well, I can't imagine what you're thinking, L. Jerome, but I hope it's not about me—you're sporting a scowl like none I've ever seen."

Hays half-turned to see the pretty teacher Lucille Morgan standing nearby. In spite of his dour mood, Hays had to smile at Lucille's chiding. She looked even prettier than he remembered. She wore a sky-blue, lace promenade dress, and sported a frilly hat adorned with feathers. He thought inanely that she reminded him of an expensive china doll he once had seen in a Montreal shop window many years ago. Like Lucille, the doll was beautiful to look at, but would no doubt shatter if handled improperly. He wondered vaguely how an ordinary schoolteacher could afford the rich clothes the Morgan girl habitually wore.

He bowed awkwardly and murmured a greeting. He had run across her several times in the past year. Once she had even come to his house seeking him. Sadly, L.J. had been away working for Crabtree's railroad crew and Tim had spoken to her. He later kidded L.J. about her.

Hays had not thought his barroom remarks funny. "She's a lady, Tim," he'd chided. "You should have more respect for her."

Tim had laughed, finding such a prim perspective unmanly. "You think all ladies are cold, L.J.?" he'd returned. "Some damn sure are, but not Lucille Morgan. I can tell. She's got blood in her veins, that's for sure. No ice water. Not a drop!"

As she stood looking out onto the Mississippi from the upper deck of the *Lakeland*, Lucille Morgan appeared to L.J. to be a perfect lady. Her stiff, almost athletic carriage, crisp features and perfect grooming acted as a kind of frame for the picture of her smile. Somehow, she was at once porcelain pure and invitingly warm, the product of breeding and an emblem of self-confidence.

It was this last that so unnerved him. For L.J. had long ago been taught his own limits, had years before discovered his own fallibility. And try as he might, he could not discern even the slightest self-doubt in Lucille Morgan. She was magnificent and knew it, bright and could prove it. She unsettled him more than mere beauty could have.

"Are you really going to St. Louis, Miss Morgan?" he asked, instantly realizing the stupidity of the remark.

"If I'm not, L. Jerome, then I *am* in trouble. This boat won't be stopping until we get there." Kindly, she didn't laugh. "Where are you staying, once we arrive?" she continued. "I'll show you all the sights."

"I'm afraid I won't have time for much sightseeing, Miss . . . Lucille. I'm on business. In fact, I haven't even decided where I'm staying."

"Well, then, you must stay with me. I insist."

"With you? You have a house in St. Louis?"

"My uncle does, and a very large one. It will swallow you up unnoticed, even if he's there. So, you must be my guest, it's settled. We can share my cab."

Hays protested, but to no avail. And it was just as well, for he needed lodging in St. Louis and if he could stay with Lucille's uncle, he would save money. He wondered about Lucille's ability to offer such hospitality until he found that a handsome carriage awaited the girl at the dock—attended by one of her uncle's servants—to take them to an absolutely stunning Victorian house north of the city.

Hays could do little more than stare open-mouthed at the house that greeted them. Set on a hill in the best residential area of the burgeoning city, Lucille's uncle's home was painted an ornate blue and white. Large balconies overlooked the river from upstairs rooms, and the home was surrounded by acres of rolling lawn and framed by tall, stately trees.

"Surprised?" Lucille pried, as they alighted from the carriage and walked up the steps to the front porch.

"Astonished, Lucille. Who is your uncle? This place must be worth a fortune!"

"Uncle Pierpont? He's . . . well, just a wheeler-dealer. He buys and sells things, you know."

"Large things and many of them, I suspect."

She laughed and took his arm. "Silly. He has places in Connecticut and Florida and a handsome townhouse in New York. And of course, one in England."

"I see," Hays replied weakly. "But if your family has such means, Lucille, why do you work as a common schoolteacher in St. Paul—or anywhere else, for that matter?"

"I'm not exactly common," she chastised, not thrilled by the remark. "But seriously, L. Jerome," she continued, recovering, "without work, life isn't worth much. I enjoy teaching and I hate city life. It's boring and people here know me too well. In St. Louis I'm attractive as much because I was born rich as because of any charm, brains or personality I happen to have. In your town I can be myself, because there are few who know who I am, or, more important, who my family is. Men who court me in St. Paul don't look past little Lucille to my family's money."

The butler who met them at the door was a small sour-faced man with sad eyes. He bowed slightly to Lucille, but looked at Hays with an expression of open disapproval after the girl told him that L.J. would be staying over and she wanted him to have rooms next to hers.

"I don't believe your uncle would approve of such an arrangement, Miss Lucille," he scolded, his sad eyes icy.

"I hardly believe a fine man like your employer would interfere with his niece's life, sir," Hays reproved mildly. "If he would, perhaps I should not even think of doing business with him."

Hays laughed inwardly as the manservant's expression changed immediately. "What is your business, sir?" he asked in more respectful tones.

"Mr. Hays is a very important man in St. Paul, Parker," Lucille interposed. "He's in the shipping business and owns Mississippi River steamboats. Now we're a little hungry. Will you see to it that the cook fixes us some lunch?"

"Of course, Miss Lucille. Right away," Parker said, and hurried away.

"Don't mind him, L. Jerome," she laughed. "He's always been a bit of a snob when it comes to my friends. I've never been quite sure if it was because he thought them after my money, or just not good enough for me."

The lunch of salmon cakes put up by the Morgan cook proved wonderful. Afterward, Lucille arranged to have the Morgan carriage and chauffeur take L.J. to the city's financial district, situated only a few blocks away from the port.

On the way downtown, Hays puzzled over Lucille's uncle. He was obviously a very rich man. From what she had said, he was probably in import-exports, though he could, of course, be in almost anything. He wondered how she could have been born with such means, yet remain so unspoiled. Like so much about her, her wealth was a mystery to him.

But Lucille was far from his mind as he began making the rounds of the banks dotting the two-block St. Louis financial district. He had anticipated that it would take several days to arrange credit, but he soon found it would take even longer, for all the banks he visited wanted time to check out his references—

Joseph Higgins at the shipyard, Phil Crabtree at the railroad and the St. Paul Shipping Company, where L.J. had formerly worked. Tim Wolfe still worked there and L.J. had mentioned to Tim that he might get a visit from someone inquiring about him for credit purposes.

"Should I lie about you, L.J.?" Tim had asked with a laugh.

"Only if they ask what I think of you, Tim," Hays had shot back.

L.J. knew he could count on topnotch recommendations from both Joseph and Phil—though he was not at all certain they would be enough. All the banks he approached would, of course, want to see his ship. He hoped the sight of it would sway things in his favor.

When the carriage arrived back at the Morgan mansion, L.J. was discouraged and exhausted. He'd listened to the fears and skepticisms of a half-dozen bankers during the day, hearing their complaints about inflation, reconstruction and the perils of steamships. Sensing Hays' mood, Lucille made him a cocktail in the study as soon as he returned to the Morgan house. She spoke little, and he not at all, as he sat reviewing in his mind the events of the day. Later, they supped alone in the ornate dining room downstairs. It proved an equally quiet encounter. After, the couple retired to connecting suites of rooms on the second floor.

Hays felt exhausted. He sat, the silk comforter atop his bed rising in swells around him, the remnants of a brandy in one hand. He thought, with a chuckle, that not only was his failing enterprise a spectacular debacle, but the scene of his ship's demise was remarkably well furnished. The room in which he sat was nearly the size of the entire Hays/Wolfe house in St. Paul. He allowed himself to admit that being invited into this wonderful home was a vicious twist of fate. Reaching into his Greek scholarship, he thought of Oedipus, the king, the rich man, housed in luxury, waiting for the stars to ruin him.

A self-indulgent gloom rose in the room and L.J. sipped his brandy, felt helpless and kicked off his shoes. In a large mirror opposite him he saw the worn face of a young man. The intensity of his labors had aged him beyond his years. But in so doing, it had marked his gaunt face with an appealing, hardened look. Clean-shaven and dark, no one could accuse L.J. of being handsome. But there was a quality to him, a kind of visible intensity that made him striking. At this moment, though, he saw only the hollowed cheeks and tired eyes of a discouraged man.

There was a rap, then, on the door connecting his room with Lucille's. "Yes?" he said, standing.

"Yes? What do you mean 'yes'?" she almost chirped.

"I mean, come in."

The door flew open and Lucille bounded into the room wrapped in a canary yellow robe. Her bright smile interrupted his dismal thoughts, even banished them, and he suddenly was aware that he stood in his stocking feet. Lucille lifted a bottle of brandy into the air and tilted her head to one side. She was lovely, as usual, but her heavy silk robe traced the contours of her trim body more closely than the schoolmarm dresses he associated with her. A thin rope, cinched tightly around her waist, made it quite clear that Lucille Morgan was a beautifully proportioned creature.

"You've had a difficult day, I gather," she inquired gently.

"Yes, very."

"Well, brighten up. Things will improve tomorrow."

"I hope so." L.J's tone was filled with doubt.

She marched across the room and poured a liberal amount of brandy into his snifter, then sat down on the bed before filling her own glass. Lucille swirled the dark liquid that was cupped in her hand, inhaled above the goblet's lip and drank.

"You'll find what you're looking for, L. Jerome," she predicted, not a trace of doubt in her voice. "I have an abiding faith in those who work hard for what they want."

"Work is never enough, Lucille. If it were, this would be a world filled with rich men."

"Oh, bosh. Most men simply toil, doing what they're told to do. Those who actually *work* at what they want almost always achieve it."

"I can understand why you think so," his gesture spanning the room, spreading to the house and grounds, somehow enveloping all of St. Louis. It was a remark spurred by envy, he knew. It was mean. He regretted it immediately. Lucille looked down into her glass, hurt, then walked slowly to the window.

"Please forgive me," he whispered toward her. "I'm discouraged and running out of money. You've taken me in and I have no right to malign your wealth."

"Tell me," she said, turning.

"Tell you what?"

"About wealth."

"I don't understand."

"Tell me what you think it is like to be rich. Tell me about wealth."

"You're making fun of me," L.J. responded, irritated.

## Railroad King

"No I'm not. Come here."

He stood and moved slowly toward her. At Lucille's side, in his stocking feet, L.J. stood only an inch or so taller than the woman.

"Being rich means having the sting removed, L.J. It means having things . . . no, *assuming* things will, ultimately, be just fine. Being rich turns life into a game, since, after all, nothing very important can really happen."

"I can't believe that."

"It's true. Look." She pointed to the setting sun, its huge, spreading, crimson lights reaching across the horizon. "I lived in this house for years without ever really noticing how wonderful are the sunsets of St. Louis. It took the mean and difficult lives of my students in St. Paul to teach me about sunsets. Believe it, it's true."

Hays looked. It was indeed a magnificent sunset, stretching across the great plains to the west. "It is easier to notice the sky if your eyes aren't stooped in labor, Lucille. Beauty, I'm absolutely certain, is a thing the rich know more about than do the poor."

"You're wrong, L. Jerome."

He shook his head. It was a peculiarly uncomfortable moment for him. L.J. Hays was, beneath the burning ambition and relentless effort of his professional life, an accomplished scholar. He had been educated in the wilderness of Canada, but had been graced with an extraordinary teacher. And his own energy had led him through vast quantities of literature, science and mathematics. Now, as he stood with Lucille, considering beauty in the abstract, L.J. wondered if beauty was something one wanted or something one admired or something altogether different. He was sure that lust, in the broadest sense of desire, lay somehow at the center of beauty. But he couldn't imagine uttering such a thought in Lucille Morgan's presence.

"One day, L. Jerome, you will be rich and you'll see."

"See what?" he sighed.

"See the warmth and safety. The bad that comes with the good of wealth. The dulling bog of riches that envelops most of those who enter it. You'll see that staying alive, alert, at risk, once you're rich is more difficult than you can possibly imagine."

He thought he heard a sadness in her voice, a weary regret. He turned from the sky he had been idly considering, and looked at her. Tears fell from her eyes.

"When I win, I will let you know." It was a feeble effort at humor, his best attempt to end the conversation that had clearly upset her.

"Hush," she sighed, tears still glistening down her cheeks. She took his hand in hers and brought it to her lips. Lucille kissed his finger tips gently. "Now, before the sun sets," she whispered and led him to her bed.

It can only be said that she made love to him. Hays had, despite his years, never been with a woman and Lucille knew it, somehow. So, as if blessed with a clear tablet on which to sketch, she introduced him to sex with a sweet and patient seduction. Neither spoke to the other. She led him, by gesture and kiss, across the mysteries of her body and finally taught him of the need she felt along with him.

Her breath warm on his chest, Lucille at last slept. L.J. listened to the soft murmur of contentment coming from her lips and stared blankly at the ceiling. He rose silently and slipped into his room.

In his dream, L.J. Hays was falling, dull lights blinking to every side in a twisting kaleidoscope of dis-

## Railroad King

traction. An undecipherable sound, a drone, the indifferent call of a deacon at some church, or the horn of a ship lost in the fog, moaned in his ear. But still he fell, helpless.

Lucille poured coffee into a cup rimmed with gold. L.J. watched her, terrified she might be either angry or disappointed in him. Wondering if he'd done something wrong. Wondering what he should say. He was bewildered by her. Lucille Morgan moved and spoke and smiled at him in exactly the same way she had the day before. He couldn't comprehend such constancy. It made absolutely no sense to him.

"So," she began finally, startling him as he sipped his coffee, "to where are you bound today?"

"In search of wealth and beauty," he answered with a smile.

Her mock frown delighted him.

"Then you will be visiting my uncle's bank," she chimed, that brilliant, shining speculation incredible to him.

"Huh?" he managed, only barely.

"My uncle's bank. He's a banker, you know." She looked at L.J. with that same frown, suggesting that he was kidding her. Looking at him, though, she realized that the handsome young man at her table was an honest, earnest ingénue in the world of business. He was, she thought with a smile, still a virgin, at least when it came to the world of finance. "You really don't know, do you?"

He shook his head.

"My uncle, whose coffee you sip and whose niece you bed, is J. Pierpont Morgan, the banker, among other things."

"Jesus!" he exclaimed.

"Did you apply for credit at the Morgan?"

He shook his head. "Not yet."

"Are you a good credit risk?" she laughed.

"Don't do that! That's not funny. I have a fine refitted steamer, a small government contract and a lot of . . ."

"Oh, shut up, L. Jerome," she cut him off. "I'm sold. I'll wire my uncle this morning and ask him to intercede on your behalf. I'm sure he'll do it on my recommendation. How much money do you need, anyway?"

"I don't believe this . . ." L.J.'s coffee was sloshing onto his lap. "I need ten thousand dollars, but I think I can make it with five."

"Done."

"I'm not sure I ought to be doing this, Lucille. I mean, considering . . ."

"You're not taking advantage of me, L. Jerome. I'm certain your ship will be a success. Now, let's talk about something else."

And that, incredibly, was that. Lucille wired New York, then escorted Hays to her uncle's bank as soon as the reply—affirmative—was received from him. The manager of the Morgan, a tall, lanky, bespectacled man, took Hays' credit application, looked it over with care for perhaps a minute, then stamped it with an energetic thump and signed the document.

"I do hope your *Resurrection* exceeds your fondest dreams," he ended.

Hays and Lucille walked out of the bank with a draft for ten thousand dollars and she accompanied him while he was making arrangements for a crew. The captain, hired after a tedious series of interviews, had served with Josh Laurence during the war. His exploits along the Mississippi, dodging snags as well as

Union gunboats, indicated to L.J. that he had both the quick reflexes, steady nerves and "feel for the water" he wanted.

A month later Lucille broke a bottle of champagne over the bow of the *Resurrection* as it was relaunched into the river. Three hundred passengers, among them Lucille and her schoolchildren, rode the ship to and from St. Louis. In the spacious cabin that L.J. had given Lucille for the trip, the couple spent hours in each other's arms. And to Hays it seemed that beauty had indeed descended upon him.

# Chapter 4

Tim Wolfe was bored. He sat in a wooden chair behind L.J.'s desk in the office of Hays Forwarding, waiting for something to happen. It was deadly dull in the dockside building, despite the *Resurrection*'s return the night before.

Not only was Tim bored, but he was unhappy, his mind far from business, as another Monday began. L.J. was, as usual, away. He was in New Orleans, drumming up business, and probably would not be back until the middle of the month. The *Resurrection* would leave her mooring tomorrow, after loading up with passengers and taking delivery on some cargo due that afternoon.

Tim had no head for figures, but knew that Hays' year-old business was neither fish nor fowl. It was not prospering in the wake of the Civil War, but neither was it foundering, as were many new businesses in the hotly competitive postwar shipping trade.

As L.J. had predicted, Mississippi River business was booming as the southern part of the country began a painful rebuilding of its stores and economies. But the large companies, many of them backed by eastern interests, were grabbing a great deal of it. They boasted large fleets of riverboats and consistently set their rates lower than the rates that a small independent firm such as Hays Forwarding needed in order to survive. At least, Tim thought, that was what L.J. said. And Tim had no reason at all to doubt him. The *Resurrection*, since its launching, had been kept busy and, according to L.J., managed to earn enough to meet expenses and produce a small profit. Tim knew it was only because of L.J.'s hard and fruitful work that the company managed to remain in business.

Hays was constantly on the move, seeking cargo from the farms springing up in Minnesota, the industries of St. Louis and the cotton plantations of the South. When cargo was scarce, L.J. had organized what he called "excursion trips" along the river, for those who wanted to get away and view life at other ports along the Mississippi. The excursions quickly became popular and the *Resurrection* had made monthly trips since the warm weather of May had arrived.

Tim had not worked as hard as L.J. since he had gone to work for his friend. Only a fool would work that hard. But the job was time consuming, and he was having far less fun than he was accustomed to having, since he got out much less frequently.

L.J., Tim thought, might not miss his poker games—Hays had played in only one game during the past fifteen months—but Tim missed his usual Saturday wenching excursions. These dalliances were lost twice each month due to the necessity of supervising the loading and/or unloading of the steamer's cargo.

L.J. paid Tim far better than St. Paul Shipping had, but Wolfe knew he deserved it and more. Although Tim couldn't help but admire L.J. for his seemingly endless supply of energy and his ability to accomplish whatever he set out to do, Tim envied his friend not a whit.

Except, that is, for the way L.J. had managed to win the affections of the most beautiful woman Tim had ever seen—Lucille Morgan. Tim envied that conquest a great deal. He shook his head at the thought of the unlikely liaison. What, he asked himself, did a beauty like Lucille see in a nose-to-the-grindstone stiff like L.J. Hays? Every man in St. Paul had, at one time or another, tried to gain Lucille's favor, but none had succeeded. None except L.J.! And the schoolmarm was forever stopping in at the office to inquire about his whereabouts and scheduled return. It was Tim's misfortune that the woman seemed totally unaffected by him, the acknowledged king of St. Paul's womanizers.

Tim's respect for Hays in business matters was no less strong than his disrespect for the man's interest and abilities with women. So, when he wondered if L.J. had bedded Lucille Morgan, he decided Hays could not have. He wouldn't, Tim thought, know what to do with a woman in bed!

Tim grinned at the thought—then jumped guiltily when the door opened and Ben Williams entered the Hays Forwarding Company office. Williams had narrowly lost the election last year to the incumbent governor, but had gained much stature in doing so. It was said to be a certainty that Williams would win the governorship on his next try. Williams stopped in front of Hays' desk and offered his hand as Tim stood to greet him. Wolfe was wary, as the banker was no friend of either the company, L.J. or Tim himself.

"Yes, Mr. Williams," Tim said automatically. "And what can I do for you on this fine day?" He turned on the wide smile L.J. always claimed was so important in a public business office.

The banker did not respond immediately, instead looking this way and that around the small office as if searching for insects everywhere. Suddenly Williams smiled. "You are Tim Wolfe, my man, correct?"

My man? Tim almost laughed, for he thought the expression asinine. "That I am, sir," Tim managed.

"Where is Mr. Hays? I wish to see him."

"I'm afraid that won't be possible, Mr. Williams. L.J.'s in New Orleans, I believe, and won't be back before the 15th. Is there anything I can do?"

Williams thought for a moment, then renewed his smile. "Yes. Tell me how goes business, Mr. Wolfe, for I've decided to buy out your employer and am formulating an offer."

Now Tim did laugh—uproariously. When at last his hilarity subsided, he saw that Williams looked unamused. "Oh, I am sorry, Mr. Williams, but you must understand that L.J. . . . well, you gotta know he don't think much of you. And he's run himself ragged traveling all over the country looking for business for the *Resurrection*. I don't believe he'd be likely to sell to you at any price."

The banker remained calm, though his expression blew stormy. "Business is so good that Hays would not entertain an offer? Come now, Tim, Mr. Hays may not like me—there's little doubt of that—but he's too good a businessman to dismiss me out of hand unless his business is prospering. And I know it is not."

Tim shrugged. He was not good with words and so would not even attempt to argue with a politician as slick as Ben Williams. "You'll have to take that up with L.J., Mr. Williams," he offered. "But I think you're wrong."

"I intend to take it up with him, Tim, as soon as

he returns. Now, tell me, how would you like to work for me?"

Tim was surprised. "For you?"

"Yes. I've been keeping my eyes on you, lad, and admiring your work. Mr. Hays has been fortunate to have such a capable and trustworthy associate. Without you he would find it even more difficult to run his business. I trust he pays you well."

Tim eyed the man suspiciously. "Well enough," he confirmed.

Williams grinned, his manner disarming. "Well, I need a good man to operate a shipping office over on the Red River. It'll be a Hudson Bay Company office, for I've an interest in that fine old firm. With the St. Paul Railroad soon to complete its spur over to Breckenridge, the Bay Company soon will be shipping goods from Fort Garry, on to St. Paul and south on the Mississippi to St. Louis and beyond. Your office will be an important spot and would pay you well."

Tim could only stare at the man. No one but L.J. Hays had ever paid court to Tim Wolfe.

"Whatever you're earning now, Tim, will be doubled when you come to work for Hudson Bay Company."

Tim blinked. With doubled wages he could really have some fun—if he had the time. He had just met a new girl—pretty seventeen-year-old Elizabeth Arton—and she could be had, if he could find a moment or two.

"What kind of time are you talking about, Mr. Williams? And where would I live? I've a house here, you know. Can't afford to pay rent over there, if I'm to come out ahead." He congratulated himself for having handled this as L.J. would have.

Williams' eyes brightened at Tim's obvious interest. "You won't have to work Sundays, and Saturdays just a half day, Tim. As for housing, there'll be quarters built right into the freight station. And besides being free to employees, they're big enough so you can entertain somebody if you want to."

Tim said nothing for almost a minute, thinking it over. "I don't know, Mr. Williams," he responded finally. "I sort of like working here and L.J.'s my friend. I hate to cross him."

Williams frowned, then played his trump card. "Oh, yes, I almost forgot to mention Rosie Simonds, the girl who'll be working for you and living at the station as well."

"Rosie? A girl?"

Williams grinned lasciviously. "She's a looker, if you know what I mean. And knows her way around, too. She likes a good time. She's the niece of a trapper I know. I'm doing her and him a favor by giving her this job—she needs it bad. She'll keep the place clean and do the record keeping."

Tim stared at the banker, but hardly saw him. His thoughts were jumbled. He wasn't completely happy with the way things were here, yet he hated to leave Hays. Still . . . doubled wages, his own place to live and now this Rosie Simonds—it all sounded pretty good. Damned good. "When do I have to give you an answer, Mr. Williams?" he asked.

"Why right now, Tim, if you will. I've got to fill this position pretty quickly and there are some others who'd jump at it, let me tell you."

"Well, I can understand that. But I really need a little time—maybe a day—to think on it."

"Well, I don't know," Williams hesitated. He could see he had sorely tempted Hays' right-hand man.

"Tell you what, Tim—why don't you stop over at the bank this afternoon after you close up here. Even if you haven't made up your mind yet, we can talk about it some more and see what objections you may have. Okay?"

"Fair enough, Mr. Williams, but I ain't guaranteeing anything." Tim stood and accepted the banker's hand, then watched him stride away.

Tim sat down and hoped the walls didn't have ears. If L.J. could have heard that conversation, he would have blown his cork, Tim thought. And rightly so! What kind of a friend was Tim, to even consider selling out his friend like this? L.J. had been good to him—great to him. And yet . . .

The tug of war going on in his mind continued for some time. Not only had L.J. been good to him over the years, but he had even promised a bonus plan once there were profits to make it possible. It hadn't happened yet, but Tim had few doubts that L.J. would keep his word.

Still . . . Williams' offer was terrific! Who could turn down double wages, let alone more freedom, less work and a pretty girl, too? Tim would have to be crazy to say no.

One thing was certain, though, Tim thought. Even if he chose to accept Williams' offer, he wouldn't go to work for the banker until L.J. got back and replaced him. Without Tim, there would be nobody to see to cargo loadings and unloadings and no one to deposit payments into the company accounts at the bank. And L.J. would have to stay in St. Paul himself if Tim left him—at least until he'd found a replacement.

The rest of the day was miserable for Tim as he agonized over the decision he was being forced to make. In midafternoon he received a telegram from L.J. in New Orleans, confirming the date of a shipment of cotton he had arranged earlier. Tim almost sent him a wire begging him to come back to St. Paul to help with his problem. But he refrained.

When at last Tim closed up the office and walked down the street to the First Minnesota Bank, Tim was still undecided. What, he thought, if the banker was offering him all these inducements just to get Tim to leave L.J. and help him destroy Hays somehow? After a short time, Williams could fire Tim and L.J. would never take him back.

A sober thought, but could it happen? Tim doubted it would, but had to admit that anything was possible. Williams did not have the reputation for being the most even-handed businessman in Minnesota.

A surprise awaited Tim when he reached the bank. The surprise was several inches over five feet tall, wore a light summer dress that emphasized a well-formed figure, and flashed a dazzling smile on a pretty face. Banker Williams introduced the surprise as Rosie Simonds.

She appeared to Tim to be the image of health. Her green eyes glistened an almost liquid invitation and her short, wavy, copper-colored hair bounced when she turned her head. Rosie moved like a child, quick and petulant, but had the full, ripe body of a woman. Thus, she was a contradiction: alert and calm, sensuous and innocent. She bewitched him.

To further confuse Tim's already addled mind, Rosie proved to be both attentive and shy. She paid absolutely unswerving attention to whoever spoke, staring intently into his eyes. As a result, it was impossible to ignore her and Tim noticed that, though he or Williams might address each other with a word or two, both inevitably found themselves talking to Rosie as though she were some sort of interpreter, or messenger. When, at last, she spoke, Wolfe melted. Her voice pealed like a bell and had a kind of clear, full tone that Tim found irresistible.

In the end, although they'd discussed carefully the job Tim was offered, none of Williams' assurances really mattered. Wolfe accepted the position with the proviso that he be allowed to work for Hays until a replacement could be found. Looking at Rosie, Tim prayed it wouldn't take long.

"Are you serious about trying to buy L.J. out?" Tim asked before he left Williams.

"Of course, I am."

"Do you think you can actually convince him to sell?"

"Eventually, Tim, eventually. But don't worry your head about it. I'll see to it that we get the station set up to your liking. Rosie'll be moving right in, so if you want to go look the place over, she'll be there to show you around."

It was an invitation Tim could not refuse and so, a week later, he took the train to the end of the line and rented a horse. As he rode toward the station in which he would one day work, Tim thought about L.J. Hays. It occurred to him that, since deciding to leave Hays Forwarding, Wolfe had become more and more concerned about his friend. He'd taken some time to think about the years they'd worked together, had recalled the struggle they'd shared, and found his recollections disconcerting. He hadn't noticed it, really, but Hays had changed.

L.J. always had been a serious young man with an indomitable will and the self-confidence of a fire-and-brimstone preacher. But, in the beginning, he'd had a naive faith in hard work and clear thinking. As though he were sure that if you tried hard enough, good things would happen to you. With time and disappointment, though, something in this faith had changed. Though L.J. knew he deserved success, it hadn't come his way, exactly. And the frustration had cracked, or tarnished, his optimism.

It puzzled Wolfe that L.J. hadn't grown bitter as a result of his disappointments, but instead had become unpredictable. He sat alone in the dark for hours, staring into the fire that burned in their living room. He once dismissed an engineer on the *Resurrection* because he didn't like the man's name. And he gave pennies to children he met along the docks. L.J. might make a major decision, concerning tons of freight, in an instant, yet then fret endlessly over some small detail of his ship's operation.

Wolfe had always shrugged off such behavior, assuming L.J. could damn well do what he wanted with his own company. But as he thought now about it all, he realized that L.J. was growing more and more strained. The pressures of a tough world and difficult industry were taking their toll on him. And, even if L.J. claimed to love the challenge of it all, some part of him was clearly hurting.

Tim Wolfe spurred the horse, trying to speed it away from the imponderable, half-digested thoughts that plagued him. He simply couldn't figure out what was wrong with L.J. And his affection for the man, colored by a very real awe, made it impossible for Wolfe to know what to do about it.

True to Williams' word, Rosie Simonds was at the station, looking just as breathtakingly beautiful as Tim remembered. She showed him around the top floor of the station, where his and her rooms were located, and they inspected the office on the ground floor. Later, she took him on a tour of the town, including stops at the three saloons already open. She had, she confessed to Tim, worked in one before Ben Williams gave her a chance to work as a bookkeeper instead of a dance-hall girl.

But if Tim expected to seduce her, he found out he could not. She could not have been nicer to him, yet firmly ignored his obvious overtures. Still, as he took his leave of the place later in the evening, Tim was not discouraged. He had no reason to be, for Rosie had kissed him goodbye with promising enthusiasm. His future with the Hudson Bay Company looked bright indeed.

In St. Paul, while he pondered L.J. Hays, awaiting his return, and looked forward to evenings with Rosie Simonds, Tim Wolfe saw nothing wrong with pursuing the dark-haired creature named Elizabeth Arton. She was a girl, even a child, to Tim, but she had a torrid way about her. A worldly nymph, she promised to be an interesting conquest. Or at least, biding his time, Tim thought of her as such.

On several occasions the young woman had agreed to visit Tim at his home. But, for perfectly plausible reasons, she had been unable to keep her date every time. Tim thought this a tantalizing game, one he could enjoy for a while, but only a while.

In fact, though, Elizabeth Arton was completely disinterested in Tim. The daughter of a cold, rigid widow, the warm, young lady had designs on L.J. Hays. She had seen him with her teacher, Lucille Morgan, one balmy afternoon the previous August. One look at the striking young man had convinced her that L.J. would go far. And she had decided, then and there, to go with him. She thought of it as love, even believed it was love, in spite of the fact she had never met him. Perhaps smitten best describes her. At any rate, Elizabeth Arton was determined to wheedle an introduction to L.J. through his friend, Tim Wolfe.

While only seventeen, Elizabeth had learned one thing from her mother: that beautiful women ought to use their beauty to obtain what they want. As if to reinforce this lesson, Elizabeth's mother had spent hundreds of hours brushing the girl's long hair in front of a mirror, intoning encouragement and praise. They had spent years, seated together in front of that huge reflection of innocence and bitterness, admiring the girl's loveliness. In the end, of course, Elizabeth had learned that her beauty, her purely radiant, sultry beauty, could be clouded with an oppressive air of wantonness, the suggestion of lust. And, armed with this peculiar weapon, she had discovered that men flocked to her. But the prize, her mother told her, ought to go to the winner. None should taste the feast until he promised the world for the privilege.

The product of her schooling, but a healthy young woman as well, Elizabeth had grown up torn between the suggestion of desire and the prohibitions her mother created. Men fascinated her. Their desires thrilled her. And she encouraged them with every fiber in her body. But she forbade herself any experimentation with boys. She would wait.

So, by the time she was seventeen, Elizabeth Arton had developed an extraordinary fantasy life. She dreamed of men worshipping her, touching her, fawning over her the way her mother predicted they must. She was consumed with curiosity and so filled that void with imaginings. A virgin, she could wish for fulfillment, even conjure it in her mind until a flood of heat ran through her and her breasts ached. But, even as her mind pictured L.J. Hays hovering over her and her hands traced the edges of her own body, Elizabeth faltered, not quite knowing what thrills she anticipated. Love and sex, future and wealth, dreams and reality confused each other in her nightly concentrations. She'd lie awake, staring at the ceiling of her small room, feeling liquid yearnings course through her, not knowing what to do about them.

Tim, it seemed to Elizabeth, was perfect. She was intrigued by his ruddy good looks and easy air, but knew she didn't intend to marry the man. He was an avenue to L.J. Hays, a means to an end. But at the same time, he was a tantalizing adult, experienced and clearly hungering after her. His desire made him interesting, even if the man himself was not.

So, bored and frustrated, Elizabeth had agreed to visit Tim at his home. His light, offhanded invitation had been met with a coquettish, flirtatious, girlish acceptance. She would drive him crazy, she thought with a smile.

Early that evening, while her mother napped, Elizabeth had slipped away to Tim's house, leaving a note that promised she would return soon. It was only a short ride from the Arton house to the one Tim shared with Hays, but Elizabeth had never made it before. She was a little disappointed to see the small stone and wood dwelling the two men owned. She had imagined a much finer dwelling. But she quickly told herself that neither really needed more until they were married.

Knocking sharply on the door, she felt a tingle of anticipation. Perhaps L.J. was at home, she hoped. But, after entering, she realized that Tim was alone.

Whatever amusement was to follow would have to come from him.

"Where's your friend, Tim?" she asked.

"Away," he replied. "He's always traveling one place or another." He didn't want to think about L.J.'s return. It promised to be an uncomfortable day.

"Where?" she persisted, walking away from him with a pert, quick stride.

Tim had suffered enough thinking about L.J. Hays. And he'd been taunted more than he could stand by his future roommate, Rosie Simonds. This young tart, he thought, was pushing her luck. "Hey," he snapped, catching her by the arm, "why are you so blamed interested in L.J.?"

"I like men," Elizabeth cooed with a smile. It was, in retrospect, a mistake. The harried, titillated Wolfe was not in any mood for tantalizing niceties. He was worn out, too tired of games.

"I can see that," he countered, taking her in his arms. She kissed him, passionately, sealing her fate.

Tim swept her off her feet, carrying the girl in his strong arms as though she were weightless. In an instant she was transported from the parlor into his bedroom. At first bewildered, then protesting quietly, Elizabeth was perplexed by this show of ardor. Like a child transfixed by a burning match, she had no idea what a single spark might unleash. But when she found herself on Tim's bed and felt his hands fumbling at the small buttons at the front of her dress, she panicked. Somewhere in her mind she knew what was happening and her imagination glowed. But, at the same time, she felt compelled to resist.

"No, Tim, please don't," she pleaded. "Please."

But he wasn't hearing her.

"Tim!" she shouted, her hands on his shoulders, pushing at him. But the effort failed.

Practiced and quick, Tim overpowered her. In moments she lay beside him, her clothes parted, lifted, askew. For the first time in her life, Elizabeth felt helpless. As his hand cupped her ample breast, glancing across her skin, she closed her eyes. It was a touch she knew, one that had excited her many times, but this came from another's fingers. It was not a dream. It was happening. Something loosened in her, some resolve vanished, as the relentlessness of his touch danced across her, over and over.

Then, lost in her reverie, delighted, irresponsible, Elizabeth heard a moan come from Tim and his hand slipped from her body.

"I'm sorry . . . sorry . . ." he mumbled, rolling across the bed until he sat, his back to her. Elizabeth looked at him, stunned. The setting sun shone through the window, filling the room with unexpected light. She blinked, speechless, then reached for him. Tim turned to the girl, a heated, frustrated apology on his lips, and found her shedding her camisole. Her trim young body glistened with perspiration and the sleek tendons at her neck and shoulders stretched as she wriggled from the lacy bodice.

Dark, almost dewy eyes looked up at him. She lay back. "Don't, please, don't," she whispered with a smile.

He drank in the sight of her, bent and kissed her hungry lips. His hands, then tongue, traveled over her and a murmur of delight echoed in her chest.

"Oh, don't," she sighed.

His hands snaked across her, quick, seeking and her knee rose. There was a shuffled skittering of starched cloth as her petticoats slid down her leg, gathering at her knees, and he gasped at the sight of her whitened thigh. He touched it and her hips turned slightly, easing toward him.

"Don't," she hissed.

Tim's head reeled, he was driven. Taunted, invited and denied by a child in a woman's body, he went blind with wanting her. Even her protests, a charade, inflamed him. The sweet, impossible insanity of it goaded him. His hand slipped under her and tore silk from cotton; he pulled again, rougher, kneeling above her. She stretched, lifting, and was suddenly naked.

"Don't . . ." she gasped, a request and question as she stared at him.

"Oh, God," he muttered, unbelting himself. He saw, at first, her childish surprise, a wide-eyed alarm as she watched. Then, lowering himself, his haste confusing her, Tim plunged against the girl and caught a glimpse of startled pain and delight in Elizabeth Arton's eyes. But then he was lost to her, moving quickly to a shuddering, desperate conclusion that left her stinging, waiting, staring at the bright light streaming through the window. Her eyes flooded with tears as she rolled away from him.

Ben Williams was well pleased with the progress of his campaign to break L.J. Hays and gain control of his forwarding company. Though still uncertain the stubborn young man would capitulate, Williams was confident. As he unlocked the front door of the First Minnesota Bank, he chortled to himself. He was especially pleased to have stolen Hays' man Wolfe with such an obvious ploy. What's more, his efforts to sabotage Hays' contract with the Army had finally proven successful: he'd received the wire confirming as much only a day before. Now he had only to wait for L.J.'s homecoming.

Putting thoughts of Hays aside, the banker lowered his sizable frame into the chair behind his desk. For the thousandth time he wondered whether to invest some of his own money in the growing Pacific Northern Railroad. The road possessed a valuable federal land grant all along its route to the Pacific Ocean and might well make a fortune in construction profits alone. He'd already sunk a substantial amount of the bank's funds into bonds for the line, but returns on this investment would be modest. If he wanted to make a killing, he'd have to own stock in the company. In so doing he would also own a piece of its subsidiary, the construction firm that would build the railroad.

But the Pacific Northern was conservatively managed and thus slow to build. It had made very little progress west. So little, in fact, that its land grants might lapse if construction wasn't hurried. And there was no way for him to know how seriously its current owners were bleeding the line for short-term profits. He'd have to investigate.

Lucille Morgan pranced into the bank looking like a freshly cut flower. Williams, who eschewed a closed office so that he could see what went on in every corner of his bank, smiled. He straightened his tie, smoothed his brown suit coat and approached her.

"Well, Lucy, how are you today?" he asked with a too-jovial familiarity.

Lucille's face bore a smile, but her eyes were cool. She nodded to him but said nothing.

"Come to borrow or deposit?" he asked.

"You must be joking," Lucille responded, turning a sarcastic smile on him.

## Railroad King

"No, no . . . really. I'm in both businesses, you know."

"I can't imagine, sir, the circumstances that would lead me to become indebted to you." This last remark contained no trace of banter, not a hint of playful conversation. It stung Williams, especially because everyone in the bank could easily hear it.

"Now, my dear Lucy, you can't mean that. With your background you must surely know the value of money borrowed in a good cause." He had recovered with a slick diversion, a conversational quirk he had long since mastered. But Lucille was piqued. His posturing bothered her.

"Mr. Williams," she fumed, facing him, "I fully understand the benefit to both borrower and lender in a sound and honest transaction. But your lending politics, if that's the right word, convince me yours is not the bank to be indebted to."

He felt the hook sink, a burning pain. The teller who was waiting to attend her listened intently to their conversation. A couple who had recently entered the bank stood, watching Lucille. His refusal to finance Hays was at the bottom of this, he knew.

"Your uncle, Lucille, is in a position to be free with his money. I am not. I have depositors to protect. I must make choices." He was stumbling.

"I am not my uncle's keeper, Mr. Williams. But, I must tell you that he seems to have made rather good choices over the years. In fact, I don't think he'd complain at all over the speculative failures of his banks." The teller laughed, then quickly stifled the outburst. Williams glared at him.

"You mean he felt safe lending to Hays while I did not, correct?"

She turned to her banking business, unwilling to answer.

"Well, I may have been right about that one. We shall see." He was talking, rather desperately, to the back of her head. "I hear that your friend Hays may have some trouble with his Army contract and, Lord knows, the loss of such a plum might prove painful to him." The sound of satisfaction in his voice spread like a purple cloud in the room. Lucille found it sickening.

"Good day, you bastard," she spat, whisking from the room. Williams stood alone in the lobby of his bank, listening to a chuckle being passed between a man and wife not far away.

L.J. Hays' stay in New Orleans was a successful one. His ship would steam full for at least another month. On August 10th, he embarked on the steamer *Mississippi* for St. Louis, where he would connect with the *Resurrection* for the trip back to St. Paul.

In St. Louis, the *Resurrection* was absent, so L.J. paid a visit to James Frye, the local banker who represented Morgan's interests. Frye was pleased to find that Hays wanted to repay the balance of his loan somewhat early. They talked, briefly, about Hays' plans to buy a second steamer and the banker indicated funding for the project should be available. That connection secured, L.J. browsed in a St. Louis bookstore and bought two volumes, one aimed at farmers, the second a brand-new illustrated volume on the building of the Union Pacific Railroad. The country's first transcontinental railroad was creating quite a stir, especially because the government had invested so much money in the project. The sums, in fact, boggled Hays' mind. The continent was being united at a cost of nearly thirty thousand dollars a mile. More impressive, there was much speculation on the success of the line and plans for others, including the Pacific Northern in Minnesota.

Hays read both books during a two-day wait for the *Resurrection*. He enjoyed such forced delays as they allowed him to read and think, to pause and reflect on his situation. And on this particular occasion it occurred to him that railroads, like steamships, would eventually encounter a problem finding enough freight. Food, it seemed to L.J., was the answer. Railroad men must, he was sure, encourage farming in order to fill their boxcars. But those men that now controlled the rails were greedy in acquiring and holding land grants. They charged too much for the property they owned and were thereby retarding the most extraordinary agrarian explosion in the history of man. Stupid, L.J. thought. Stupid. He decided, watching the rain fall on the Mississippi, to become an expert in wheat and cattle.

After two days of watching the docks for the *Resurrection*, L.J. visited the small office he maintained in the city. Cliff Spencer, his man in St. Louis, was there. "Where the hell is the *Resurrection*?" he demanded.

Spencer, a quiet, friendly sort, shrugged. "I expect she's at the Higgins yard, L.J. Boiler blew the other day, from what I hear. Tim wired me."

Spencer had no idea how long it would take to get the *Resurrection* back on the river, so L.J. caught the next steamer heading north. It was a tidy little ship and made good time. As it churned up the Mississippi, Hays paced the deck, anxious to be home. Lucille, he thought, ought to be back from her trip to the West Coast. She'd ridden the Union Pacific and he had a score of questions for her. And it would be pleasant to tell her that Hays Forwarding had repaid her uncle's loan.

L.J. thought of Lucille often. She was the most exciting woman he had ever met, beautiful and intelligent. And self-assured. If only she weren't so self-assured. L.J. found her independence intimidating, somehow. Like an animal, a bejeweled cat, she seemed to prowl the world, taking from it what she wanted. She was unafraid, always unafraid, and the thought of such a magnificent creature completely unconfined, utterly capable of doing anything she wished, remained unsettling to L.J.

For he felt comfortable only when he was grappling with the hazards of an uncertain future. He was happiest when conjecture and estimation, promise and prediction surrounded him with uncertainty. The art of defining the proportions of such risks thrilled him, and the element of the imponderable, the unseen, the unknowable, set his mind whirring like a top. Lucille seemed indifferent to this great, yawning aspect of life. She was amused, even occasionally delighted by the unforeseen. But she never was afraid of it. Hays wondered if she were simply a jaded rich girl or a special sort of genius. Perhaps, if he were rich, he'd understand her.

Then and only then could they marry. Only when her wealthy independence was equalled by his own could L.J. Hays consider such a step. He would drown in her riches, he thought. Suffocate in the sheer possibilities of her world. Before they could wed he must erect his own universe, build it out of nothing so that it would surround him, an empire he both understood and controlled. Then, perhaps then . . .

His mind turned to the Red River. He had long thought of taking the Hays Forwarding Company northwest to the Red so that it might compete with the Hudson Bay Company. He had learned, of course, that the Bay Company was immensely powerful in the region, that it possessed—in effect—a monopoly. But it had abused its position and now charged much more to ship goods than was necessary. If Hays could move into the Red River, he could underprice them. A fortune could be made.

Halfway home to St. Paul, L.J. was heartened by the sight of the *Resurrection* moving smartly along down river. He waved to her and his salute, to his surprise, was greeted only a few moments later by a blast from the ship's whistle. Billy Henry, the *Resurrection*'s skipper, had seen Hays through his field glasses. L.J. waved, delightedly, heedless of the odd looks his fellow passengers offered.

It would be good to arrive home.

# Chapter 5

L.J. Hays marched across the wooden dock, the sound of his heels like drumbeats on the dried planks that hung above the river. He was in a hurry, anxious to talk to Tim Wolfe about the explosion aboard the *Resurrection*. But, more important, he was back at his home base and so strode the familiar waterfront with particular satisfaction. His steely eyes surveyed the dock hands, the mule-drawn wagons, the sea of barrels and mountains of lumber that were stacked on shore. Men stood about talking, or cursed to themselves in complaint over the endless parade of goods to be toted. The waterfront surged with activity.

Hays loved it. The damp, windswept scene filled with the merchandise of a continent always struck him as something of a miracle. The logistical coordination, the transportation phenomenon taking place, was awesome to him. But, while the economic miracle that was the opening of the Northwest never failed to impress Hays, it was the smell and noise, the motion and color of it that he truly loved. The constant lapping of the river's waves against hulls, the whistles, like signatures from each ship, the surly men and drunken engineers were all warming to his heart.

So, as he walked toward the Hays Forwarding Company office, his mind felt clear and hopeful. L.J. Hays was sure he knew what he was doing.

Tim Wolfe seemed startled when Hays burst, buoyant, into their office. The big, blond, strapping man rose quickly from his chair behind the desk at the sight of his friend. Hays couldn't help but notice that he wore an odd expression, an uneasy posture.

Hays shook Tim's hand and scanned the room. The mirror, always cocked just off vertical, was still crooked. The great, cracked school clock still ticked in the corner. Two battered pine straight-back chairs sat before the desk. And the roll-top, an ancient thing, was squeezed into one corner. It displayed the color of faded rust and was littered with scraps of paper, notes, bills, reminders. Tim was a slob, L.J. thought.

Reflexively, Hays moved to his most familiar position in the room. He slid to the corner, propping his elbow on the shoulder-height top of the desk. There he noticed a deep white stain, a ring left by L.J.'s coffee cup over the years. And, on the desk top itself, he saw the second ring, this one deeper, whiter, the evidence of Tim's countless cups of tea while working and talking to L.J. The heat and moisture of steaming mugs were ruining the desk, L.J. thought, but neither of them cared. The marks somehow told Hays just how long he'd stood while Tim sat, drinking and considering the future.

"Am I glad you've got back," Tim declared. "We sure got trouble. You ain't gonna like it much, L.J."

"Sit down, Tim. I already know about the blow in the *Resurrection*'s boilers. When and where?"

"Two days ago."

"And where?"

"Lucky there. Only a half hour out when it went.

Joe Higgins took her under tow and brought her back to the yard to fix her up. He just got her out today."

"Bad timing, don't you think?" L.J. smiled. It was easy for him to be relaxed now that his ship was on the water again. But his humor didn't seem to warm the room. Tim was acting strangely. He hadn't smiled. Still, L.J. thought his serious demeanor must be the result of all the bad news Tim bore.

"Higgins don't think so," Tim offered, a tentative choke in his voice.

"What?"

"Joe said somebody rigged it, L.J. He says there's not much question about it. Somebody blew her up."

Hays' good spirits vanished. "Sabotaged? I . . . really . . . was anybody hurt?"

"The fireman just missed getting his head blowed off, but lived to talk about it. He ran for his life at the smell of something weird. Quit the ship the next day. Nobody else was hurt."

"The passengers?"

"I fixed 'em up with a Cruise Line boat headed for St. Louis. Had to pay cash for jacked-up rates, so we're a little short."

Hays nodded. Tim had done the right thing. "Where did Higgins find the new boiler so quickly?"

"He ripped it out of that half-finished steamer he's stuck with. A damned good thing it was there."

"Damn good thing." Hays pondered the news Tim had delivered. Williams, he thought. That son of a bitch. "Williams," he muttered.

Tim shuddered, the spasm of a man at the edge of hysteria.

Hays glowered, furious. His adversary was playing very rough, indeed. "Is there something else, Tim?"

Wolfe squirmed in his chair, refusing for a moment to look at L.J. Finally he forced his eyes up and met his friend's perplexed stare. "I . . . I don't know how to tell you, L.J., but . . . I'm, I guess . . . I'm gonna . . . that is, you're gonna have to find a replacement for me."

"I'm what?"

Tim nodded.

"What happened?"

Tim sucked in a huge breath of air, at once relieved and frightened. His eyes fell to the top of the battered old desk. "I'm gonna be workin' for somebody else. I got another offer and I'm takin' it. It's for double the wages you can pay me . . . double, did you hear that?"

"When . . ." Hays sighed. "Double?"

Tim nodded.

"Can't figure that one, Tim. You sure?"

He nodded again.

"Well, I guess the trick is to make sure you're going to be all right. So, tell me, where you headed?" L.J.'s warmth beamed at Tim, his concern like a beacon.

Tim shook his head and swallowed. "Ben Williams came in here last week. He's hired me to be an agent for him up in Hudson Bay country, over in Breckenridge. Says I'm experienced . . ."

Hays tugged at his mustache and felt a numbing breeze flow through the room. His jaw muscles exercised, locked against one another, and a cloud descended over his eyes. Silence prevailed in the small room, invaded only by the painful ticking of the school clock.

"L.J.?"

Hays heard the noise as if from a great distance, but, groping in his mind, couldn't decipher it. He was suddenly a child again, remembering another betrayal from long ago.

"L.J.?" Tim almost pleaded.

The Reverend appeared before the twelve-year-old L.J. Hays. In his memory, it was as vivid as any vision could be. In the blackest cloak, that mad raven of a man seemed to bluster, windswept, about the room. He moved like a great, bony bird, the caw of his commands shrill, deafening to Hays. The lesson at hand was mysterious, a puzzle Hays could not master, and his teacher persisted with it.

"Why did he do that?" the Reverend asked. "Why?"

"Because he was angry?" L.J. guessed, praying his boyish explanation would satisfy the man.

"No. He wasn't angry."

"But he killed him. He must have been angry."

"No. He wasn't angry." Then the Reverend asked again, "Why?"

Hays stopped, his mind vacant.

"Why?" the question louder now.

Still, for all his effort, nothing came to L.J.

"Why?" the query now a shout.

Tears came to the young Hays' eyes. "You tell me, sir, why?"

"Think about it," the Reverend demanded. Then he was gone, his cloak billowing like wings as he swept from the room, a bird escaping.

L.J. Hays turned to Tim Wolfe, his friend, and asked him, "Why?" Sweat pearled on his brow as his eyes riveted Wolfe to the chair.

"You all right, L.J.?"

"Why?" he asked again.

"L.J.?"

Hays appeared frenzied, possessed by a nightmare

beyond speech. His skin glistened in a cold sweat, a drop at the tip of his nose, his neck reddening. Hays retreated. He backed away from the horrified Wolfe as though the man were carrion, a grimace racking his face. The question, "Why?" still echoed in his mind, but not a sound came from his lips. He was terrified, stunned. He stumbled, tripping over a chair as he backed up. He turned and kicked it, the thing scraping across the floor, clattering into a corner.

Hays stared at it, then lifted the rickety chair in both hands and crashed it against a wall. The legs broke away, splintering, but the back held together limply. Again he battered it, a mirror tumbling as he did so. The third blow left L.J. Hays standing with a bit of chair in each hand, the remnants like fallen flags against his legs. The numbing wind rose in the room once again and Hays stood silent.

Tim turned away, the bizarre display far worse than anything he had imagined. "Mr. Williams wants to buy you out, L.J.," he explained, not able to look at Hays.

"I'll just bet he does," the stunned employer responded acidly. "What else did he tell you? What has he paid you so far? Are you enjoying the work?"

Tim didn't know what was going on.

"Did he tell you he was going to sabotage the *Resurrection*? Did he pay you to do it?"

Tim was aghast. "Hey, L.J., that's not even worth the breath it takes . . ."

"Well," Hays interrupted, a fire burning in his temples that could light a city, "did you blow her up?"

Tim saw the man, twitching like a leaf in the wind, sweating like a pig in the sun, and wondered if L.J. were sick.

"L.J.?" It was a plea, not a question.

"You bastard, you sold out. You tried to sink my boat. You bastard."

Tim Wolfe, righteous, honest, a decent if fun-loving man, cracked. In an instant he towered over L.J. and then brought his huge, balled fist around and down against his face. As he watched L.J. reel from the blow, Tim prowled the floor like a tethered tiger. When L.J., bleeding from one nostril, gathered himself up and looked at Tim, the blond, livid and shuddering, shouted, "You're an idiot, Hays," and walked from the office.

After Tim had disappeared, Hays sat for a long time at the desk, a garbled stream of thoughts flowing through him. He struggled to concentrate, but every image that came to him rushed quickly away. And so, to escape the nightmare, he hid among the vagaries of his business, the maze of finance, and tried to make order out of his future. He hurried there, to the world of risk that always distracted him.

What would Williams do next? Come to Hays with an offer? And be turned down? Hays unraveled thought after thought in a flurry of threads. Tim had said the Hudson Bay Company was expanding. Had Tim said that? A railroad? At Breckenridge? How many miles? How much track? How soon? The railroad at Breckenridge, he repeated in his mind. When?

The Hudson Bay Company had only scratched the surface of the trade to be had over on the Red. With the railroad there, goods could come all the way from Canada to Breckenridge, then on to St. Paul and ports along the Mississippi, all the way to New Orleans. Stations, routes, transfers, rates, warehouses, mines, lumber, furs, wheat, coal, all appeared in his mind. The Red. The corridor to Canada, the connecting link, the future. Blood poured across L.J.

Hays' chin and onto his shirt, but the vision of trade he imagined totally obliterated any pain.

Hays grinned. It was time. Watch closely, Reverend, he thought. A boat on the Red. Joe Higgins' unfinished disaster. On the Red. The thought captured his imagination. Higgins' albatross would be worth a fortune if completed and moved to the Red River. Nearly as big as the *Resurrection,* it could haul tons of goods out of Canada.

An hour later, L.J.'s face began to show the signs of Tim's powerful fist. Deep blue, edging to purple, spread under his eyes and the flesh at the bridge of his nose swelled. He was pale, tired, the color of a man who had fasted for days, but Hays wore a weird grin as he plodded along the river toward Higgins' shipyard. Cleaning himself at a mirror and changing his clothes, L.J. had worked out his plan. He had a vision of a ship, a great ship, traveling across dry land. It moved slowly, but steadily, and Hays stood on the bridge.

"What happened to you?" Joe Higgins asked, pumping L.J.'s hand.

"Tried to break a man's hand by hitting it with my face."

"You all right?"

"I'll be all right."

Higgins frowned as L.J. produced two cigars from his coat and offered one to the shipbuilder.

"What are you after now? You haven't given me a cigar in a long time."

"You're a dreary old skeptic, Mr. Higgins."

"I am like hell. You've got that look in your eyes."

"What look?"

"That same lunatic kind of stare you had the first time you told me about your plan to raise the

*Cuyahoga* with railroad engines. That same look you had when you asked me to trust you for the finishing work on her. The look you get when you have your mind set on something colossal and impossible."

"You've a good memory for expressions, Mr. Higgins." Hays grinned and a pain shot through his nose. "I wish you hadn't, though. I'd hoped to sneak up on you with my proposition. But, no matter. It concerns your white elephant over there." Hays waved to the right, toward the hull of the uncompleted steamer on the river side of the yard.

As Joseph Higgins puffed on his cigar, L.J. related his scheme to bring the steamer—after it was complete—to the Red River. The shipbuilder, stunned, said nothing for several minutes. Then, shaking his head, noted, "That's a trip of two hundred miles, L.J."

"I know."

"Have you thought about the stresses on a boat during that kind of journey?"

"Yes, and I'm sure you can rig a way to truss her so she'll make it. I thought some kind of temporary scaffolding, both internal and external bracing . . ."

"Now wait a minute, L.J., not so fast. You have to talk to Phil Crabtree about such a move. There isn't a railroad line within a mile of my yard. Then you've got to figure some way to load her on a pair of flatcars, so she'll pivot around turns and, speaking of which, I have to think of a way to pick her up and put her on the blamed cars in the first place. Lord, L.J., I'm not sure it can be done."

Hays smiled. Higgins was clearly intrigued. "I think you know better. Should we complete her, we can sail the ship down river to the new siding that the railroad's putting in south of the city. We'll build a temporary way, haul your hoists over . . ."

"Mr. Hays," Higgins interrupted, "you are a maniac."

"And you, sir, love to watch lunatics at work."

Joseph Higgins answered with a guttural "Hurrumph."

"But the real question," L.J. continued, "is your willingness to go along with the idea. I can borrow the money we'll need to move her to the Red, but I'll have to owe you for most of the work necessary to complete her. Are you willing to finish the steamer on speculation?"

That Higgins was doubtful would be a huge understatement. He was a carpenter, not a shipper. He didn't know much about freight rates. Still, he respected Hays and knew the young man was not only ambitious, but also superbly capable.

"I don't know, L.J.," Higgins finally replied. "To run a steamer over on the Red—if you can get this one over there—won't be easy. I'm more troubled by Calhoun and Williams than by your scheme. Calhoun's general manager of the Hudson Bay Company and I hear he's a mean one. He's not likely to be pleased to see you moving in on his trade."

"I'm worried about them, too, Mr. Higgins," Hays agreed, "in case you haven't noticed. But not afraid. I beat the banker to the *Cuyahoga* and I can beat him again over on the Red. As for Calhoun, we'll see how tough he is when he's challenged. Hudson Bay's had everything its own way there for a long time—too long.

"There are a lot of trappers and farmers over there who, I'm sure, will welcome Hays Forwarding, for I aim to pay fair prices for furs and charge reasonable rates for freight. I doubt if our steamer will ever sail with less than a full hold. And with the railroad finished to Breckenridge . . ."

"What about the railroad, L.J.? Ben has powerful friends and he won't hesitate to get them to refuse your business. If I know Ben, he'll . . ."

"I know Phil Crabtree, Mr. Higgins. He's an honest man and won't let either Williams or Calhoun use him—against me or anyone else."

"He may not have much to say about it, L.J. He's the general manager, but he does have superiors. If Ben or Calhoun gets to one of them, Phil's honesty won't mean a thing."

"I believe he'd buck them on something like this, Mr. Higgins. And he'd win, too, because he's not just the general manager, but the most capable railroad man in the whole Northwest. They'd have a damn hard time replacing him."

Higgins nodded, then half-turned to look across the shipyard at the unfinished steamer. He'd received a couple of offers to finish it, but not nearly what it was worth, and while he sorely wanted to get rid of the ship, he wouldn't give it away. But he wasn't at all sure he wanted to get into the freight business, either, directly or indirectly. Finishing the steamer would mean investing a lot of his own hard-earned money in it. And should Hays be wrong, should his scheme go sour, Higgins could lose it all. Or could he? Actually, he thought, the finished steamship would retain its value as long as it wasn't destroyed or severely damaged.

"I don't want to be involved in a partnership, L.J.," Higgins judged. "If I went along with you, it would have to be on a lease—I'd finish the steamer and lease it to you. If you go under, I keep the boat."

Hays neither smiled nor frowned as he digested Higgins' offer. At last he held out his right hand.

"Agreed," he said, "if I can have an option to buy the boat for a stipulated price after, say, two years."

Higgins broke into a grin as he accepted Hays' hand for a firm shake. "I believe you've just bested me in this arrangement, L.J., but I will abide by it. I imagine you also have a rental figure in mind—which you must, of course, guarantee to me?"

Hays nodded. "I thought four percent of the ship's cost to you for each of the twenty-four months prior to the option date. What do you think?"

"Make it five and I agree."

"How can I refuse you, Mr. Higgins?" Hays rejoined.

"You can't, L.J., since we both know that you were no doubt figuring six was reasonable. But I'll take the five and be happy. You want that in writing?"

Hays' eyes gleamed. "I believe in handshakes and strong personal friendships, Mr. Higgins, but I also know my memory isn't perfect, so I think you'll agree that writing it up will save me embarrassment."

Higgins laughed. "Or me, for I'm older than you and my memory's probably a lot worse. All right, L.J., you draw it up and I'll sign it."

When Hays left the shipbuilder, both men were pleased. Now all Hays had to do was talk to Crabtree and get him to agree to cart his ship, and, of course, agree to accept L.J.'s business. And he would have to go to St. Louis to see James Frye about the financial backing he'd need. Then there was the matter of a replacement for Tim. And calculating the freight charges he'd have to charge between Breckenridge and Fort Garry. And L.J. would have to hire a man in Fort Garry to find cargo for the steamer on its return trips from Canada. Preferably somebody who'd fallen out of favor with the Hudson Bay Company.

If L.J. Hays had been an ordinary man, the crush of things to do might well have weighed on him. Instead, he was lightened, released. Once again at odds with logic and caution.

But his concentration forced his mind away from Lucille Morgan, and that cost him dearly.

It was a week after L.J. returned to St. Paul before he remembered he had not yet called on Lucille. When he rode to her small house on the north end of town, he found it empty, a note pinned to the door with his name on it. He unfolded it and read:

> Dear L. Jerome,
> I understand you returned to St. Paul last Tuesday. I trust you had a good and successful journey, although I had hoped you would find time to call on me soon after your return. Since you did not (or could not) I have decided to take Uncle Pierpont's invitation to join him in New York, where he's opening a new office. My best wishes for a pleasant and profitable summer to you.
> Lucille

Hays muttered an inaudible curse, refolded the note and turned away from the door. Furious with himself, L.J.'s eyes swept the narrow street, seeking a place where Lucille, hidden, might observe him. Was she playing a trick? Or had she really gone away? Again he cursed, this time out loud, as he stood in uncertainty on the porch. He stared at the oak door. Why, he lamented, had she not been a little more patient?

He reached into his pocket for her note. Unfolding

it, he glanced at it again and confirmed that there was no date on it—none at all. When had she written it? How long had she waited for him to visit her? Had she gone that very morning, or the day after his return? Whenever it was, she would have had to go by steamer and could easily have bidden him good-by at his office at the dock. Why had she not done so?

If Lucille had left only yesterday, she'd have had to take the *Resurrection,* for it was the only ship to dock and take on passengers for another trip to St. Louis. She'd have had a perfect excuse to come to his office, without humbling herself, for a ticket. This woman, he thought, is inscrutable.

Phil Crabtree was worried about L.J. Hays. And about the risk his friend, Joseph Higgins, was taking. "Seems we can get your boat to the Red," he informed L.J. "I've studied Joseph's plans and they are sound."

L.J. nodded, as though he had been certain the undertaking was manageable all along. But his mind raced at these words. His dream of a ship inching along dry land might actually become a reality.

"Joe Higgins thinks a great deal of you, L.J.," Crabtree told him. "You know that, don't you?"

L.J. was taken aback by the remark. He'd never considered the shipbuilder as anything other than a resourceful supplier. "He's made a sound business deal, Mr. Crabtree, and you can be sure it'll turn out well. I'll see to it that his investment in me is secure."

"Perhaps."

"No, absolutely. When a man borrows, he'd best repay."

"That's really not the question, L.J." Crabtree waved a hand, dismissing Hays' approach. "The man is sinking his fortune in you and your outrageous plan.

You could ruin him. Calhoun and Williams may see to it."

L.J. didn't want to think about the jeopardy his venture was forcing on Higgins. He cast the thought from his mind as though it were a leech, a wretched annoyance best salted away. "I'll not ruin him, Mr. Crabtree. Only you can manage that."

The railroad man's eyes narrowed.

"My problem, and Joseph Higgins', will be filling that boat with freight. Our competition will try to keep us from doing so and the only way they can stop me is to apply pressure on you. If you and your railroad refuse to accept my goods, I'm finished. It's that simple."

"I'll carry your freight, L.J., rest assured. But I'm not the only way that pair will try to get to you. Mark my words. The Red is locked up tight and won't pry free easily."

Hays grinned. "They have the Red now, Mr. Crabtree. But if I have anything to say about it, their control will soon pass and be lamented by no one. The Hudson Bay Company has made a lot of enemies over on the Red River, enemies who'll soon be my best friends."

"I hope you're right, L.J. It won't be easy, though—not if I know Ben and Calhoun. Ben fancies himself another Jay Gould. They figure they can build the Bay Company into an empire. Just between you and me, Ben's got ideas about buying the St. Paul one day. If he does, I'll be gone. I'd rather work for the Devil than work for that man."

"Tell me about Calhoun, Mr. Crabtree. Who is he and what is he? Everyone says he's someone to fear, yet I know very little about him. If I'm going to incur his enmity, I need to know."

"Got one of those good cigars of yours, L.J.?"

Crabtree asked. Hays produced two from his coat, handed one to the railroad man and lit both.

Crabtree chuckled. "That's good luck," he predicted. "Well, L.J., Calhoun is tough as railroad spikes. I believe he would cut off his mother's hand if he caught her using goods not carried by the Hudson Bay Company. Right now he's only general manager of the company in this region, but there's no doubt he's destined to move up within another year or two. All he needs is to succeed in doubling the Bay Company's Red River profits—as he's promised to do—and their directors will let him do anything he wants."

"And how does he expect to double the company's profits up there?"

"By increasing rates and by getting the Canadian government to charter a transcontinental railroad," Crabtree informed Hays. "He's already increased the rate by one half. As for a Canadian Pacific railroad, it's only a question of time before that becomes a fact. If you're serious about competing with Calhoun, you're going to find out he's formidable. And he ain't too damned concerned about doing things the legal way, either, from what I hear. Soon as he finds out what you're planning, he'll come down on you like a boxcar filled with bricks."

Hays was silent for a moment, thinking over Crabtree's warning. "You don't think I ought to upset Mr. Calhoun's apple cart, Mr. Crabtree?"

Crabtree laughed. "I surely do think you ought to, L.J., if you can. All I'm doing is telling you what you're up against—as you asked."

"If you're a betting man, Mr. Crabtree, I would *not* suggest you bet on either Mr. Calhoun or Mr. Williams. Neither will take my measure, of that you can be certain."

The railroad man smiled because he believed in this soft-spoken young man. L.J. Hays' stature and outward appearance would impress no one, but the young man had a quiet strength of will which Crabtree found almost awesome. "I believe you, L.J.," Crabtree replied at last. "And I wish you well. If you can lick the Hudson Bay Company monopoly, you'll have a great many souls beholden to you. If you ever decide to involve yourself in my business, do come see me, will you?"

"I will, Mr. Crabtree. I most certainly will."

That night L.J. Hays sat alone in the tiny, rough parlor of the Hays/Wolfe house. The fire burned low at his feet and a single kerosene lamp glowed on the table behind him. His hands, long fingered and thin, held an unopened envelope, addressed to him in Tim Wolfe's unmistakable scrawl. He opened it with a peculiar sort of caution, as though afraid it might burn him.

> Dear L.J.,
> I'm in Breckenridge and started to work. You can have the house to yourself while I'm here. All I ask is that you keep a room for me so I can have a place when I'm in St. Paul. Only thing bothers me is you were wrong about the boiler.
> Tim

The simplicity of Wolfe's message cut L.J. to the quick. Its affection obvious, its tone simple, the truth of his denial clear. Hays wept. Not so much from a sense of guilt as from a self-pitying regret. The big, laughing Irishman was gone, abandoned L.J., left him

# Railroad King

alone to listen to the walls creak and the fire spit. Left him in the dark confines of his home to ponder the threats that surrounded him. Tim had taken the easy way out, quick money in a soft job. He'd lost faith in L.J. just as things were becoming hot. Hays sat, bitterly angry with Tim for having left him so very alone. And now, with the note, Hays knew the man was still a friend, honest and fair. He was, thus, furious with the loss. Angry that the friend was still a friend.

The next day, just before noon, a wire came from the Army in St. Louis, canceling Hays Forwarding's grain contract. The shipping concern would not be bankrupted by the contract loss, though of course it would not be aided by it, either. Hays was not surprised by the action. He assumed that Williams was at work.

Shortly after the wire, a trim and leathery, blond Scandinavian named Chris Christiansen appeared. Christiansen wanted work, he said. Though he spoke with an accent, he seemed to handle the English language well, L.J. noted.

"What kind of work?" L.J. asked, his eyes appraising the man, his rumpled clothes and large hands.

"I will do anything you ask of me and I will do it well," he responded, self-assurance brimming from him.

"Where do you come from, Mr. Christiansen?"

"Oslo, Norway," the man replied. "I come to New York first. Then I hear about this part of land and decide to come. I would like buy some land and grow wheat, as my family does in Norway. But for now, I just need work."

Hays needed someone to replace Tim, but wondered if this brawny, inexperienced immigrant could do the job. "What kind of work did you do in New York?" he asked.

"I work on New York docks," Christiansen informed Hays.

"All the time you were there?"

"We are in New York two years," Christiansen told him. "I work on docks for one year, then . . ." His sentence stalled, unhappy as well as uncertain.

"Then what, Mr. Christiansen?" Hays prompted. "If I am to employ you, I must know your background. All of it."

"I am put in jail, Mr. Hays, but it was not my fault. I only do what I have to do. A very important man—a bad man—try to seduce my wife, my Irmgaard."

"They put you in jail for that?"

The big Norwegian shook his head, then held up his hands, which seemed the size of pumpkins. "I use these to show this man he should not bother Irmgaard and . . ."

Hays grinned. "You hurt him?"

"He will not be bad any more. Not for a while, anyway. I put him in hospital with just two swings, but before he go, he . . ."

"He had you arrested," Hays finished for him. "I see. Well, you need not be embarrassed. There are such people everywhere in this country and, I'm sure, in Norway. Your wife is here in Minnesota with you?"

Christiansen nodded. "She is right outside, waiting for me. We must find place to stay after I find work."

"Can you read English?"

"Yes. I learn it from a good friend in New York. He help me lots. I read now—many books."

Hays liked what he saw in Christiansen. He was strong and eager to learn, and Hays Forwarding could use him. The Norwegian's English was good, good enough for the work at Hays Forwarding.

"Very well, Chris," L.J. declared, "you can work for me. I can't pay you a great deal, twenty dollars a week to start, but I can offer you a place to stay. I've a house a short distance from here. Would you and your wife like to use the spare bedroom?"

"Ya, but how much would it cost us?" Christiansen wanted to know.

"Nothing at all, Chris, if your wife is a good cook. Is she? I'm tired of taking my meals out. I live alone, you see."

"My Irmgaard is fine cook, Mr. Hays. You will see. She will keep your house clean, too." He thrust out his hand and Hays shook it gingerly, expecting a bone-breaking squeeze from such big hands. To his surprise, the Norwegian was gentle, shaking his hand firmly. L.J. gave Chris a key to the house and directed him there. The next time he saw Tim, he would speak to him about using his quarters. If Tim refused, L.J. would make him an offer for the entire building.

If Christiansen worked out, it would be a good deal for L.J., since he had been paying Tim thirty dollars a week. Even with the increased cost of stocking the pantry with food for his new employee and Irmgaard, which he planned to foot, he would save a few dollars. And Chris seemed strong enough to do anything that Tim could.

Just before L.J. closed the office, Williams arrived. He looked dapper in a new brown suit and seemed ebullient. He offered L.J. his hand, but Hays refused it.

"If I took your hand," he told Williams mirthlessly, "you'd no doubt use the other to harass what defenseless flanks resulted from the gesture, Mr. Williams. I understand you've a mind to, shall I say, 'acquire' my business as well as my most valued employee. Tell me, what did you use to tempt Tim—a girl?"

Williams laughed. "He told you then. Well, I'm surprised, because I didn't believe he had the intelligence to recognize it."

Hays sat down behind his desk and motioned the banker into the only other chair in the room. "Tim told me nothing. He didn't have to. You had to have offered him something more than money, for Tim values our friendship. Unfortunately he also values flesh and so, I assumed you offered him that."

"Quite right, L.J. The girl's name is Rosie Simonds and she's a very comely wench." Now Williams frowned as a thought occurred to him. "She is not, of course, of the Morgan quality, but was more than sufficient to charm your Mr. Wolfe. Or should I say my Mr. Wolfe."

"Please state your business, Mr. Williams, for I do have important things to do. I can save us both time, I suppose, by telling you that neither my ship, nor my business, is for sale—to you or to anyone else."

Williams' face showed dismay at L.J.'s bluntness. But he had a number of arguments ready for this meeting. "See here, Hays," he began anew. "You aren't making any money with the *Resurrection*. Your freight rates are too low, your expenses too high, especially when you blow a boiler, as your ship did recently. Now if you had the contracts I could arrange, your ship would be all but minting its own money.

"Of course, you can't have those, because you don't have the connections I have. And therein lies the reason I am here. I don't want to buy either your ship or your company, L.J. Not anymore. Instead, I ask you to consider making me your partner, say for fifty percent of your profits. Your greatly expanded profits, once I'm in. I can guarantee your share will be at least three times as much as you're earning now."

Hays said nothing for a moment, then stood and walked to the window, turning his back on the banker as he looked out over the Mississippi. An icy chill overcame him. Williams was clearly behind the boiler incident and the cancellation of the Army contract. And now he had the brass to walk into Hays' office and try to talk himself into a partnership? Incredible. Worse yet, Williams was probably right about his contacts. Hays had few doubts that the banker could increase the *Resurrection*'s profits substantially. Perhaps even more that he was promising. But L.J. would sooner sink his ship than see Williams earn a dollar off it.

He turned on his heel and faced the banker once more. "You don't interest me, Williams," he blurted. "If you've said all you have to say, I suggest you be on your way."

The banker's expectant look became a scowl. "You're turning down my offer?" he asked, incredulous.

"I heard no offer," Hays replied coldly, "only a fool's banditry."

"You're shortsighted, Hays. Can't you understand that? Do you have something against money? Lie down with your enemy and be fulfilled. After I'm elected governor of Minnesota, things will be better still. You can say no to that?"

"I surely can. I don't need you or your contracts. I didn't need you to raise the *Cuyahoga,* I didn't need you to finance my operations. I don't need you now."

Williams frowned angrily. "You've been damned

lucky up till now, Hays," he blurted, "but don't expect Lucy Morgan to bail you out every time your ship springs a leak. She's left you. She's gone back East. You're on your own."

Hays despised Williams' sneering tone. "Miss Morgan," he shot back, "is none of your concern and I will not discuss her with you. Suffice it to say that I am well aware of the aid she has given me. As for my ship springing a leak, you had better watch out for your own. Now good day. I must be going."

L.J. walked to the door and held it open, his eyes cold as they met the banker's. Williams hesitated, then sighed and retreated past Hays at the door. "If you come to your senses, you know where to reach me, Hays."

"Don't hold your breath waiting for me to change my mind, Williams. You've heard the only answer I can give." Hays wanted to add: "And stay away from my ship," but did not.

L.J. closed the door behind Williams, went back to his desk and wrote himself a note to caution Captain Henry about the possibility of sabotage. As he walked home, Hays' mind dwelt on Lucille. He missed her more than he would admit, even to himself.

August became September almost before L.J. realized it. His days were filled teaching Chris Christiansen the things the Norwegian needed to know to do a good job for Hays Forwarding. Chris, a rapid learner, proved to have a good memory and L.J. found he rarely had to tell the man anything twice. Soon Hays felt free enough to travel and so, early in September, he left Chris in charge of the office and warehouse and took the *Resurrection* to St. Louis to arrange the financing of his Red River undertaking.

## Railroad King

As he stood at the railing encircling the top deck of his steamer, Hays was once again struck by the ship's beauty. Higgins had done a good rebuilding job and had done an even better job keeping the *Resurrection* in good repair. Hays smiled at the memory of his first view of the ship and thanked God and the Union Navy for delivering it into his hands.

As Captain Henry backed the *Resurrection* away from the dock and took it out into the river, Hays looked toward Higgins' shipyard and there caught a brief glimpse of the big steamer which, he hoped, would soon carry the Hays Forwarding Company flag on the Red River. His eyes stayed on the new steamer as the *Resurrection* swung around and headed north toward the docks of Minneapolis to pick up passengers. When they were halfway there, Hays' attention was diverted by the sight of a six-car St. Paul Railroad train heading for Minneapolis from St. Paul.

The train, idling in the station when the *Resurrection* left its berth, was rapidly closing the distance between them. Before the steamer began its docking procedures at Minneapolis, the train was nowhere in sight, having rushed past at least five minutes earlier.

Hays wondered if what he had just seen was some sort of omen. Crabtree had often spoken of the superiority of railroads over steamers and Hays himself was already convinced that rails would ultimately be more profitable than anything afloat. But his present and immediate future had to remain in steamers. He was forced to so limit himself for a great many reasons, not the least of which was money. Railroads cost enormous amounts—millions of dollars! Hays had read somewhere that the Union Pacific expected to spend more than fifty million before reaching the West Coast. He shook his head at the thought.

And yet . . . Hays stared at the St. Paul Railroad's small Minneapolis station as the *Resurrection* nosed into berth. The train, already having taken on passengers and freight, was pulling out and heading west for the Red River.

Rails. There was something spectacular, something eternally enchanting about the whole notion of a road. The idea that you could build a string of gleaming iron that would carry you through civilization, to and through any wilderness and again to civilization. Such a road could transport thousands of tons—even millions of tons—without recourse to water or wind or weather.

As the *Resurrection* left Minneapolis, Hays made his way to the pilothouse, bid Captain Henry a smiling good day and went through the door leading down from the house to the private office he'd had Higgins build for him. It was accessible only through the pilothouse so as to ensure his privacy while working.

There he made detailed notes on the financial good health of Hays Forwarding's Mississippi River operation, as well as a calculation of the total amount of cash he'd need to finance the Red River undertaking. Including the construction of a warehouse and station in Breckenridge, the cost of transporting the steamer by rail from St. Paul, the cash required to hire a crew and begin operations, Hays figured he'd need somewhat more than $45,000—a not-inconsequential amount. Would Jim Frye grant it? Hays thought so, though it was possible the man might require him to settle for less.

L.J. again went to work with pencil and pared his cost estimate to the bone to see what minimum figure he needed. What he came up with now—$33,000—was still a great deal, but a lot better than the first figure. He was glad he'd cleared his accounts with Morgan's bank quickly after his much smaller piece of financing for the *Resurrection*. It would stand him in good stead. J. Pierpont Morgan was not likely to grant Hays the sizable amounts now needed merely to please his niece.

But Hays was more than a little worried when the ship docked at St. Louis. Perhaps he was too optimistic, too confident.

It was midafternoon and the sun flared bright as he hired a carriage for the short trip to the financial district. The balminess of the seventy-degree St. Louis day was comforting to Hays as he alighted from the carriage and walked into the Morgan bank. An auspiciously wonderful day, he thought to himself.

The offices of the bank were plush, and thick, red tufted carpeting, polished mahogany furniture and a matching French provincial settee set off the reception room of Mr. Frye's suite. Frye, though a bookish man, possessed one of the sharpest minds for figures Hays had ever come across. Frye himself came out to escort Hays into his office.

"I've a surprise for you, Mr. Hays," Frye said with a smile as they shook hands. "Mr. Morgan is in town and he's awaiting you inside."

Morgan here in St. Louis? Hays didn't know if his presence was a blessing or a curse. At least Frye knew L.J. from their earlier dealings. Would the man himself be difficult to deal with?

Morgan's father, Junius Spencer Morgan, had founded the family's fortune. But J. Pierpont was almost, at thirty, as rich in his own right as his father. In 1864 the young man had bought out the George Peabody London firm and renamed it. J.P. had since severed his affiliation with Peabody's to found his own firm in New York. It was said that within a decade Morgan could well become the country's foremost financier. Still, L.J. thought, Morgan must put on his trousers one leg at a time.

Whatever Hays was expecting, he found a mustached man only a little older than himself, a little taller and a little heavier. Neither a giant nor a flashy presence. Morgan was a man, however, whose bearing and manner spoke of great wealth and self-confidence, whose clothes were impeccable and whose grooming was fastidious.

The financier smiled and offered his hand as Hays was introduced. He seemed at ease, a hint of amusement in his eyes. "Well, L.J. Hays," Morgan began in a strong voice. "At last we meet. Lucille has told me a great deal about you and I must confess you don't look to me like the genius she says you are." He laughed. "But then, I suppose there are those who might say the same about me. In any case, I must tell you that you are both fortunate and unfortunate at the same time in your choice of Lucille as a paramour. She is as fickle as I."

L.J. was stunned by Morgan's blunt choice of words. "Where is she, Mr. Morgan? I was under the impression she—and you—were in New York. She left me a note . . ."

"To tell you she was in a rage at you because of your terrible neglect, I gathered," broke in Morgan with a laugh. "She mentioned it to me while we were in New York. But she is there no longer. Would it please you to learn that Lucille is here? That she could not bear to stay away from you?"

L.J. tried unsuccessfully to hide the delight Morgan's words inspired. "It pleases me almost as much as it would—hopefully will—to obtain your backing in my latest venture." L.J. thought to himself he should press on quickly, take advantage of the good humor in the air. "I come to St. Louis to seek your help in breaking the monopoly of the Hudson Bay Company in the western part of Minnesota."

"Good man, Hays! Stick to business!" declared Morgan. "The Red River is what you're talking about, unless I miss my guess. Shall we discuss your venture before lunch?"

Hays nodded.

"And, you'll be happy to hear, I'm expecting Lucille to join us in about an hour. So, we'd best get to the business which brought you here, before any distractions divert us. Now tell me all about the Red River. It is on the border between Minnesota and North Dakota, I believe. You propose to put a ship in the water there?"

Hays struggled to put the thought of dining with Lucille out of his head. "I will put one in the water there," he declared. "The Bay Company has had things all its own way for quite some time, but I intend to change that."

"With my help."

"With or without your help, Mr. Morgan. I have other sources now and will use them if I must. What I propose to do on the Red River is something that someone will accomplish. I simply want to be that man."

Morgan was impressed. Here, the banker thought, was an arrogant young man. Just the sort to get things done, whether or not he had Morgan backing. Morgan listened intently as Hays outlined his plans. Afterward, he stood and began to prowl Frye's office.

"Need I remind you of Jay Calhoun's reputation? He will not tolerate your intervention in Red River affairs without making your life difficult. He and your friend Williams form a deadly tandem."

"I'm well aware of that, Mr. Morgan. I will expect the worst and try to provide for safeguards. The risks are great, but so, too, are the rewards—for both of us."

Morgan nodded. "One cannot gain greatly," he declared, "unless one is willing to take great chances as well. I like your ideas, L.J., and I believe you've a good chance to carry them out in spite of the opposition. I'm willing to extend your line of credit up to $50,000—assuming you do not wish a silent partner in your undertaking."

Hays grinned. "Not if I can help it," he informed Morgan.

Morgan grunted. "I thought as much. Well, you can keep me as a creditor, if you wish. In fact, I think it is time I opened up a branch office in St. Paul. If you like the idea, I shall have my lawyers arrange it as soon as possible."

L.J. was astonished and pleased by Morgan's proposal. He had been prepared to ask for no more than one half of what the banker was offering. An open line of credit was ideal. He could borrow only as much as he needed, when he needed it. As for Morgan's decision to open up a branch bank—Hays was beside himself with joy at the notion, and said so.

"Having your bank in my town will aid me greatly, Mr. Morgan. Williams and his cronies have a strangle hold on banking in St. Paul. You can break it."

"I'd calculated as much, L.J. No sense letting the enemy be privy to all your financial affairs. They'd be a step ahead of you all the time. And we can't have that, can we?"

"It does leave one on the defensive, and that's a terrible position to be in, whether engaged in war or in business."

Morgan laughed. "There's a difference?"

Hays could see why Morgan had already exceeded, though barely over thirty, the success that most men would consider as much as they could expect. Morgan would, Hays thought, have been a formidable enemy. He was thankful the financier had become his ally. It even seemed that the man might become a friend. Before they left Morgan's office and rode in his carriage to the poshest restaurant in St. Louis—the famed Diamond Club—Hays asked Morgan if he had any predictions as to the kind of problems Calhoun and Williams might cause him on the Red River.

"Well," Morgan spoke slowly, stroking his mustache, "if I were in their shoes, I'd no doubt pray for your boat to have an accident long before it reached the Red. Say on the trip across the state. Or even at the shipyard."

Hays had anticipated such problems already. "And if such an accident couldn't be arranged?"

Morgan smiled. "Then I'd harass you unmercifully, drive off your passengers by making them feel unsafe, see that your freight is damaged or destroyed—things like that."

"I'd say your powers of prediction are excellent," L.J. grinned. "By the way," Hays continued, "I must say I'd rather face Calhoun and Williams than you."

Morgan beamed. "L.J.," he responded, "you could not have given me a more sincere or flattering compliment. To thank you for it, I'm going to treat you to the best food served in St. Louis and a view of the harbor second to none." He chuckled. "And of course, the presence of my niece."

Hays pinked slightly, but took Morgan's teasing good-naturedly. He was more than a little anxious to see Lucille again, and had been for a long time.

The Diamond Club lived up to the tributes accorded it by Morgan. It was contained in an ornate three-story gabled structure overlooking the St. Louis harbor far below. From the moment the Morgan carriage arrived at the Club's main entrance, the service and looks of the place said it was for royalty, not commoners. As impressive as the Club was, however, Hays today found it uninteresting, for as he, Morgan and Frye were being escorted to a private room on the top floor, his thoughts were only of Lucille. To his disappointment, she had not as yet arrived and so he had to suppress his excitement as Morgan extolled the view through the large picture window next to their table.

"It's nice, Mr. Morgan," Hays mouthed half-heartedly as the two stood near the window looking down on the harbor crowded with ships.

"You must visit me in New York sometime, Hays," Morgan offered. "St. Louis is busy but New York puts it to shame. And . . ."

"Well, what have we here?" came a voice behind them. "I don't believe it! I thought you'd been swallowed up by the Mississippi, L. Jerome!"

Hays had turned at the first sound of the familiar voice. His broad smile was almost childishly warm. If Lucille Morgan's words exhibited her continuing pique with him, he didn't care, for she was here! For a moment all he could do was stare at the tall, beautiful woman. Turning to his host, he began, "Will you forgive me, Mr. Morgan, if I . . ." Morgan's delighted chuckle cut him off.

"Just don't make love to her here," the financier kidded. "They frown on such things at the Diamond Club."

But Hays hardly heard the last. He crossed the room to Lucille, took the hand she offered and kissed it, his eyes never leaving her face. "I'm so glad to see you again, Lucille," he murmured in a low voice. And he had never spoken truer words. He longed to sweep her off her feet—up into his arms. To carry her off somewhere where they could be alone.

Lucille's expression softened. "You're a rat, L. Jerome," she chided, "but . . . I believe you mean it."

"I do. I can't tell you how miserable I was when I found you'd left St. Paul. I was tempted to follow." It was true, though the temptation had been suppressed quickly by the crush of Hays' business.

"I'd have liked that, L. Jerome."

"You will forgive me, Lucille?"

Now Morgan's voice interrupted the conversation. "For God's sake, Lucille, stop toying with him. He's a businessman and you know very well that his neglect was justifiable. Not exactly gallant, but justifiable. You even admitted as much to me."

Lucille shot J.P. Morgan a quick, good-humored glare. "True, Uncle," she rejoined, "but men who neglect their women deserve to suffer at least a little, business or not." She turned back to Hays. "Have you suffered enough, L. Jerome?" she asked.

"Far too much, dear Lucille," he sighed. As his answer was somehow a key to her affections, she flung herself in his arms and kissed him. His reprimand was concluded.

Although dinner lived up to expectations, he could only wish it over and done. Morgan found L.J.'s obvious lust for his niece amusing and as they were leaving, went out of his way to introduce Jim Fiske to the party. Fiske, who with Jay Gould had gained control of the Erie Railroad, kissed Lucille's hand and held it unnecessarily long—to Hays' supreme displeasure.

"Don't mind Fiske," Morgan told Hays as their carriage stopped in front of the Morgan mansion. "He's far more interested in Morgan money than he is in Lucille's body."

"I can't imagine that," Hays replied.

J.P. Morgan had to leave for New York that evening, but insisted that Hays stay over in his house. "My niece," he told L.J. with a wink, "will be glad to serve as your hostess. Even I will admit she will prove more amusing than I could ever hope to be."

Hays laughed. He was certain Mr. Morgan was correct.

When the financier had finally departed, Lucille led L.J. to the parlor off her bedchamber. They embraced, then L.J. suddenly backed away from Lucille, wondering if the turmoil that clambered through his veins was visibly shaking him. He sought a seat, searched for something to say but managed only a kind of awkward stammer.

"First the lust, then the talk," she whispered.

Her hair, longer than when he had seen her last, spread across the creamy sheets like silver rivers. It cascaded down her shoulders, curling over her breasts. L.J.'s hand traveled through hair and down flesh, listening to the quick breaths from her mouth half open, watching the rise and fall of her ribs. Her finger traced his side. His grip locked on her. "Jesus," she muttered, her eyes closed.

Later, she lay on her stomach, that long, silver-blonde hair clinging, moist, to her back. L.J., his hand propping his head to gaze at her, idly stroked her back, then slid his hand gently between Lucille's white buttocks. There was a murmur of distant pleasure, a hum of encouragement from her and so his touch lingered there, teasing and wandering down her thighs. Her legs parted slightly and L.J., fascinated by her quiet, steady sighs of delight, persisted in the silent, delicate game, his touch like a feather on her skin. She stiffened, then relaxed as he toyed near the mark. She murmured again, the meaning of her words lost to her pillow.

Then, in a fury, she was on him, an enraged woman, leaning back, taking what she wanted. He watched her, magnificently taut, grimacing with desire, heeding the call of something beyond his vision. She thundered above him, her hands on his thighs, head back, like the most perfect figurehead ever to grace the bow of a ship.

"Did you miss me?" she asked later, still struggling to catch her breath.

"A stupid question."

"Not really." She frowned in mock displeasure. "You haven't exactly been the most steadfast of pursuers."

"Don't," he said, a kind of helpless plea.

"I know you're busy, L.J.," she continued, "but I don't see why you can't hire someone to solicit for you. Then at least you would have more time to spend at home."

"I can't afford to hire a person of quality and ability to solicit shipping. It's that simple, Lucille. And, anyway, no one would expend the efforts I must in order to survive in this business. That much work can't be hired. And I cannot depend upon others for my success."

She sighed. "Why is success so very important, L.

Jerome? Why must you have it so fast? You're wasting your youth, and a good part of mine, I might add. My uncle has the right idea. Even though he works as hard as any man, he still travels, wenches, plays, enjoys."

"Your uncle was born into money, Lucille. I was not."

Lucille's eyes sparkled. "You are still two of a kind," she declared, running her hand over the stubble of his beard, which by this late hour had covered his chin and the sides of his face. "I believe Uncle Pierpont senses that in you. He does not take kindly, in business at least, to those who are timid or slow. The confidence he has shown in you by backing your new venture confirms it. But what has all this to do with your rush to success? With not finding time for me?"

"Everything, Lucille." He paused. "A teacher once put it best, I believe, when he told me that not everyone respects the successful man, but absolutely no one looks up to a failure. I cannot have your respect as well as your love unless I can also be the success your family is used to. I must, in short, prove myself. And to prove myself, I must devote all of my energies to business—for the moment, at least.

"Perhaps, when I've done what I've set out to do on the Red, I'll have more time to enjoy my youth, Lucille—and yours. I must tell you, though, that I've little hope to pin you down to anything permanent, for your uncle says you're as unlikely to settle down with one person as he is."

Lucille fell silent. "He's right about one thing," she said at last, "I'm only twenty-three and would be quite uncomfortable if I found myself chained to one place. I guess . . . I've a few wild oats I still must sow. I can sow them, I suppose, while you're turning the Red River into the L. Jerome Hays Bank." Now she kissed Hays fervently. "You will be careful, L. Jerome? My uncle says Calhoun and Williams will be out to strangle you. I wouldn't like it if you were hurt. Not at all."

"Nor would I, Lucille."

# Chapter 6

While Joseph Higgins went to work in earnest on the half-finished sternwheel steamboat, L.J. journeyed to Fort Garry to find and hire a former Hudson Bay Company shipping agent named Thomas John Short. Short's task was to establish a Hays Forwarding Company office and to seek out cargo for the newly named *Manitoba*.

Short was a tall, spindly, scarecrowish man with dirty straw-colored hair, an elongated face and a dour disposition. He was a good talker, got along well with people and knew the territory, for he had lived here all his life. He was also as clumsy as a thirty-five-year-old man could possibly be. This almost comical flaw caused his dismissal by Jay Calhoun. Short had the misfortune to drop a crate of expensive Canadian whiskey while getting it ready for shipment in full view of his boss. He was dispatched immediately.

The accident was not the first time Short's clumsiness had caused a loss for his company. So his firing wasn't really capricious. Still, Thomas John was not an easygoing sort and took his dismissal poorly. He made no bones about his bitterness toward Calhoun and the Bay Company—a long point in his favor when Hays interviewed him two weeks after L.J.'s meeting with J.P. Morgan.

Short had a number of other things going for him. He, like many of his fellow Canadians, was bilingual, having mastered both French and English. This fact pleased Hays, for he had almost no opportunity to speak his own second language. Having left Canada nearly ten years earlier, Hays had not spoken a word of French for years. The two men chatted for almost an hour in the language before Hays offered Short a position.

Even more important, Thomas John knew the Hudson Bay Company from the inside, having been an active part of its operation for more than seven years. He told L.J. how Calhoun would react to threats to the company's supremacy.

"Calhoun's a mean bastard," he warned. "He won't hesitate to do you dirty. Down and dirty. Anything it takes to get your ship off the river. I wouldn't blab the fact that you got a ship until you can hide it no more."

Although he was impressed with Thomas John, Hays knew the job would be a difficult one. He decided to push a little. "Can you give me a good reason why I should put you on, Thomas John?" he asked.

Short looked Hays straight in the eyes, a feisty expression on his face. " 'Cause I can do a lot of good, my friend," he declared, "and 'cause I'll do everything I can to show Jay Calhoun he made a big mistake in letting T.J. Short go. He's my enemy, Mr. Hays, even more than he is yours!"

Under normal circumstances, Short's final statement might have put Hays off and caused him to think twice before hiring the man. But these were not normal circumstances and, as J.P. Morgan had opined, there was, after all, little difference between business and war. One thing appeared to be certain—Calhoun would surely come down hard on his Red River competition as soon as he discovered it was there. So it seemed to L.J. that Short's bile might stand him in good stead.

It was late in the evening and Hays was exhausted when the train pulled into the small St. Paul station, returning from Fort Garry. L.J. had slept fitfully in the uncomfortable seat of a St. Paul Railroad coach and so was anything but alert and refreshed when he climbed down from the railroad car and started for home. He had taken no more than five steps when he raised his face and sniffed the air. Was something burning? It surely smelled like it.

He half-turned in the direction of the shipyard, just north of the docks, and saw a glowing crescent in the sky. Without hesitation, he took off on the run toward the yards.

What he saw started his blood boiling—the steamer, his new steamer, the *Manitoba,* was in flames!

He raced across the yard to the cabin Higgins occupied and banged at the oak door with his small suitcase. Joseph staggered out in a nightshirt. Higgins took one look at Hays' face, glanced quickly at the *Manitoba,* cursed, and disappeared for barely five seconds. Immediately a whistle sounded—an emergency signal the shipbuilder had installed to summon help when he needed it fast.

Higgins wasted no time in conversation. He raced to the *Mighty Mite,* which contained his pumps. He dug into the hold for a long length of fire hose and attached it to the pump. Soon water from the Mississippi was pouring onto the top deck of the *Manitoba*. Hays had no time to appreciate the shipbuilder's quick work.

He was busy shoveling coal into the tug's engines. By the time the pressure built up and the pump was operating at its maximum rate, L.J. could hardly stand. Coal dust coated his sweating face as he went to the tug's rail and watched smoke and flame spiraling upward from his steamship. The great pumps in the tug's belly spewed river water over the *Manitoba*'s deck. Smoke wafted in the light wind and steam rose in the flames that flickered in the yard. The sight of the burning steamer was eerie, a dream.

Higgins' men were hard at work, hooking up a second hose and starting another of the tug's pumps. Two men had climbed onto the *Manitoba*'s burning deck and were chopping away planking at the edge of the fire to keep it from spreading. Hays watched silently.

An hour later the fire was out, but it was not until the next morning that Hays and Higgins could assess the damage. It was a bleak day, the sun obscured by thick clouds, the threat of rain weighting the air. As Hays and Higgins picked their way around the badly burned areas of the top deck, Joseph said little. Hays agonized over what he saw, moving in complete silence. Any hope of moving a finished steamer over to the Red River before spring had now vanished, he thought.

"She's a bloody mess," Higgins observed as they climbed down for a look around the hull, "at least the top deck is."

Hays said nothing.

The hull seemed sound, though in places it had been blackened by flames. Higgins grunted as they climbed to the top deck for a closer look. Near the wheelhouse, Higgins found an empty metal container. The builder's eyes turned black with anger. "The sons of bitches!" he declared. "They torched her! Did a crappy job of it, thank God, but they tried. If they'd started the fire down inside her hull, we'd never have saved her."

Hays lit a cigar and tried to think, his own rage a white-hot furnace deep within him. So, he thought, Calhoun and Williams had started their game.

"I'll post guards over the *Manitoba* from now on, L.J.," Higgins offered, "though I doubt they'll try again."

"I'll bear the cost, Mr. Higgins," returned Hays, "since those we guard against are my enemies."

"We'll share the costs, L.J.," responded Higgins. "They are *our* enemies, not yours alone."

But Higgins was right—no further attempts were made on the *Manitoba*. It nonetheless proved to be a long and restless winter for L.J., in spite of the growing sense of excitement he experienced as the steamer drew closer and closer to completion.

The long nights seemed unendurable to L.J. and he missed Tim Wolfe. Hays was more than pleased with Tim's replacement, Chris Christiansen. The man was able to do anything Tim could, physically and mentally. But Chris was not the friend Tim had been, and never could be. Chris was loyal, but the good-humored affection Wolfe wore on his sleeve was missing. To make matters worse, Lucille Morgan had traveled to Europe. Often L.J. thought about her as he lay in bed at night trying to sleep. Was she as fickle as her uncle suggested? Was she even now in bed with another lover? Hays' scalp prickled at the thought and he forced his mind to abandon the speculation.

True to his word, in mid-November J.P. Morgan had opened a branch office of the Morgan Federal

Bank in St. Paul—right across the street from First Minnesota. Williams was furious. And he fumed when L.J. Hays and Joseph Higgins moved their accounts from First Minnesota to Morgan Federal.

It was shortly before the unsuccessful attempt to burn the *Manitoba* that Williams had journeyed to Fort Garry to meet with Jay Calhoun. There, he apprised him of L.J. Hays' plan to extend his business to the Red River. Calhoun, a barrel-chested man with matted, pale skin, red hair and simmering temper, was silent as he thought over what Williams told him. His finger scratched unconsciously at his oversized, veiny nose. "You say he means to transport his steamer from St. Paul to Breckenridge by rail, Ben? Is it possible?"

"I guess so, Jay. I hear Phil Crabtree thinks it can be done."

"And you know for a fact that Hays has J.P. Morgan's backing? Incredible!"

"Morgan's planning to open a branch of his bank in St. Paul and it's hurting me already. I won't be able to keep track of how Hays' business is doing. And I'll probably lose the shipbuilder and the railroad, too."

Calhoun frowned, his eyes now beginning to wander aimlessly about his small office. "Don't you hold a fair-sized interest in the Pacific Northern Railroad, Ben? And doesn't the Pacific Northern hold an interest in the St. Paul?"

Williams shook his head. "We do own PN bonds, Jay, but they never got around to buying St. Paul Railroad stock. I know some of the powers in the PN, though, and they ought to have some friends on the St. Paul Board of Directors. What did you have in mind?"

"We can't have Hays bucking us on the Red, Ben. See if you can persuade somebody to get the St. Paul to refuse to move his boat. No railroad, no way to move the steamer to the Red—it's as simple as that."

"And if we can't arrange that? I can arrange an unfortunate fire at Higgins' yard, I think. How does that strike you?"

"I've no objection, but why bother? If we can get the St. Paul to do what we want, it won't be necessary."

"I'm not sure anybody can keep Crabtree from fulfilling a promise—and make no mistake about it, he's promised Hays."

"He's only the general manager over there, isn't he?"

"So are you, Jay. But there's nobody I know of who can shove *you* around."

"Just so, Ben," replied Calhoun. Only a flicker of a smile bespoke the Bay Company man's pleasure at Williams' undisguised flattery. "All right. See if you can burn the damned boat. If you can do that, it will solve our problem. But go ahead and see if you can find a way to pressure Crabtree, just in case you fail."

So it was that Williams arranged the fire at Higgins' shipyard, then went after Crabtree at the railroad. He failed at both.

Early in December L.J. boarded the *Resurrection* for a business trip to St. Louis—followed, unbeknownst to him, by Elizabeth Arton. But at the halfway point to St. Louis, she had not seen Hays once. Finally she asked a crewman where she could find him and was told he had a private office, accessible only through the pilothouse where he worked while traveling.

She quickly formulated a plan. If the ship's captain was a man, he would not say no to her simple request for an audience with Mr. Hays.

She took herself up the stairway to the high-perched pilothouse and paused before entering to open her wrap. The attractive figure beneath her gown could hardly go unnoticed by the captain. She opened the door and entered. Captain Henry stood at the wheel, a long clay pipe in his teeth. When he saw his visitor, it nearly fell from his lips.

"Captain," Elizabeth said with a nod, "I am here to see Mr. Hays. I'm told his office is through that door." She pointed to the side of the pilothouse.

"Mr. Hays doesn't like being disturbed when he is working, Miss," the captain offered. Then he grinned. "Will I not do?"

She laughed nervously, noting the captain's dark eyes. "You are certainly a handsome man, Captain, but it is Mr. Hays I must see."

Captain Henry knew he should send the girl packing. But he also knew that, like himself, Hays was a bachelor. The lady was young and pretty and might well present even the serious-minded Mr. Hays with a pleasant moment on a chilly day.

"What's your name, lass?" the captain asked. "If you'll tell me that and give me an idea of your business with Mr. Hays, perhaps I can see my way clear to let you in to see him."

"I'm Elizabeth Arton of St. Paul," she replied. "As for my business—it's really rather personal and I cannot discuss it."

The captain laughed and regarded the girl with new respect. She was clever, to be sure, though he was certain she was barely old enough to travel alone. "Very well, Miss Arton," he declared, "go through the door there, down the stairs to the door on the right. I would ask you a favor, however. Should Mr. Hays not be pleased to see you . . ."

Elizabeth's answering smile was brilliant as she anticipated his request and interrupted it. "Don't worry, Captain, I assure you he'll be delighted to see me."

Captain Henry was not satisfied. "Of course, my dear. But should he not be, please tell him you sneaked down there while I had my back turned. Agreed?"

She nodded and was gone before he could change his mind. Reaching the door to Hays' office, she paused to gather herself together, for she was scared, her heart fluttering.

Hays must not think her a fool. Or a child. He must see her for what she was—a sweet young woman who admired him and wanted to tell him so. This was her chance.

As before, when she met Captain Henry so successfully, she inflated her lungs with air and felt the bodice of her gown tighten against the thrust of her breasts. She knew she was not as pretty as Mr. Hays' Miss Morgan. But her teacher, though tall and beautiful, did not have what men seemed to admire most—the comfortable fullness that gave a woman presence and dignity. Men knew when a woman sensed her own power: they responded to the radiance of her style and carriage.

Could she hope to compete with Miss Morgan for Hays' favor? She had asked herself that question many times. She felt a pang of jealousy, a lingering unease. Each time she compared herself with Miss Morgan, she had felt discouraged, for Lucille was not only beautiful, but smart, too. And being the niece of J.P. Morgan certainly was no drawback.

It wasn't fair that a girl should be as pretty as Lucille Morgan and rich as well. Elizabeth had spent hours trying to decide how to compensate for her plain, direct ways, her youth, her lack of means. In the end she'd decided she would just be herself—but a more interesting version of herself. If she could not be as smart, witty and worldly as Miss Morgan, she could still be more attractive to Hays, simply by being more interested in him than anyone else could be! Young men might be put off by having a girl show an overearnest interest in them, but not so a mature man like L.J. Hays.

Now she smiled. L.J. had a nice ring to it. She must ask him what the initials stood for and why he didn't use his given names. Miss Morgan, she suspected, already knew what those initials stood for.

Miss Morgan! Elizabeth made a face. She had never liked the woman. There was an air about her—a sort of nose-in-the-air snootiness that Elizabeth had seen right off. Elizabeth recognized that Miss Morgan always called on her to recite poems that dealt with poor folk.

At last Elizabeth roused herself from her thoughts, squared her shoulders and knocked on the polished mahogany door.

"Yes, who is it?"

In answer Elizabeth turned the latch and swung open the door. "Mr. Hays?" she bubbled, smiling as sunnily as she could. She stepped over the high metal ledge at the cabin's entrance and approached Hays, who sat behind a desk littered with papers.

Hays matched her smile, not only because she was a pretty girl, but also because he thought she was a potential customer. He stood up to shake her hand.

"Mr. Hays," she began, "I can't tell you how glad I am to meet you again."

Hays frowned. "I confess I'm at a loss, Miss," he responded. "For I don't remember you—and it's clear I should. I don't forget such attractive women as yourself." He kissed her hand.

His chin was prickly with whiskers. Elizabeth hated that. One of her former beaus had grown a beard, and she thought L.J. might look good in the same.

"I'm Elizabeth Arton," she explained. "I was with Miss Morgan's class when you launched the *Resurrection*. I never did get a chance to thank you for the trip. I enjoyed it very much."

"Oh," Hays remembered, "yes, I think I recall you now, although there were a number of you. You were a bit younger."

"Actually, I've always looked younger than I am. I was seventeen even then." Elizabeth prayed Hays would not detect her little lie.

"Really? Well, I do appreciate your finding your way down here to thank me, but it really wasn't necessary. I'd promised Miss Morgan I'd give you all a free trip and was most happy to do so. Are you enjoying your trip today?"

"Even more so since I've had a chance to see . . . the boat again, Mr. Hays." Her cheeks flushed pink as she almost revealed her reason for being on the ship. "It's a beautiful boat and comfortable, too. I understand it's called *Resurrection* because you raised it from the dead."

"From the deep, Miss Arton—or perhaps from the shallows would be more accurate; she was at the river's edge. But yes, that is why I called her what I did."

It was a dumb name, Elizabeth thought, but she didn't reveal what was in her mind. "I've always been fascinated with steamboats, Mr. Hays. Perhaps, if you could find the time, you might tell me more about the *Resurrection*. I'd really love to hear how you came to be her master."

"I'd be glad to, Miss Arton, but I'm afraid I'm a little busy right now. Tell me, where will you be staying in St. Louis?"

Elizabeth could have kissed him—and congratulated herself for having wormed out of Irmgaard Christiansen where Hays would be staying in St. Louis. "Why, at the Trent, Mr. Hays."

"Say, that's wonderful," he enthused, "I'm staying there, too." He scratched his chin. "Would you care to dine with me tonight? I have business in the middle of the evening, but I'm free for supper. We can discuss steamers or whatever you like."

Elizabeth made a show of thinking it over, her eyes averted shyly. "Well, I suppose that will be fine, Mr. Hays. Since we're both registered at the Trent, no one's tongue will wag about us."

Hays chuckled. "I should hope not. And you have my word we'll give no one reason to speak badly of us."

Elizabeth was giddy as she left L.J.'s office; he had kissed her hand. And at last, she had a date with him!

She hummed softly to herself as she passed through the pilothouse. Captain Henry grinned, wondering what had transpired between the pretty coquette and his young, serious-minded employer.

As might be expected, L.J.'s fancy was taken by the luscious young Elizabeth. She was, he thought, just the tonic he needed to relax before tonight's appointment. What he found truly diverting about her was her genuine interest in the *Resurrection*. If she truly cared about his ship, she had to be a remarkable person.

He also had to admit to himself that he was taken in by the large, swelling breasts straining at the front of her yellow satin gown. He couldn't help but wonder what they must feel like compared to Lucille's tiny mounds.

He stopped grinning when Lucille came to mind. Don't worry, Lucille, he now thought, she's only a momentary amusement. After resolving to behave himself while in the company of Elizabeth Arton, he managed to resume his work.

When Captain Henry steered the *Resurrection* smoothly into the berth at St. Louis, Hays was so deeply wrapped up in his work that he was not even aware of the slight bump of the ship against the pier. Only when Captain Henry knocked on the door was L.J. aware of the journey's end.

"We're in St. Louis, L.J.," spouted Henry with a crooked smile. "Say, I hope that cute little girl didn't pester you. She was eager to see you about a personal matter, she said."

"No trouble at all, Billy. But don't get in the habit of sending down every pretty young thing who decides she wants to meet me. Such women are very disrupting, to say the least."

Henry laughed. "I can sure as hell understand that, L.J. I wouldn't mind being disrupted a little myself over someone as cute as Miss Arton. I've told my mate to have a carriage wait for you. Will you be long?"

"Only a few minutes. Has that girl left yet? I could share the carriage with her."

"I don't know; I'll see if she's still about."

## Railroad King

But the Captain did not find Elizabeth and L.J. rode alone to the Hotel Trent. When he reached his destination, however, he found Miss Arton sitting in the lobby reading a newspaper.

The Trent was not as grand as some of the hotels in St. Louis, nor as expensive. Its carpeting was a bit frayed and some furnishings had seen their better days, but its rooms were large and comfortable.

Hays smiled as he bowed and tipped his hat to Elizabeth. "I hope you are not too tired to keep our little dinner date?" he asked.

"Not at all," she responded eagerly. "You have a most comfortable ship, Mr. Hays, much more comfortable than some of the other steamers sailing the Mississippi."

L.J. wondered how many ships this young lady had been on. "Since it's already close to dinner time, Miss Arton, why don't we take it now?"

Elizabeth agreed, so L.J. escorted her into the small dining room of the Trent. Like the rest of the old hotel, its furnishings were old. But the food was excellent—the best in St. Louis.

Throughout dinner, Elizabeth asked Hays all sorts of questions about himself, some regarding business, others rather personal.

Hays couldn't help but be flattered. He told her everything she wanted to know. And whenever he paused for fear of boring her, she earnestly encouraged him to go on. Never before had L.J. confided so much about himself to anyone. No one had ever shown so much interest in him—not even Lucille Morgan.

He found his pulse racing a little faster in Miss Arton's company. She was as delectable as she could be and he was growing more than just a little interested in her.

After dinner, as L.J. was about to ask Elizabeth if he could see her after his business appointment with Jim Frye, she told him of her plans to meet her aunt at the opera.

Disappointed, Hays said nothing about a later tryst, and left her with a little bow. "I thank you," he said honestly, "for an enjoyable evening. Perhaps we can meet back in St. Paul."

"Oh, I would like that, L.J.," she told him, "very much! Do drop by my mother's home. We live on the southern edge of town."

"I promise you I will just as soon as I can." L.J. meant it, for the girl, who was a stranger only hours before, now seemed capable of arousing him with just a look, a word, a smile. She was less sophisticated than Lucille, but a great deal more sensuous for it. And though L.J. felt a twinge of guilt, he could not deny the desires Elizabeth Arton had aroused in him.

More than once that evening in Frye's office did Hays find his attention wandering away from his discussion with the banker and to pleasures with Elizabeth.

It was just after ten o'clock when he returned to the Trent. Promptly he asked the desk clerk if Miss Arton was in. To his chagrin he learned she was not even registered! He hoped that the girl's meeting with her aunt had something to do with that.

Hays didn't see Miss Arton in St. Louis again. Extremely disappointed, he had to continue on to Washington D. C. to conduct business with Senator Jed Tidrow—one of Minnesota's two senators—about the railroads and land grants.

Though neither subject was urgent to him right now, Hays believed that any knowledge he gleaned about railroads would serve him well. In Washington,

Tidrow told Hays a great deal about the St. Paul Railroad system, for which he had been an attorney when it was formed in 1864. What L.J. found most interesting was that its founder, Barton Cunningham, had spent "far too much money" in constructing the roadbed between St. Paul, Minneapolis and later, Breckenridge.

"He owned property along the route, didn't he, Jeb?"

Tidrow laughed. "You *are* perceptive, Mr. Hays. Yes, of course he did—they all do. It's part of the railroad game. Railroads don't come to towns—except in the Northeast, where it's heavily populated. Towns come to railroads. And you'd better believe that, for it's the gospel.

"To have power, all you gotta have is the right to pick and choose a railroad route. Bart and his friends have done all right for themselves. A good thing they sold most of their capital-improvement bonds over in Holland. If those bondholders knew how their greenbacks had been squandered by the St. Paul, that road would've been tossed into receivership already.

"Only good thing about that railroad is Phil Crabtree. He knows his business and gets the job done without any bullshit. His biggest trouble is his boss, Cunningham."

Tidrow also educated L.J. about land grants and how they affected the railroads. Tidrow believed that they encouraged waste by tempting otherwise astute investors into buying railroad bonds and thereby placing millions of dollars into the hands of those who ran the roads, who in turn used the money without restriction or accountability. The bondholders were merely serving as bankers for the railroads, and once they had loaned the roads their money, they had no say over how it was used or for what. To hear Tidrow tell it, the result of the federal and state land-grant system was to cause two-thirds of the country's railroads to be undercapitalized—have too much debt for the road's assets, in spite of the land acquisitions resulting from track laying. According to Tidrow, the St. Paul, while having no federal land grant, had one in Minnesota consisting of fifteen million acres of land—and much of it in the rich Red River valley!

More than ever Hays was eager to get his freight lines going on the Red River, for he knew now that if the St. Paul Railroad ever extricated itself from its financial difficulties, it might well continue its main line up the Red to Canada. And if so, it could mean the end of all of Hays' dreams.


Back in her mother's small home, Elizabeth Arton was delighted with the results of her trip to St. Louis. And she was sure she had interested L.J. Hays greatly. And well did she earn his interest; she had worked hard enough for it! All that talk about steamers—it had flown straight over her head. She was glad she had managed to hide her ignorance by simply keeping him talking.

There was no question that Hays lusted after her. She could see the spark in his eyes. She giggled at the thought. He was a handsome enough man and had, she thought, an aura that was stimulating—at least to her it was. The idea of keeping him company on his trips sent her spirits flying. So did the hope that he could be a good lover, and make her body happy as she wanted it to be. He wanted to, she was sure of it.

Elizabeth laughed at that thought. Then she ran into her mother's room to inspect herself in the full-length mirror her father had brought all the way from New Orleans.

She was alone in the house, having convinced her mother that she could take care of herself while her mother visited a sister in Memphis for a fortnight. That, Elizabeth now thought, would give her just enough time to lure L.J. Hays into her bed.

While admiring herself, she remembered her first time with Tim Wolfe. It had not been good. It had, in fact, been just plain awful! Would L.J. be better? She hoped so, for she wanted to *win* L.J., not just be his bed partner.

She was certain she could marry the steamboat owner—if she could coax him into her bed, for Hays, unlike Tim, was a real gentleman. Once he had bedded her, he would not thereafter spurn her. She would make him believe she was still a virgin. A gentleman did not take a lady's maidenhead, then spurn her.

Warmed by these thoughts, Elizabeth shed her robe and looked at her body. Her flesh was smooth, she thought admiringly, and there was just enough of it to please a man. More than enough of her breasts, she knew.

She closed her eyes and stood motionless before the mirror, her arms hanging limply at her sides. Her tongue snaked out to moisten her lips as her mind began to work. Her hands moved to her thighs, then upward to her breasts, which she gently cupped and caressed. The nipples grew hard and she touched them with the heel of her hand.

One of her hands moved down across her stomach, to dive into the space between her thighs. In her head now were visions—of herself as she was being touched by men, manipulated by men, men whose faces were blank, and whose bodies were large and strong. She loved her visions. She had known them even before Tim had deflowered her. They always brought her satisfaction.

Elizabeth, her eyes still closed, swayed before the mirror as her left hand teased the hard nipples of her enormous breasts and the fingers of her right hand worked the soft, pink flesh folded beneath the dark hair between her legs. Soon a moan came from her half-open mouth and she sank to her knees. She bit her lip as an exquisite cloud of delicious pleasure coursed through her from her legs to her neck. Slowly, her sweet visions faded away.

The *Manitoba* was coming along well, L.J. discovered when he returned home to St. Paul just after the new year was born. The fire hadn't done as much damage as first thought. "Soon our only task will be to get her to the Red River," L.J. enthusiastically told Joseph Higgins on a snowy day in mid-January.

"A small task," observed Higgins dryly, his eyes on the snow-covered steamer, which now occupied a long, flat car built specially by Higgins' men for the job ahead.

"Do you think you can have the *Manitoba* ready by the end of March?" Hays inquired.

"No question about it, L.J. I figure by then the weather'll be a little better and we can get her moving."

"Good. My man in Fort Garry has sent word that he can have a full cargo for us within two days of the *Manitoba*'s first trip north."

"Do you expect any trouble from Williams or Calhoun on the trip from here to the Red River?" Higgins asked.

"I surely do, Mr. Higgins, but I'll be ready for it.

I've already spoken to Crabtree about getting some railroad detectives out from Chicago to serve as guards."

"You expect an out-and-out attack? I suppose it's logical—after the way they tried to burn the ship I guess I wouldn't put it past them. Still, I hate the idea that there might be killing over any boat."

"So do I," Hays agreed. "But if there is to be killing, I aim to make sure it'll be their blood that's spilled, not ours."

That night, Hays wrote a long, rambling letter to Lucille, telling her of the impending battle with the Hudson Bay Company, of the coming completion of the *Manitoba,* of his appreciation for her uncle's help in making it possible for him to begin trade on the Red River.

He also mentioned his loneliness for her, made clear by his encounter with one of her former students—the charming Miss Elizabeth Arton. He stated that Miss Arton did not remind him of Lucille in any way, but confirmed the loving desires he held for her from the first moments of their love.

After writing the last, L.J. seriously reflected on what he thought of Miss Arton. Clearly, she was no child. He knew it would be judicious of him to make every effort to avoid her in the future—for if he did not, he would surely wind up in her bed.

L.J. had not seen Elizabeth since his return from Washington, but he had thought of her many times. On a number of occasions he had almost sought her out, but found something to divert himself. Lately Hays was in the habit of rising early, and setting out on morning walks that took him to the boatyard to check the *Manitoba*'s progress.

Elizabeth had learned of this routine from Irmgaard Christiansen. So one Saturday morning in early February, she awoke even earlier than Hays, took her mother's wagon and horse, and set off for Higgins' yard. If L.J. would not come to her, she would go to him!

It was bitter cold and snowing lightly, and Elizabeth was immediately sorry about her choice of mornings, but she gritted her teeth and urged the horse on until she reached the hill that overlooked both the yard and the river. There she pulled a blanket around her and waited for Hays, praying he would not be too long.

Finally, just as Elizabeth, shivering and wet, was ready to leave, her quarry showed up. The moment she spotted Hays' red-jacketed figure striding purposefully through the swirling snowflakes, Elizabeth focused her eyes on the steamer far below and pretended to be fascinated by it. At the last possible moment—when she could hear the sound of his boots crunching the icy particles of snow into the frozen earth—she half-turned and looked straight at him.

"Oh! Mr. Hays! You frightened me! I . . . I didn't think anybody was up at this hour."

Hays was perplexed to find Elizabeth Arton here at such an early hour and in this ungodly weather. "Well," he said, a smile appearing on his wind-whipped, rosy cheeks, "I've been meaning to look you up for more than a month. As a matter of fact, the night of our dinner back in St. Louis I returned early to the hotel and asked for you. They told me you were not registered."

It was Elizabeth's turn to be surprised, for she had not anticipated that he would return to the Trent and ask for her. But she would not tell him that she had left at nine p.m. that evening to return to St. Paul on the Cruise Line steamer. Or that she had to go

## Railroad King

home because she had only enough money to pay for her return trip.

"I stayed with my aunt, Mr. Hays. She insisted, as I expected when I decided to postpone taking a hotel room."

"And what brings you here, Miss Arton?"

Elizabeth smiled in the way she had practiced so many times in front of her mirror these past few weeks. It made her look a lot prettier, of that she was sure. "Why, I just found that I couldn't sleep, so I dressed and decided to go for a ride in Mama's carriage. As I was riding, I thought of you and decided to come up here to see how your new boat was coming. It looks like it will be done soon. Is it as big as the *Resurrection*? Will you be sailing it on the Mississippi?"

"The *Manitoba*'s somewhat smaller than the *Resurrection,* Miss Arton, but she won't be used on the Mississippi. We're shipping her over to Breckenridge soon as she's finished, to sail the Red River between there and Fort Garry."

"I didn't know they had steamers over there. It must give you a lot of pleasure to see your very own boats on the river, L.J. And I can't help but admire a man who's so successful at what he does."

"Success is a relative term, Miss Arton . . ."

"Honestly, L.J., won't you please call me Elizabeth. I hate it when people are formal with me."

"Of course, Elizabeth. As I was saying, success for one man could well be deemed failure by another. I have done well up until now and I suppose some people would think me a success. But I don't. I've a long way to go yet."

Elizabeth's answering smile was dazzling. "I'm sure you'll make it, L.J. May I give you a ride back to your home—or down to the dock?"

"Much obliged," L.J. replied as he climbed aboard and took the reins from Elizabeth. Now L.J. surprised her. "Tell me, Elizabeth, am I the reason you're here? Because I had not kept my promise that I would see you in St. Paul?"

She could have made a denial, but decided against it, for Hays seemed flattered rather than angered. "Yes," she said coyly. "I wasn't sure of the reason you hadn't come over to see me. I figured meeting you here would be . . . well, less embarrassing, if you were to tell me you don't like me."

Elizabeth looked at the ground and held her breath. She had rehearsed the essence of what she had just told him, because she was convinced that the one quality L.J. admired over any other was honesty. If she was right, his reaction to her honesty would be to want to reward her.

More than his words, his expression confirmed her belief. "You're an honest and interesting girl, Elizabeth. I think . . ." Hays hesitated, his eyes on her face, "I'd like to see you again and will—even though I'm extremely busy these days."

"You'd only *like* to see me?" she rejoined, with a show of disappointment.

"I'll love seeing you again," he continued with an answering chuckle. "But I must tell you," he said with some uneasiness, "that my relationship with Lucille Morgan is . . . quite meaningful. And although we're not engaged . . . we will . . . probably someday . . ."

He trailed off uncertainly. Elizabeth merely shrugged. "I've no claim on you, L.J.," she replied. "And I see no reason why you can't continue your, uh . . . relationship with Miss Morgan, and see me as well. Of course, not at the same time."

Hays chuckled. "That," he noted, "is for sure."

"Will you let me entertain you tonight? My mama says I'm a very good cook and she's right! She says people can hardly wait to come back to dinner for some of my cooking."

"Tonight?" Hays asked. "Well, I was going to the Riverboat after work to play poker but . . . What time?"

"Seven?"

Hays agreed. They had reached the dock, and after climbing down from the buckboard, Hays told Elizabeth, "I look forward to seeing you later."

"Don't be late," she returned.

"I wouldn't dream of it." And he meant it.

It was warmer, but snowing heavily at six-thirty as L.J. and Chris finished off-loading cargo from the *Resurrection,* which had arrived in midafternoon.

L.J. had been looking forward to the evening visit all day, and, in spite of the deepening snow, arrived at the Arton's two-story frame house on the south side of town at five minutes before seven.

He put his horse away in the small barn next to the house, and after finding some oats and water for his horse, Hays waded through the deep snow to the front door. The memory of how Elizabeth had looked in his ship's office and later at the Hotel Trent warned him—perhaps all too much, for with her mother there, he would surely have to be on his best and most proper behavior.

Elizabeth awaited him at the door, dressed in a low-cut frilly gown of cream-colored mohair and silk, which fit her snugly, and bared her shoulders. Hays wondered how her mother would allow her to wear such a gown in the presence of a man to whom she wasn't married.

"Where's your mother?" he asked as she took his coat and made him take off his boots.

There was a hint of luster in her eyes as she replied, "Didn't I tell you she was away?"

She had turned her back and was leading him into the parlor before he could reply. A grin appeared on his face as he thought either Elizabeth was not as young as she seemed, or she was not afraid to reach out for what she wanted.

Indeed, Elizabeth delivered what she had promised—a sumptuously delicious beef-and-dumpling dinner. "I ought to hire you to replace the cook aboard the *Resurrection*," he observed.

"I would love that, Mr. Hays. Cooking is my second favorite pastime."

L.J. had a feeling he would find out what her favorite pastime was before the evening was over, and held in the obvious question.

After dinner, they took brandy in the parlor, which was sparsely lit by candles. Elizabeth sat so close to L.J. on the settee that he could feel the warmth of her breath as she spoke. The scent of her perfume made him want to kiss, to taste, her neck and shoulders. But he refrained, and they just talked.

It got late and Hays knew he had to go, though neither he nor Elizabeth made a move. Finally, he checked his pocket watch, and stood up. Their bodies touched. He touched her elbow with an apologetic gesture, turned and took half a step away, then impulsively and surprisingly turned back and gathered her into his arms, kissing her hungrily. Elizabeth responded with more than just a return kiss. She rubbed and pressed her entire body against his—her knees, her thighs, her groin and belly, her bosom.

When their lips parted, Elizabeth gasped for air.

Hays kissed her neck, her shoulders, her chest flushed pink with passion. Quickly he undid her bodice, taking her lovely breasts into his hands. He kissed her breasts, caressing her gently.

At the same time, Elizabeth reached down and touched him. "To my room," she whispered as she nipped his ear.

Hays tenderly picked her up and carried her up the stairs to her bedchamber. He laid her down on her bed and easily removed all her clothes. Never had he seen such an ample, sensuous body, aching for his touch. As Hays removed his clothing, Elizabeth smiled at the sight of him—as large and as perfect as she had wanted him to be.

For a time, L.J. teased her breasts, her belly, her buttocks, the curves and lines of her body with quick kisses. Elizabeth, yearning for him, fondled him, begging him softly to come to her. Hays obeyed gently, entering her as she sighed her welcome.

Tears came to Elizabeth's eyes. "I love you, darling," she whispered. "Kiss me, sweetheart, please kiss me."

L.J. kissed her, and together they rocked, gently at first, then gradually a near frenzied arching and thrusting. With a throaty sigh and a shudder, Hays lost himself in her, which brought a cry of joy from Elizabeth. Spent with ecstasy, they lay together, limbs entwined.

At last, a real man had done more for Elizabeth than her visions ever had. If she did nothing else with her life, she vowed to keep this man forever.

Remembering one of the Reverend's lessons—"You must please yourself before you can please others"—Hays chased away the demons of guilt. Never before had he known such carnal pleasure; it was unearthly. He promised to see Elizabeth very soon, then left her for beer and poker at the Riverboat.

At Breckenridge, Tim Wolfe was baffled by Rosie Simonds, who tormented him with her behavior. She could not have been nicer to him—often acting as if she were mesmerized by him—yet she would not be coaxed into his bed. If Rosie only would be more cooperative, he thought, *everything* would be perfect. She did her work well, kept the Hudson Bay Company station clean and was doing a good job with the ledgers. But she was driving him to drink, something he was doing a lot as spring came to the Red River valley. Tim was out nightly, returning to the station staggering drunk.

One day late in March when Jay Calhoun and Ben Williams came to Tim's office in the station to pay him a visit, Tim had a tremendous hangover. It was the banker's first visit to Tim since he had hired L.J.'s only St. Paul employee.

"Well, Tim," Williams began after introducing Calhoun, "how are things here with you?"

Tim watched Calhoun move around him and sit down in the chair behind his desk. "Everything'd be great, Ben, but for Rosie. She's a looker, all right, but she's damn sure not a doer. She won't let me so much as touch her!"

Williams sniffed Tim's breath. "You hitting the bottle?"

"Rosie's driving me to it, damnit! Outa my head, that's what!"

"I didn't say Rosie was a whore, Tim," Williams shot back. "I thought you were supposed to be a ladies' man."

"Rosie's the toughest one I ever met up with,

Ben. I can't figure her out nohow. Don't know what she wants. Usually I can figure a woman without any trouble at all. Sometimes all she needs is a couple of nice words. Other belles need to be forced the first time they do it with you. But not Rosie. She's cold as the Red River in January!"

"I'll speak to her, Tim, though I can't promise you anything. Now, Jay and I have a job for you. Your friend L.J. and Joseph Higgins are getting ready to move a new steamer over here to compete with us."

Tim frowned. "What's that got to do with me?" he asked.

"Everything," replied the banker. "If Hays gets that boat over here and establishes himself on the Red, we'll lose a lot of our business—plus we'll have to cut our rates. Which means we also may have to cut your pay—or worse, maybe let you go completely."

Tim looked from Williams to Calhoun, then back at Williams. "Christ," he muttered. "You're serious, ain't you?"

Williams just nodded.

"So what do you want me to do?" Tim finally asked.

Calhoun cleared his throat. "Nothing at all, Tim. Not yet. But as soon as we find out when Hays' boat is coming across from St. Paul, we want you to arrange something—just a minor little accident. One that'll turn the steamer into scrap. You won't have to do it alone—we'll bring in some professional help for you. But you'll have to be the guide."

Tim was shocked. The news had sobered him up real quick. He shook his head.

Calhoun raised an eyebrow and fixed a stern look. "You'll have no choice, mister, so do not shake your head. You will do *what* we ask, *when* we ask it."

Tim's throat turned dry. "I can go back to St. Paul," he argued. "L.J.'ll take me back."

Suddenly Calhoun's right hand held a pistol, its hammer cocked. The general manager of the Hudson Bay Company stood and brought the barrel of the gun to the middle of Tim's face. "Ever see somebody get their head blown off?" Calhoun asked. "If I pulled this trigger now, your brain would just sort've explode."

Even Ben Williams showed surprise at Calhoun's tactics, but the banker recovered quickly, to grin evilly. "Even if we let you go back to Hays," Williams added, "which we won't, it wouldn't prevent us from doing what's got to be done. We'd just find someone else to do it, that's all."

Just then, Calhoun's finger squeezed the trigger; the hammer struck. "Bang!" shouted Calhoun, as the hammer struck an empty chamber. He roared with laughter.

Tim felt as if he had jumped out of his skin. His heart raced like a locomotive and he had trouble catching his breath. Calhoun holstered the gun, then wrapped a friendly arm around Tim's shoulders. "Do what we ask, Tim. You won't be sorry. There will be a substantial bonus for you, I promise. Say around . . . five hundred dollars?"

Williams nodded approvingly. "And I'll see to it that Rosie's a good deal friendlier to you, Tim."

In the end Tim agreed to be a guide for Calhoun's man Steve Wilson, who would be arriving in Breckenridge the next week, after a successful detail in the Texas Panhandle. Later, Tim tied on his worst drunk yet and fell down the flight of stairs leading up to his room.

Hours after, when Tim awoke in his bed, Rosie was sitting beside him on the bed, her large, dark eyes focused on his face. She was holding a cold, damp towel against a lump on the side of his head.

"How . . . how'd I get up here?" Tim asked.

The girl did not answer that question. "When are you gonna stop the boozing, Tim? You'll surely kill yourself if you don't."

Tim grimaced at the pain he felt throughout his body. "I got reasons. Reasons I need to drink, 'cause drinkin' helps me forget."

"I'm one of 'em, right, Tim? Mr. Williams said . . ."

"I don't give a damn what Williams said!" Tim snapped, then groaned at the pounding in his head. Panicking Rosie, he lost consciousness once more.

He awoke several hours later, still in bed, with Rosie at his side, and unaware that he was awake some time ago. When he saw Rosie, he cried out in joy, "Rosie!"

"Hello, Tim," she whispered. "How're you feeling?"

"Am I dreaming? Are you really here—in bed with me?" Rosie wore a yellow robe over her nightgown.

"Reach over here and touch me," she answered with a smile.

Tim groaned as he turned from his back to his right side so that he could see Rosie better—and touch her cheek.

"What are you doing here?"

"I got you up here after you fell down the stairs. You were staggering drunk and could hardly walk."

"You did that? Impossible! I'm too big."

"I didn't carry you—you walked yourself. But I kept you upright. You passed out when I got you up here and into bed. I had a heckava time gettin' your clothes off, though." She grinned as Tim confirmed that he was nearly naked.

"I come from a big family," Rosie explained, "and my pa and my three brothers used to drink like you. So I've had practice pickin' 'em up. But you're the first one I ever picked up who got stinkin' in the first place just 'cause of me."

Tim blinked as his eyes took her in. "That's because I need you, Rosie. I want you. Bad."

"How bad?"

"Real bad. More than I've ever wanted anyone—ever." Tim's hand dropped from Rosie's face to her breast. She made no attempt to stop him from fondling her.

"Enough to get married?" she asked.

"Jeez!" He released her breast and stared at her. "Married?"

"A lotta men actually like it, Tim. It's not so bad."

"They're lunatics. Is *that* what you been holdin' out for, Rosie? To get me to marry you?"

Rosie shrugged. "I like you, Tim. A lot. Maybe I love you, I don't know. But you're one of the nicest guys I've ever known. You think I *didn't* want to climb into bed with you? The heck I didn't! I wanted you the first time I saw you. But . . . I knew if I bedded down with you, you'd never marry me. You'd think I was a tramp, a whore. Well, I'm not. And I want you, but there's only one way I'll have you."

"Married."

"That's right, Tim." Rosie moved over close to him now, hugging him, nuzzling her face near his neck. "I'd be good to you, Tim. I can help out more than most wives, 'cause I got a job and plan to keep it. I'm real good with figures and Mr. Williams pays me good. I cook pretty good, too—in case you haven't noticed."

"No reason to get married," argued Tim.

Rosie put two fingers over his mouth to shush him. "I ain't through yet," she reprimanded. She moved as close to him as she could. "How do I smell, Tim? Pretty good, right? My mama was a bug on stayin' clean and so I wash up a lot. Almost every day. What's more, I got me some good smelling perfume and that's what you'll be smellin' right now."

Tim nodded weakly, feeling the effect of their closeness.

"I got a mind to be a mama myself one day, Tim. I'd love to have two, maybe three little ones. And I'd sure raise them good. They wouldn't be no trouble to you, Tim. All you got to do is give 'em to me. You know how to do that." She giggled. "You seem like the kind of man who might enjoy having a coupla kids around."

"Maybe. Maybe not," Tim countered.

Suddenly Rosie got up and stood beside the bed. She shed her robe, revealing the outline of her body against her cotton nightgown. She was a small girl, lithe and tawny. When she pulled the nightgown over her head, Tim felt his groin grow warm.

"Is this a reason to want to get married, Tim?" she asked softly, standing within inches of him, her knees against the bedframe.

Tim swallowed. "God, Rosie, you are beautiful! And I want you, more than I ever wanted anybody before."

"You can have me, Tim. But only if you want me forever."

Forever. He had never thought much about getting married. There had never been any reason to—all the girls he saw usually let him do what he wanted to. Married? Tim and Rosie Wolfe? "Can't I think about it a while, Rosie? And while I'm doing that, we can . . ." He reached for her, but she stepped out of his grasp.

"No, Tim. If you want me, you can have me—but only one way."

He had to make a decision now, for forever. Since he had known her, Rosie had become much more to him than a potential roll in the hay. He genuinely liked her, which made his yearning for her that much more frustrating. And what she'd said was true—she was an excellent cook, quite good at figures, and seemed very practical, which would make her good with children. She was ideal, Tim could not deny.

"All right," Tim answered in a low voice.

Rosie closed the distance between them with a little leap and smothered him with kisses. "Oh, Tim," she gushed. "You won't be sorry. I promise you. I will take good care of you, you'll see. You won't ever need to take another drink on my account. I'll be good to you—so very good!"

"Be good to me now, Rosie."

"Oh, yes, yes, yes. . . ."

He winced as he struggled to position himself over her. Her eyes showed concern, but she said nothing, her own flesh as eager to receive him as his was to take her.

It was good—tender, exciting, comforting—as she knew it would be. And Tim had never known such a caring, responsive sex partner. He had made the right decision. He fell asleep immediately afterward, with his left arm wrapped around her. She snuggled against his shoulder.

Rosie did not sleep, but rather studied his ruddy features, the large yet well-formed nose, the wide mouth with straight white teeth, the strong chin. Tim should have been born rich, she thought. Rich, like that friend he was always talking about—L.J. Hays. It was a shame Tim always got the leavings while other men took the plum pudding. Poor Tim. Rosie kissed his shoulder and he stirred but did not wake. Now she began to think about the family she wanted so desperately.

She had lied to Tim. She had not come from a large family; there was no family. She had been an orphan, and had been raised by her Uncle Seth. At least that was what she called him—Uncle.

He had raised her in the timberlands north of St. Paul, west of Lake Superior. But he was more interested in his whiskey than being a good father to her. Only when Rosie had turned into a pretty little thirteen-year-old had Seth paid her much mind. It was then that she learned her body could get her a lot of things she wanted, like pretty clothes and book-learning.

But after a while, she became disgusted with being "nice" to her uncle, and made up excuses to get out of her "family duty." It was shortly after that that Seth started to drink heavily and regularly beat her up. The last time he had tried to beat her, she kicked him unconscious. It was then she left the old coot and went down to St. Paul.

Her hand stole across Tim's thighs, stroking the soft hair at his groin, then stroking him, rousing him. Her fingers teased hair and flesh. Soon Tim began to move, responding to the fingers that held him prisoner.

"There now, Giant," Rosie whispered the name she had dreamed up during the long months of her abstinence. "Be nice and Rosie will make you happy."

Tim awoke fully when he felt the surge of warmth

from Rosie's mouth upon him. No woman had ever done that to him before. And though it felt wonderful, he was compelled to ask her to stop. But Rosie ignored him.

# Chapter 7

The sun shone brilliantly through a cloudless blue sky on the morning of All Fools' Day—the day when L.J. Hays' new steamer *Manitoba* would journey by land to the Red River. Only yesterday had Phil Crabtree's track layers completed the short section St. Paul Railroad spur that now ended at the single section of track beneath the flatcar, specially designed by Joseph Higgins.

The *Manitoba* had been built on a high ridge on the Mississippi side of the shipyard, its prow pointed toward the Mississippi seventy-five feet below and to its right. Had her destination been that river, launching her would have been simple. But the Red River was far away from the Mississippi. Getting there presented some problems. The ground to the steamer's stern and port side was level, but a slight downgrade commenced about twenty-five feet to its rear.

When Hays arrived at his friend's yard at seven o'clock in the morning, Crabtree had two 4-4-0 class wood-burning locomotives already lined up and coupled to the flatcar holding the steamship. Hays stood spellbound for a moment, as he saw his new ship from just inside the gate of Higgins' yard.

The *Manitoba* was a gaudy two-stacker now, painted red and white with a touch of light blue here and there, including the lettered name across the side. It had three decks: the main, where the central hold for freight was located amidships; the boiler deck, where huge boilers and paddle wheels were located; and the top deck, consisting of cabins for passengers and crew.

Rising high above the top deck, in the exact middle of the ship, was the pilothouse, from which Captain Sam Meyer, the new skipper, would navigate the *Manitoba* through the shallow and sometimes treacherous waters of the Red River. Meyer, a one-time sailor aboard a Hudson Bay Company Red River steamer, represented another piece of Hays luck. He had not been able to gain a command on the Red because the Bay Company's steamers all had irreplaceable captains, men who had spent years with the company and were good friends of Jay Calhoun. So Meyer had left the Red and gone to St. Louis seeking a ship. It was there that Hays found him and snapped him up. Meyer's command was a lock when Hays learned Meyer knew the Red inside and out.

Another bit of good news came from Thomas John Short, who was confident that he could attract plenty of freight in Manitoba Province, in spite of the threats of violence made against potential Hays Forwarding Company customers by Hudson Bay Company thugs.

And finally, Phil Crabtree had sworn on his mother's grave that the rails his men had laid to Higgins' shipyard would hold the great weight of the *Manitoba* "as if it were a butterfly!" The railroader also guaranteed that the locomotives would have no trouble pulling her.

## Railroad King

All this left Hays with only one concern—sabotage. Trouble in the form of one Canadian and one Minnesotan—Jay Calhoun and Ben Williams. Not trusting either man as far as he could spit, Hays had made arrangements to guard against any surprises they may have had in store for the *Manitoba*.

Hays now discovered, however, that the first of the arrangements—his attempt to conceal the ship's departure date—had not worked. By eight o'clock, the time set for the *Manitoba*'s leaving, a number of St. Paulers were on hand to view it. Williams stood among them.

From his position near Joseph Higgins on the steamer's top deck, Hays raised his hand and began windmilling it to signal Crabtree's engineers to open their throttles and release their brakes. Phil had not wanted either man on the ship at this stage of its journey, but Hays had insisted, saying, "If we are to have an accident, it will ruin me, Mr. Crabtree, so I might as well go down with my ship."

Higgins, finding the remark funny, also noted that as the builder, he too had much to lose if the big ship did not make it to Breckenridge, and he chose to ride with Hays.

Now, as the locomotives began to pull, Hays held his breath and clutched at the railing before him. He kept his eyes glued to the track between the lead locomotive and the slight downgrade which would lead the ship across the width of the shipyard and onto the St. Paul Railroad's main line a half mile to the southwest.

The engines pulled the ship forward only an inch or two, but then gradually began to pick up momentum as they reached the downgrade. The onlookers cheered at this strange procession travelling across the shipyard.

Hays and Higgins, however, restrained their glee. Their concern right now was that the ship might sail right off its flat car as the train travelled along the downgrade. Not until the train passed out of the shipyard and was level again did Hays and Higgins breathe more easily.

The train was moving along at a smart ten miles an hour when it reached the main St. Paul line leading north and west toward Minneapolis, heading toward Breckenridge. The plan was to shuffle the locomotives at Minneapolis to place one behind the ship to help the one in front. That would give the train its maximum power on the grades between Minneapolis and Breckenridge. The switch was accomplished without trouble by separating the lead locomotive and running it off on a siding while the second locomotive and steamboat passed through, then reattaching the first engine to the rear.

Before the train left Minneapolis, a St. Paul Railroad handcar arrived, operated by the muscle power of eight strong, armed men. This was another one of Hays' preventive measures for trouble. The leader of the eight railroad detectives, Will Rutledge, a quiet man who looked like he could out-armwrestle a lumberjack, talked with Hays on the *Manitoba*'s deck. He and the others had been borrowed by Crabtree from the Chicago, Burlington & Quincy Railroad in Chicago. They were to serve as "point riders" for the train—to spot and hopefully head off any trouble before it reached the engines and ship.

Rutledge said he would use flare guns to signal any trouble. The tone of his voice made Hays think that trouble was inevitable.

As the engines moved out again, L.J. took his position beside Higgins on the top deck. He eyed the countryside far below, which was turning green with new grass and foliage. To his right was the Mississippi, to his left hills and farms.

"Beautiful country," Hays observed, "but wait till you see the valley of the Red east of Breckenridge, Mr. Higgins. It isn't heavily cultivated yet, but I'm certain it will be one day. It's gorgeous country, with rich, black dirt just made for farming. The farmers who'll eventually settle there will be important customers of mine."

"Let's just hope we reach your Red River Valley without incident, L.J. There are rumors flying around that the *Manitoba*'s earmarked for accident."

"An accident? Hardly, Mr. Higgins, and we both know it. Anything that befalls us will be no accident." L.J. nervously fingered his mustache. His and Higgins' careers were riding on their getting the *Manitoba* to Breckenridge safely.

High above the St. Paul Railroad tracks running through a narrow mountain pass due west of Melrose, two men formed a welcoming committee for the train bearing the *Manitoba*. One of the men was Tim Wolfe, and though resigned to the circumstances that caused him to be there, he was not happy about being a part of it. And neither did he like or trust Steve Wilson, the explosives man Calhoun had brought up from Texas.

Hours ago Wilson had finished planting explosives all along the rocky hillside, a hillside strewn with hundreds of huge granite boulders. He had only to light the long fuses to start what could only be an enormous landslide.

Tim was altogether gloomy over what was about to happen, although he said nothing to Wilson, who sat back against a boulder and whittled with a long, sharp knife. Tim watched the track to the east through field glasses for signs of the train.

It was midafternoon. If Hays' steamer had left St. Paul this morning, as Tim had been led to expect would be the case, the train ought to be nearby.

Tim focused the glasses on the tracks some five miles to the east, then swept them to the west. He saw nothing. He panned back one more time and was about to put down the glasses when he was momentarily blinded by a brilliant reflected glare. He quickly lost the glare, but brought the glasses around again and found the source.

On the tracks about a mile or so to the east was a handcar filled with men, all of them with rifles. One man stood on either side of the car and scanned the countryside with field glasses. The man on the easternmost side of the car had his glasses focused directly on Tim, or so it seemed.

"We got trouble out there," the big Irishman warned, handing his glasses to Wilson.

The explosives man zeroed in on the handcar, studied the armed men, then, with a shrug, handed the glasses back. He sat back against the boulder and rolled a cigarette.

Tim was unnerved. After another few minutes of watching the handcar, he turned back to Steve. "Let's set off the charges right now and get the hell out of here. I don't like the idea of us being the bull's eyes for their target practice."

"They won't spot us. Stop worrying."

"But what if they do? They're armed to the teeth! If they come up here after us, we're gonna have to ride for our lives."

Wilson laughed. "Brave son of a bitch, ain't cha?"

Tim glared at him and took a threatening step in his direction.

"We're high here, Wolfe," Wilson explained. "Even if they caught a look at us—which won't happen unless we're careless—I've got plenty of time to blow the mountain before we ride for it. By the time they get up here, we'll be long gone. And that's assuming they don't get buried in the slide itself."

"I'm for blowing the explosives right now," Tim argued.

Wilson ignored him and continued to smoke. The job he had to do for Jay Calhoun was simple enough—or would have been had it not been for Wolfe. He was tempted to send Tim back and would have, if it had not been for the fact that Calhoun wanted the big shipping clerk implicated if it became necessary.

Will Rutledge, a veteran railroad detective, had guarded dozens of trains in his time. He had never lost a train and was determined to keep his perfect record intact. He toyed with his black, bushy mustache while experiencing a familiar uneasiness. Someone, he was certain, was out there, watching and waiting, biding his time.

Rutledge kept his eyes on the passing countryside. The thought of the big ship behind furrowed his brow. The *Manitoba* was an immense target. An attacker could hardly miss, no matter how he went about it. Yet, he was impressed with the ingenuity of the vessel's transportation.

Rutledge brought the glasses back up to his eyes and studied anew the territory. The land was deserted in these times, the Indians having been forced by the Great White Father in Washington to move along so that the white man had a place to live. Once, Rutledge thought, a white man riding through this territory would have taken his life in his hands with the Sioux or the Chippewa Indians who hunted and fished and lived here. But not now, and Rutledge had mixed emotions about that. He had, in his youth, fought the Indians in the Minnesota Territory, and they were as tough an enemy as could be found, as numerous as they were fierce. But they had surely been taken advantage of by the Great White Father in Washington.

Now he turned his thoughts back to the problem at hand: how to prevent an attack on the *Manitoba*.

There were many forms of attack possible, some of which could cause much more serious damage than others. A derailment would do damage to the ship, but Rutledge was not at all sure that would cause sufficient damage for a determined enemy. A derailment across a bridge or in a narrow pass would be better. But where? He had yet to come across any one place the enemy might logically lurk. There were a thousand places, but no probable ones.

Rutledge's assistant, Hank Barr, was keeping a close eye on the tracks ahead, making sure that they had not been mined or otherwise sabotaged. It was another way the train could be wrecked with its huge cargo.

There were still other ways. A land or rockslide could be created out of the hills and low mountains that bordered the track. Such an event might well sweep the magnificent *Manitoba* off the track and off the flatcar, wrecking her completely. Rutledge kept his sharp eyes on the high ground in anticipation of just such an "accident."

Like the detectives he had hired, L.J. Hays was ever vigilant as the big ship was pulled slowly onward toward the Red River. Occasionally where the roadbed narrowed, the sides of the ship scraped the trees or ground that sloped away, causing Joseph Higgins to yelp in anguish over the damage to the ship. With the trip now half over, they would soon reach the northern plains, a relatively flat area with few trees, and rich, fertile soil. Once there, Hays thought, he would feel a lot better about things, since the ship wouldn't be vulnerable to attack from above.

While watching the high ground, Hays thought he saw something bright flash several times some miles to the west. He called Higgins' attention to it, but saw no more flashes.

"I don't like it, Joseph," L.J. warned. "It seems to me that if Williams or his crony Calhoun were going to pull something, it would be certain to happen while we're still in the hill country. We're almost out of it now."

Higgins smiled without warmth. "Perhaps," he thought aloud, "we've misjudged the good gentlemen."

"There's about as much chance of that as there is that the fire in your yard was an accident."

L.J. fell silent as he recalled the layout of the track ahead. Hays had been on the construction crew that laid that track, and if he remembered correctly, there was a sharp dip in the level of the roadbed up ahead due to granite in the rocky soil. Rather than waste time and money blasting through the granite, Crabtree had opted for a sharp curve to the north, then a gradual fifty-foot drop through a valley.

Granite. That meant there was rock up ahead hard enough to open gaping holes in the wooden hull of the *Manitoba*; boulders the size of a railroad locomotive; rock that could be moved only with explosive power. Dynamite!

Hays cursed under his breath and strained his eyes to catch that glint again in the hills up ahead. Suddenly, out of the corner of his eye, he saw something move and quickly swung the glasses toward it. He was just in time to see a pair of deer—a small doe and an even smaller young deer. They had stopped and were alert, as if they could see him, even though he was miles away.

In spite of his bad case of nerves, Hays managed a grin. But the grin lasted only a few seconds, as again he keyed on the danger he could smell. The danger he was beginning to taste in the dryness of his mouth.

"Oh, my God! Will you look at what's coming toward us? Weird seeing it on dry land! Look how big it is!" Tim Wolfe's eyes bugged as he saw the huge blue and white steamship come into view far to the southeast.

Wilson glanced at the *Manitoba*, but said nothing, content to wait for the moment when he would make mincemeat of it. Soon the procession would have to slow for the sharp curve and downgrade which was the narrowest part of the roadbed, some four hundred feet below the two men. Then the *Manitoba* would be in a straight line with the rockslide Wilson's explosives would create.

Tim, his glasses again at his eyes, swallowed hard when he saw two familiar figures standing on the deck of the entrained steamer—L.J. and next to him Joseph Higgins, the shipbuilder. Tim's scalp prickled as he realized the rockslide could kill his old friend and the harmless old carpenter.

"Hey, Steve," Tim cried out, "there's people on the deck of that ship—two of them. If we start the slide, they're liable to be killed!" He offered Wilson the field glasses. The explosives man shook his head.

"That's their tough luck," Wilson said, "not mine."

"Hey, one of them's an old man. I don't want to be responsible for killing an old man."

"If he dies, he dies," Wilson shot back. "My orders are to blow that damned ship right off the tracks and see that it don't make it to the Red River. That's what Calhoun's payin' me for and that's what I'm gonna do. Now forget about those people and stay out of sight. The handcar's down there, too."

Tim hadn't figured on hurting anybody, yet it now seemed all but certain that the slide would kill both Hays and Higgins. He couldn't be a party to it. Yet what could he do about it now? Wilson carried a pair of six-shooters and looked like he wouldn't hesitate to use them.

Rosie had sized up the man correctly the very first time she had seen him. She had told Tim, "I think the man is bad news—I can feel it."

Tim couldn't let on to Rosie what was about to happen, so he told her that Wilson was a troubleshooter for the Hudson Bay Company. When he and Wilson left Breckenridge, he had told her only that he had to do an errand for Calhoun.

He was doubly glad now that he had not confided in her. There seemed little chance now of his not becoming a murderer. He tensely watched Wilson roll still another cigarette. The ground around the explosives man was already littered with burned-out butts.

"Don't you care that we're about to kill a couple of people with your dynamite?" Tim asked.

"Do you?" Wilson replied, tossing the used match to the ground just short of the end of the fuse.

"Yes," Tim affirmed, "I do. And I'm not gonna do it!" He took a step toward Wilson, too late—the man's right hand had already dropped to his six-shooter.

"*You* don't have to kill anybody, big fella," Wilson snarled. "*I'm* gonna do it and you're gonna be a good boy and not make any trouble. Now why don't you just get on your horse and mosey on back to Breckenridge? If you do, maybe I won't tell Jay Calhoun how you turned yeller."

Tim turned red with anger. "It's not a matter of bein' scared, Wilson! Calhoun didn't hire you to kill nobody! And I won't let you do it!"

Wilson's gun leaped into his hand before Tim could close the distance between them. "Stand back," Wilson ordered, "or I'll give you the honor of being the first one to die today."

Tim stopped and stared at Wilson. "You don't dare shoot," he warned. "If you do, the men on that handcar will sure as hell hear the shot and you'll lose your chance to surprise anybody."

Tim took another step forward, praying he was right. In a hand-to-hand fight, Tim figured he could hold his own with Wilson, even if Wilson tried to level him with the butt of his revolver. Tim was six inches taller, fifty pounds heavier, and a great deal stronger. If he could get close enough to get his hands on the man . . .

Rutledge's handcar was a half mile past the narrow pass where Tim Wolfe and Steve Wilson were holed up. In a matter of moments, the country suddenly flattened out, as the last of the mountains fell behind. Now Rutledge snapped his fingers as he realized what he should have known earlier—that any attack on the train had to be mounted in the high ground, in the mountain country they had just left and the steamer was just passing through!

Quickly he ordered the handcar stopped and reversed. Soon the little car was careening back toward the train as fast as it could go—perhaps fifteen miles an hour.

Rutledge unholstered his flare pistol and pointed it skyward. As the car came back around the tight curve, Rutledge caught a glimpse of a man standing among the rocks high above the track. He was walking slowly toward a big boulder next to him.

Then the man vanished from view and at the same time, Rutledge heard the sound of the train's whistle. It could be no more than a mile away, Rutledge guessed. Now the detective ordered the car stopped right in the middle of the curve, and deployed his men to the right and left. Pointing it skyward, Rutledge pulled the trigger of his flare gun.

Moments earlier L.J. had signaled the train's engineer to slow down. Up ahead lay the last possible place for a sneak attack. But the engineer signaled back that if he did, the train would come to an absolute stop because of the great weight it was carrying. So Hays had resignedly allowed the train to go on.

Now, when he saw the warning flare up ahead, he was not surprised.

Tim Wolfe was right about one thing—Steve Wilson did not wish to alert the train or its detective guards by firing a shot to stop him. But Tim had miscalculated Wilson's quickness and agility. He sprang to one side as Tim rushed toward him. The butt end of Wilson's gun came crashing down on Tim's head. Wolfe went down in a heap, but he did not immediately lose consciousness. Wilson cracked him again—this one a crunching blow to the temple. Tim fell motionless to the rocky turf. Wilson wondered briefly if he had killed the big blond.

Steve Wilson, breathing hard, stood over the big man for just a moment to make certain he would not move, then hurried back behind the boulder shielding them from scrutiny. He was just in time to see the detectives disembark from the handcar stopped on the tracks in the curving pass below.

He swore when the flare high overhead caught his attention. Now beginning to panic, Wilson picked up Tim's field glasses and brought them to bear on the train. It was not moving, and the two figures who had guarded the steamship's deck now were standing beside the lead locomotive talking with the engineer.

Wilson swung the glasses around to check on the men on the handcar. They were gone. The car lay still and empty. He swept the field glasses back and forth, but still could not find a single armed man.

Where the hell were they? Were they climbing the mountainside? Or just hiding somewhere, waiting, perfectly aware of where he was? And how had they learned he was there in the first place?

Wilson, a single-minded man who earned a good living doing dirty jobs for dirty people, had not earned the attention of people like Calhoun and Williams by failing in his undertakings. If he could not destroy the *Manitoba,* he could still at least delay its arrival at the Red River.

He lit the main fuses leading to the explosive charges. He watched them just long enough to make certain that the flames were making their way down to the dynamite, then turned to beat a retreat to where he and Tim had left their horses tied to a tree.

Chief Detective Rutledge had directed his men to climb the mountainside and close in on their assailants. "If you see any fuses lying around," he told his men, "yank them before you move on. Then move further right or left, or you'll be pushing daisies before your time. And move fast, but try to stay out of sight of that boulder up there." The boulder he pointed to was large enough to hide a small locomotive.

Rutledge was leading half of his men up the mountainside when the first explosions came, some fifty yards to his left. He took one look to see where the explosion had been, then motioned for his men to hit the dirt.

L.J. ordered the engineers to move the train and wait with it back in a heavily wooded stretch of track about a half mile to the rear. He climbed back up on the steamer's deck and began searching the mountainside for further signs of trouble. What he quickly found was the shower of rocks and dirt sent up high by the first blasts of dynamite. The mountainside became instantly alive with big, granite boulders racing down its side.

Hays closed his eyes and said a silent prayer of thanks for the warning that had kept the train out of the line of fire. Had Rutledge not warned them, the train most certainly would be battered with rocks at this very moment.

"Looks like we did not misjudge Ben or Calhoun, L.J.," Higgins said quietly as Hays looked up from his prayer.

"If we did not, Joseph, it would appear we've another enemy to reckon with. A formidable one, though he has failed to destroy our ship."

The first blasts brought Tim Wolfe back to consciousness. He dove behind a boulder a few feet away and prayed that the shaking of the ground from the explosives would not cause it to dislodge. More blasts punctured the air and Tim hugged the boulder more closely.

Now with the deafening sounds of huge rocks jumping down the mountain, Tim cautiously peeked out from behind the boulder. He saw no sign of Wilson, so he swiveled and shot a glance down toward the tracks. They were gone—buried by tons of rock and earth! And there was no sign of either the steamship or the locomotives!

Suddenly, Tim heard shouts and saw men climbing up the slope after him. The men from the handcar!

Tim quickly dodged out of the line of sight of the men and headed for the other side of the mountain, where he had tethered his horse. He prayed that Wilson was gone. He also hoped the explosives man had not turned his horse loose.

His heart leaped for joy when he found his horse, untethered, but munching on fresh spring grass not far from where he had been tied. Tim mounted the animal and frantically urged him downward toward Breckenridge.

Rutledge was only half surprised when the mountainside began exploding around him. As soon as the pattern of the explosions could be readily seen, he motioned his men to follow and began skirting the rock-slide area, his eyes on the spot he wanted to reach.

He was the first to reach the boulder, but found only a pair of field glasses to confirm that this was the spot from where the train was being observed. But the man or men were gone. Quickly, from the tracks at the site, he deduced there were at least two.

He and his contingent of detectives raced to the top of the mountain and began scanning the bottom lands far below for signs of the saboteurs. Far off to the west, Rutledge got a quick look at a lone rider headed for Breckenridge. The only thing Rutledge could tell about the rider before he disappeared behind a rocky abutment several miles away was that he was a fairly large man, dressed in dark clothes. Rutledge waited for the rider to emerge in a clearing to the northwest, but to no avail. The rider had disappeared.

Now the detective was joined by several of his men. "No sign of the ones who did it, Will," his assistant informed him, "but take a look at what the buggers did to our handcar."

Rutledge saw that the railroad roadbed was no longer there, nor the handcar. Both had been covered with tons and tons of rocks and earth. But that was all right; Rutledge had been hired to see that no harm came to the *Manitoba*. Surely, it would have been demolished had it been where the handcar had been when the slide began.

Both Hays and Higgins were relieved when they saw Rutledge's two flares, which signaled the danger was past. Night was falling by the time they arrived at the scene of destruction. L.J. was appalled when it became clear that their journey would not resume for quite a while—not until work crews could clear a path through the mountain of granite and dirt, repair the roadbed, and lay new track.

L.J. told Rutledge he was sending him back to St. Paul with the rear locomotive. "Tell Phil Crabtree we'll need as many men as he can assemble to do the clearing, Will. And tell him I said we'll pay their wages."

"You're going to remain here, Mr. Hays?" Rutledge asked. "Those thugs may be back."

"Perhaps, but I'm staying. I'm betting that you and Phil's people get back before the criminals. Did you see who was responsible for this?"

"I only got a couple of quick looks," Rutledge said. "One just before the explosions went off, but I couldn't describe him. And I had a look at a lone rider heading north away from here afterward, but he was a couple of miles off and had his back to me. All I can say about him is he was a pretty good-sized fellow. But we're sure there were two of 'em. We found two sets of hoof prints."

As L.J. climbed back up on the *Manitoba*'s deck, he knew there was little chance that the men would ever be apprehended—though there was little doubt in his mind for whom they worked.

He slept poorly that night, his mind on the huge cleanup job and the delay it was causing him, and his formidable enemies Calhoun and Williams. L.J. did have a poignant dream, however—involving the Reverend.

L.J. was a boy again, and the Reverend was lecturing to him again, ranting and raving in his usual way, cracking his long pointer to strike an idea.

"Why did he do it?" the Reverend asked.

"I don't know, sir."

Crack went the stick. "What do *you* intend to do about it?"

"I . . . I don't know, sir."

The Reverend whirled about, his black cloak flying behind like a huge black wing. In a tone he might reserve for the Devil himself, the Reverend spewed forth his message, " 'He that doeth wrong shall receive for the wrong which he hath done! . . . Whatsoever *ye* do, do it heartily, as to the Lord! . . .' "

When Hays awoke the next morning in his office on the *Manitoba*, this dream was as clear in his head as sparkling crystal. It inspired him to formulate a plan, a plan of risk that warranted his asking Higgins just how much he cared about the ship, and just what he expected to get out of it.

"Do you still feel it wise to lease the *Manitoba* to me?" he asked Higgins. "You stand a greater chance of loss if our opponents, shall we say, succeed in damaging or destroying her. If you were my partner, you would at least have a share of the profits now generated by the *Resurrection*. I will gladly agree to the change, if you wish it."

Higgins, who had been leaning on the rail as the two men talked, now straightened and turned to Hays with a smile. "A deal is a deal," he said, "but I do appreciate your kind offer. You are an honorable man. I not only like you, but I trust you."

Hays laughed, a gleam in his eyes. "I am also a good businessman, Joseph. You are the only man in St. Paul I would trust as a partner."

"What about Mr. Big?" Higgins inquired. "Your Mr. Morgan?"

"J.P. Morgan has aided me greatly, Joseph. I cannot testify to his honesty with others, but he has always dealt fairly with me." Hays paused, then grinned. "Nonetheless, I've a feeling he would not hesitate to deal from the bottom of the deck if he felt it expedient to do so."

"You would not have him as a partner, L.J.?"

"I would prefer not to."

"He could not be a poorer partner than a Jay Calhoun or Ben Williams."

"I don't know which is worse: having Calhoun and Williams as suitors or having them as enemies."

Higgins smiled at the remark. "Only time will tell," he replied. "But it seems to me that we are soon to discover what uncomfortable adversaries the pair can be."

Hays nodded a stern, thoughtful agreement. "It's for just that reason that I've prepared a little surprise for them and their friends," he muttered, almost to himself. Higgins grilled Hays unmercifully about his "surprise," but L.J. refused to reveal it. "When the time comes..." was all he would say.

Crabtree's work crews labored for more than a week clearing rubble from the twisted ribbons of track which lay before L.J.'s riverboat. Immense boulders were rolled aside or split and carted away. Mountains of sand, stone and the splintered shards of brittle rock ledges had to be hauled to either side of the roadway. And, after a week of backbreaking work, the weather turned grey and chill, then the wind mounted and everyone on the scene knew that the last of the great spring storms would soon be howling down on them.

The men, railroaders, work crews and shipbuilders alike, huddled in the dark, spacious rooms of the riverboat and watched the snow fall around them. It fell dry and cold, blowing in the wind until drifts as tall as a man swirled around them. They were stranded, cut off from both St. Paul and Breckenridge. Though none of the men spoke of their fear, each felt helpless and immobile, an easy target.

But the freak storm had been a blessing in disguise. It had stopped the Hudson Bay Company "trouble-shooters" dispatched by Calhoun to finish the job botched by Wilson and Wolfe. The very toughest men available to him in Fort Garry had been sent to burn the *Manitoba*. But when the storm hit and temperature dropped to near zero, they were forced to abandon the mission.

The railroad crew spent the morning after the storm digging out. L.J. Hays and Joseph Higgins took turns at the shovels, to the delight and surprise of the crewmen. But, for all their efforts, the *Manitoba*'s journey could not be resumed for four more days, and only then because warming air and light rain cleared the tracks ahead. On the 16th of April, the *Manitoba* reached Breckenridge and, via a special spur laid by the St. Paul, was immediately launched into the muddy waters of the Red.

# Chapter 8

It was nearly a month before the *Manitoba* made her maiden voyage up the Red to Canada—a busy month indeed for L.J. Hays.

Hays set up shop on his new steamer to book cargo and begin freight operations. Even before the captain and crew of the steamer arrived from St. Louis, the *Manitoba* was a veritable anthill of activity as dozens of local trappers, farmers, and businessmen swarmed over its decks.

A small army guarded the steamer night and day while Hays anxiously awaited his "little surprise" for Calhoun, Williams and company. It was actually two very unpleasant surprises, to be precise.

Fifteen days after the *Manitoba*'s launching, two large crates arrived from a major munitions company in St. Louis. They were accompanied by four employees of the company, whose task was to guard the crates and instruct the purchaser on their use. That night under a close veil of darkness, Hays, Higgins, and the four men broke open the crates on the deck of the *Manitoba*.

Hays felt both a thrill and a chill at the first sight of the contents. "So this is Mr. Gatling's gun," he en-

## Railroad King

thused, reaching out to touch tentatively the short, stubby barrel.

Higgins was silent, almost in shock. These rapid-fire, revolving machine guns were the most deadly weapons ever devised by man and had only just come into use at the end of the Civil War. He wouldn't have guessed this was Hays' surprise, not in a million years.

Later the company stood in the wheelhouse of the *Manitoba* discussing the placement of the two guns and their value in the type of battle most likely to be launched by the Hudson Bay Company.

"What you have here, Mr. Hays," lectured Louis Dunn, the head of the munitions company contingent, "is a standing army. Two men at each gun can stand off a hundred, even a thousand men, as long as they're supplied with enough ammunition. And I brought plenty of that. These guns can throw lead out so fast the world's worst sharpshooter could not miss his targets."

"My hope is that their biggest value won't be in their killing power," explained Hays, "but rather in their ability to deter and discourage the opposition—keeping them from fighting at all. And so, we shall have a demonstration of our army's effectiveness. It will be open to all who might be interested—especially those of the Hudson Bay Company. I want invitations engraved, Joseph, and sent over to Messrs. Jay Calhoun and Benjamin S. Williams. I want notices posted in prominent places, like at our new Red River shipping office and on board both the *Manitoba* and the *Resurrection*. Even if neither Calhoun nor Williams attends, some of their hirelings are bound to report back to them of the power of our Gatling guns."

So it was that invitations were duly printed and

sent out, and posters nailed in place, all of them announcing:

> A FEARFUL DEMONSTRATION OF THE POWER OF THE "HAYS FORWARDING COMPANY" TO REPEL ANY MARAUDERS INSANE ENOUGH TO WISH TO DEFILE THE STEAMER *MANITOBA* AND TO PREVENT IT FROM PERFORMING ITS LAW-ABIDING FUNCTIONS OF SHIPPING ON THE RED RIVER OF THE NORTH.

The two weeks following his attack on the *Manitoba* were weeks filled with terror for Tim Wolfe. All the way back to his freight station he had worried about being ambushed by Steve Wilson. To prevent such an ambush, he took a route which circled the town before he finally entered it. Tim had seen nothing of Wilson, however, for the explosives expert, Tim later learned, had headed back to Texas, afraid that his failure to destroy the *Manitoba* might well decree his own death.

Back in the Hudson Bay Company station, Tim was confronted by a worried Rosie Simonds. But she did not question him about where he'd been or why, or even about the bruises on his temple and the lump on the back of his head.

On his third day back, Tim quaked as the steamer *Alberta* arrived from Fort Garry with Jay Calhoun on board. When the Hudson Bay Company general manager came by to see Tim, he brusquely ordered Rosie out of the office.

"Why wasn't the Hays steamer buried?" Calhoun demanded.

"We had bad luck, Mr. Calhoun," Tim stammered, wondering what Wilson might have told his boss. "We did the best we could, but . . . somehow they got wind that we were there waiting for them. They stopped the train short of the stretch we'd mined, then the ones on the handcar came up the side of the mountain after us."

"Who?"

"Railroad detectives, I'd guess. They'd been riding that damned handcar up and down ahead of the train—looking for us, I guess. They were armed and ready for trouble, that's for sure."

It became clear to Tim that Steve Wilson had not reported back to Calhoun. It was obvious that Calhoun knew little more than the end result.

"What happened to Wilson?" Calhoun asked.

Tim could have laughed in joy. "I've no idea, Mr. Calhoun," he replied. "Steve set off the explosives early on account of . . . well, he said he didn't want to get caught by the dicks. Then he took off like a shot. I tried to tell him he should've waited on the explosives, but he wouldn't do it. And he damned near shot me."

Calhoun was quiet for a moment, then shook his head and rose from the chair to look out the window onto the Red River. For several minutes he stared at the *Alberta*, one of the three small steamers the Hudson Bay Company operated on the Red. Calhoun knew that if he didn't do something about it soon, the imposing *Manitoba*, a bigger, better, and faster steamer than any of his three, would begin taking away some of his business.

Calhoun slowly walked to the station door to leave. Before opening it, he turned to Tim and with hate and revenge in his voice said, "The *Manitoba* will *never* reach Fort Garry. You can tell Mr. Hays that, Tim. Whatever I must do, I'll do."

On the night the printed announcements of the Hays Forwarding Company's "power demonstration" arrived from St. Paul, L.J. ran into Tim Wolfe. It was the first time the two men had spoken to each other since Tim had left for his new job.

Tim and Rosie were at the Red Rooster Cafe, the best eating place in Breckenridge. L.J. was eating with Dan Salter of the munitions company at a nearby table. Neither Tim nor L.J. saw each other at first.

It was Salter who saw the beautiful Rosie and pointed her out to Hays. "Now there," he confided, "is a lucky man. Look at the lovely lady sitting beside him!"

L.J. grinned the moment he saw Tim. "It so happens that I know that lucky man, Dan. He used to work for me, and I still consider him my friend, though he now works for the Hudson Bay Company."

"That looker can't be his wife! Do you know her?"

Hays started to shake his head. "I may, now that I think of it. Would you excuse me?"

"See if she has a friend hereabouts, Mr. Hays," the Gatling man grinned. "My guns aren't very much company and I'd much rather sleep with a woman than a gun."

Hays smoothed his mustache and new growth of chin whiskers as he crossed to Tim Wolfe's table. Halfway there, he saw Tim look up. His old friend looked as if he wanted to bolt and run.

"Tim!" L.J. cried as he arrived at the table. "It has been a long time. How are you?" He held out his hand, and Tim took it hesitantly.

"I've been all right, L.J.," Tim replied, lowering his eyes. "This here's Rosie, L.J. She's my, uh . . . we're gonna get hitched soon."

"Say, that is good news, Tim," declared L.J. "It's about time you found a woman who could tame you." He smiled at Rosie, finding her fresh, young beauty as striking as the flowers of summer. L.J. took Rosie's hand, which she thought he would simply shake. But he brought it up to his mouth and kissed it instead. "I won't congratulate you, Rosie, if you don't mind, for from what I know of him and what I can see of you, he is certainly getting the best of the bargain. I do wish you both nothing but good luck in the future! If I can ever help you, please remember I am not only Tim's friend, but yours, as well."

A look of irritation crossed Rosie's face. Tim's friend was certainly forward. What gave him the right to take such liberties? Was he quite the ladies' man?

"And how're you doing with the ladies, L.J.?" Tim asked. "You still goin' round with Lucille Morgan?"

Hays shook his head. "She's in Europe, Tim. Left her teaching job in St. Paul and hasn't been back here since December. And I surely do miss her. But I manage to keep my sanity by keeping busy."

"Yes, I hear you just brought a new ship over here."

L.J. frowned. A body would have to be blind not to see the *Manitoba* in her berth on the Red. "You hear right, Tim, though your employers made another attempt to demolish her during the trip over from St. Paul."

"My employers?" repeated Tim warily. "Gosh, L.J., the *Gazette* said it was a rockslide. What makes you think somebody tried to do your boat in?"

L.J. could hardly believe his ears. Tim knew damned well Calhoun and company were after him! "They mined an entire mountainside trying to stop us,

Tim. I'm thankful for the railroad detectives I hired; they spotted one of them and warned us off."

"Well, hey, L.J., I'm glad you made it all right, anyway." Silently Tim sighed, realizing his part in the affair—however hesitant—hadn't been recognized.

"I'm damned sure your bosses Calhoun and Williams wouldn't agree with you, Tim. They'll try, I'm sure, to keep the *Manitoba* from sailing for Fort Garry. But I've got bad news for them. Tell them to come to my little demonstration."

"What demonstration, L.J.?"

"Just tell 'em to come, Tim. It's posted all over town. Take care, Tim; and you, too, Rosie."

Later, as Tim and Rosie were preparing for bed, Rosie said, "Mighty friendly, your friend Mr. Hays. Doesn't seem as bad as you'd told me, Tim."

"He's dull, Rosie—all work and no play. He don't even play cards much anymore, I hear. Years ago, when him and me both worked as clerks for Josh Laurence over at St. Paul Shipping, we'd go out together on weekends. He'd play poker and I'd . . . well, you know, have me some fun."

Rosie did not look at him. "I'll bet you always found your fun, didn't you, Tim?"

"Never one as nice as you, Rosie, or as pretty. Glad as hell you're mine." He put an arm around her waist and squeezed her.

But in bed that night, after Tim had made love to her, Rosie tried to recall the man she'd met that day. Hays wasn't handsome. Wasn't even rugged or otherwise impressive in his appearance. But there was something about him . . . something that Rosie couldn't understand. A sort of magnetism, she supposed.

Whatever it was, it had caused Rosie to look away

from Hays. It had incited thoughts in her head that she neither liked nor could justify, in view of her impending marriage to Tim Wolfe. She resolved to steer clear of L.J. Hays.

The tenth of May was an unseasonably hot eighty degrees in Breckenridge. The sun was dazzling in a cloudless blue sky as hundreds of onlookers gathered on the docks built by the Hays Forwarding Company near its brand-new warehouse. Tacked up everywhere were printed circulars that read:

TO ALL RESIDENTS OF THE RED RIVER VALLEY:

WE HOPE YOU WILL BE OUR GUESTS ON THE TENTH OF MAY AT 11:15 A.M. TO WITNESS AN AWESOME DEMONSTRATION OF THE ABILITY OF THE *MANITOBA* TO DEFEND ITSELF AGAINST ANY HEREABOUTS (OR IN CANADA) WHO WOULD ATTACK HER.

WE WILL HAVE TEA AND SANDWICHES FOR ALL, AND ANY WHO WOULD LIKE TO SEE FOR THEMSELVES HOW SEAWORTHY IS OUR NEW STEAMER CAN JOIN US FOR A SHORT TRIP NORTH. WE WILL LEAVE AT 12 O'CLOCK NOON SHARP. EXCURSION TRIPS TO CANADA WILL BE OFFERED LATER THIS SUMMER ON A FIRST-COME, FIRST-SERVED BASIS.

/s/ L.J. HAYS

At eleven o'clock a well-groomed L.J. Hays stood on the top deck of the flag-bedecked *Manitoba*, megaphone in hand. In the crowd far below he spotted Tim, and that pleased him, but when he picked out Ben Williams and Jay Calhoun, he was tickled.

Both Gatling guns, draped with tarpaulins, had been securely bolted to the *Manitoba*'s deck, and each had been enclosed by a metal structure designed to protect the two men required to operate the weapons.

On the river, anchored several hundred yards from the *Manitoba*'s mooring, were two old wharf boats, which would soon be the objects of everyone's attention.

The crowd was in a festive mood and happily gorging their collective gullets with the fare prepared by the French cook Hays had hired in New Orleans to fill out the *Manitoba*'s crew. Captain Sam Meyer sounded the ship's whistle to quiet the people long enough so that Hays could be heard.

"Ladies and gentlemen," Hays began through the megaphone. "I have asked you here today to show you that the Hays Forwarding Company will, in the name of free enterprise, carry out the transportation of goods on the Red River, and that the company plans to protect you and the goods you entrust to us. I'm sure you are all aware that there is in Breckenridge a competitor who is not at all reluctant to do us violence—one who has already made several attempts to destroy the *Manitoba*. Now, if you will direct your attention to the far ends of the upper deck, you will see two of the most awesome weapons ever devised by man."

The crowd gasped as the Gatling representatives pulled off the tarpaulins and unveiled the gleaming machine guns.

Hays suppressed the mad desire to smile at the reaction. He continued, "Now, folks, I'll have to describe exactly what you see, for unless you fought for the Rebels in the West, it's probable that you never have seen such a weapon. These are Gatling guns, named after their inventor, the brilliant Richard Gatling." The crowd applauded, and L.J. warmed to his speech.

"This gun can shoot at a fantastic rate of speed and must be seen to be appreciated. I'm told that in service it fires six hundred shots *per minute!* But let's suffice it to say that Gatling guns can spew out hot lead faster than an entire army could in attacking it. And Hays Forwarding now owns two." Hays paused to let the information sink in.

"Out on the river are two old, green-hulled wharf boats with hulls reinforced at the waterline—reinforced with iron, folks. Sinking those boats ought to be as difficult as picking up a rattlesnake by its tongue."

Hays waved toward the boats, then pointed to them with a finger. "Take a look at this, folks. It's something I hope you never see again!"

Suddenly the munition reps sprang into action, the guns smoking, firing a rain of steel-jacketed bullets into the two wharf boats, ripping large splinters of wood out of their hulls, more than a few bullets making a metallic noise as they encountered the iron Hays had mentioned.

A stunned babble swept over the onlookers as water rushed into the riddled sides of the boats. After a full minute, the guns fell silent, and the wharf boats began to sink.

Absolute silence overtook the crowd. Hays, too, said nothing for a time. Even he could not have fully appreciated the power of the guns until now. Finally he spoke, in a low, somber voice. "I am not a violent man. But neither am I one to turn the other cheek. When others try to hurt me, I hurt them back. Back in St.

Paul somebody tried to burn the *Manitoba* in the dead of night. Thank God they were bunglers and didn't succeed! On the way here from St. Paul by rail, they almost buried us with a mountain. Our vigilance saved us that time.

"Now, I want to warn anyone who may be listening with hatred in his heart for me or my ship: Pay heed to what you just saw, for I will have no hesitancy—I will show no mercy—to use these Gatlings against you. And they will send you to the fires of hell for all time!"

Hays paused just long enough to let this threat sink in, then announced that any wishing to board the *Manitoba* for a short voyage north could now board.

There was a scramble as people began to flow up the gangplank. But Hays was less concerned about that than he was about Jay Calhoun and Ben Williams, whose eyes were still fixed on the gleaming Gatlings.

L.J. wished he could be privy to what the two were discussing.

Whether or not it was fear of the Gatlings, the *Manitoba*'s first summer was successful indeed—and passed without violence of any kind.

The response to Hays' avowed policy of paying the highest prices possible for furs and to charge the lowest rates possible for freight transport was little short of phenomenal. The Hudson Bay Company had been gouging its customers for years and lost a number of them even after the company responded to Hays' prices with a substantial rate decrease.

By the time the Red River froze solid and the *Manitoba* was moored for the winter, Hays had a bulging bank account. And he turned the ship into a saloon, with of course plenty of gambling and entertainment—an idea of L.J.'s that made the winter only a little less profitable than the summer. L.J. soon was making plans to have a second steamer built in Breckenridge, by Higgins, of course.

Also, Hays was making plans to marry.

L.J. had continued to secretly see Elizabeth Arton through the summer and into winter, whenever he was in St. Paul, which was about half the year now that he had to pay attention to the Breckenridge freight office and warehouse operation.

He had met Elizabeth's mother and formed the opinion that the older woman was rather cold. He wondered how such a cold mother could raise such a hot-blooded daughter. On three different occasions Elizabeth had taken the St. Paul Railroad to Breckenridge to see him. Each time they had made love in the living quarters Hays maintained there in his warehouse.

In early December, she announced that she was pregnant.

L.J. might have felt guilty about his secret trysts with Elizabeth, if it had not been for articles he read in the New York newspapers about Lucille Morgan. She had, it seemed, managed love affairs all over the European continent—wherever she went on her "sabbatical." In London Lucille had, according to the papers, vamped a prince and received for her trouble several priceless rubies. In Paris, a painter drew her attention, and she was rumored to have been painted in the nude! On her uncle's yacht in Rome, she conducted such a heavy affair with an Italian count that there were hot rumors she would marry before she returned to the United States.

Although disgusted with the reports of Lucille's conquests, L.J. felt that he had only himself to blame for her infidelities. For it was Hays' reluctance to affiance himself to her because of the difference in their financial capacities that had caused her to go abroad in the first place.

But if he would otherwise have felt guilt over Elizabeth, Lucille's meanderings expiated that guilt.

Early in January, L.J. Hays and Elizabeth Arton were married in a Roman Catholic church in St. Louis. Right after the wedding, Hays had bought a tract of property in the best section of St. Paul and had built on it a fair-sized mansion. It was obvious that he expected to start raising a family. Hays and Elizabeth moved into the house in mid-April. The following July while Ben Williams was again busy running for governor, Elizabeth delivered a seven-pound boy whom they named Paul Jerome.

Less than a day later, in Breckenridge, Rosie Wolfe delivered a son, Billy Sean Wolfe.

# PART II

# Chapter 9

The decade of the 1870s began with great promise for the Hays Forwarding Company. By the spring of 1871, L.J. had half a dozen steamers working the Red. The company had earned such an outstanding reputation that it had become a very real, bona fide competitor of the Hudson Bay Company. And that's when the trouble began. Not the overt "seek and destroy" trouble, but a more subtle form designed to hit L.J.'s pocketbook—manipulation of freight prices.

When Phil Crabtree left the St. Paul Railroad to work for the Chicago, Burlington & Quincy (known as "The Big Q"), Jake Bronson, nephew of the new Governor of Minnesota, Ben Williams, was appointed general manager. Through persuasion from Williams, Bronson saw to it that Hays' customers paid a much more substantial rail rate on the Breckenridge-to-Minneapolis/St. Paul line than Hudson Bay customers. On top of that, the Bay Company was getting the overcharge as a kickback.

It was the first serious problem Hays had encountered since he'd set up shop on the Red River, and one that L.J. would not tolerate. The first thing he did was pay a little visit to Bronson.

"What you're doing here is patently illegal, Jake," L.J. told him, "and will no doubt get you put in a federal prison. My next stop after here is at the marshal's. You'll save me a trip if you'll agree to revise those rates."

Bronson shook his head and scratched his chin. "I ain't doin' nothin' illegal, Hays," he drawled. "If you can prove I am, go ahead and try."

"I intend to, Jake. And when I do . . . I'm sorry to tell you that your uncle Ben won't serve your jail term for you."

Hays tried, but could not substantiate his charges of criminal collusion between Bronson and his uncle, the Governor. Nonetheless he lodged a civil suit in Minnesota Court. For months, however, the case did not come to trial, as the railroad kept requesting and obtaining new trial dates.

One day while Hays was talking to Joseph Higgins at the shipyard about a new steamer, the topic of Ben Williams and problems with the railroad crept into their conversation.

"Well," Higgins said, a twinkle in his eyes, "what are you waiting for? Why don't you buy the railroad? Anybody who can build a successful business simply by finding a sunken steamboat ought to be able to do just about anything."

If Higgins was being funny, Hays did not laugh. Instead he half-turned to stare across the yard at the railroad track Crabtree's men had laid nearly five years ago for the *Manitoba*'s trip to the Red River. "You know how often I've thought of doing just that, Joseph. But do you know why the St. Paul stopped laying track at Breckenridge?"

Higgins frowned. "Why, they've no need to go farther, L.J. With the railhead through to the Red, they get trade from Canada by way of yours and the Bay Company's steamers."

L.J. shook his head. His expression was serious, though his eyes glittered. "They stopped, Joseph, because of money. Phil Crabtree told me so a couple of years ago and so did Jed Tidrow down in Washington. Both Phil and the Senator said St. Paul's profit picture is terrible, that it's barely able to stay in business because of the payments on something like thirty million dollars' worth of first-mortgage bonds.

"The St. Paul's profits do come from Canada, Joseph, but they're infinitesimal compared to what they could be if the road were extended all the way to Winnipeg. The railroad would be king of all it surveyed—including, by God, half of Canada. Can you imagine that? Half of Canada—and those western Canadian provinces are rich, rich as any territory in the United States. The St. Paul could get so rich . . ." L.J. stopped there. Higgins didn't need to know everything he was thinking—specifically that if he owned the St. Paul, he'd take it straight up to Canada, then westward to the Pacific!

"If the St. Paul built to Winnipeg, it would hurt you badly, wouldn't it, L.J.?" Higgins now asked.

"Probably turn the *Manitoba* into a full-time excursion boat, Joseph. That's another reason why I've been checking into the St. Paul's operations for some time now. Eventually somebody's going to gain control of it, reorganize it, and make it really pay."

"But how? If, as you say, the road is heavily in mortgage-bond debt, it seems to me that further expansion is impossible."

Hays pulled a cigar from his inside coat pocket and lit it. "Not impossible, Joseph," he explained as he puffed to get an even burn on the cigar. "But possible *only if* the bondholders become convinced that they have to take a loss in order to make a profit."

"Can that happen? Sounds strange to me."

"It can. But it'll take time, and some persuasion. A great deal of persuasion." Now Hays grinned, because he had just talked himself into a momentous decision. "It seems, Joseph, that I really have no choice but to go after the St. Paul Railroad. Because if I don't, one day it'll swallow me up and spit me out in little pieces."

Hays was deep in thought as he drove his carriage back to the docks. When he reached the main office of Hays Forwarding, he found Chris Christiansen seated behind his desk, up to his elbows in paper. With the opening of the Red River access route to Canada, the company's warehouse was bursting at the seams with freight awaiting shipment dates. Keeping track of it had become a monumental job—Chris' job.

The Norwegian had done it well, in spite of occasional difficulties with the language. Hays had doubled, then redoubled Chris' wages, for he knew the man was a bargain. Christiansen had managed to save money and buy acreage for a farm, though he and Irmgaard still lived in Hays' old house in St. Paul. They had been blessed with two boys since Hays had married and moved out.

Chris looked up from his paperwork at the sound of L.J.'s entrance, and started to rise. Hays motioned him to stay where he was. "How go things?" he asked Chris, taking a seat in a rocking chair.

The big Norwegian shrugged. "Mostly they go bad, Mr. Hays. We need more ships. We lose money because we must hold freight here too long."

It was true. Hays had long ago established a policy of discounting charges on goods which could not be moved by steamer within seven days of their receipt in St. Paul, and lately there was so much freight coming in from Canada by way of the railroad that Hays' *Resurrection* could not handle it all.

That Chris possessed a sharp business sense to understand what this meant in terms of profits made him invaluable to Hays. L.J. was afraid he would lose Chris one day—perhaps to Hudson Bay, with Tim.

If he managed to gain control of the St. Paul Railroad, Hays swore he would use Chris in a way that would keep him so happy he wouldn't want to leave.

The railroad. It all came down to the railroad. Was he suffering delusions of grandeur? Even if he somehow convinced the bondholders (who had the power of foreclosure over the St. Paul) to sell, it would still take millions to acquire control. But Hays did not have millions. He had thousands, tens of thousands. He could even get his hands on a couple hundred thousands. But not millions. Nor did he have easy access to millions, in spite of his dealings with one very substantial millionaire, J.P. Morgan. Morgan had granted him credit, but the largest sum his bank had risked for Hays had been a paltry fifty thousand dollars.

The thought of the complex problem confronting L.J. discouraged him and he shook his head sadly as he reflected on it. He looked up to see Chris looking at him. What, Hays wondered, would he think of the scheme? Insanity? Or merely a foolish dream?

Hays stood up from his rocking chair, stretched, then walked over to the desk to offer Chris a cigar.

The Norwegian enjoyed cigars occasionally and readily accepted it. After he lit his cigar, Hays blew a perfect smoke ring and watched it move slowly across the room in front of the window, growing ever larger as it passed farther and farther away.

"What do you think of railroads, Chris?" Hays asked.

Chris' eyes narrowed as he dragged on the cigar and loosed a small smoke ring of his own before replying. "They are big. And powerful. In New York they are all-powerful."

"Have you ever considered that the St. Paul could hurt us badly?" Hays continued. "Not by the current overcharges Jake Bronson is hitting us with, but in other ways."

"How?"

Hays explained to Chris what he had to Higgins. And like the shipbuilder, Chris understood.

"That is bad, indeed," Chris observed. "Can we do nothing about it? Can we not make an agreement with the railroad? Or perhaps . . . maybe—?"

"Maybe buy the railroad, Chris?"

The Norwegian nodded.

"That's what I've a mind to do, Chris—except it's going to take a great deal of money. Far more than I've got and maybe more than I can raise anywhere."

Chris tapped the ash from his cigar, then studied the glowing end for a moment. "You can raise the money," he said. "My Irmgaard says you can do anything."

Hays could not help but grin. Irmgaard Christiansen was one of the most thoroughly pleasant people Hays had ever met—and for some reason worshipped the ground he walked on. While Hays was still living in the house with the Christiansens, she had fussed over him like a mother hen, cooking his meals, mending his clothes—anything to help him. She had hugged him so enthusiastically when, a year ago, he had helped Chris get credit to buy land in the Red River Valley that he thought for sure she would crack one of his ribs.

## Railroad King

"I wish I was sure she was right," Hays said.

"You will do what must be done because you can see what you must do. Many others cannot because they cannot first see."

Chris' encouragement raised L.J.'s spirits, and he began working in earnest to understand what he must do.

He decided the St. Paul was actually worth about twenty million dollars against almost thirty million in bonded debt, two-thirds of which was in first mortgages against railroad properties. Gross earnings of the road last year had been five million dollars, against 5.2 million in debt service and operating expenses, resulting in a net loss.

Although the St. Paul showed a negative net worth when its real assets were matched against its huge liabilities, the unrealized Minnesota land grant was like a pot of gold at the end of a rainbow. If the road could lay track to Canada, a large part of the fifteen million acres promised by the Minnesota lawmakers would be turned over to it. The land then would be worth a great deal more than a few dollars an acre. This was the main reason the St. Paul Railroad bonds could be sold in the first place.

But at present the railroad could raise no more cash for track laying, and was in default on interest payments to some of its foreign bondholders—a crime considering its monopoly on being the only railroad carrying freight to St. Paul for shipment east and south. One of the reasons it was doing so poorly, Hays knew, was the private arrangements Bronson had made with the Hudson Bay Company. But a more important reason by far was the huge debt service—more than three million dollars yearly—on the railroad bonds.

Hays mulled over his analysis of the St. Paul and

its problems for weeks before reaching the conclusion that in spite of its difficulties, it could be saved and turned into a tremendously profitable property—*if* it could be restructured to reduce both its bond obligations and debt service, and *if* new monies could be brought in to finance track laying.

They were two monumental ifs, Hays knew.

Because they owned first mortgages on all railroad assets, it was the St. Paul bondholders who held the power of life and death over the road, not the few common stockholders who controlled it. Foreclosure of the first mortgages could at any time throw the railroad into receivership and wrest control out of the stockholders' hands.

Therefore, Hays decided to inform the bondholders of their extreme jeopardy. That would be simple enough. But then he would have to win their confidence by offering them something good for something bad. Finally, he had to get them to foreclose on their defaulted bonds and grant control to him.

A small order, Hays thought with a not very optimistic laugh. Still, he might accomplish it, especially if he could guarantee the interest due the bondholders for the immediate future. For Hays, that meant building—as quickly as possible—the necessary track. With that track, he would enrich the railroad with land-grant holdings as well as Canadian profits.

Canadian profits and Red River land. They were the key, Hays knew, and the railroad could obtain neither without money. And without money, he could not get the railroad.

In the end, Hays knew he had to go where the money was—to New York, to J.P. Morgan. He wired Morgan that he was accepting the man's invitation to see the town. The next day Hays received his answer that he was welcome and should expect to be Morgan's house guest. The financier ended his wire with a bit of humor. "HOPE YOURS TRULY WILL SERVE AS ACCEPTABLE HOST SINCE YOU-KNOW-WHO IS AWFULLY ANGRY AT YOU."

Hays did not find the allusion to Lucille funny, but could think of no response and so immediately put it out of his mind in favor of the more serious business at hand. He thought about wiring John Kennedy in Boston for an interview. Kennedy was the American agent for the Dutch syndicate that owned the very important St. Paul Railroad first-mortgage bonds. Hays decided to wait until after he'd spoken to Morgan.

Knowing that J.P. might well be skeptical of his ability to run a railroad—especially since the financier had only two years ago outfoxed Jay Gould and Jim Fiske to gain control of the Erie Railroad—Hays wired Phil Crabtree in Chicago and made a date to stop in for a chat on his way east.

That week, when L.J. told Elizabeth he was going to New York, she leaped into his arms to kiss him. "Oh, I've always wanted to see New York," she murmured against his neck.

"I'm sorry, Elizabeth, but this is a business trip and I can't take you. Anyway, you've young Paul, little Nora Jean, and the baby to take care of." Joani, the baby, was barely three months old and Hays did not like the idea of her being left only in the care of her nanny.

"I can leave them with Mother," Elizabeth argued, still clinging to him, although her smile was gone and there was anger in her eyes.

"I just cannot have you along, Elizabeth. You must understand. I won't be staying in New York very long—perhaps a day, two at the most. And I may well have to go up to Boston for another day or two. My business in both places is urgent and I can afford no distractions or dalliances."

Elizabeth backed away as if she had been slapped. "Oh!" she said, glaring at him. "I'm a distraction, am I? A mere dalliance! And I thought you loved me." Tears began to flow instantly and Hays, as always, hated it. He had been through scenes like this all too frequently these past couple of years.

Regardless of what Elizabeth said or did, though, he would not bring her on this trip. He had much to accomplish and knew that it would take twice as long if she went along, for she would insist on seeing everything.

He hadn't minded taking her along on quick trips to St. Louis and even once to New Orleans before they were married. In those days, she rarely showed the selfish, stubborn streak which had first manifested itself soon after Paul's birth. But nowadays Elizabeth seemed not to care at all that he had business to attend to— important and necessary business, which had paid for the beautiful mansion he had built for her, the maid she had demanded so she could devote all her time to the children, the latest fashions from New York and Paris she insisted on so that she could be the most beautiful woman in all of Minnesota. Saddest of all was that she no longer stirred the embers of lust within him. What, he wondered sadly as he packed a single suitcase, had happened to that saucy young thing who barged into his office on the *Resurrection* and applied for a job as his mistress? The hot-blooded young woman who lost herself in passion when he merely touched her? Whose cries of pleasure had filled the bedchambers at the climax of their lovemaking? Where had that Elizabeth gone?

# Railroad King

L.J.'s biggest disappointment with Elizabeth, however, was not her selfishness, nor her coldness, but rather her absolute lack of interest in what he did. Where once she had asked interminable questions about him, about what he did, whom he knew, and so forth, now she showed next to no interest at all. Whatever a good wife should be, L.J. was convinced, she must be an interested and good listener. Elizabeth now was neither.

He closed his suitcase and placed it on the floor beside the canopied bed he and Elizabeth had shared since April of 1870, when they'd moved into the mansion. While undressing for bed, he thought about making love to his wife to try to make things right.

He lay awake when Elizabeth came to bed. L.J.'s pulse quickened when she smiled at him and began to undress. She had not done that since they were aboard the *Resurrection* four years ago. She turned coyly away when the last garment came off, but did not put on a nightgown before climbing into bed next to him.

Hays was quite ready for her. It had been nearly six months since their last try. Reaching over with his left hand, he traced her face, her neck, her breasts. Elizabeth sighed.

He turned on his side and looked down at her, fondling her more intimately. Her eyes were closed, her mouth slightly open—the way it used to be.

Forgetting his pique, he kissed her, tongued her, touched her everywhere. He eased himself atop her, and was just about to enter her when she spoke.

"You *will* let me come with you, won't you darling? I've already had Hannah pack my suitcases and we can pick up Mother in the morning on the way to catch the *Resurrection*."

Three days later L.J. was in New York—alone. Elizabeth's reaction to his obstinate refusal to take her on his trip was to not allow him to make love to her. But Hays had lost his desire to do so in any case. She had not taken kindly to his telling her that, however, and he wound up sleeping alone in the canopied bed.

Morgan was his congenial self as he greeted Hays. The two men retired to his book-shelved study furnished with comfortable red-leather easy chairs.

"You don't owe me money," the financier said with a laugh. "You've got a fleet of steamers. What brings you to me? More steamboats? Gold mines? Steel? Tell me."

L.J. explained his interest in the St. Paul line. He tried to read the banker's expressions, but he could not. Morgan always maintained an advantage when hearing out deals by keeping an absolutely placid face. Morgan did not say a word when Hays had finished his presentation, but instead rang his butler for more wine. At last he looked Hays in the eyes and shook his head.

"Railroads?" he asked.

Hays had only to hear the way Morgan pronounced the word to know that the financier was not enthralled with his idea. But he said nothing, awaiting Morgan's additional comments. He had long ago learned that the sound of his own voice taught him nothing, whereas the sound and words of another could teach him much.

"Half the railroads in this country are skating on thin ice, L.J. They've borrowed too much and spent too little on the track they borrowed it for. And the money you're talking about is too damn much for a run-down little railroad like the St. Paul."

"I can make it a great little railroad within five years. Maybe the best in ten."

Morgan lifted his crystal wine glass and drained it. His eyes keyed in on a painting adorning the wall of his study opposite the brick fireplace. "Invest in fine art, L.J. It won't give you nearly the heartaches that a railroad will. And as you know, I'm more than a little up on rails these days."

Hays drained his own wine and looked hard at Morgan. "I want that railroad, J.P. I'll do whatever I have to to get it."

Morgan shook his head. "Aside from everything else," he continued as if he hadn't heard Hays, "your timing's terrible. Wait a year, maybe two. Money's tight right now and a stock-market break's coming one of these years, and that'll throw a helluva lot of railroads into the hands of receivers. Mark my words. And your St. Paul's going to be one of them."

L.J. sighed. "Aside from the fact that I really believe the St. Paul can be the start of an empire for me, J.P., I have another problem that won't be solved by waiting. My dear old friend Governor Williams has me over a barrel because he's got his nephew—the railroad's new general manager—under his thumb. Now the nephew's putting the screws to me with his railroad rates."

Morgan's eyes gleamed, and as the butler brought in a decanter of wine and refilled both glasses, the financier suggested, "Why not just have the bastard killed?"

"Wouldn't I like to!" Hays said, though realizing Morgan was joking.

But Morgan wasn't smiling. "I'm more than half serious, you know. Williams and his nephew are playing with dynamite. If they pulled that crap here in the East, somebody'd pull the rug out from under them—

fast. And they'd fall so hard they'd never operate another business in this country."

"But I don't play that way, J.P. I'm not averse to taking every advantage I can get in a business situation—or a game of poker. But as for anything violent, it's not for me. I'd sooner lose."

"You didn't feel that way a few years ago when you bought those Gatling guns for your steamer *Manitoba*. Remember?"

"That was different. They'd tried to . . ."

"Look here, L.J., you're your own man and I respect you for it. But I can't help you right now. If you want I can extend your line of credit—double it, maybe even triple it. But I can't let you have the kind of money you'll be needing to buy the St. Paul. Not right now. And for a couple of different reasons, one of them being that my money's pretty well tied up for the next year or two. And as I said, L.J., your timing's bad. Wait for the stock-market break. It's coming—everybody knows it."

Suddenly Hays had an idea. "You say everybody knows the market's in for it, J.P. What about Kennedy? Can he be smelling it?"

"I don't like him much, L.J., but sure, he's no cigar-store Indian. Why?"

"He's the American broker for the syndicate of Dutchmen who own a bunch of St. Paul first-mortgage bonds. Suppose I went to him and told him his bondholders were going to take a bath if things didn't change on the St. Paul? What do you think his attitude might be?"

"Ask him. He's a canny one, though, so don't expect to fool him. And don't expect him to act right off the bat. He doesn't work that way. Doing what you're suggesting could be a big help to you later, when repercussions hit Wall Street."

Hays was thoughtful for a moment. "Well, I believe I'll do that, J.P.," he concluded. "Now tell me, how is Lucille? Last time I heard from her was a couple of years ago and she didn't sound very happy."

"When she found out you'd married, she started throwing things. I got out of the way in a hurry. She told me, confidentially, that she would have gladly married you. Really was stuck on you, but you told her she was too rich."

"Which she was," Hays said. "Call me stubborn, but I couldn't marry her then, J.P. If I had, it would've been on her terms—at a time when I couldn't meet those terms."

"Could you meet them now? Will you *ever* be able to meet them?"

"I don't know. But Lucille is a sweet, wonderful woman. And I miss her. Where is she, by the way?"

"I haven't the faintest idea. New York, London, Paris. She hasn't written to me recently."

"Well if she does, do tell her I was asking for her, will you? Tell her . . . that I'd like to see her again."

Hays traveled to Boston, disturbed by thoughts of Lucille. What would his life be now if he'd married her? Was he too proud and foolish? He had to shake clear these thoughts as he met with John Kennedy, a tall, humorless man with a commanding presence. The two men met in Kennedy's sunny Back Bay office on Commonwealth Avenue. The Bostonian was also an intent listener, good at masking his feelings. Nevertheless Hays tried to be as convincing as possible about the Dutch bondholders' "shaky property already in default and on the verge of bankruptcy, which could force the St. Paul into receivership at 'almost any time.' "

"In which case," Hays concluded, his eyes locked with Kennedy's, "their bonds would be valueless."

Kennedy was most disconcerting, Hays thought, as the Bostonian sat behind his desk, mute, the fingertips of both hands forming a bridge beneath the dark eyes that never wavered in their stare—more a glare—at him.

Kennedy at last looked away for a moment. When he turned back he wore what for him must have been a smile. "You have something in mind, Mr. Hays. What is it?"

"Three million dollars, sir," Hays replied. He was surprised at his own temerity, for he was not at all certain he could raise even one of the three million. But his own expression gave no hint of his uncertainty.

"The face amount of the bonds my Dutchmen own is substantially greater than that. What would you expect for your three million dollars?"

"Control of the St. Paul Railroad, Mr. Kennedy. The money would pay up overdue interest and retire about one-third of the bonds. Once the bonds have been foreclosed and I have gained control, I will reorganize the railroad and issue your clients new bonds—but in an amount consistent with the real value of the road."

Kennedy scowled. "What you're suggesting, young man, is that my clients give up a substantial percentage of their holdings—about eight million dollars' worth—for your three million and new bonds totaling about sixteen million. Would you guarantee that the new bonds will not be watered with new issues to finance track laying?"

"We will do no watering, Mr. Kennedy, and I will gladly make that an integral part of our contractual agreement. Therefore, your clients will suffer no real loss of interest."

"You call at least five million dollars no loss?"

"We both know the St. Paul is worth substantially less than its bonded debt alone, sir. What I'm proposing is to peg its debt to its real market value. It will hurt your clients little, since there is no way they can currently or in the foreseeable future obtain full value for the bonds." L.J.'s confidence gained momentum and he continued. "As things stand, the St. Paul is in an impossible position because of its overindebtedness. It must expand in order to survive, in order to increase profits even enough to maintain timely payments to bondholders as well as to pay for operations. Yet the burden of the bonds is so heavy that it cannot obtain financing to make the expansion possible."

"And how would you propose to expand, Mr. Hays? To assure a large profit increase?"

"The St. Paul," Hays explained, "must open Canada to year-round trade. Where now the Red River steamers transport goods only during the months when there is no ice, the railroad could carry goods and passengers the year round. And, as you must know, Mr. Kennedy, the railroads have virtually unlimited hold space compared to steamers. To increase load space, simply add more boxcars.

"I estimate we can more than double the railroad's profits once the main line is extended to Canada—assuming we charge rates substantially lower than what shippers are now paying for the combined steamer-railroad services. By having *one* mode of transportation and charging *one* fixed fee, our customers will be happier and more secure, and business should increase."

Kennedy remained skeptical. "What you say

sounds very reasonable on paper, Mr. Hays," he ventured. "But how will you raise cash to lay the necessary track? You've said you'll do no stock watering. And what about the Minnesota land grant?"

"We'll sell all unnecessary railroad-owned land right at the outset, Mr. Kennedy. The present ownership has been holding onto some good-sized tracts in hopes of selling at inflated prices later. What additional moneys we need—and I'm certain we'll require some—I will personally raise."

Another bold statement, Hays thought, at the same time knowing full well that the meek might inherit the earth, but would never drive a deal with John Kennedy. He turned the discussion to the subject of the Minnesota land grant. Most railroad investors were far more interested in the land offered the roads for laying track than in the railroads themselves.

"We'll realize the full land grant once we've completed the line to Canada," Hays declared. "Selling much of it as soon as we get it will bring in large numbers of farmers who will use our trains to ship their grain to markets and that, of course, will add to our prosperity."

Kennedy seemed impressed with Hays' arguments, but now suggested that they break off their discussions to have dinner. They would eat, he said, at his Walnut Street townhouse on Beacon Hill and finish their talks later. It was more of a command than an invitation, and Hays could hardly refuse, even had he wished to do so.

It was a short ride in Kennedy's elegant black and gold coach, past the historic Public Gardens and Boston Common, (a campground during the early days of the Revolutionary War), up the charming shady lane arched by spreading elms to Kennedy's four-story gray brick townhouse. Kennedy lived in an exclusive district among "the famous," including authoress Louisa May Alcott, a "good friend of my wife's," the Bostonian told Hays. All the homes had fine gardens, and Kennedy's was no exception. Because of the slope of his property, the large tree-shaded garden was high above the street and fortified by a stone wall.

When Hays stepped out of Kennedy's coach, his hat in his hand, he was shocked at the sight of the windows in Kennedy's house. They were purple.

Kennedy, noticing the look on Hays' face, chuckled. "Like the windows, Mr. Hays?" he asked. "My wife had those imported from Italy. I understand they were once in a Rome basilica."

Hays grinned a trifle sickly. "They are . . . very interesting and unusual." They were, Hays thought, a horror! As they proceeded up the stone steps, Hays was astonished to see across the way two other mansion-sized houses with violet stained-glass windows. Were all these rich Bostonians daft? he wondered.

Now he had still another reason to be glad Elizabeth was back in St. Paul. For sure, their house would be the first in Minnesota with purple windows!

Nothing was said of business as they repaired to a luxurious gas-lit hall to dine on lobster prepared exquisitely by Kennedy's cook. L.J. quickly became a lobster enthusiast and overindulged—to Kennedy's delight.

After dinner they retired to Kennedy's library on the second floor for sherry and more talk.

The room, like Kennedy himself, reeked of wealth. It was paneled in rich mahogany and featured walls lined with thick oaken bookshelves encased in gleaming glass. Inside the recessed bookshelves were rich leather-bound volumes, some quite old and delicate and probably worth a fortune, Hays thought. Two floor-to-ceiling windows were draped with maroon velvet to match the thick rug under their feet.

Leather easy chairs were situated beside the stone fireplace, two others near an imposing mahogany desk fronting one of the windows. Atop the desk was a crystal decanter filled with sherry. Kennedy took two tall wine glasses from a liquor cabinet near his desk and filled them from the decanter, handing one to Hays and keeping one for himself.

"To railroads," Kennedy toasted, lifting his glass.

"To profitable railroads," Hays countered with a smile, "especially the St. Paul under new ownership."

The two men drank and their talks resumed. Kennedy's eyes contained a hint of amusement as he drank steadily, refilling Hays' glass each time he refilled his own. Hays, a moderate drinker, found himself forced to down more than he was used to in order to keep up with Kennedy. Hays also felt that Kennedy wasn't getting to the point of their meeting, that he was just prattling on about things they already discussed in Kennedy's office.

Only when he thought Hays had downed enough sherry to loosen his tongue did Kennedy get down to business by asking the question Hays feared most: "Where will you raise three million dollars? I've done some checking and it seems your net worth is a fraction of that."

Hays smiled and shook his head, as if to clear it. He was a long way from being drunk, though it wouldn't hurt to let Kennedy believe he was already there. "Like yourself, Mr. Kennedy," he said, "I've my sources. If I invested only my own funds, I would be limited indeed."

Kennedy was not to be put off so easily. He

nodded as he poured Hays a refill, then did the same for himself. Now he looked straight into his guest's eyes and grinned. "It's Morgan," he said with an air of triumph. "That's who you've got in mind—old Junius Morgan. Well, I can tell you he's not going to back you, for he's not in the game right now. And I have that on the best of sources."

Hays laughed a trifle drunkenly. "Not *old* Junius Morgan," he said, "but *young* J.P."

"But Morgan nonetheless, Mr. Hays." Kennedy now looked pleased. "And he won't back you."

Hays shrugged, on the surface undisturbed by Kennedy's remark. "I can neither confirm nor deny my sources, Mr. Kennedy. If I did, they would not long remain my sources."

Hays parried a number of Kennedy questions about his ability to run a railroad as both men grew heavy with drink. The Bostonian became more jocular and good-humored with the spirits in him. Late in the evening, however, Kennedy suddenly launched into a sharp attack on the idea that the bondholders should have to take a loss at all. They had, he declared, invested hard-earned cash in the St. Paul and it had bought the rails on which St. Paul trains now operated. "Without my Dutchmen," Kennedy concluded, "there would be no St. Paul Railroad at all!"

Hays had been prepared for such an outburst; he'd made some inquiries about Kennedy's foreign clients. "Your Dutchmen," Hays announced with a knowing grin, "are fat cats whose money comes more from shrewd investments made through cagey traders like yourself, John, than from hard earnings. They take their chances, just as you and I do. I feel no sympathy for them, though I most assuredly understand that you must keep their best interests in mind. I would expect no less."

Hays now sat up in his easy chair and leaned closer to Kennedy's chair. He dropped the level of his voice and became deadly serious.

"But John," Hays nearly whispered, "you know the market's down and money is tight. The smart money is ready to dive for cover when the break comes—as it surely will in the next year or so. Do you know what that'll mean to your clients? I'll tell you, sir. Their holdings in the St. Paul will be wiped out. Their bonds will be hot-damn worthless! Nobody'll want them. Not me, not anyone.

"You say the Dutchmen's money lies in the St. Paul's rails? There's no arguing with that; it's true. But you know it costs ten dollars to lay a dollar's worth of rail and the only way you can ever see that labor money is if the road earns profits.

"Well, the St. Paul isn't earning enough profits and won't—not until I'm at the throttle, with the dead-man control in my hand."

Hays had been watching Kennedy through eyes that were mere slits as he tried to convince the Boston Irishman that he'd succeeded in drinking his guest under the table. But Hays still couldn't assess the effect of his words on the man, for Kennedy's expression had hardly changed. He was, Hays thought, a capable and crafty thinker.

Now Kennedy suddenly changed his tack and said, "Well, Mr. Hays, what you say may have some truth in it, but I'm still concerned about your inexperience in the railroad business. You're in steamers, they tell me, and I don't see how you can know the problems of railroads. Even the Commodore—Cornelius

Vanderbilt—had his troubles when he made the transition from boats to locomotives."

"I make it my business to know a lot of things, John," Hays said thickly. Quickly he went over in his mind some of the things Phil Crabtree had told him in Chicago. "I know most of the men who run the railroads waste millions. I know that they lay their roadbeds crooked, rather than straight, in order to benefit themselves and their friends who own adjacent land. I know they build track and roadbeds so poorly that the cost of maintenance is enormous. I know they economize on bridges—another big, costly, long-term mistake. I know they waste money burning wood in their locomotives, when coal's cheaper and a devil of a lot more efficient.

"I also know the 4-4-0 is a good locomotive, but it's not as strong or as fast as it can be. It needs more driving wheels. Conversion to a 4-8-0, or maybe a 4-10-0 or a 4-12-0.

"And I think the smart railroad in my part of the country will build up its freight by importing the people who produce it—farmers and miners. No doubt we'll eventually import some of your real hard-working Dutchmen, John, to grow wheat out my way, or dig for gold, or silver, or whatever."

The talks broke off soon afterward without any deal struck. Hays retired to his room to sleep fitfully. He was confident he'd done a good job in presenting the problem and a good, solid solution to Kennedy, but had no idea of his host's reaction. Kennedy, he thought, was a sponge, who took it all in, but would not give anything unless squeezed. And L.J. felt the time wasn't right for squeezing—not yet.

Before drifting off to sleep, Hays tried to sort out his troubled mind. Could he *really* raise three million, even with J.P.'s help? What would it take to convince the bondholders to see his argument if J.P. and Kennedy were so reluctant? Was he truly capable of running a railroad? There were so many more variables than in running steamers. Hays' last thoughts before slipping over the edge into sleep were oddly enough, not of Elizabeth, or even Lucille, but of Chris and Irmgaard Christiansen.

Hays awoke the next morning, feeling more confident than he had in months—despite his heavy head. Over a fine breakfast of eggs, sausage, biscuits, and coffee, Hays wanted to squeeze Kennedy for an answer. But the Bostonian never gave him an opening. All he talked about was how the city of Boston was changing, how the growing numbers of poor were affecting the quality of life there.

At South Station to see Hays off to New York, Kennedy left L.J. with a final word that neither buoyed nor discouraged him. "I will reflect long and sincerely on your offer," he stated. "There are questions I must resolve before I can submit the matter to my principals. This is a complex deal and will take time. Considerable time. I will be in touch."

"I eagerly await your word," Hays closed, shaking the man's hand.

As the train pulled out of the station, Hays was already focusing on his next problem—where and how to raise the cash he had offered. He thought that, with luck, he could get by with one-third to one-half of the three million figure. But even that was considerable, he realized.

Upon his return to St. Paul, Hays sought out Joseph Higgins. When L.J. asked half seriously if he had "a spare million or so lying around somewhere,"

Higgins chuckled and shook his head, but offered to buy into Hays' new enterprise with $100,000. That was a start, and L.J. thanked his friend sincerely.

A few weeks later L.J. visited a Canadian banker he had once met in Jim Frye's St. Louis office. The banker, Pierre Richaud, was a director of the Canadian Pacific Railroad, a new transcontinental planned to span Canada from Vancouver in the west to New Brunswick in the east. Richaud was impressed with Hays and liked his ideas. He agreed to invest with Hays, but cautioned L.J. that his must be a silent partnership in the St. Paul because of the possibility one day that the Canadian Pacific and St. Paul could become competitors for business.

Hays readily agreed, deciding not to worry now about if and how the Canadian Pacific would compete with his road. *His road.* Hays grinned at the thought. It had a nice ring to it. But if it was to become reality, he had so much more to do.

Higgins' and Richaud's money guaranteed Hays $200,000. Adding to it what he himself could spare, barely another $100,000, Hays amassed $300,000 in no time. But he knew this fell far short of what he needed and continued his search for capital.

Nearly six months passed with no word from Kennedy. During the fall of '71, while still awaiting Kennedy's word, L.J. devoted his attention to cornering the market on coal, a far more efficient fuel than wood, and used by both steamers and trains.

Elizabeth remained upset and jealous over L.J.'s extended trip to New York and Boston. She claimed he had left her behind "only so you could pay a visit on my old teacher, Miss Lucille Morgan." She had hurled a New York newspaper at him in which a columnist had written "Hays dropped in to see J. Pierpont Morgan and his pretty-as-a-picture niece for a little tête-à-tête." Hays was so angry at this cheap ploy that he didn't bother denying it or discussing it.

When Elizabeth saw that she could get no reaction from him on this, she started in on the railroad. "The railroad, the railroad!" she complained so often. "That's all you ever think about, is that dumb railroad! You never spend time with the kids. You never spend time with *me*. Sometimes I wonder what we are to you, L.J. Hays. Are we a front, a façade of the happy American family for the great and powerful L.J. Hays to hold up to his cronies? I swear, L.J., unless you start acting like a decent husband and father, I'll leave. I swear it; I'll take the children and leave you!"

L.J. saved her from taking that drastic step by removing himself to the other side of the house, out of sight, out of mind. The funny thing was, he liked his new quarters. He set up a small office and turned a small servant's quarters into his bedroom. Finally, he had peace and quiet from Elizabeth, but could still see his children.

He could also receive clients and visitors without Elizabeth's knowledge. One day an interesting visitor dropped by unannounced—Rosie Wolfe. She had changed a great deal since he'd seen her last three years ago—all for the better. As if he'd seen her only last week, Hays kissed her hand and welcomed her into his office.

Rosie was plainly nervous as she answered Hays' gently probing questions about her family—little Billy and her husband Tim—and about hers and Tim's health. When he asked about Tim's employment situation, Rosie wrung her hands in anguish and broke into tears. "He's been let go, Mr. Hays. And so have I. Just like that—after we gave Calhoun the best years of our lives. He says he can't afford us anymore."

Hays told her he was genuinely sorry to hear it. He had not seen Tim in two years, when he came to St. Paul to sell to Hays his half of the old Hays/Wolfe house and property so that he could buy a tract of Red River farm land.

At that time Tim seemed in a hurry and not very friendly. L.J. had wondered out loud what was bothering him, but Tim denied anything was wrong. Had L.J. not been so preoccupied with business matters, he might well have pressed Tim more.

"Is there anything I can do?" Hays now asked Rosie. "I'm afraid I have no job openings at present."

"Oh, isn't there something you can do for Tim? We built a house on the land he bought, but had to take on a big mortgage to finish it. We figured we wouldn't have any trouble meeting the payments with both of us working, but now, we could lose the farm to the First Minnesota Bank!"

L.J. studied Rosie. She was still an awfully attractive woman. Her clothes were plain—not like the ones Elizabeth wore. Yet Rosie looked far prettier. In spite of her present difficulties, Rosie's smile was warm when she heard what Hays said next.

"How much is your mortgage, Rosie?"

"Two thousand two hundred dollars. The payments . . ."

"Suppose I take over your mortgage payments, Rosie. Just for now, until you get on your feet again. You can take as long as you want to pay me back. And . . . well, I don't need another man right now, but I can use someone to keep my books. I've been keeping them myself all these years and I find I'm really too busy. Are you willing?"

Rosie's face lit up with joy. "Why, that would be . . . just great! But would it be possible for me to keep the books over in Breckenridge? I can't be away from home for too long. I've got little Billy to worry about and don't have anyone to leave him with."

"You can work in the office there, Rosie. No problem. I'll keep two sets of books, one you'll keep up to date over there and the other which I'll keep with me. Whenever I come over to Breckenridge, you can update and balance them. How's that sound? I can pay twenty dollars a week."

"That sounds awfully good, Mr. Hays," Rosie declared. "You're so . . . sweet and kind and . . ." She suddenly buried her face in her hands, as tears began rushing from her green eyes.

L.J. came around his desk and put his hand on her shoulder comfortingly. "Tears are unnecessary, Rosie," he offered awkwardly. "I'm glad to help. I only hope it's enough."

Rosie dried her tears, then stood and looked straight into his eyes. Before he could anticipate her, she kissed him, then buried her head against his shoulder.

It took her a few minutes to collect herself before she could leave. L.J. watched her departure with a strong sense of attraction toward her. She seemed so helpless, and L.J. wanted to take her into his arms and tell her everything would be all right. At least the job would help financially. But she seemed to be a woman in need of emotional support as well—something Tim obviously could not provide.

The new year, 1872, came with still no word from Kennedy. L.J. spent many solitary hours in his office at home, going over the books Rosie had set up and making plans for his entry into the railroad business. Hays was now more convinced than ever that his destiny lay in railroads. He was still confident that as soon as Kennedy gave his okay, working out the financing on the St. Paul would be no problem. Of course, it all would have been so simple had Morgan not said no. Not that L.J. could blame Morgan. Already the giant Union Pacific was tottering because of the millions of dollars in railroad bonds issued to finance track building—and mostly wasted.

Federal land grants and loans, Hays knew, encouraged the worst type of spending excesses. The roads, flush with government money and the money of a railroad-fascinated public who bought railroad bonds, spent the funds lavishly, without first making the new lines pay for themselves. The idea was to lay track to gain title to land, regardless of profits. That was a huge mistake. Without profits, the largest of businesses had to wind up in receivership.

The land grants promised millions of acres of land to the building roads, the only proviso being that the railroad had to lay a mile of track along its chartered route for every so many acres. The land's value was nil without the railroad, and all too frequently, not worth much more with the railroad. The railroads often hung on to the granted land too long in an effort to sell it at an inflated price. Hays thought that policy entirely dumb, since, occupied by farmers, the land would produce real and quick profits.

Well, Hays would not make those mistakes. He would not, he swore, lay a foot of track that could not support itself. He would sell all but the most desirable land along the St. Paul's state land grant route—and sell it at reasonable prices. The monies from the sale would help to finance additional track building and, at the same time, make the track beside the land profitable.

The more Hays studied the railroad's operations, the more convinced he became that he could create an empire, if only he got his hands on the St. Paul. If only the Dutch bondholders would consider his offer!

Meanwhile, Hays had lost his suit in State Court against the St. Paul and general manager Jake Bronson, but won it on appeal. A rollback was then ordered. So Hays Forwarding Company was again operating its Red River branch solidly in the black, and Hays' bank balances grew steadily.

That spring Hays at last received a letter from John Kennedy. The Bostonian was cautious with his words, but what he said, in essence, was that Hays should put together his offer in some kind of "definite" form, raise his capital, then present it.

The news left Hays ecstatic! But just for a short time because he still lacked the full capital he knew he would need.

He spent the next three months updating his studies of the St. Paul, deciding on its real value, and that of the properties it owned and those it *could* own, like the Minnesota state land grants, if it met the track-building deadlines the state had laid down. Then he redoubled his efforts to raise cash, knowing if he could not raise at least another million, the bondholders would most likely not consider his offer, even though times were not as good as they might be with the world's stock and bond markets.

For all of his time-consuming efforts, L.J. came up empty. And so late in the fall of 1872, he wrote Kennedy a long letter, begging for more time because of the poor state of money markets in Minnesota at the present. He felt only half-bad at having to do so, since many analysts were not freely predicting the long-anticipated market break. When that happened, it would only further depress the market value of the St. Paul, making his bid much more desirable.

That December, landlocked with lots of time on his hands and waiting for the market to crash, a curious thing happened to Hays. It happened at the freight station and warehouse in Breckenridge while he went over the books with Rosie Wolfe.

From the beginning of her bookkeeping chores, Hays had kept his distance from the beautiful Rosie, and this time was no exception. They were both very tired after finishing the books and while Rosie left to go home to the Wolfe farm, some twenty miles north of Breckenridge, Hays decided to stay over in the quarters above the station. Needless to say, he was caught off guard when Rosie returned less than a half hour after she'd left. She apologized profusely, saying she had neglected to make a necessary change in the Winnipeg accounts of Thomas John Short.

It took her but a minute to write in the corrections, but Hays asked if she'd stay and have one glass of wine with him. To his surprise, she accepted. They chatted a bit about business, about the ice on the river breaking up soon, about last year's wheat Tim had grown and how well the farm was doing.

When Rosie refused a second glass, she stood and said, "I really must go, Mr. Hays. As it is, I've stayed too long and Tim may be angry. He's very jealous of you, you know."

Hays frowned. "Tim, jealous of me? *He's* the lucky fellow—landing you after a succession of floozies with their adulterous 'A's' written indelibly on their foreheads. Not one of them was good enough to lick your boots."

Hays took both of Rosie's small hands in his own and squeezed them familiarly, his eyes squarely on hers.

Rosie's cheeks turned bright red as she tried to back away. "You're awfully nice, Mr. Hays..."

"L.J., Rosie. For God's sake, call me L.J."

"Well, all right, L.J. You're sweet and it's a shame I have to go, but I do."

But she didn't move. Her eyes remained locked with L.J.'s, and they were drawn irresistibly into each other's arms.

"No," Rosie murmured just before L.J. brought his mouth down upon her soft lips. She did not withdraw or push him away. Nor did she resist when he led her to his bed. She even helped Hays remove her clothes. Without hesitation she climbed into his bed to receive him.

Though their lovemaking burned with the excitement and freshness of a first encounter, it was quiet, sensible, to the point. Rosie and Hays seemed to know each other like old lovers—knew where to touch, how to stroke, what to caress to give the other the greatest joy and satisfaction.

Afterward, they lay together for nearly an hour, warm and snug in each other's arms. Then suddenly, without warning, Rosie jumped out of bed and dressed quickly.

Suspecting that he had just done the ultimate in cruelty, he babbled over and over, "I'm sorry, Rosie, I'm sorry. Please forgive me. I should have known better."

Rosie simply put a finger to Hays' lips, kissed him, and smiled good-by. Thereafter, over the next several months, Rosie and L.J. regularly used the bed over the Breckenridge freight station. Neither seemed to have any guilt over their actions; on the contrary, their trysts, looked forward to by both with great enthusiasm and anticipation, seemed to spur business.

In the spring, however, Rosie felt the presence of another baby within her and she called a halt to their affair. But she didn't tell Hays why, hoping that he'd never know the baby was his. She herself was not absolutely certain whether the baby born in September of '73 was L.J.'s, or Tim's, for she had not completely curtailed her lovemaking with Tim during her affair with Hays.

Hays had taken the breakup well, believing that she had succumbed to guilt. "Whenever we make love," she said, "I just can't . . . can't get enough of you. But then I have to go home and I feel so guilty I can't look Tim in the eyes."

Hays worked hard all that summer to raise more capital. Though he didn't achieve his magic capital figure of three million—or even one million—Hays' break came just a few days after Rosie delivered another boy. The bottom of the stock and bond markets fell out that September, thereafter to be known as the "Panic of 1873." The crash depressed the values of nearly all businesses—especially railroads.

# Chapter 10

Half of the railroads in the United States were thrown into receivership by the great panic that slashed millions of dollars from the value of the once-prized railroad bonds. One of the affected roads was the St. Paul. Its bankruptcy broke the backs of Kennedy's group of Dutch bondholders. They instructed their agent to look for "any reasonable offer," and with that in mind, Kennedy not only wired Hays looking for his offer, but also sent a night letter to the chairman of the board of the Hudson Bay Company, an old Kennedy friend, seeking an offer from him "since the St. Paul Railroad might well be a profitable adjunct to your trading business." Fortunately for L.J., the Hudson Bay Company chairman was an ultraconservative man who thought railroads a "preposterous" business and gave the matter little consideration.

But even the panic could not short-cut a lengthy procedure. It took L.J. nearly a year and a half to finally secure an agreement on terms and round up the necessary cash to prove good faith.

First they could not get together on price. Then there was the matter of dealing with other creditors, then the necessity of Hays' offering bonds in a new corporation rather than cash. To complicate matters, the St. Paul, under its receiver, showed a substantial profit increase during the first nine months of its second bankrupt year. Had this information been passed along to Kennedy and the bondholders, negotiations might have broken down completely, so Hays spent some frustrating hours convincing the court-appointed receiver that the profits were not profits at all, but rather capital expenditures. That L.J. succeeded was a tribute to his persistence and business acumen, for the receiver was stubborn, if not especially learned.

In the end, though, it was a threatening gesture by the Pacific Northern toward running a line north to Canada on the western side of the Red River that goaded Kennedy into forcing the issue with his principals. And so, late in December of 1874, Lynne Jerome Hays and two partners, Joseph Higgins and Pierre Richaud, took over the St. Paul Railroad. They entered the scene just in time to face another crisis.

It was just after the first of the new year, 1875, that Hays and Higgins set out upon a tour of the facilities of their new property. Hays was taken by a pulse-pounding excitement which made up for Higgins' skepticism. Their first stop was at the roundhouse where were kept the four locomotives the road owned. As was railroad custom, they bore the names of the engineers who ran them. They were all of the hardy 4-4-0 wood-burning class made by Baldwin in Philadelphia. The 4-4-0 was designated so because its four wheels in front provided steering, and four driving wheels for power were at the back. The "0" simply indicated that there weren't any wheels under the cab, the way there used to be. Two of these 4-4-0 engines were in need of repair.

They moved on to the St. Paul station, which

handled both passenger and freight traffic. It was fairly large, but dirty. The station agent was an old railroad engineer taken off locomotives years ago because of poor hearing. He was bitter and seemed to take out his feelings on anyone who chanced to stray into the station.

Hays immediately moved him out of the station and into the St. Paul freight yard, to work with another engineer whose hearing was not flawed. Then he hired a young, personable man and instructed him to clean up the station, paint it, and smile at the passengers who used the facility.

Minneapolis, St. Paul's growing sister town a few miles north, had a newer, though smaller station, and a substantial freight yard.

Sauk Rapids, Melrose, and Breckenridge (where the main line ended), each had a tiny train station, but invariably a fair-sized freight yard. Each station, of course, had its own telegraph lines. None of the small stations, however, was manned after dark, for no St. Paul train, freight or passenger, was scheduled at night.

The line's scheduling was, as Hays put it to Higgins, "simply atrocious" and designed more to accommodate the St. Paul's employees than to maximize service. The railroad had two principal freight customers—Hays Forwarding and the Hudson Bay Company.

"Now," Joseph advised, "we must service our former enemies better than they have ever been serviced—if we are to be successful."

It was true, but as Hays said, "Without the Hudson Bay Company our railroad would turn little profit, for they still control a large share of the Canadian trade."

"That must change," returned Higgins thoughtfully.

"It will," Hays concluded, "as soon as we've extended the main line into Canada. Then we can not only compete with the Hudson Bay Company, but can become its irreplaceable ally—or put it out of business on the Red River if it doesn't lower its charges to customers."

"No one will cry over that, L.J."

Hays chuckled. "I hear Williams has his eye on the Pacific Northern, by the way. If he should take control of it, I've a feeling he'll try to compete with us along the Red. The PN is already complete to Fargo across the river from Glyndon. Though it doesn't have the right to build on the Minnesota side of the river, it would be simple enough for the PN to go north from Fargo on the western side."

"Let's hope that doesn't happen."

"Amen, Joseph. Especially since the PN would have a shorter distance to go to reach the border than we do."

After Joseph left, L.J. went back to the roundhouse, to look over again the gleaming black-and-red locomotives. They weren't as pretty as his steamships, he decided, but there was a sleek sort of beauty about them. And the power in those four huge driving wheels was awesome. He felt goose bumps crawling as he recalled the time Phil Crabtree agreed to help him pull the *Cuyahoga* out of the Mississippi mud. If engines as big and powerful as these could not do such a job . . .

Yet, he now thought, the locomotives before him were the beginning, nowhere near the end of the railroad engines. Someday there would be other locomotives twice as large and twice as powerful, which would carry goods and people from one place to another faster than anyone could possibly dream.

L.J. resolved then and there to make certain that

his railroad—already in his mind extended to Montana and beyond—would be equipped with the fastest, most powerful locomotives on the market. They would be expensive, but the savings in time on each trip would, in the long run, save money—more trips, fewer man hours per trip.

The next day Hays learned for the first time that not only did he have to move his main line northward to the Canadian border, but that he had to do it as quickly as possible. The St. Paul Railroad's most valuable asset—its fifteen-million acre Minnesota land grant—was in danger. Its terms stated that the railroad had to lay track to the border by July 1, 1875!

Hays had known about the date from earlier investigations, but had understood that the date had been extended by five years by an act of the Minnesota legislature during the past year. Now he was shocked to learn that the governor—Governor Williams—had never signed the measure, thereby exercising what was called a "pocket veto," a veto which could not be overturned by the legislature because the measure was not returned to it.

Apparently, he now realized, Williams had even then had his eyes on the Pacific Northern Railroad, for the PN's only competition in Minnesota was the St. Paul. To remove the St. Paul land grant would be to break the railroad. Hays had to pull off a miracle and complete the St. Paul to the border in five months with only three of those months guaranteed warm-weather months.

After he had checked with friends in the legislature to confirm that Williams had enough power to block a new measure to extend the land grants, Hays went to work planning the extension. While doing so he had his attorney review the original legislation granting the state land to the St. Paul to make certain he could comply with all of its provisions.

When he received the attorney's report on the legislation, he found it mind-numbing, for not only did the St. Paul have to build to the border to protect its grant, but it had also to "connect with" a spur of the as-yet-unbuilt Canadian Pacific Railroad from Winnipeg to Pembina at the border! Thus, he not only had to build his own line north, but had to somehow see that the CPRR was there to join with the St. Paul when he got to Pembina!

A week later he was in Montreal, discussing the matter with his silent partner, Pierre Richaud, who was on the CPRR Board of Directors. Pierre told Hays that the Canadian Pacific had already agreed to build the spur "to coincide with the completion of the St. Paul's main line to Pembina."

Hays was not entirely satisfied with that, but extracted Pierre's promise that his partner would bring the matter up at the next directors' meeting and let it be known that the spur would have to be started immediately in order to coincide.

As always, money remained a problem, so L.J. had to spend a substantial amount of the little time he had in raising cash and credit to begin track-laying operations along the Red River. He held a public auction in St. Paul to sell land owned by the railroad—land previously acquired under the Minnesota land grant. The auction was successful but left Hays still short of the necessary capital to complete the more than two hundred miles of track to Pembina.

Hays even asked his friends in the legislature if they might sponsor legislation to grant the St. Paul a low-interest loan, but they feared the Governor too much to even try. A state senator told L.J. that Williams and his nephew, Jake Bronson, now his uncle's aide in St. Paul's State House, had their eyes on the bankrupt Pacific Northern Railroad, whose lines ran from Duluth on Lake Superior across the state to Brainerd, then to Glyndon at the Red. Hays was not pleased over this last piece of news, but was not surprised, either. The Pacific Northern could well be a business plum, if the right owner controlled it. It had valuable federal land grants across the Dakota Territory, Montana and Idaho and Washington—provided it could reorganize and lay track across that route to the Pacific.

In March Hays traveled to New York to talk to J.P. Morgan. Morgan claimed he had been hurt by the stock market and could not, therefore, help Hays out. But, he said, Hays could try Lucille.

"She has, you see, at last received her inheritance from my dead brother's estate, and it is substantial. Certainly enough to help you out—providing, of course, that you can convince her to do so."

With mixed emotions, Hays decided to see Lucille. He swore to keep their meeting strictly business, but he could not deny that he still felt something for her.

She literally greeted L.J. with open arms at her new husband's New York townhouse not far from J.P.'s Fifth Avenue home. "L. Jerome!" she exclaimed, hugging him. "My God, it's really you! I thought the snows of St. Paul had swallowed you."

Holding her in his arms, Hays suddenly recalled everything about her—the sweet fragrance, her tender body, her lovely smile. Then he stood back and looked at her. She was older for sure—just past thirty. Yet the years had only changed her from beautiful to dazzling!

Her hair had been restyled charmingly. Her figure seemed fuller and more womanly; her legs as long and shapely as ever. And, of course, her smile made him feel glad that he had come. They spent their first hours having tea and crumpets, reminiscing about the old days in Minnesota.

When her husband arrived home from Wall Street just past five and found them together, he didn't seem particularly surprised or put out that Lucille was entertaining a former beau. "You will stay over, Mr. Hays?" Jeff Lions asked Hays. "I insist."

After dinner, Lions excused himself to visit his ailing mother in Southampton, kissed Lucille on the forehead and shook L.J.'s hand. Watching the sterile parting kiss, L.J. wondered how they had ever managed to become a couple. But of course, he could hardly claim that his own marriage was a match made in heaven.

Now, alone in the big townhouse, L.J. told Lucille of his acquisition of the St. Paul. He was pleased when she seemed genuinely excited. He knew, however, it was time to talk business when she said, "But tell me, darling—isn't the railroad business a bit risky these days? My Uncle Pierpont says there are too many of them already and only a few are making a reasonable profit."

"J.P.'s right, Lucille, but that's the fault of the fools who run the government, and the rascals who *own* the fools who run it." Hays grinned. "Your uncle, by the way, is one of those rascals. But seriously, Lucille, my railroad—the St. Paul & Winnipeg is what I've renamed it—will sure as hell make a profit! It's a damned sight better than the ones cluttering up the East."

Lucille laughed. "Why, L. Jerome! You have certainly changed. I don't ever recall you cursing before."

"I've never owned a railroad before. I'm told that one of the requisites for being a railroad tycoon is learning how to curse in genteel company."

Lucille laughed again.

"Here's my problem, Lucille. I've got a great little road, with simply fantastic prospects. But no money, unfortunately! If I'm to make the St. Paul & Winnipeg pay, I've got to raise money to lay track. There's no getting around it. And that's where you come in. I'd like you to invest in me."

Lucille's expression changed minutely. "In what, railroad bonds? Dear me, L. Jerome, I don't know what to say. My husband handles my money and he has often told me what poor investments railroad bonds are. He'd think I was daft if I told him to sell something good to buy something bad."

Hays' eyes narrowed. He couldn't believe he was hearing Lucille correctly. The Lucille Morgan he remembered didn't have a concern in the world for money. If she'd had little money of her own, she had never worried about it. But this was a different Lucille.

"Well," he stammered, forcing a smile on his face that he did not feel, "I guess I can't fault your judgment based on recent history. I won't press the issue, since I wouldn't dream of taking advantage of our friendship to get you to do something you don't wish to do."

He changed the subject of their discussion, trying to hide his disappointment. If he didn't know better, he'd say it was a seething resentment behind Lucille's refusal to invest with him—a resentment centering around his marriage to Elizabeth.

Deftly Hays avoided a confrontation with Lucille

over his marriage and everything else. By the time he thought it proper to break away, he felt she had softened considerably in her manner. He even got the feeling she was looking for a renewal of their affair.

She seemed shocked when abruptly he insisted that he had to leave. He hoped she was.

Lucille's rejection, however disheartening, only strengthened L.J.'s resolve to make good his boasts about making the St. Paul & Winnipeg pay. Returning home to St. Paul, he mustered a construction gang and on the fifteenth of March began track-laying operations at the Breckenridge terminus of the present road.

On the first day, the crew managed to lay only a little more than half a mile of track, a record that would have brought shame to the worst construction gang in the country. He spoke to the foreman, an ex-Pacific Northern construction man, and was assured that the crew would do better "once they got used to each other."

Hays hoped so. He refrained from interfering through the first week of work—when the crew managed only eight miles. Then Hays acted; he fired the foreman. He did not replace the man, however. Instead, he ran the crew himself while looking for someone capable of taking charge. In the next two weeks, as the weather went from bitter cold to hot and from snowy to rainy, the crew laid only twelve additional miles of track. Hays was ready to fire himself.

Then, on a Monday morning early in April, a stoop-shouldered white-haired man in his early fifties (looking at least in his upper sixties) showed up at the railhead dressed in wrinkled but clean Pacific Northern work clothes. Beside the man was a thin, frail-looking girl of no more than eleven, with clear blue eyes and golden-yellow hair that slipped haphazardly from two long braids.

Hays was curious about the man, but said nothing to him as he and the little girl stood around and watched Hays' crew form up and go to work on leveling and cindering the roadbed, laying railroad ties, and lugging in the fifteen-foot sections of steel rail to be spiked down.

L.J. had no idea where the man and girl disappeared to when the workday ended at dark, but the two were back the next morning. This time the man wore a different work outfit—a striped one with "Chicago, Burlington & Quincy" stenciled on it.

This time, after the men began forming up, the man was suddenly at Hays' elbow. L.J. turned to look at him. The man was as tall as Hays, though much heavier. He looked like he had had a hard life.

"My name's Andre," the man said in a matter-of-fact tone, his hands on his hips. "Andre Pelletier. I been watching your crew work." He shook his head. "They're pretty damned slow. You know that?"

L.J. knew it only too well. His eyes went from the man to the freckle-faced little girl, then back again. "Your work clothes say you once worked for the big Q. That right?"

Pelletier nodded. "The Pacific Northern, too, but it's a lousy road. The big Q was a good one. I was foreman of the construction gang for a while."

"Why did you leave that job?" Hays asked.

The man hesitated, but the little girl beside him did not. "Papa likes the bottle," she stated matter-of-factly. "But don't worry—he's off it now."

Hays' eyebrows arched upward at the little girl's bold statement. When he looked at Pelletier for a confirmation, Andre shrugged, but made no effort to chasten his daughter or show any sign at all of disapproval. Nor did he lower his eyes from Hays'. "It's true," he concurred, before loosing a stream of French, shaking his head as he did so.

Although his own French was rusty, Hays understood what the man was saying—a tirade at himself as a "drunk and a bum." Finally Pelletier came back to English and said, "The Q fired me because of my drinking and so did the PN, bad road that it is. Now my wife is dead and my little girl knows me only as a drunk."

"Does the child speak French?" Hays asked him in French.

Pelletier showed his surprise, then smiled for the first time. "A little," he answered. "I have been remiss in her schooling because of my traveling about. After Chicago, Danielle took lessons only from her mother, then from me. And now . . ."

"Your wife is dead. And so you drank."

"No!" Pelletier paused for a moment, then added softly, "Although it has been worse since she died. At first I drank only with the men, but then . . . Where did you learn French?"

"I was born in Canada," Hays answered, "and am still a Canadian, although I live here, work here and have married an American. But we waste time—my men are ready to work. You need work, I am sure, but I fear I cannot hire you unless you can give me a good reason to do so. You say my crew is slow and you're right. But can you tell me why? Or what to do about it? I must build to Canada and fast, for I have a state land grant to protect. To keep it, I must finish the road by the first of July."

"You will put me on, even knowing I have had a bad history?"

Hays studied the man for a long moment. He had no use for drunks; they were bad business in every way. Once a few years ago, a drunken crewman had almost succeeded in wrecking the *Resurrection* by running it aground while tending the wheel. A half-drunk poker player years ago had tried to call Hays out after being beaten in a fair game of poker, and only the interference of another player—the marshal—had saved Hays' life.

"I've no respect for drunks," Hays told Pelletier.

"And I've no respect for myself for being one," returned the old man. "But I am on the wagon and have been for the entire winter—since I was let go by the Pacific Northern. And when I am sober, as I now am, I am as good a railroad man as you'll find in the Northwest."

"I can use such a man as that," Hays affirmed, "but only if he will lick old John Barleycorn permanently."

"He will, sir," the little girl broke in in French. "Papa has promised he would stop this time and he has never gone as long as this before. I will watch over him, never fear."

Pelletier grinned. "Danielle is a smart little one," he boasted. "But never mind about that. You asked me why your crew is slow and what to do about it. I can only say they are poorly organized and therefore wasting time. If you will allow me free hand, I will reorganize them and the results will speak for themselves."

Hays nodded. "You've a job, Andre, but only if you can improve the efficiency of our track laying by fifty percent. We must lay not less than two miles of track each day if we are to meet our objective and reach Pembina before the first of July."

"Your crew—our crew—will do that and more,

## Railroad King

Mr. Hays. How much more I cannot say. Now, if you will tell the men they must take orders from me?"

Before Hays could climb up on one of the construction wagons to call the men together, little Danielle threw her arms around his neck and kissed him on the cheek. "Thank you, Mr. Hays," the little girl gushed. "My papa will be the best foreman you could ever get, you'll see. And I'll make sure he stays away from . . . you know what."

Hays chuckled. "You've an irrepressible little manager there, Pelletier," he said, beaming at the little girl. "When she grows up, I've a feeling she'll be a difficult young woman to deal with."

"She is very much like her mother, Mr. Hays. As you say, she will be strong and difficult. But she will also be beautiful, both inside and out, for that is how her mother was."

L.J. remained on the site only long enough to assure himself that Andre had been running no bluff. It took only five minutes for the man to demonstrate his skill and knowledge. He gave orders crisply, brooked no back talk, yet seemed to relate well to the men. Soon they were hard at work and looking surprisingly well organized.

Hays rode back to Breckenridge to tend to some business, then returned to the railhead in midafternoon. He was pleased and surprised to find that the crew was past the mile-and-a-half marker and would, at its present rate, easily exceed the two miles Andre had promised.

The 4-4-0 locomotive which now carried number 75 on its cab and front, in honor of L.J.'s takeover of the railroad this year, had just arrived with a new supply of ties, rails and spikes. It had backed its load—four cars full—to the railhead and was now shut down as the crew loaded the ties onto a wagon pulled by mules.

Sitting on the bright red cowcatcher in front of the locomotive was the child Danielle. As Hays dismounted from his horse, he heard her singing, loud and clear:

"My Daddy builds the railroad,
Makes it nice and strong;
My Daddy builds the railroad,
To run those trains along.
Can't you hear my Daddy shoutin':
Lay those rails out right!
Can't you see the men a-workin',
Right on through the night?"

Hays looked around at the men and saw that they all wore grins at the sound of the spirited little girl's voice. They worked steadily, three men at a time banging down the spikes in rhythm with Danielle's song.

Andre was everywhere. At the moment, he was working with the grading crew, showing them how to level and mold the ground more efficiently. The sun was unseasonably warm for April, so Pelletier had tied a red bandanna around his forehead to keep the sweat from dripping down into his eyes.

Three hours later the sun disappeared over the Red River and the day's work was ended. They were two and a half miles north of where they'd started.

Hays watched in silence as Pelletier moved from man to man and group to group, talking briefly to each, then departing.

When Andre saw Hays, he came over. "They did better today, Mr. Hays," he judged.

"What were you just saying to them, Andre?"

The French-Canadian shrugged. "I only told them they had worked hard and accomplished much, but would do even better tomorrow, and with less effort. I thanked them for their cooperation and asked if they had any problems."

"Well, you've a job with me as long as you want one, Andre. I'm delighted. You think you can reach Pembina by July 1st?"

"You've my promise that we will, Mr. Hays. I will not fail you; Danielle will not let me."

Hays laughed. "She was in good voice," he commented. "She's obviously proud of you, Andre, and with good reason. I've a son not quite her age, and two daughters a bit younger, so I can appreciate how you must feel about Danielle."

"You hear that song? She made up her own words for it. I suppose she is proud of me, Mr. Hays, but I am even more proud of her."

Andre now had it within his own power to redeem himself, and had begun doing it today. For his sake, Hays hoped the man would make it.

Soon after hiring Pelletier to head the construction gang, Hays had to find a replacement for the man who ran the Breckenridge freight operation, which was now combined with the railroad business.

Though sorry to see the old man go, Hays was pleased, too. For it now gave him the chance to hire Tim Wolfe to run the combined operation. Tim's wheat farm was doing well, but with two sons and a daughter to raise, their money was always tight. Every so often, Rosie would ask L.J. to put her husband on his payroll.

"Are you sure he'll be willing to come back to work for me, Rosie?" L.J. had asked. "The last time I saw him he seemed . . . well, not really friendly. And that was way before what happened between you and me."

"Come on out to the house and ask him yourself, L.J. I'll cook you a fine supper."

Rosie had outdone herself with that meal. After all the whiskey and claret and brandy, Tim readily agreed to L.J.'s job offer. Also for the first time, L.J. saw the Wolfe boys, Billy and Mark, and their little sister Judith. Hays noticed that there seemed little family resemblance between the boys, though the girl looked as much like Billy as anyone could.

Pleased that the construction gang was under good direction and that the new freight-railroad operation was in Tim's hands, L.J. was inspired to return home to St. Paul to see his own children. But it was a short stay, and thirty-six hours later he was out seeking new avenues of financing to carry the line through to Canada.

Hays had enough money to finance things as far as Crookston, a little better than halfway up the Red to Pembina. But that would exhaust his supply of rails, ties, and spikes. The company that supplied them had already refused to extend him credit, crying that half the railroads in America owed them money.

It was Joseph Higgins who pointed out to Hays that he had a lot of capital tied up in the *Resurrection*—and that perhaps it could finance the rest of the Red River line.

A day later, Hays was on the Hays Forwarding Company's first steamer, heading for St. Louis to visit Joshua Laurence, who had recovered from his Civil War wounds and imprisonment, and was back in the shipping business. It was a sad trip for Hays. The thought that it might be the *Resurrection*'s final trip under the Hays Forwarding Company's banner dampened his spirits immensely.

But sentimentality couldn't stand in the way of

progress. Already a good deal of freight once hauled by steamships was being carried in railroad boxcars, Hays knew. And much, much more would go that route because railroads could carry freight much more economically than the largest and most efficient of steamers.

Still, as Hays sat down in Josh Laurence's office near the St. Louis docks and began discussing the *Resurrection*'s sale, he felt as if he were deserting an old friend.

Governor Ben Williams was furious when he learned of Hays' acquisition of the St. Paul Railroad. As Hays had surmised, Williams had in the works a secret deal that would soon gain him control of the Pacific Northern from the receiver who had been operating the road since 1873.

Jake Bronson had already hired a bridge-building outfit to put up a wooden span across the Red River at Pembina to hook up with the spur the PN would lay on the western side of the river. This spur would then hitch up with the Canadian-Pacific track, which the Canadian transcontinental would lay down from Winnipeg.

Williams was even more furious than he had been on the day so long ago when he'd lost the *Cuyahoga* to Hays. The pain from the *Cuyahoga/Resurrection* affair was still with him and he cursed silently each time he saw the Hays Forwarding Company pennant flying from the *Resurrection* at its St. Paul berth.

But now the Governor had more power than before and was grimly determined to crush Hays this time. Williams would see to it that his Pacific Northern construction crew completed the line from Moorhead, across the river from Glyndon, to Pembina before

Hays' track layers could push north from Breckenridge to the border. With a head start of some forty miles, Williams was confident that it was a sure thing. In beating out the St. Paul construction crew, the PNRR could cause Hays to lose the Minnesota land grants that were promised to Hays.

As soon as he assumed control of the PN, Williams met with its board of directors and gained easy agreement that they must oppose Hays along the Red River. Canadian trade, they agreed, was vital to their interests.

That accomplished, he halted the PN's construction program designed to reach the Pacific and brought all construction crews to Moorhead to build the road north on the west side of the Red. Then he set about harassing the St. Paul directly.

Using the threat of blackmail over the dynamite incident, the governor learned from Tim Wolfe when the next shipment of Hays' vital supplies of track, spikes, and railroad ties were due, then instructed Jake Bronson to make sure that the supplies got lost. When Hays returned to Breckenridge from his sad but successful trip to St. Louis, he found construction halted because a shipment of rails and ties had gone astray.

"How in hell do you go about losing a railroad car full of rails and ties?" Hays demanded.

Tim could only shrug. But Andre Pelletier suggested that the cars may not be lost at all, but perhaps "intentionally misdirected."

"Explain," demanded Hays, his blood boiling.

"It is an old trick, Mr. Hays," Andre remarked, "to hide a car by simply attaching it to a train going somewhere else, or putting it with a group of empty cars off on a siding. The Pacific Northern has begun laying track from Glyndon, and it would not surprise me if PN paid some men to divert our supplies."

Hays bristled. "All right, then, Andre. Where should we look?"

"You have yards at Sauk Rapids, Melrose, Minneapolis, and St. Paul. They could be in any one of them—or all. New numbers have, no doubt, been painted on the cars, so the contents of each car will have to be checked."

Within ten minutes, Hays and Andre were riding in a caboose attached to number 75 and on their way southeast to Melrose. Hays and Pelletier discussed who might carry out such sabotage other than the Pacific Northern. But they both felt strongly about the PN's involvement.

"Even while I was working for the PN," Andre noted, "there was talk of a northern route along the Red River to Canada. The only reason it was not begun long ago was that the former management wished to pursue the federal land grants they could get between Moorhead and the Pacific."

It now became clear to Hays that the new management had taken over from the PN's receivers, though it had not yet been given a title. The smart money, L.J. had read in a St. Louis newspaper only the other day, was betting that Governor Williams was their number-one man. Hays didn't like that at all. If Williams were involved, trouble was just around the next curve in the track!

Finally L.J. advised Andre, "I think you'd best send Danielle back to Breckenridge. There's liable to be trouble if and when we move ahead of the PN construction crew. I hope I'm wrong, but I can't trust that crook Williams not to launch a small scale war against us."

"Danielle will not like leaving me. She is more possessive than her mother ever was."

"What happened to your wife, Andre?"

Pelletier shook his head ever so slightly, but said nothing. He just stared out at the track behind the caboose.

At first, Hays wondered if Andre had heard him. But he let it drop. "Rosie, my bookkeeper—Tim Wolfe's wife—I'm sure would be glad to look after Danielle. I'll ask her when we get back."

"Very well, but *you* tell Danielle; I do not wish to face her."

Hays grinned. He could well understand Andre's reluctance, from what he already knew of the precocious Danielle Pelletier.

Now the train began to slow, as it reached the station at Melrose and headed for the freight-yard siding. Andre and L.J. followed the brakeman off the caboose before it stopped rolling, and together inspected every freight car stored in the Melrose yard—without success.

Off to Sauk Rapids they went, where their search was again fruitless. Likewise the Minneapolis yard, where its few cars turned up nothing.

They went on to St. Paul, and it was in this yard that Hays and Andre found what they sought—two boxcars, both with new numbers painted on their sides. From a distance or at night, the altered numbers would not easily have been detected.

"You were right, Andre," Hays said, "now let's hope our supplies haven't been tampered with or stolen." He swung up onto the boxcar and was about to unlock the sliding door when the door was suddenly thrust aside and he found himself face to face with a six-gun.

"Back off, man," barked the tall, bearded man inside the freight car.

Hays stepped back off the car so awkwardly that he almost fell at Andre's feet. As Andre moved to catch Hays, he slipped his hand into his pocket, pulled out the small derringer pistol he always carried there, and palmed it in his meaty hand.

"All right, now, turn around and face the other way," the bearded man ordered.

Hays hesitated, then turned. He was unarmed and knew he could be killed before lifting his foot to make a move toward the man. Andre turned, too. But he already had formulated his plan. The man was forcing them to turn so that he could jump down from the car without fear of being attacked. Once he came down, Andre figured the man's options were few. He could knock them both out and tie them up somewhere, or he could kill them. Andre figured the second option was the one this man would opt for. A chilling prospect, but the most likely under the circumstances. This man had been paid to guard, for Ben Williams, the vital Hays tracklaying supplies. His instructions were, no doubt, to kill anyone who tried to retake them. And it was clear that he wasn't going to ask him or Hays what they wanted.

Now Andre placed his thumb on the hammer of the little pistol. He tensed himself to whirl and fire at the bearded man the moment he heard the scrape of his boots on the railroad-car floor, indicating he had jumped. He knew he wouldn't get a second chance with this hired killer.

Hays, meanwhile, unaware that his foreman carried the deadly little derringer, had already made up his mind that he would not die without making a struggle. When he heard the telltale grunt the man made as he jumped, Hays swiveled and hurled himself at the gunman. His hand clutched the other's gun arm before he could swing up the barrel and fire. The outlaw's gun went off, and its bullet ricocheted off the dirt by Hays' left foot. The explosion jarred Hays, but he managed to hang on.

Then he heard Andre's excited voice call out, "Let him go, Mr. Hays! I've got a gun aimed right at his heart!"

Andre had been about to fire when Hays leaped, but now could not get a clear shot as the two men struggled.

But the outlaw was not through. With a grunt, he exerted all his strength to send Hays sprawling into Andre, dropping his gun as Hays took a wild swing at it. As the man fled for a string of freight cars a short distance away, Andre fired at him but missed badly. The derringer was accurate only at short distances. He then started to follow the man, but Hays stopped him.

"Let him go, Andre. We've got what we came for. No sense either of us getting killed. He left his gun, so he's not likely to come back. Let's get these cars back to the railhead."

Half an hour later Hays and his construction foreman were on their way back to Breckenridge, the two freight cars now in tow behind the locomotive.

"You've earned yourself a bonus, Andre," L.J. enthused. "And you deserve it. If you hadn't had that little gun—"

"I deserve nothing," Pelletier said. "You disarmed the outlaw. If you had not, we both might have met our maker."

"Perhaps, Andre. But were it not for you, we'd not have found the cars in the first place. So I think what I will do is invest a hundred dollars on your and

Danielle's behalf in the St. Paul & Winnipeg Railroad."

"For Danielle? Well, I thank you, Mr. Hays. And one day she will, too."

Back in Breckenridge, Hays obtained handguns, rifles, and ammunition from the local gunsmith and gave them to Andre to take back to the railhead. "Let's hope you won't need them," he told Andre. "And bring Danielle back by train tomorrow. I'll make arrangements with Rosie Wolfe."

"No, no, Mr. Hays. *You* come out and bring her back."

Hays had to laugh. "I'll be there, Andre," he agreed.

The next morning Hays telegraphed Thomas John Short in Winnipeg, instructing him to check the Winnipeg office of the Canadian Pacific to see when the CP would begin laying track south from Winnipeg. Just before noon, Hays received the reply from Short:

LINE TO PEMBINA IN DOUBT STOP PACIFIC NORTHERN SEEKS TO BUY RIGHTS STOP PN ALSO TALKING TO CP WHAT TO DO QUESTION MARK ADVISE SOONEST END TJS

Hays responded immediately:

INFORM WHOMEVER WE WILL TOP ANY BID BY PN RR STOP I WILL BE IN WINNIPEG TOMORROW TO TALK TO CP PD END LJH

The *Manitoba* was scheduled to dock later in the evening and would be making a return trip to Winnipeg tomorrow. Hays would be on board.

Now Hays sent a telegram to Joseph Higgins in St. Paul:

CONTACT PHIL CRABTREE IN CHICAGO AND OFFER HIM WHAT HE WANTS TO RETURN TO WORK FOR US STOP TELL HIM WE

NEED HIM DASH I UNDERSCORE NEED HIM DASH TO HELP ME PULL ANOTHER SUNKEN STEAMER OUT OF WATER PD END LJH

L.J. had planned eventually to bring Crabtree back to the St. Paul anyway, but the impending conflict with the Pacific Northern convinced him to jump the gun.

In midafternoon L.J. rode out to the railhead to get little Danielle. Pelletier's crew was having another good day—the rails were down for another two miles of track. Danielle was perched in the cab of the 75 locomotive. As usual, she was singing.

Andre reported to L.J. that there had been no trouble, but that two men left when they learned of the possible conflict. "I told them they could go, if they felt they had to. They felt they had to, so good riddance. I told the others you would pay a thousand dollars to the family of any who might die. They are with you all the way."

"Have you told Danielle?"

"I tried, but I cannot. I think she knows it must be, for she heard what I told the men. But she will not be easy to handle."

Hays found Danielle watching the men spike down fifteen-foot sections of rail. She smiled when she saw L.J.

"Hi, Mr. Hays," she bubbled. "Did you know it takes 352 sections of rail to make a mile and Daddy's crew is laying more than ninety an hour?"

"You planning to be a track layer when you grow up?" L.J. asked.

She shook her head. "I think I would like to work on the railroad, though. Would you give me a job?"

"Only if you grow up pretty," Hays said, kissing her freckled forehead.

Danielle giggled. "I hope I do. And it makes sense, too—a pretty railroad deserves a pretty conductor."

"You want to be a conductor?" Hays asked.

"Unless I can figure out some way to *own* the railroad."

Hays laughed and swept the little girl up off the cowcatcher. "You are priceless, princess. But we've got to go."

"I know you want to take me away from here, Mr. Hays. But you can't—Daddy needs me."

"You heard what your father told his men, honey," Hays argued. "There's going to be trouble here—bad trouble. People may be hurt and both your daddy and I want to make sure that you aren't one of them. That makes sense, doesn't it?"

The little girl thought about that. "Yes," she said finally, "I guess it does make sense. But I don't want to leave Daddy, either. Where'll I stay?"

"I have some friends, Danielle. Rosie and Tim Wolfe. They've a farm just east of here and Rosie's a wonderful lady. She has two boys, one named Billy, and another named Mark. They also have a little girl named Judith."

"Well," Danielle spoke slowly, her eyes sweeping the railhead, "let me say good-by to everyone, will you?"

Hays watched her go around saying good-by to all the men, as if she were one of them. She also said good-by to the locomotive. When she came back, she looked up at Hays and asked, "That lady Rosie doesn't have a dog, does she? I've never had one of them."

"I'm afraid not, hon," Hays said, holding out his hands to her. "Come along now. We've got to be going. Don't want to be late for supper." Hays swung her up onto his horse, then climbed up behind her and put his arms around her waist to take the reins.

She giggled. "I never did this before."

Hays rode over to Andre who stood talking with some of the track layers. Danielle leaned down to hug him, then straightened up once again. "Mr. Hays says I have to stay with Mrs. Wolfe for a while, Daddy. But I won't be far away, so if you need me, just whistle."

"Whistle?" Andre repeated. "You'll be twenty miles from here."

Danielle laughed. "With the locomotive whistle, silly!"

But as Hays rode away with the girl, her brave front crumbled and tears came to her eyes. He tried to cheer her up. "It won't be for long, princess," he soothed. "How's your daddy doing with his problem?"

The little girl sniffed and wiped her tears. She turned to see Hays and shot back, "What problem? His only problem is figuring out how to get the men to lay track faster."

# Chapter 11

Thomas John Short did not look too happy at the dock the next day at noon when he met Hays stepping off the *Manitoba*. "We got trouble, boss," he told Hays as the two men walked away from the pier. "Guess who's on the Canadian Pacific board of directors."

"Jay Calhoun."

"Right. The only thing we've got going for us is that he hasn't the power there that he has with the Hudson Bay Company. As it is, he must've been doing some lobbying against us, because the directors didn't want to talk to you until I told them that if they didn't, you'd probably go to Parliament as a Canadian and ask for their Charter."

"Not only good thinking, Tom," Hays complimented, "but exactly what I *would* do if they refused to do business with me."

"You still may have to do just that, L.J. I have a friend on the board and he says Governor Williams has them boondoggled. He and Calhoun must be quite a combination, 'cause between them, they've got the directors convinced they ought to wait to see who lays track to Pembina first before they commit to which American line gets first rights to their spur line."

So that's Williams' game, is it? Hays thought. He fell silent, and he and Short didn't speak again until they reached the temporary offices of the Canadian Pacific.

The board was already in session and from the outer office, L.J. could hear the sound of loud arguing from inside. He smiled at the bespectacled clerk who greeted them. "They fighting for the privilege of greeting me? Or over when to get out of the talking business and into the railroad business?" Hays could not imagine how the men who had formed the CP could call themselves a railroad when they had laid so little track to date.

The clerk looked as if he had been personally insulted. "I beg your pardon, sir. We are very much in the railroad business," he argued. "And who might you be?"

"I am L.J. Hays of the St. Paul & Winnipeg. I'm here, of course, to meet with your directors."

The clerk's attitude didn't change. "I'll see if they're ready for you." The clerk scurried across the floor like a rabbit, eased open the door to the inner office, and edged inside.

They wouldn't see Hays for half an hour. When they called for him, he was seated at a long, narrow table, where he listened to Francis Smythe-Barlow, chairman of the board, explain why the CP could give Hays no commitment to merge its Winnipeg-to-Pembina line with that of the St. Paul & Winnipeg. As Short had suggested, the CP decided against choosing either the St. Paul or Pacific Northern until one of them reached the Canadian border. It was a race and to the winner went the spoils! A race, in spite of the fact that the CP had previously agreed to build the spur to connect with the St. Paul, which alone had the Red River building rights in Minnesota.

And just as bad from Hays' viewpoint was the condition that the winner would be required to sit around at Pembina waiting for the Canadian Pacific to lay its track, for Barlow seemed to have absolutely no idea when the spur would be started!

Hays checked his anger, though he raged inside. A display of temper would only make things a good deal worse. And in spite of his good reasons to scorn these inept men, he knew he needed them. With the Winnipeg spur, the St. Paul & Winnipeg would bloom like a beautiful summer flower. Without it, the blossom might never open up to show its beauty.

When he was given a chance to say his piece, Hays calmly rose and looked carefully over the men before beginning. "If we are to serve the people of Canada as well as those of the United States, your connecting line to the border is all important. When can we count on you to begin work? Tomorrow? Next week? Next month? Next year? Next century?"

Barlow was not pleased at the asking of this question. He glared at Hays, then looked around the room to assure himself that all present were disgusted with their guest. At his left, Jay Calhoun sat, his expression plainly saying: Give the upstart his comeuppance, Frank.

"The connection of which we speak," Barlow began at last, "is one which is of more importance to the United States than it is to us Canadians. We are just beginning construction at Vancouver and in New Brunswick and neither section of the main line will reach Winnipeg for a long time."

"That's all the more reason to move with

dispatch, Mr. Barlow," Hays interjected amiably. "We can serve central Canada while its citizens are awaiting the main lines of which you speak. I'm sure the goods we can bring in and the service we can offer Canadians will not go unappreciated or unwanted."

Barlow was piqued and showed it. "Canadians have gotten along quite nicely for a hundred years without railroad service to the United States," he sneered. "I'm certain they can do so for another year or two."

"If what you say is true, Mr. Barlow," Hays shot back at the chairman, "then why bother to build your railroad at all? Canada has, as you say, gotten along without the Canadian Pacific, too."

Now Pierre Richaud, Hays' good friend and owner of a chunk of St. Paul preferred stock, stood and tried to mediate the struggle between Hays and Barlow. "Now, now, gentlemen. We must calm ourselves. Mr. Barlow, sir, what Mr. Hays is asking seems not at all unreasonable to me. We have, after all, previously agreed to build this link with America to provide Canadians with rail service. And I expect Mr. Hays, if necessary, could go to our government and acquire rights to build the spur on his own.

"So let us be reasonable. We have told him our position on which railroad we will favor—a position which I, incidentally, do not agree with. But since it is our position, I will go along with it. We can hardly drag *our* feet, however, since we are making it clear that the Americans cannot afford to drag theirs. Let us here and now set an early starting date on the spur. We have the crews available and the funds to pay their wages. Why not do it?"

Before the directors had a chance to speak on Richaud's proposal, L.J. jumped in to say, "Gentlemen, I am willing to commit myself right now to helping you finish the spur when we have reached the border. That way we will both get what we want." He paused as the group digested his words. "And I will charge back to you only the cost of materials. But my offer will stand only if you agree to begin work on the spur not later than one week from today. I calculate that will allow your people to complete something like three-fourths of the track by the time I reach the border."

"That sounds very generous, Mr. Hays," returned Richaud.

"Not to me," yelped Calhoun. "He can't afford to do that, unless . . . Ask him what's in it for him?"

"A completed line is what's in it for me, Jay," declared Hays. "And it will be a boon to both of our countries. And a moneymaker for the Canadian Pacific, once we put the entire line into operation."

The directors sent Hays out in order to go into a closed session, but to his joy, L.J. learned late in the day from Richaud that he had won. The CP would begin its Winnipeg operations in one week. "Let us be damned glad that none of my associates on that board know that I have a vested interest in the St. Paul & Winnipeg," Richaud told Hays.

"As if none of the others aren't on the take and protecting their hides. Look at Jay Calhoun—carrying Williams' banner."

A week later Hays got confirmation, via telegram from Short, that the CP had indeed begun laying track. What would have pleased him more would have been if his construction crew had made up ground fast enough to suit him, in spite of Andre Pelletier's fine supervision.

Andre suggested that the men might accomplish their tasks faster if they could be given periodic breaks during their long, twelve-hour day. Accordingly, Hays paid visits to the burgeoning cities of St. Paul and Winnipeg, seeking workers to labor as relief men. He had no trouble hiring whom he pleased, and in the process put on a strong, harmonica-playing cowpuncher named Cole Younger—who unbeknownst to Hays had only a few days earlier been hired by Governor Williams.

As L.J. sailed downriver aboard the *Manitoba* with Younger and the others, Williams was steaming for Winnipeg aboard the Hudson Bay Company's steamer *Alberta*, following a trip from Pacific Northern's headquarters at Brainerd to the port of Glyndon.

The Governor was in high spirits. At last everything seemed to be breaking his way. He now had a bank and a railroad to go along with the highest office in his home state. He had tremendous advantages, not only over his nominal competition, L.J. Hays, but over any railroad executive in the country. His First Minnesota made possible easy, short-term financing when the Pacific Northern needed it, while his position as governor could and would make possible state grants in both land and money to the road. The fact that it was clearly unethical—if not outright illegal—for Williams to use his power to favor his own railroad bothered him not a whit. And no one had the guts to blow the whistle. After all, his old friend Leland Stanford had done it in California, so why couldn't he?

As he stood at the rail of the *Alberta* looking west toward the Pacific Northern's track, Williams chortled over his coup in the battle against Hays and his St. Paul Railroad. With Jay Calhoun's help, he had arranged the "race" to the Canadian border, in which the Pacific Northern already had a substantial head start. A hundred-yard run with only sixty yards to go was how Williams looked at it.

So far, at least, Williams' PN construction crew had been able to hold the lead it had started with. The Governor's lone regret was that he had not been able to take control of the Pacific Northern until after the St. Paul track layers had already covered twenty-five miles.

But Williams had made arrangements to once more slow down the St. Paulers. He had hired a professional from Kansas, who bragged about his record of never having failed to do what he was hired for. Jay Calhoun had suggested Younger. Now Williams was confident of obtaining that ten-year exclusive contract the Canadian Pacific Railroad directors promised to the first American railroad that reached the border at Pembina.

He had had, until the previous night, just one more victory he wanted to score over Hays. It would surely be the *coup de grâce*: the seduction of Elizabeth Hays.

Hays' wife was a beautiful woman, and obviously unappreciated by her husband, Williams learned. If he played his cards right, he might convince the lady to leave Hays and become the First Lady of Minnesota. He was sure Elizabeth would like that. He was equally certain Hays would not.

People were always asking Williams why he had never married, a question which he never had a truly satisfactory answer for; it had almost cost him the election. How could he tell people that the only women he ever felt passion for were those he had to buy?

The Governor at once admired Hays' lovely wife

at the Governor's Ball last year. Elizabeth's escort was not Hays, who was away on business in New York. She was most unhappy for it, but Williams paid off her escort and tried to show her a good time. They had spent much of the evening talking—mostly about him. Elizabeth had a way, he thought, of drawing him out with a flurry of questions. Then, after she had laughed at one of his small jokes (he loved to tell them), she suddenly became very serious and looked a trifle uncomfortable.

"What's wrong, my dear?" he had asked.

She shook her head and looked like she was fighting back tears. He took her hand and patted it, saying, "Tell me what's wrong, Elizabeth. Perhaps I can help. At least allow me to show my understanding side. As Governor I'm not allowed to be understanding, you know."

But Elizabeth had not laughed at the joke. Instead she told him that she shouldn't have come to the Ball at all, that L.J. would not approve.

"Oh? Is he jealous, my dear? Possessive? I don't blame him. You are a beautiful woman. If I owned you—as a wife, of course—I'm afraid I, too, would wish to keep you to myself."

"It isn't that, Ben," she had sniffed, tears appearing in the corners of her eyes. "I'm sorry, I must leave."

He could not talk Elizabeth into staying, and a few moments later, she left the Governor's mansion with her escort. Later, Williams sent an aide to make sure she'd arrived home safely. With the aide, he sent along a short, hand-written note:

Dear Elizabeth:
    I can't tell you how I enjoyed your company tonight. You dance delightfully and

## Railroad King                                                285

are certainly a fine listener as well as a beautiful woman. I am sorry you saw fit to leave, but I can certainly understand your discomfort. Please think of me now as your friend—someone you can trust to be a sympathetic listener should you feel the need to confide in someone.

Love,<br>Ben

Williams now grinned as he recalled that Elizabeth Hays had the most sensational figure he had ever seen. And during the six months he had been quietly seeing her socially, he had longed to sleep with her.

Last night he actually had done so. The thought of the soft, curved beauty of Elizabeth Hays filled him with an intense feeling of heat. Even though Elizabeth had made it clear in the aftermath of last night's tryst that she could not see him again, he was certain she would. They had made love twice last night. Her talents had exceeded his wildest dreams. The resulting ride had been as satisfying as any he had ever experienced. Hays was a foolish man.

Afterward Williams had said words he'd never before uttered: "I love you, dear Elizabeth."

They had a strange effect on the lady, however. She had jumped up from his bed and begun dressing. And that was when she insisted they would not see each other again. Williams was sure Elizabeth didn't mean it, not after her obvious enjoyment of their coupling. He thought she could be coerced into becoming at least his mistress, even if she would not or could not—because of her Catholic religion—divorce Hays. Perhaps, he thought, that would be best, for there were certain advantages to being a bachelor governor.

Though he had enjoyed Elizabeth and would like to do so again, there were others whose charms he still enjoyed sampling.

Returning to the moment at hand, the Governor frowned as he saw, on its way downriver, the high-decked, double-stack *Manitoba*, more than twice the size of the *Alberta*. The two steamers passed little more than fifty yards apart in the narrow river, allowing passengers on both boats to see those on the other.

Williams saw L.J. Hays standing on the top deck at almost the same moment L.J. spotted the Governor. Williams cursed the man. But as the two ships passed, he burst forth in giggles as he thought of how he'd just cuckolded old L.J. Hays.

In Winnipeg, Williams was met by his nephew, who outlined the results of Hays' recent visit to the Canadian Pacific directors' meeting. The Governor's good mood was immediately broken by what he heard. When he and Jake Bronson reached Calhoun's office and were ushered inside, he lit into Jay.

"You losing your touch, Jay?" Williams burst out. "I hear you let Hays buffalo the board—let him have his way."

Calhoun shook his head. "All he got was an earlier start date for our section of track down to the border. No big deal. Anyway, there was no way I could stop him, not after he offered to help the CP finish the job at almost no expense to us. Hell, Ben, he was giving us money and the others just couldn't turn that down. But I don't know why you should be so unhinged about it. I understand your track is ten to twelve miles ahead."

"True enough, Jay, but I damn well refuse to spend a pot that isn't yet in my hands. Not this time. I've beaten that bastard before, only to lose in the end.

I'm not going to let it happen again. Hays has a deadline to meet if he's to keep that land grant and I aim to make doubly sure he doesn't make it."

"What difference does the land grant make, Ben? If the Pacific Northern gets the contract with the Canadian Pacific by making the border before Hays does, you'll have Canada's Red River trade and he won't."

"Not true, Jay. Are you growing senile? He'll still have his steamers and can use them to carry freight between the end of his line at Pembina and Winnipeg. And he will, if I let him stay in business. On the other hand, if he loses the land grant, he'll be effectively out of business and I'll be able to buy up his road for the price of a keg of beer."

"I see," Calhoun said. "So what do you want me to do?"

"I want that damned CP spur south to Pembina delayed, Jay. So badly that there's no way Hays can hook up to it until July 2nd, no matter what he does."

Calhoun shook his head. "I don't know if I can do it, Ben. My neck's on the chopping block up here with the Hudson Bay Company and I've got my eyes on becoming top man of the CP. If I get in trouble there, I'm liable to find myself looking for another job."

"Use your head, Jay, and you won't get into trouble."

"I'll try, Ben. Can you handle Hays' construction crew on the Red?"

"I can and will," Williams boasted. "Just see that you do your part. If you do, we'll both be rich."

# Chapter 12

Phil Crabtree was at the railhead just north of Glyndon when L.J. rode into camp. The two men embraced warmly. Grinning, Crabtree said, "Just like old times, L.J. But where's this old steamer I'm supposed to pull out of the water?"

Hays laughed. "There it is, Phil," he said, gesturing toward the track being laid by Andre's crew. "We've got a race on our hands—one we can't afford to lose." L.J. went on to explain the whole situation to Crabtree.

"And you're expecting trouble?" Crabtree asked, eyeing the rifles neatly stacked on a wagon near the track crew.

"I wish I could say 'no' to that one, Phil. But I've little doubt that Williams will stop at nothing to break me this time."

"What happens if the Canadian Pacific lets up on its part of the bargain? A start is no finish."

"With Calhoun on the CP board, you're right about that. Thomas John Short will keep me posted on CP's progress. Right now I'd like you to give me your ideas on how we can catch that PN crew."

"Let me look things over, L.J. Ten miles is a lot

of ground. There's only so much track you can lay in a day."

"Maybe we'll have to start working at night too, Phil."

Both men knew it might well come to that before they could drink victory beer in Canada.

Two days later Phil came up with a new system of track laying which, he said, had worked well recently at the Chicago, Burlington & Quincy. It made use of the new men Hays had hired as relief men.

It also made use of the offer of a bonus. The next morning Hays stood on a stack of five hundred-pound steel rails the men had carried from the flatcars behind the locomotive and outlined a new program.

"Men, you've done me proud up until now, and I hate to have to ask you to do better. But I must. If we lose the fight to reach the Canadian border before the Pacific Northern, we may be put out of business. And that means you'd lose your jobs."

"Once we get to Pembina," one of the crew called out, "we ain't gonna have jobs anyway, 'cause there won't be any more rail to lay!"

Hays heard others in the crowd echoing the man, a veteran track layer who had hired on with a dozen railroads in his time.

"Shorty," L.J. said, addressing the man, "you've just made a good point—but one that's invalid here on my railroad. Because Pembina is not the end of our line. I'll have track-laying work for every man-jack of you—for at least ten years—if we win this blasted race."

The men erupted in a gaggle of sound. When they finally quieted, Shorty piped up again. "Does that mean you're goin' to strike out for the Pacific?"

Hays grinned and held up his hands for quiet as

again the men began talking back and forth. "I can't tell you anything more than I just have. Now in addition to that, I'm going to give each of you a hard cash bonus when we get to the border—first, of course. How's a fast hundred dollars sound?"

How indeed!

Hays' words had a magic effect on the construction gang. So did the changes Crabtree had worked out for their fifteen-hour day: in addition to the hour's relief, every man now got two half-hour breaks, one every six hours.

On each of the next three days, the men laid more than three miles of track—a truly prodigious feat. According to a man Hays had hired to keep an eye on the progress of the PN crew, it had made six miles in the same three-day period—a gain of three miles for the St. Paul gang!

Hays and Crabtree were jubilant. "I believe that extra effort they're putting out comes from being rested," Crabtree argued as they sat around a campfire drinking "Bitsy" Walsh's coffee. (Bitsy, the cook, was six feet around as well as high.)

"I believe it to be the profit motive," opined L.J. "Money always has been a mover of men."

Only one member of Hays' construction gang was unaffected by the new arrangements. Cole Younger was expert at keeping his feelings hidden. He played constantly on his mouth organ. It was his greatest pleasure when not plying his trade as a hired troubleshooter. Troublemaker was a better word for him. Once he'd been hired to call out and kill a gambler on a Mississippi riverboat. The gambler was not only a card cheat, but had won the affections of the wife of the ship's owner, which was worse. Cole slew the gambler with a single shot.

Most of his work was perhaps a little less romantically dramatic, but no less unscrupulous: cattle rustling in Texas; investigating a private range war in Arizona; assassinating a politician in Kansas City; robbing a bank in Albuquerque—this at the request of the bank's owner, who had embezzled considerable amounts of money.

This job was simple for Younger. All he had to do was stop the St. Paul crew from reaching the Canadian border.

That night at the PN railhead, Ben Williams listened impatiently to the construction foreman explain why his crew had not averaged better than two miles a day, why *no* crew could be expected to do better. Williams could only shake his head in disgust.

"If what you say is true, then how in hell are we losing ground to Hays? How is it his crew is doing *three* miles a day—and sometimes more?"

The foreman, a big Irishman who'd once worked for the Erie Railroad in the East, shrugged and said, "Maybe Hays has hired a bunch of Chinese coolies, Governor. I surely don't have the vaguest idea."

Williams' look could have killed. Younger, he thought, would have to make his move soon. The question was, would his actions be enough?

Williams walked down to the river's edge and stared upstream. A three-quarter moon shone down upon the water, reflecting a cloudless sky. But the Governor paid it no mind as he racked his brain for a deadly scheme. Suddenly from around a curve upriver, Williams saw the brightly lit upper deck of the *Manitoba*. The *Manitoba*. Williams spit into the river.

Then in a flash he remembered that she still carried the two Gatling guns Hays had installed to keep away attackers. Williams had been impressed by the scene at the Breckenridge dock when Hays' gunners ripped open the two wharf boats.

The Governor held up his hand and waved stingily as the *Manitoba* passed by. He laughed softly at the beautiful irony that he would use Hays' own steamship to bottle up Hays short of the Canadian border.

Early next morning, he and Jake Bronson rode the PN locomotive over to Glyndon, then caught the Hudson Bay Company steamer to Winnipeg. He needed men—some rough, tough ones—to carry out a task which would guarantee the Pacific Northern's ten-year lock on the Red River Valley trade.

The St. Paul track layers continued their torrid pace, and less than a week later, Phil Crabtree spotted the Pacific Northern crew across the river. The men of Crabtree's crew let out shouts of delight as they spotted their opponents as well. By the end of the day, they had overtaken the PN crew by half a mile.

While Hays himself was exultant at having at last passed the opposition, his feelings were tempered by the knowledge that it was still a long way to Pembina. The month of May had barely begun. There was, he knew, plenty of time for Williams—or even one of his men—to make a move against the St. Paul crew.

For weeks Hays had tried to decide in advance in what form an attack might come from the Governor. He thought there was a strong possibility that some night a party of attackers might creep up and rain down destruction with dynamite. Hays ordered Phil to post guards at the perimeters of the railhead to protect against that possibility.

It was as if a saboteur had been listening over Hays' shoulder. Early that morning, an hour before sunrise, an earth-shaking explosion shattered the silence of the camp, followed by a second, third, and fourth explosion in quick succession.

Hays, who slept in a sleeping car attached to the now-empty freight cars that had brought railroad ties and steel rails up from St. Paul, was knocked out of his bunk by the first explosion. Hays leaped out of the car just in time to see the beautiful 4-4-0 locomotive being torn asunder, its pieces sent flying high in the air. L.J. dived under his sleeping car for cover and stayed there as the third and fourth explosions shook the ground.

When all the dynamite had exploded, the camp looked like an earthquake had leveled it. The wagons holding steel rails and railroad ties were no more, their pieces scattered here and there around the camp. The rails were torn and twisted like pretzels, the railroad ties ripped into large splinters.

But the locomotive was simply unrecognizable, its four driving wheels nowhere in sight, its cab torn loose and hurled near the river, its bell lying in the roadbed a half mile upstream.

It was sheer good luck that only two men were killed by the explosions. The rotund cook, "Bitsy" Walsh, was decapitated by a fifty-pound piece of steel rail that pinwheeled at him. And one of the trackmen took giant splinters from a railroad tie directly into his heart.

At first, Hays could not believe what he saw. How, he asked himself, could someone have slipped through the posted guards, plant explosives where they could do the most damage, then simply vanish?

Or did they need to vanish?

A shiver passed through him at the thought that one of his own men might have done the deed.

Quickly Hays gathered his wits. He sent a courier on a fast horse to Glyndon, to send off a message by telegraph. Tim Wolfe was to order another locomotive and new supplies, to be delivered to Hays as quickly as possible.

Then L.J. had Phil and Andre muster the men, who were very badly shaken. Hays looked at each one of them before finally speaking his piece:

"It looks like our opponents have decided they can't beat you fairly, men. You see what they've done with their dynamite. Two good men are dead. I can't tell you how bad I feel about that, and I'm sure you share my grief. I've sent for more supplies and another engine. We'll lose some valuable work time, but I'm sure we can make it up. The question is, will you quit because of this? Or will you stiffen your backs and work that much harder? Which is it, men?"

There was silence around the stunned group for a moment, and then Shorty sounded off, "I'm for workin', Mr. Hays. They don't scare me none."

"We're with you," hollered a grizzly old bear of a Minnesotan who'd served with L.J. under Phil Crabtree.

"And me," added Cole Younger.

"All right, men, now listen carefully to what I have to say. Chances are whoever did this came from the PN camp across the river. But there is the chance it might have been done by one of our own people." There were angry murmurs. "Does that surprise you?" Hays asked.

When the men had again calmed, Hays warned, "I would therefore suggest that you be wary in the days to come. Come to Andre or Phil or me if you see anything that looks suspicious. We're going to double and maybe triple the guard to make sure this doesn't happen again. Let's have a moment of silence for 'Bitsy' and Albert, who had the misfortune today of being in the wrong place at the wrong time. I'll be sending their survivors each a thousand dollars, by the way, though I know it sure won't make up for their loss."

After Hays stepped down, Andre set the men to work cleaning up the mess. L.J. and Phil held a council of war.

"So," Phil said as they walked along the river's bank, "we have a traitor in our midst."

"It looks like it, Phil," agreed L.J. "None of the guards heard a thing suspicious, though they weren't keeping their eyes on the camp's interior. I don't see how an outsider could have done this."

"All the men's tents are quite a distance from where the explosions destroyed the supplies," Phil observed. "One of the guards might have seen some movement across the camp."

Hays thought for a moment, then asked, "Are any of the men especially early risers? Check with Andre and see if he knows of anyone seen skulking about. We've got to unmask our killer before he decides to eliminate our men along with the supplies. We can replace supplies, but not men."

Andre and Phil were in a fevered discussion when two surprise visitors rode into camp. Both of them were speechless when they saw the aftermath of the explosions.

L.J. was chewing on the stub of a cigar when he saw Lucille Morgan and Rosie Wolfe ride in. He was stunned to see Lucille.

"L. Jerome!" Lucille cried. "I'm so glad you

weren't hurt. I was coming out to see you, but when your message was received in Breckenridge, the train let us all off and then headed back to St. Paul." She stopped, waiting for some reply from Hays. "Well, aren't you going to lie and at least tell me you're glad to see me?"

Now L.J. smiled and hugged Lucille. "Of course I'm glad to see you," he confirmed, "though neither you nor Rosie should be within a hundred miles of here. What happened may be only the first shots of an all-out war."

"We had to come, L.J.," Rosie piped up. "Tim says he sent Hiram back on 76 for supplies. We have only a couple of days' worth of rails and ties back in the warehouse, but it'll keep the men working. And there's a shipment due any day now."

"Good work, Rosie. Tell Tim I appreciate it."

Rosie gave L.J. a look that told him she had more to say, but wouldn't say it in front of Lucille.

"Why don't you go over and deliver any messages you have from Danielle to Andre, Rosie?" L.J. said. "I'll talk to you later."

"I'll be glad to, L.J., but first I have a message for *you*. Danielle said I should be sure to kiss you for her, but I guess I'll just tell you about it instead."

Hays reddened slightly as Rosie walked away. He turned to Lucille. "It would've been better if you hadn't come, Lucille."

"I understand, L.J. I'm terribly sorry about what happened."

"Two men were killed and all our supplies destroyed."

Lucille shivered. "Who did it?"

Hays shook his head. "We have no idea. But

there's little question it was one of Governor Williams' men."

"Good Lord, L. Jerome! The Governor? You can't mean it. He wouldn't do something like this!"

"I wish I didn't mean it. He's got control of the Pacific Northern and they're trying to break me by stealing my Red River line."

Lucille's look was more significant than her words. "I'm sorry I turned you down when you asked me to invest with you, L.J. I was wrong. Dead wrong. I came today to tell you I'll let you have as much as you need—whenever you want it."

"Provided that . . . ?"

"No provisions, L.J. No strings at all."

"What about your investment adviser—your husband?"

"I'm divorcing him. I left him last month."

"May I ask why?"

Lucille laughed for the first time. "I might've left him over you, had you cared enough to try to make love to me! I wanted you to, you know."

"I stay away from married women," Hays offered.

"Oh. But a 'Rosie' by any other name is still a married woman, L.J!" Lucille quickly tried to make light of it. "Oh, damnit, there I go again, letting skeletons out of the closet!"

"Lucille," Hays fumed, "tell me why you left."

"Must I?"

Hays nodded.

"Well . . . the last time I saw a woman look at a man like Rosie just looked at you was back in New York at the Governor's Ball. The woman was the Governor's pretty little daughter and the man was my handsome little husband."

Hays gave her a sympathetic look, but her eyes were out on the river.

"L. Jerome, this is marvelous country," she sighed, "much more beautiful than the Seine. Listen. I agree that a look isn't necessarily a confirmation of *anything*. *Every* woman wants her man to be admired. But if the two involved have had the opportunity—and if the man looks at the woman the same way she looks at him—well . . ." Her palm swept upward pointlessly.

"I see," Hays replied meekly.

"Tell me, L. Jerome," Lucille continued, "why do you stay with that conniving little prig you married? You can't be happy with her. I'm told you're almost never at home. And of all the little girls I've taught, she was one of the few I *never* liked."

"Why not?"

"She was like a counterfeit gem. She could shine and sparkle like the real thing, but when you scratched at the surface, you found that Elizabeth was only a cheap imitation."

There was nothing Hays could say; Lucille had, unfortunately, described Elizabeth perfectly.

"Would you walk with me up the river a little?" Lucille asked now. "I want to be alone with you—just a moment. Come with me, please?"

Hays couldn't help himself and went along. The moment they were out of sight of the camp, Lucille stopped and held out her arms to L.J. He took her in his arms and kissed her hungrily. Their mouths furiously worked at each other and it was joyous. No, it was much more than that. He had not felt so at ease with a woman since . . . since the last time he had held Lucille Morgan in his arms.

"Now," he said dryly, "it appears I am seducing another married woman."

"I was right about Rosie?" Lucille giggled, then added quickly, "No, don't tell me. I really don't want to know. It isn't my business."

She kissed him again, but then Hays withdrew. "We must go back, Lucille. I've much to do and it isn't safe for you and Rosie here."

"Will I see you again, L. Jerome?" she asked as they walked back.

"I don't know. My railroad must not be stillborn—and it could easily be. Right now she's both my mistress and my wife. She keeps me very excited and satisfied. Later . . ." He shrugged. "I can't see beyond tomorrow right now."

"You *are* obsessed, L. Jerome! It seems the only good thing I can say about you is . . . I like your beard."

A short time later Hays was alone with Rosie, and she told him some frightful things. "I know you'll be furious, L.J. I'll understand. But I must tell you that Tim made a confession to me the other night. He's been tortured by this for a long time, so perhaps you can find a grain of compassion in your heart." Rosie paused, then let out a deep sigh. "Tim is your man—at least one of them. Now I don't know if he's responsible for this. I don't think so. But he told me that on several occasions he passed along some vital information about your operation to Williams and Calhoun. He said he was forced into doing it because of his participation in the *Manitoba* landslide some time back. Blackmail, he said. Tim is a good man, L.J., and I know he feels terrible about . . ."

"*Terrible*? Death and damnation!" Hays thundered to the heavens. He was so furious he couldn't speak, but just stomped around and around in a circle, hands clenching and unclenching like mechanical clamps. "I'll *kill* him! I swear it! I'll *kill* the bastard! When did he tell you this?"

When Rosie took her hands away from her face, Hays saw that tears were flowing down her cheeks. "Night before last, but I know . . ."

"A confession for a deed not yet done, damn! *This*!" Hays got right up into Rosie's face and said in a vile, throaty voice, "I'll never forgive him. *Never*."

Rosie squared her shoulders and said, "Hold on, Mr. L.J. Hays. Don't forget that *you* took something of his much more valuable than information. You have committed the insult of insults by taking another man's wife. Don't worry; Tim will never know. I'll not tarnish your good reputation. But I think you should at least let a man speak for himself before you condemn him. When you talk, I think you'll find that he is as much a victim of Calhoun and Williams as you have been."

"No thanks to your monstrous husband." L.J. took a deep breath. "All right. All right, what do you expect of me?"

Rosie blinked and shook her head. "I don't know, other than talk to him. I suppose you must fire us. I just . . . I just thought you should know. I owe it to you."

"Well, thank you very much. At least *you* show some semblance of sense. I can't believe it. What kind of information has he been giving to Williams?"

Rosie drew in a lungful of cool air before replying. "The location of your supply of rails, L.J.," she said. "And that's the last piece of information he said he'll ever give them. He swears it."

L.J. stared at the woman for a long time, exerting every bit of self-control he had to conceal the rage he felt coursing through his veins. Finally, he stomped away, muttering to himself. Rosie followed, her tears gone, but concern a dark cloud on her face.

Hays was nearly a half mile south of the railhead before he stopped suddenly and whirled on Rosie. He pointed across the river, to the Pacific Northern railhead.

"You see how close the Williams track layers are, Rosie?" he asked. "This is the most important race I'll run in my life. And I don't intend to lose it. What we have right now is about a half-mile lead. Damn little, isn't it?"

Rosie nodded, still staring across the way.

"Williams knows he's got to beat me. He'll stop at nothing to do it. He'll use Tim again. He'll use anyone who can help him. Do you understand that?"

"Yes, but..."

"So I have no choice but to get rid of Tim. I can't afford to keep him around. I'll leave whether you want to stay up to you. But I won't let Tim." Hays trailed off as Rosie moved up close to him.

"I understand, L.J.," she said, "but before you let Tim go, I must tell you that Tim said he's going to try to make it up to you by finding out what Williams will do to try to stop you."

"That's pretty clear, isn't it, Rosie?" Hays scoffed.

"You don't think it'll stop here, do you, L.J.? You said yourself that Williams won't be satisfied until he's *ruined* you. Please give Tim a chance; I know he can help you."

"No, Rosie, I just can't trust him. It wouldn't be fair to my men. Do you know how I feel right now? Knowing that this race, and the bastard who caused the explosions this morning, killed two of my men? I can't have the safety of the others depend on an admitted turncoat."

"There's nothing Tim could have told Williams that could've caused what happened, L.J. And there's nothing he can tell Williams now that could possibly endanger your men more than they are already. But just maybe Tim can find out something that will help you—tomorrow, or next week, or next month."

Rosie was right, Hays now thought. There was no way Tim could further endanger the men or their struggle to win this race. The damage had been done. And he *was* the only link Hays had to Williams. Maybe it was worth a try.

"You're sure he's sincere, Rosie? That it isn't a trick Williams put him up to to jeopardize me further?"

Rosie stepped back to look up at him sincerely. "I can tell you one thing he found out long ago, L.J. That . . . well, it's real bad and I hate to pass it along to you."

"What? Let's have it, Rosie."

"It's about . . . about Elizabeth, L.J."

Hays stiffened. "Elizabeth? What about her?"

"Williams claims . . . He's bragging that he's having an affair with her."

Hays stared at Rosie for one long moment, in his mind a cauldron of thoughts. Elizabeth? Bedding his worst enemy? It seemed impossible. Yet Hays knew Elizabeth was capable of it, and that Williams would dearly love to embarrass him. And hadn't Hays learned quite by accident recently that Elizabeth had visited the Governor's mansion? Hays had thought little about it at first when Elizabeth described a beautiful painting she had seen depicting a railroad engine in the wilds of Minnesota. The painting, Hays remembered, hung on a wall in the Governor's home; he had seen it there before Williams became governor.

Elizabeth. Hadn't he tried, in spite of their differences, to maintain decent relations with her? True, he was away from home a great deal, but that was unavoidable. And true, he no longer occupied the same bed with her, but Elizabeth's hunger for sex had long ago disappeared—to surface only now and again when she wanted something from him. Once it had been the trip to New York, another time for his approval for redecorating their house. But how could he be expected to be the all-loving, all-forgiving, all-understanding husband? He hadn't the time; he had a railroad to build.

"I'm sorry to have to be the one to tell you, L.J.," Rosie sighed.

"It's all right, Rosie," Hays said softly. "I suppose I should have seen it coming. It matters little, in spite of everything." He now looked straight into Rosie's eyes. "You're sure Tim will help?"

"He won't betray you again, L.J. I know it."

L.J. hesitated, looking deeply into her eyes. "All right, Rosie," he decided, "I'll give Tim a chance. But I want you to tell him that you've told me, so he'll know there's no turning back. And if he gets mad at you for telling me and hurts a hair on your lovely head—"

"He won't, L.J. I'm sure of it."

When Rosie and Lucille rode away, Hays was more despondent and lonely—and tired—than ever before. Rosie and Lucille, though very different, were both fine women. He loved them both, he thought, though in different ways. Would he see Lucille again? He knew he would, as soon as this race was over. As for Elizabeth . . . Cuckolded by Williams! Well, let the whore sleep in the Governor's mansion if she so desired.

That day, with the entire camp idle waiting for

supplies, L.J. Hays recalled something he hadn't thought about in a long, long time: the Reverend. He could see the old man, now very tired, preaching a lesson. This time he was saying, "And the Lord God said unto the woman, 'What *is* this that thou hast done?' And the woman said, 'The serpent beguiled me, and I did eat.'

"Let *your* conversation be without covetousness; and be content with such things as ye have. For he hath said, 'I will never leave thee, nor forsake thee.' So that we may boldly say, 'The Lord is my helper, and I will *not fear* what man shall do unto me.'"

These words would sustain Hays through the duration of the race.

# Chapter 13

Ben Williams was furious as he faced a grim Jay Calhoun in Jay's Hudson Bay Company office in Winnipeg. Calhoun had just told Williams he had been unable to keep the Canadian Pacific from continuing its track-laying operations to the border.

You dumb son of a bitch! Williams thought to himself. How'd you ever get to be anything more than an office boy? But the Governor held his tongue. He needed Calhoun—for the time being, at least. Jay had clout in Canada and could easily find the kind of muscle Williams needed.

"I hope you *will* make sure the line isn't finished before Hays' July 1st deadline," Williams hissed, as calmly as he could.

"I think so, Ben, but as I told you, I have to be careful."

"How will you do it, Jay?" Williams asked, in the way an adult asks a child a question.

"The rails we're using are coming in by boat, Ben—Bay Company boats. I'll see to it that when the spur gets low on rails, the new shipment gets delayed. Nothing to it."

"I hope you're right, Jay. Now, I want you to find

me about a dozen good men who'll do what I tell them. I've got a dandy idea that'll stop Hays and company for good, but I can't afford to be connected with it, you see. And of course, I can't pull it off myself."

"What have you got in mind?" Calhoun asked.

Williams carefully laid out his plan for using Hays' steamer, the *Manitoba*, and enjoyed Calhoun's childlike astonishment.

"You mean you're really going to use Hays' own boat to bottle him up?" Calhoun said, his eyes wide. "I love it! And you will have the men sink that damned ship when it's over with, won't you?"

"With pleasure, Jay. Now, can you get me the men I need? Jake will run the show up here, but I'll be a long way from the railhead when it happens. As a matter of fact, I expect to pay a visit to Rosie, Tim Wolfe's wife, the night we decide to take the *Manitoba*. She'll give me the best possible alibi, since she works for Hays, and at the same time . . . well, I've been wanting to sample her biscuits, if you catch my meaning."

Calhoun frowned. "You'll have a hard time with her, Ben. I once tried to get her into bed, but she wasn't having any. Told me I could fire her, and Tim as well, but I'd not get into her drawers."

"Is that why you fired them?"

Calhoun laughed. "I can't have the hired help sassing me, Ben—or refusing me, either. Anyway, I wish I hadn't. Tim was a good worker and what can you say about Rosie? She kept the books a lot better than the clerk I've got doin' them now."

You are an idiot, thought Williams as he left. Back in St. Paul, Williams acquainted Jake Bronson with his role in the plan, then sent him to Winnipeg to take charge of the men Calhoun was to give him. The date of the operation would depend on the way the track laying was going on both sides and on the schedule of the *Manitoba*. Williams thought the ideal place for the execution of his plot was a few miles below the Canadian border, where Hays' track would pass within a hundred yards of the river over a small ridge. There was little cover there, only a few trees dotting the terrain.

Back at the State House in St. Paul, the Governor spent time working on legislation that would provide financial aid to any Minnesota-based railroad proposing to open commerce with territories as far west as the Pacific. There was, of course, only one railroad that could qualify to benefit from the bill: the Pacific Northern.

When reporters from various Minnesota newspapers asked the Governor about the recent explosion that had slowed the St. Paul Railroad's track laying along the Red, Williams told them he was "shocked" and that it was "a shame that human life was lost because somebody got careless with explosives over there."

Late that same day he had a caller—Elizabeth Hays. She was, she said, lonely and he had just the medicine for that: he dined with her, then made sweaty, grunting love to her in his bed. He was again astonished at how sensual she was and how passionately and thoroughly she threw herself into their couplings. He swelled with pride when she confessed in an impassioned moment that she had never before achieved such satisfaction with any man.

Early in May Williams got word from the PN railhead that the St. Paul track layers had again forged ahead in the race to the border. He quickly decided that the time had come for him to arrange the fatal stroke to Hays. Within an hour he was on his way to Breckenridge on the St. Paul Railroad. There he sought out Tim Wolfe in the railroad station and asked him casually about the *Manitoba*'s schedule for the next two weeks.

Tim frowned. "You planning on riding the *Manitoba* to Canada?" he asked. Williams always rode Hudson Bay Company boats.

The Governor shrugged and said he might, it was a free country.

Tim reluctantly gave him the *Manitoba*'s schedule, since the information was not at all secret and could be obtained at any of Hays Forwarding's Red River freight stations.

Williams shoved the monthly printed schedule into his coat pocket, barely giving it a glance. "How's our good friend Hays doing, Tim?" he asked, to cover for time.

"Good enough," Tim replied cautiously.

Williams creased his brow. "A pity about the accident at Hays' railhead."

Tim had to look away to hide his disgust. He knew that Williams himself had not directly set off the blasts, yet he had unquestionably caused it. And that made him a murderer!

"Two men were killed, Governor. Do you have any information on who's responsible?"

"Haven't heard a word, Tim. I was in Winnipeg when it happened. I was just as shocked about it as anyone. Well, keep in touch, Tim. I may be your employer again soon."

"You fired me once before, Governor, after you talked me into leaving L.J. to work for you. I did your dirty work, remember?"

"And not very admirably, if I recall, Tim. But

you must know it wasn't I who fired you, but Jay. I don't run his business and he doesn't run mine."

"What're you gonna do if Hays wins the race? He's ahead of your crew again."

Williams remained placid. "The race won't be over until his crew or mine reaches the border. I can assure you, Tim, that mine will be there to greet his!"

"From what I hear, Governor, Hays' crew is a mile or more ahead. Do you have another accident arranged?"

"Now, Tim," Williams popped with just a touch of anger, "I don't do things like that and I would appreciate it if you didn't let your filthy little tongue suggest it."

"So you had nothing to do with trying to bury the *Manitoba*, right?"

"I was in St. Paul, Tim. *You* tried to do the deed, not me."

Williams walked out, leaving Tim to seethe at his condescending attitude. From the railroad station Williams walked down to the docks, where the Hudson Bay Company station once run by Tim Wolfe was located. He sent a wire to Jake Bronson in Winnipeg:

DATE IS JUNE 20 STOP SUBJECT WILL
BE IN WINNIPEG ABOUT SEVEN PM
STOP DON'T FAIL PD END
   BW

Then, a grin on his face, Williams hired a rig and drove north to call on Mrs. Rosie Wolfe.

In St. Paul, a troubled Elizabeth Hays awaited response from the Governor confirming that he would see her tonight; she didn't know he was out of town. The children had been a trial to her even though they had a capable nanny looking after them. But tonight she had to see Ben as badly as an alcoholic needed a drink.

Ben Williams. At first it had been exciting for her to receive the attentions of the Governor. And why not? Ben was not bad looking, and he was certainly the most important man in the state. He was unattached. But best of all, he paid lots of attention to her—so much so that he left her feeling young and giddy. She had never felt more a woman than on that evening of the Governor's Ball.

She had let Williams beguile her, for she had needed it, even though she knew well that Williams was her husband's worst enemy, sworn to wipe L.J. Hays off the Minnesota map. Or perhaps that was the reason she let the Governor woo her; she herself had grown to despise Hays. She already had resolved to enjoy Ben's attentions and love, the flowers and gifts he had sent these last six months. And she simply adored the flattery Ben was forever engaging in, telling her how pretty she was, and how interesting, too. He had even intimated he would marry her if she were free.

Of course, she wasn't free and, being a Catholic, would never be free to marry again, even if she could bring herself to divorce Hays. Still, it was nice that Ben felt the way he did, for it made her feel much less dirty about carrying on the affair.

What an ugly scandal would erupt if L.J. should ever find out she was having an affair with his arch rival! Elizabeth shuddered at the thought. She prayed word would not leak out about it, and had made Ben promise he would never let on about it to anyone.

Where was that messenger from Ben? She had sent a message over to his office hours ago and still had received no reply. She rose from the settee in the Hays' drawing room and walked out into the central hallway to look at herself in the mirror just inside the front door. She was not happy with what she saw. The Governor might think her pretty, but she did not. Aside from what she considered the very plainness of her features, she saw lines in her skin that had never been there before. And she had never taken off the last five pounds of weight she had put on with little Joani. That, too, she found distressing, though it seemed not to bother Ben at all.

The Governor seemed to glory in her. He could never get enough of her, it seemed. And she never believed she would ever enjoy making love as much as she did with Ben. So what that he hated L.J.! It didn't matter, for wasn't she entitled to some enjoyment out of life? If L.J. wanted her to be faithful, why didn't he pay more attention to her?

She made a face at her reflection in the mirror. How, she wondered, was a sinning harlot supposed to look?

That was the very thought in her mind when a messenger knocked at the door. His simple message, the Governor was unable to see her tonight because of business that had taken him out of town.

Moments after the messenger left, Elizabeth Hays lay on her bed, crying.

Two days after the devastating explosions at the St. Paul railhead, Hays' supplies started to arrive—minus rails. They received all the ties and spikes they needed, but no rails. Barely containing his rage, L.J. told Andre and Phil it was what he expected from Williams, and that he was sure Tim Wolfe had given Williams the information necessary for the theft of the rails.

Fortunately, and in no small part due to Hays'

foresight, he had earlier ordered a new shipment of rails even before the last one arrived. They arrived by steamer in St. Paul the very next day. Still, Hays' track layers lost four miles by their forced inactivity.

Andre drove his track layers hard, however, and within two weeks—by the 17th of June—they had again caught and passed their rivals by more than a half mile. There remained less than fourteen miles to go to the border!

Hays could not take pleasure in this, however, because the identity of the man or men who had blown up the locomotive and supplies remained unknown. This, coupled with a visit from a distraught Rosie a few days ago, increased Hays' worry. She was certain, she told him, that Williams was planning some master stroke against him. He had come to the farm when Tim was at work.

"What plan is this? Do you know something for sure?"

"No, but he was so confident about beating you, L.J. He . . . he tried to seduce me, and I played along for a time, trying to get him to say something I could pass along to you. Instead, all I learned was that he was dead sure he was a winner and you'd soon be a loser."

"He tried to make love to you?" Hays was truly disgusted. "First Elizabeth and now you? Did he?"

Rosie shook her head. "I wouldn't have let him, no matter what, L.J., though the children made it easier. He said he'd be back this week—Friday night, the 20th, he said. I'm supposed to make sure the children are bedded down and that Tim won't be home. But don't worry—I'm sure going to make sure Tim's home early that night. I want nothing to do with that slug."

"Thanks for the information, Rosie."

"Oh, and one more thing. Tim said Williams came by the office; it was earlier the same day."

"What the hell did he want?"

"He just wanted the *Manitoba*'s schedule."

"What the hell for?"

"Tim said he didn't know."

"He didn't give it to him, I hope."

"He did, L.J."

"That idiot bastard! I'm telling you, Rosie . . . !"

"Anybody can get that schedule, L.J.! Anywhere in town!"

Hays ran his hands through his hair. He was boiling mad, but he knew he was angry at Williams this time, not Tim. "Did he say anything else?"

"That's all, other than he implied that he could still blackmail Tim. But didn't I say Tim wanted to help?"

"Yes. Thank you, Rosie. You better get on back now."

*Now* what did Williams have planned? Blowing up his steamer? He would tell his crew to be extra sensitive to new passengers over the next several days, and to especially be on the lookout for Williams and Calhoun, though he was sure they'd hire strangers to do their dirty work.

Would he try to sabotage their supplies again, now that he had enough supplies to finish the line? Enough, even, to lay track northward to the Canadian Pacific's spur line, if necessary?—though it looked like the CPRR would reach Pembina right on time, if Tom Short's most recent message could be relied upon.

All the supplies and the work train at the railhead were guarded now by no fewer than three men, the theory being that if three guards were posted, a single traitor couldn't overwhelm the other two—assuming, of course, that there was just one traitor, an assumption Hays hoped was correct. As an extra precaution, however, Hays, Andre and Phil served as extra guards, each one alternating with the others on a sleep shift.

But nothing more happened. Except that on the morning of the 20th, one of the relatively new men turned up missing. His name was Cole Younger.

When Andre and Phil confirmed Younger's disappearance, L.J. asked if they thought he was the killer. Both men shook their heads. "I don't know what to think, L.J.," said Phil. "Younger was a good worker, got along well with everyone. None of his friends thinks he could've had anything to do with the explosions."

Andre's assessment was similar. If Younger was the man they had sought, he had done a wily job of covering up his intentions as well as his actions. Now even more cautious, Hays did not relax the guard, in spite of Younger's disappearance.

When the track layers finished work that day, they were about eight miles from the border, and a full mile ahead of the PN gang. The camp was filled with a quiet sort of confidence, and no one but Hays, Phil, and Andre truly worried about any more snags.

As Hays downed a mug of steaming coffee while sitting on a wagon near the river, he calculated that whatever was going to happen—if Williams had something up his sleeve—would most likely happen tonight. Williams couldn't risk any more time.

When Phil Crabtree suggested that Williams could really wait two-and-a-half more days, Hays disagreed. "No, Ben Williams promised to call back on Rosie Wolfe tonight—the 20th."

"I don't see . . ."

Crabtree stopped when L.J. suddenly snapped his fingers and exclaimed, "Phil, think! Knowing how fast we're working, Williams could easily have predicted our completion date was going to be between the 20th and the 25th. Agreed?"

Crabtree nodded. "So what?"

"So when would be the ideal time for him to stop us cold? A day or two before we're due to reach the border! So, if you wanted to stop someone in their tracks, what would you use?"

"If I knew that, I'd have told you by now. The Army?"

"Close, but they're busy over in the Dakota Territory keeping the Sioux under control. No, Phil, I believe Williams has his eyes on another army—*my* private one."

"What in hell are you talkin' about, L.J.? You don't have any private army."

"How about the *Manitoba*, Phil? The two Gatling guns are still mounted on her top deck."

Crabtree's eyes grew large as the immensity of what L.J. was suggesting reached him. "God!" he exclaimed. "That's why his asking for the schedule bothered you! If he could take control of your ship, uncover the guns and man them, then sail down here . . ."

"Anchor just off the river's edge and hold us completely under his thumb. Exactly, Phil. It's the *only* way guaranteed to stop us—if he can bring it off."

"Can he take the ship? We've got to do something and quick! Where is she now?"

"Somewhere between St. Paul and Winnipeg as far as I know. I've passed word along to the crew to keep their eyes open for explosives and odd characters. But my guess is, if they catch Captain Sam and his crew unawares, the ship's theirs. Look what they did to us! We've got to send another message to Sam quick to expect a takeover. I'm figuring that Williams needs an alibi to keep himself from being implicated, and that's why he'll use Rosie to prove where he was when the *Manitoba* was taken. So I have to believe tonight will be the night. The first thing I've got to do is get to the telegraph key at Glyndon Station and find out from Tim just where the *Manitoba* is right now. Tell Casey to fire up the boiler on 76, Phil. I'll be needing her right away."

As he climbed aboard the caboose, L.J. told Phil to get together with Andre Pelletier and "try to figure out what we can do if I can't warn the ship in time."

One very long hour later Hays arrived at the temporary one-floor station at Glyndon. He found the door locked, for Kenny Steves, his telegrapher, had gone over to the saloon for supper. Steves never ate his supper.

# Chapter 14

As was his custom, Winnipeg Agent Thomas John Short was at the dock when the *Manitoba* eased into the mooring upon returning from Breckenridge. He personally secured the ropes, then hurried on board to greet his good friend Captain Sam Meyer and give him the manifest for the return trip.

Short drank a tall glass of beer with the captain, then watched the crew unload the ship's cargo before walking back down to the Hays Forwarding office only fifty yards away.

He sighed wearily as he wrote "delivered 6/20/75" across the face of the old manifest and tucked it away inside his battered oak desk. Business was good and Short was happier than he'd been in a very long time. Working for Calhoun and the Hudson Bay Company had been the most hateful period of his life. Working for L.J. Hays had been so much better that it was almost like a vacation.

He pulled out his pocket watch and saw he had time to light a cigar before going home to his wife and the four little Shorts to dine and take things easy for the rest of the evening. He had just brought the match up to his cigar when a bell sounded, indicating the telegraph was about to receive a message. Short sighed again, laid the cigar on a metal ashtray, and crossed the room to take down the message. It was a message from L.J. Hays that read:

> TJS: IF *MANITOBA* THERE CMA ORDER IT TO GLYNDON IMMEDIATELY PD DANGER OF SEIZURE BY WILLIAMS AND PN THUGS PD REPEAT CLN TELL CAPTAIN SAM TO UP ANCHORS IMMEDIATELY AND SAIL GLYNDON PD ACKNOWLEDGE THIS MESSAGE END     LJH

Short sent a quick acknowledgment and the telegraph began to chatter immediately thereafter.

IS THAT YOU THOMAS JOHN QUESTION MARK

Short responded: YES PD

IS *MANITOBA* THERE

Short hesitated. If there was indeed a plot afoot against the ship, oughtn't he make certain it *was* Hays on the other end of the telegraph wire? He tapped out:

WHO WISHES TO KNOW

HAYS

WHAT IS YOUR YOUNGEST CHILD'S FIRST NAME

JOANI CMA NOW RESPOND EXCLAMATION POINT

*MANITOBA* REACHED HERE 8 O CLOCK PD REPEAT INSTRUCTIONS PD

MOVE HER OUT DASH NOW EXCLAMATION POINT WILLIAMS MEN AFTER GATLING GUNS PD

ON MY WAY PD WILL WATCH *MANITOBA* ON WAY THEN RETURN

TO CONFIRM PD IF I DO NOT GET BACK WITHIN HALF HOUR SUSPECT I WILL BE UNABLE TO PD END SHORT

Short started to run out of the office, but stopped quickly and returned to his file cabinet to get his old six-shooter and a short, sharp, stiletto. He stuffed the gun into his belt, then raced out without locking the door behind him. He ran up the dock toward the half-darkened silhouette of the *Manitoba*, sweating as he approached the ship, wondering if Hays was right about the attack. The huge steamer seemed no different than she'd been twenty minutes ago when he'd left, though there was no way of telling by just looking.

The engines were shut down, making only the banging sounds always present in cooling boilers. From where he stood, Short could see no one on the main deck where there ought to have been a guard. Still, the deck was shrouded in semidarkness and he supposed the guard might be lurking in it, perhaps smoking.

Cautiously Short stepped onto one of the steamer's two gangplanks and moved across it to the ship. His heart was pounding as he stepped onto the main deck. He stopped for a split second as the boat creaked. He looked around, but there was no one in sight. The hair on his neck seemed alive as he stood uncertainly where he was, listening but hearing precisely nothing. It was so very quiet he knew something had to be wrong. Even at anchor, there were always sounds to be heard around the *Manitoba*. And there were always guards. But not now.

Short moved over to the open stairway curving upward to the steamer's white-railinged passenger deck, which also housed the six boilers and operating engine. At the top of the stairs, he stopped and listened some more, again hearing nothing.

The captain's quarters and office were on the top deck, and so Short climbed the ladder on the port side of the boat and crept down toward Sam Meyer's office. Captain Meyer would be either in his cabin or the office, for he was in the habit of remaining with the ship when she was in port—unless she was to be shut down for two or more days. Most steamer captains had girl friends in Winnipeg, a good town for women, but not so Captain Sam. He was a good family man—like Thomas John—and straight all the way.

Short now stopped dead in his tracks at the sound of voices coming from the Captain's cabin.

"I asked you where the key to those gun houses are, Captain, and I expect you to tell me now!" threatened Jake Bronson.

"You'll have to forgive me, gentlemen," retorted Captain Sam in a calm voice, "but I haven't the faintest idea where those keys are now. We haven't had occasion to . . ."

Crack! The sound of a man's hand striking another's flesh made Short wince. He glanced about him, deciding to hide behind one of the two big, black smokestacks not far away, if he had to.

Again Bronson spoke. "Give me those keys, Captain, or your wife won't recognize you when she sees your body at the undertaker's."

"I honestly don't know," Captain Meyer argued. "Have you looked in the pilothouse? We used to keep them hanging from a nail up there. I just don't . . ."

Crack! "You're lying, you son of a bitch! All right, if you're going to make us hunt for those keys, we might as well kill you now."

Short thought about attacking the men but decided it was too risky, not knowing how many men were with Bronson. He was sure the men wouldn't kill the captain, since navigating the shallow Red River was a tricky proposition at best. They would need him.

The sounds of men climbing the ladder at the end of the boiler deck stirred Short to action and he concealed himself behind the big stack nearby. He watched as three large men, none of whom he recognized, came over the top of the deck and made their way to the captain's cabin.

At Glyndon Station L.J. Hays paced the floor and willed the telegraph key to begin clicking out a message from Short. At the key Ken Steves was clearly nervous and unhappy. And, of course, hungry.

But Hays cared not at all about Steves' hunger. What he cared about was what was happening in Winnipeg, what was happening with Short and the *Manitoba*. It had been nearly an hour since he had communicated with Short. Hays glanced at his pocket watch one more time, then decided he had to assume the worst—that Williams' people not only took Short prisoner, but also had the *Manitoba*—the *Manitoba* and its two Gatling guns!

Hays muttered an oath. If Steves noticed, he said nothing, continuing to sit at the telegraph key as Hays had instructed him to.

"All right, Steves," Hays said now, "I want you to stay right here and wait for a signal from Short or until I send you one from Breckenridge. I'm sorry I spoiled your dinner, but trouble never picks a good time. And I got more trouble right now than you'll ever dream of having!"

It was nine-thirty when Hays reached the Breckenridge Station. When he walked in the door, Tim

Wolfe jumped like a scared rabbit. "L.J.!" Tim cried none too happily. "What . . . I hadn't expected . . ."

"Telegraph Ken at Glyndon," Hays interrupted sourly, "and let him know I'm here."

Tim, grateful for the chance to turn away, did so and quickly tapped out the message on his telegraph key. He wondered how long Hays would stay—and how angry he still was. Rosie had been truthful about Hays' reaction when he'd asked her how L.J. had taken the news about his helping Williams.

As he completed the message, Tim was sure Hays remained in a rage—the man's eyes were two gleaming black daggers, his mouth below his mustache as stern as Tim had ever seen it. Tim met the eyes only briefly, before dropping his. "Any other messages?" he asked.

Hays shook his head. "Do you have a horse or carriage here?" he asked. "I need to reach the marshal."

"I've got a horse out back. Want me to go over and roust the marshal for you?"

"Yes, Tim. Ask him to come back here right now. There's trouble brewing at the railhead . . . as I'm sure you're aware," Hays added softly.

Tim frowned as he stood up. "What kind of trouble?" he asked sincerely.

L.J. looked away, a scowl on his face. "Trouble trouble," he growled. "Just get the marshal."

Still Tim hesitated. He forced his eyes up to Hays' and moistened his suddenly dry lips. "Listen, L.J.," he started in a low voice, "you got reasons—good ones— not to trust me. I guess even to hate me. I know Rosie told you about . . . what I've done. And I know she told you how sorry I am for it. I am! I really meant what I told her about not lettin' the Governor or Calhoun use me anymore."

"Rosie said you were going to find out what Williams was planning, Tim. So what have you found out?"

Tim swallowed hard, but continued to meet Hays' eyes. "Nothing, L.J. I wish . . ."

"Nothing more about my wife?" Hays spit out, his voice truly nasty.

Tim blinked. "Oh! She told you about that? Gosh, L.J., I'm sorry. That Williams is a damn skunk! Any man who'd fool around with another man's wife—he ought to be tarred and feathered!"

Hays turned away to hide the slight touch of red that came to his face. "Get the marshal, Tim. Your friend has arranged to capture the *Manitoba* and use her Gatlings at our railhead. At least that's my guess. Can you confirm that?"

Tim's eyes widened. "The *Manitoba*? Christ! So that's why he wanted her schedule! You know, he was in here a couple of weeks ago . . ."

"I know, Tim," L.J. interrupted, still keeping his back to Tim.

"I'll go get the marshal," Tim blurted, and was out the door.

At the railhead, Phil Crabtree and Andre Pelletier spent the hours following Hays' departure for Glyndon planning countermeasures in the event L.J. did not reach the *Manitoba* in time to prevent her takeover.

"If L.J. doesn't head them off," Phil told Andre, "we've lost. Even an Army can't long survive a Gatling attack."

"If I were not on the wagon, I would need a drink right now at the thought." Andre spoke mirthlessly.

Crabtree pulled a flask from his pocket, uncorked it and took a long draught. "I'll drink to that, Andre, if you'll forgive me."

Pelletier nodded. "I don't blame you. Do you think we might bushwhack the *Manitoba*? We have enough men and a kind of advantage. We could place a group of men beside the river where they can await the *Manitoba*. Once the ship moves into shore here, the men could swim out and board her, then attack the gunners."

Crabtree just looked at Andre, but took another swig from his bottle. "First off, my friend, look up there." He pointed to a sliver of a moon.

Andre nodded. "Even so," he said, "if the enemy believes he will surprise *us*, he will not be expecting a counterattack."

"Do you think your men are willing to risk their lives in the dark, unable to see, not knowing what to expect?"

"This line is as much theirs as yours. Come, let us go talk to them."

Soon the whole camp was assembled and listening as Andre launched an impassioned plea for volunteers to attack and take the *Manitoba* if it was in enemy hands. After he had spoken, the track layers, roadbed levelers, and railroad tiemen broke off into small groups to think quietly over what he'd said. Andre had touched their emotions when he asked the men if they were willing to let the "bastards of the Pacific Northern" steal their bonuses "without a fight."

Shorty, all six-feet six inches of him, was the first to come forward. Andre and Phil placed him in charge of the volunteers, then suggested a plan of action centering around the need to capture the Gatling guns. Andre would kick off the plan by trying to get on board the ship upriver. All the men seemed pleased and were willing to go along with this—all but one. Phil Crabtree was aghast when Andre outlined his plan—to paddle upriver, pretend to be drunk when the steamer came into view, and try to get picked up.

"You're insane, Andre!" he shouted. "If they figure out who you are, you'll be killed!"

"I am in Mr. Hays' debt, Phil," Andre argued, his dark eyes flashing with pride. "If I can help the men, then I will be happy. If not . . . then I shall miss all the fun."

"Fun? Well, I suppose you could call it that, if you're a former keeper of the guillotine or a depraved medieval torturer!"

"What I am is a former drunk, Mr. Crabtree. I must do what I can for the man who has helped me become once more a man. Say no more. I am going." He grinned. "Now, if you don't mind, I will sample your flask. I will need it if I am to be once again a drunk."

Along with the flask, Phil wanted to give the man a six-gun as well, but Andre refused it. "It will do me no good, for I expect to have to fall drunkenly into the river before I can be properly rescued. A wet gun is of no value."

Crabtree watched dolefully as Andre took a canoe into the river and headed north. That, he thought, was a brave man, regardless of his drinking history.

Andre rowed until he felt his arms would soon fall off. A couple of miles or so north of the railhead he shipped his oars, tied both of them together and dropped them overboard. Then he uncorked Crabtree's flask and drenched himself with it—his face, his neck, his arms, his clothes, every part of him. When he had but a single swallow left in the bottle, he brought it to his lips and poured it into his mouth. Closing his eyes, he swished the whiskey around, let but a trickle into his throat, then spat out the rest over the side. He then crossed himself and thanked God for his precious little girl, who had helped him throw off the chains forged by old John Barleycorn.

Now Andre scanned the horizon northward, looking for a sign of the *Manitoba*. Heading north had been a calculated risk for Andre, since he could not be certain the steamer was north of the Canadian border. But he had a vague recollection of a boat passing on the river yesterday afternoon and he suspected it could well have been the *Manitoba*. If it was not . . . he could do little about it now.

Around eleven o'clock he heard dim noises far upstream. A short time later the twin gaslights attached to the *Manitoba*'s superstructure came into view. Andre was no expert on steamships, but he knew the *Manitoba* was the biggest steamer on the Red. The boat coming toward him was quite large. He began to sing in a loud, drunken voice—in French. In one hand he held his empty flask of whiskey and as he sang, he occasionally brought the flask to his mouth. The whole time, he kept his eyes on the ship, and when it veered toward him, his heart skipped into his mouth. Were they coming to pick him up—or run him down?

The *Manitoba* did neither, closing to within twenty yards as it passed. Andre heard vague voices from the ship as it slid by, its keel barely four feet out of the water. As it moved past, Andre shifted his weight to the left and fell out of the little boat, then began screaming as if in terror.

"Halp! I be drowning!" he yelled. "I no can swim! Please, somebody save me!"

Andre continued to holler, but the steamer moved on, its speed unabated. He had all but given up when he suddenly realized the *Manitoba* had slowed and was lying almost dead in the water. He allowed himself to go under again, as if drowning, then surfaced and began to yell louder.

In only a minute a small boat from the steamer reached him, just as he slipped under for what he wanted to look like the last time. A man dived in from the boat and grabbed him by the shirt. He came up sputtering, held firmly in the grip of the swimmer.

For effect, Andre renewed his struggles and his drunken cries and very nearly succeeded in drowning both he and his would-be rescuer. He wanted the man to do exactly what he did—slam a fist into his jaw to quiet him. He had not counted on the force with which the man struck him, however, and instead of feigning unconsciousness, he actually found himself going under.

When he awoke, Pelletier found himself lying on his stomach on the main deck of the *Manitoba*. The man who had sent him to dreamland was nowhere to be seen—nor was anyone else. He wondered if, as he had counted on, the captain of the steamer had forced the vessel's conquerors to pick him up. But Andre was destined never to know that Captain Sam Meyer had deliberately steered toward the drunk in the river, then told his guards they could navigate the rest of the way themselves if they didn't save him.

In the dim light of the moon, Andre studied his surroundings—the stairway leading up to the boiler deck, the flagpole at the end of the foredeck, the two gangplanks now raised high in the air, the railing and porch looking down over the stairway, the top deck above it.

As his eyes grew accustomed to the semidarkness, he saw several men on the far side of the stairway, not more than twenty feet away. Fortunately they could see him no better than he could see them, so they couldn't know he had regained consciousness.

Andre had no idea that he had an ally already on board the vessel. Thomas John Short was hiding in a small closet—a weapons locker, actually—two doors down from the captain's cabin on the top deck. Because he was the Winnipeg freight agent, Short carried a key to almost every door on the *Manitoba*. He guessed no one had heard the jangle of his keys, which he tried to suppress as much as possible, when he let himself into the locker. Still, he kept his hand on the six-gun holstered in his belt. Suddenly finding himself in this unprecedented situation, he was sure he could force himself to use his gun, despite his peaceful nature. He also thought that to contest an armed force of more than a dozen would be suicide. He decided to mark time for a while and await an opportune moment to make his presence felt.

South of Glyndon, the work train containing L.J. Hays was traveling north at its top speed—twenty-five miles an hour—while the railroad boss sat looking out the window of the caboose into the darkness, despondent and beset with worries. It was just before eleven o'clock and he was alone.

Marshal Ray Burgess was away and so Hays could not bring the law back to the railhead. It was, he reflected, a loss, but no great one, for he knew Williams' thugs held no regard for the law. And the marshal's talk would have had little effect on the *Manitoba*'s deadly pair of Gatlings. What could he or his men do against those awesome weapons? Hays wondered, should he have had the guns dismantled when it looked like the *Manitoba* would not need them? Even as Hays asked himself that question, he knew the answer. He hadn't dared dispose of the guns, for their value lay in just having them. Remove them and the deterrent would be gone—and that would be an open invitation to trouble. His thoughts turned to Tim Wolfe, and to Rosie, who was supposed to have a visitor tonight. How would Tim like it when he found the Governor with *his* wife? Hays frowned. Rosie had assured him she would not face Williams alone, yet Tim had said nothing of going home early. Had Rosie forgotten to tell him of Williams' intentions? Or had she purposely not done so out of fear that Tim might get hurt? Not so much physically, but Williams could make the rest of Tim's life miserable.

Hays wondered if he was being too harsh on Tim. The big Irishman could not have been more unhappy when he realized he had unwittingly given Williams a new weapon when he gave the Governor the *Manitoba*'s schedule. And Tim seemed genuinely contrite over his participation in Williams' previous plot against the steamer. Tim had been a good friend for years—until the Governor had tempted him with Rosie Simonds and wooed him over to the Hudson Bay Company of Jay Calhoun. It had been Tim who defended L.J. from outlaws back in '57 and perhaps saved his life. And Tim who had agreed years ago to let L.J. build them a house on the land his father had left him. As far as the fling with Tim's wife was concerned . . . What was past was past, Hays told himself. He must bury the past, both the good and the bad, for it counted neither for nor against him now. What Tim had done for him was ancient history—and so, too, was what Tim had done against him, willingly or not.

When this was all over, Hays now promised himself, he would make up with Tim, for his own sake as much as the Irishman's. The hatred he had been feeling toward Tim was eating him up and left L.J. disgusted as much with himself as with Tim. Friends were not easy to come by and Tim had been a good one. Perhaps he could be one again.

Now Bagshaw, the brakeman, interrupted his thoughts with a mug of coffee he had brewed on the coal stove in the center of the caboose.

"Thanks, Jim," Hays said. "It looks like a long night ahead."

A long, long night.

Phil Crabtree awaited him when the train pulled in at the railhead. L.J. listened as Phil quickly outlined Andre's plan to put a team of St. Paulers aboard the *Manitoba* from the river.

"That crazy Canadian!" Hays exclaimed. "He hasn't been hitting the bottle, has he?"

Crabtree shook his head. "Maybe if he'd had a drink or two he wouldn't have gone. Anyway, he raised a dozen volunteers to wait north of here for the ship to show up. They're at the river's edge waiting now."

Hays frowned. "They're going to try to board her?"

"And take the Gatling guns. It's dangerous, but the alternative is to sit still and let Williams herd us like cattle."

"Agreed. Say, why don't we try to lay some track away from the river. We probably couldn't get far enough to be completely out of range, but it might make things more difficult for Williams' thugs. What do you think?"

"I thought of it an hour ago, L.J. Figured it would keep the men's minds off what was happening, too, so I got them started. Look over there." Phil waved toward the former end of the line and Hays now saw that a section of track was already in place leading well off to the right away from the river. Thus far they had laid only about two hundred yards of rail, but they were picking up speed.

Their work, however, was soon to stop, for now came a yell from the men Crabtree had posted as lookouts. The *Manitoba* was in sight!

Hays hustled over to the locomotive, which was parked barely fifty yards east of the river, and watched as his own big steamer, looking like a gigantic white whale floating on top of the water, approached.

A knot of nausea tightened in his stomach as a sense of violation came over him. These filthy animals had control of his ship! He thought back to when the *Manitoba* was only a half-finished hull of a ship, then a burned-out hulk of a finished one. A wave of nostalgia took him at the memory of the *Manitoba*'s launching day, when the ship slid down the temporary track and slipped into the Red River with a gentle splash. It had been the proudest moment of his life.

Yet he realized he would now blow her out of the water, if necessary, to save his precious railroad and the 4-4-0's that would work for him. His eyes went from the chunky red-and-white form of the steamer closing in rapidly to the huge, sleek black-and-red beauty of the locomotive next to him. With black tender, three brown-and-white freight cars off on a siding, flatcars, sleeping cars and caboose, a train was a stirring sight, he thought. It could travel so far, accomplish so much!

Hays' scalp prickled and he blinked back the moisture that began to form in the corners of his eyes. He had loved his steamers—all of them—but especially the *Resurrection*, now owned and operated by Josh Laurence, and the *Manitoba*, for which Hays held the warmest spot in his heart.

But L.J. had not fully realized what he had dedicated his whole life to. He had yet to build his empire. He had success with his steamers, but he *knew* his goal lay in the railroad. The Reverend had always said, "Sentiment has no place in success; nostalgia impedes progress." He tried to remember that always, ever since he was a child. Although he didn't analyze the thought, it did sometimes occur to him that perhaps he was so obsessed with making something important of his life that he left no room for making something important with people—with women. With his wife. But he didn't dwell on this, he had made a choice to make his work the focus of his life, just as he was sure Vanderbilt had done, and John Jacob Astor, and Whitney —anyone who had built an empire!

The Reverend had said it in one of his lessons: "Cut you an empire out of this cruel, cruel world. The world has no room for average men; just men who are *great*. Spend your time, your strengths, your love to build that empire. Pleasures of the senses are but temporal; don't dally with sensual satiation. But an *empire*, built by the strength of your hands and the sweat of your brow, lasts forever, long after we are gone. *Work*—pure, unadulterated, heavenly work—is the key to a perfect life. Make it the meaning in your life, for man's life on this Earth is all too brief."

Hays would not give up now. If necessary he would sacrifice his steamer for the empire. He watched the *Manitoba* slow and nose closer to shore. Hays said a mental prayer, his volunteer assault force was at the river's edge no more than twenty yards from the ship's new path!

Suddenly the steamer's shrill whistle filled the air. Captain Sam, he thought, had no doubt sounded the whistle to warn him. A good man, Captain Sam Meyer, a good man indeed. Hays glanced over toward his

## Railroad King

track layers and saw that they still were working. L.J. had instructed Phil to keep them at it as long as possible.

Because of the spring runoff, the Red was high and the *Manitoba* was able to close to within fifty yards of the railhead—close enough that Hays, from where he stood next to the locomotive, could see the two Gatling guns at the opposite ends of the ship, both manned by two of the insurgents.

Now a man's voice came from the pilothouse, a boxlike structure squarely amidships, with windows all around. Inside at the ship's wheel was Captain Sam Meyer, along with his two guards, one of whom was Jake Bronson.

"Call off the track layers, Hays!" Jake yelled. "Or I'll order my Gatlings to give 'em a permanent layoff!"

"What do you want?" L.J. yelled back, stalling for time. He wondered who the other man was.

"I want the track laying stopped—and now!" Suddenly the quiet of the night was shattered by the metallic sound of the rotating muzzles of the forward Gatling.

The track layers dived to the ground as lead from the Gatling zinged overhead.

"Next time we'll shoot a bit lower, Hays, so you better start following orders!"

The swimmers would be in the water by now, Hays thought, and could take advantage of any diversion he could create. So he left the protection of the locomotive and crossed the track to the river, to stand directly in front of the *Manitoba*.

"Well, look who's here!" called out Bronson. "If it ain't the boss of the whole bloomin' railroad!"

Hays said nothing as he studied the situation and awaited Bronson's next remark, order or whatever. The

*Manitoba* lay anchored broadside to the railhead, her prow pointed south, her stern in the north. A half-dozen men with rifles and hand guns were stationed on the inland side of the vessel's main deck: two stood in the prow, just below the Hays Forwarding Company pennant, which still flew from the stanchion there, the other four near the cargo hold. There were guards all along the inland side of the top deck, their rifles clearly visible over the white picket railing. Several men stood near the Gatling housing on the prow, but only the two gunners attended the stern Gatling. It was an imposing array and Hays had huge, huge doubts about the safety of his attacking force. He wished he could see the other side of the ship, for his volunteers hoped to board it from there.

"Where's the Governor, Jake?" Hays called out, throwing caution to the wind. He had to concentrate Bronson's attention on him, not his ship or his men.

There was a heavy silence and then Bronson answered, "Stow it, Hays, or I'll have you cut to little pieces with your own guns."

"Piracy is a serious offense, Jake, even on a river. When they catch you, you'll likely be sent over to that new federal prison in Kansas—Leavenworth, they call it. I hear it's not a very nice place to be, and I doubt Ben's going to like his new Governor's mansion."

"In one more minute I'm going to shut you up permanently, boy! I swear I will!"

Clearly Bronson was tottering on the edge of his control, so Hays tried to calm him. "I won't say another word if you want, Jake, but I have to tell you the marshal from Breckenridge is on his way over here with a posse. You ready to fire those guns at a marshal?"

"You can't buffalo me, Hays. We only just got

here a few minutes ago. There's no way you could have known enough to go lookin' for a marshal."

"I guess you're right, Jake. I couldn't have guessed you were going to steal the *Manitoba* and come here. Just like I have no way of knowing where your uncle is right now—over at Tim Wolfe's farm in Breckenridge trying to use Rosie Wolfe as an alibi."

Bronson now fell silent, and Hays was alert, ready to jump if there was any telltale movement on the part of the two Gatling crews.

"Where's the captain?" Hays asked, "and the crew?"

"None of your damn business!" retorted Bronson.

Hays, noting Bronson's increasing agitation, tried another tack. "Why don't we parley, Jake? Let me come aboard and talk things over."

"We got nothing to discuss," came Bronson's reply.

"Then we can socialize, Jake. I know where Captain Sam hides his liquor supply and . . ."

"Hays, you are daft!"

"I've been called worse. Look, if you won't let me come on board, why don't you come over here. Right where I am. Your gunners can cover us, so I can't trick you. There are things you should know and I know you'll benefit from learning them."

"I know all I need to know right now, Hays. I know you're in trouble and your railroad ain't gonna be yours much longer. I know we can keep you here for a week if we have to. I know you never did find out who blew up your supplies."

"Do you know, Jake?" Hays said.

Bronson laughed, pleased that he now had the advantage. "I know all I need to know, you bastard!"

"Did Ben happen to tell you about the party he's

planning for you when you sail my boat back to Breckenridge?"

Bronson grew silent again. "What in hell are you talkin' about?"

Hays chuckled. "The Governor's gonna shower you with thanks when you dock, Jake—the kind of thanks you can't survive: hot lead. He's going to have you killed, Jake. You and all of your men, but especially you, because he can't afford to leave you alive to point a finger at him."

Andre Pelletier and Thomas John Short had different reactions to the long-range conversation between Hays and Bronson. Andre recognized Hays' tactics for what they were, for he knew his track-layer volunteers would be in the water by now and soon try to board the *Manitoba*. As for Short, an eternal optimist, he hoped that Hays' request for a parley would lead Bronson into surrendering.

Andre now decided Bronson would be his objective. If he could neutralize the Governor's nephew, maybe his thugs would throw down their weapons.

For several minutes Andre had been watching a large cloud formation move toward the moon. When it arrived, to bring total darkness for a short time, he planned to move up the staircase little more than ten feet away. Just then, one of the *Manitoba*'s guards walked over to him, nudged him with his foot, then left when Andre showed no sign of life.

Now the clouds arrived and quickly blanketed the main deck. Hays and Bronson continued to talk. Andre sprang to his feet, made the stairway in three light, flying steps, and noiselessly raced up to the forward boiler deck. He paused there long enough to make out the one guard at the railing on the inland side, then moved silently to the ladder up to the top deck. He took the rungs carefully, then stopped short of the top, to peer over it at the group of hired guns clustered around the Gatling.

He was just about to climb over and try to reach the ladder up to the pilothouse when the clouds passed and the ship was again lighted by pale moonlight. Directly in front of Andre, toward the rear of the ship, were its two black fire stacks, where hot cinders from the fires heating the ship's six boilers were vented high in the air. Some twenty feet past the stacks was the pilothouse. On the forward end of the deck and behind Andre was the Gatling and its attendants, all of them looking away from Andre, towards Hays, a solitary figure on the bank.

Andre could go no farther, for Bronson could not fail to notice him were he to race down the deck to the pilothouse ladder. And if he did, it would take but a moment for the crew on the Gatling to swing around to face him.

He shot a look upward and cursed as he saw that the sky now was cloudless. He decided to wait for the arrival of his men.

In his refuge Short was wondering if he could slip out of the locker, mount the pilothouse ladder and get inside before one of the pirates used him for target practice. Like Andre, he knew if he could take the group's leader prisoner, the chances of ending the engagement would become real.

But he was not agile, not quick. He was clumsy. Chances are, he thought grimly, that he wouldn't take two steps out of the locker before they would be all over him. And then he would be no good to anyone. Perhaps he should wait. Perhaps the leader would leave the pilothouse. Then Short could take him. In the meantime, he should try to get a better idea of what was going on, he thought, and so eased open the door to the locker and looked outside.

# Chapter 15

Rosie Wolfe sat in a rocker by an open window, sipping a cup of tea, keeping an eye out for the Governor. She had long ago put her children and Danielle Pelletier to bed.

Until an hour ago, she was sure that the Governor would keep his appointment with her. Now she wasn't so sure, it was so late. Although she had promised L.J. she would have Tim come home early this night, she decided not to mention tonight's little make-believe tryst to him. She was sure Tim would not have stood for it. Instead, she decided that she should just keep Ben here for as long as possible and pump him for as much information as possible, and hope that Tim wandered home while Ben was still with her. Now, it seemed likely that Tim might come home any time and foil her plan completely.

She had decided to put her six-shooter within easy reach in a drawer in her dresser—just in case the Governor got a little rough. Tim had bought the gun for her when they first moved out to the farm.

"No tellin' who's liable to show up out here," Tim had told her when he handed her the gift-wrapped package. "We're rid of most of the Indians now, but who knows if a couple of bucks from the Dakota Territory might get drunk and come wandering back here looking for some great-looking woman like you." Not put off by guns at all, Rosie had quickly learned to load and fire the pistol.

Her thoughts were interrupted when she heard a buggy pull up outside. It could only mean that Ben Williams had arrived.

She ran into her and Tim's first-floor bedroom and glanced at herself in the mirror over the dresser. Then she opened the drawer to double check her six-gun. She hoped she would not need it, not even have to *show* it—but it was a good idea to be prepared just in case.

Williams, as always impeccably dressed in a business suit, took off his top hat and held it over his heart at the sight of Rosie. "Well, dear lady," he greeted, "here I am, as I promised. May I come in?"

"You may, Governor," she replied. She checked the yard before shutting the door behind him. "I was beginning to think you might not come." She followed him into the small living room.

He turned back to her and smiled wryly. "You look as tasty as buckwheat cakes in the morning, Rosie," he purred, his eyes on the bodice of her plain black dress.

"I'm a lot tougher than that to chew, Governor," she warned with a half smile. "And so is L.J. Hays. I believe he's almost finished . . . can practically spit to the border."

Her statement, designed to rouse the Governor, didn't. In fact, Williams' good humor improved instantly. "So can I, Rosie," he chortled. He moved closer and tried to wrap an arm around her, but she backed away.

"I hear L.J.'s a half mile ahead of you, Ben. And Tim says you can't make it up."

Again Williams closed in on her. Dropping his hat to the settee, he backed her against the side wall. She edged sideways to get away but he moved with her. "Tim's dead wrong," the Governor breathed, his mouth darting to her neck. "By noon tomorrow, Hays and his damnable railroad will be finished."

Now Williams suddenly seized her arms and twisted them behind her back. Holding them in place with one big hand, he slowly brought the other around to her ample breast.

Rosie, with a huge effort of will, managed to smile as she endured his touch. She even let him kiss her. When she seemed to be warming to him, Williams released her arms. Then he suddenly swept her off her feet and carried her straight into her bedroom across the hall. There he fell on the bed with her, his hands busily exploring her intimate places, his mouth trying to do likewise.

Frantically she tried to push him away, but could not. Williams was fumbling with the ties securing her bodice.

"Ben," she said in a low voice, her eyes closed, "I want to do it standing up, so you can *really* enjoy seeing it."

He stared at her for a moment, then grinned widely. "Take 'em off slow, Rosie honey," he said, releasing her.

She kissed him lingeringly, hating every moment of it, but knowing it was necessary for her charade. Now she slowly rose from the bed. The Governor's eyes watched her every step as she backed toward her dresser, at the same time loosening the ties that held her dress together.

Then she turned coyly to the dresser, pulled open the drawer, then leveled the six-gun at his belly, its hammer cocked in firing position.

Williams blinked dumbly, dismay sweeping over his face.

"What's the matter, Governor," she sneered, "where's all the pretty words now?"

"What do you think you're doing?"

"How does it feel to be caught with your pants down? To be tricked, threatened with your life?"

"Now, Rosie," Williams blurted, struggling to get to his feet while keeping his eyes glued to Rosie's gun, "you wouldn't kill a man in cold blood—you know you can't. It isn't like you. And especially me, the Governor. Be reasonable, Rosie." He moved a step closer to her.

"Stay right where you are, Ben, or I'll let all the air out of you with a single whoosh! I know how to use this six-gun good enough to shoot off your ear lobes. Want me to show you—for starters?" She grinned and raised the gun. "Or maybe you'd like to take your trousers back down and I'll fire away at something much more valuable to you." She lowered the pistol to his groin.

"By God, I believe you would. You . . . you harlot!"

"That will be enough of the name calling, Ben. So tell me how you know Hays won't be beating you to Pembina," she threatened, "or you *will* be sorry."

Williams' tongue snaked out to moisten his dry lips, his eyes still on Rosie and her gun. Then his eyes moved left—to the doorway. He nodded in that direction and said, "Who's that little tyke?"

Rosie was not a gunfighter. She looked to the

doorway, and that was just the advantage Williams needed. He hurled himself across the floor like a big cat, knocking the gun from her grasp, then struck her head with his balled fist. She collapsed, unconscious.

When she awoke a few minutes later, Rosie found Governor Williams tying her to the four-poster bed—her wrists tied to the bedposts at the top, her ankles to those at the bottom. But not only was she tied—she was naked as well.

She could taste a dab of blood at the corner of her mouth, but she was otherwise not seriously hurt. Not yet.

Rosie groaned as she tugged at her own garments that bound her. "My God! You beast!"

"Beautiful," Williams declared as he pinched a rosy nipple. "I'm so glad you decided to cooperate."

"You rotten . . ." She shut her eyes tight as Williams opened his belt and dropped his pants to the floor.

"And now, little lady, you are about to be had by the number one man in all of Minnesota, so cry out in delight!" With that he fell upon her and, without preliminary, forced himself into her.

The pain was horrible, but Rosie gritted her teeth and bore it. She would not give him the satisfaction of a cry.

"Your friend Hays right now . . . is just as helpless as you are, love. I'm screwing him as well as you . . . but in a different way."

He continued to thrust hard, burying his rigid male organ deep inside her. He then gave a deep-throated villainous chuckle. "Hays' very own ship is holding him prisoner right now—with those marvelous guns of his. What do they call them again—Gatlings?"

The Governor pounded away with renewed fury, feeling like he was conquering the whole world!

Williams did not hear the noise made by an interloper in the room, not until she had picked up Rosie's gun and, with two hands, leveled it at his back, saying, "You'd better stop that right now, mister, or I'm going to pull this trigger."

Tim Wolfe was miserable after L.J. left Breckenridge to ride back to the railhead. And he had not a drop of whiskey to ease the pain he was feeling—pain caused not by L.J., but by Ben Williams. Were it not for the Governor, he and L.J. would still be best friends. Tim's big hands curled into fists at the thought of Williams. He cursed and kicked futilely at the coal stove near the window. If only there was something he could do to help L.J. He wanted to; he had to!

Finally he sat down at the desk and stared at the silent telegraph set. It was just midnight—quitting time—but because of the gravity of the situation, Tim decided to stay on for just a few minutes longer in case some late urgent message came through.

Two minutes later came the sound of the telegraph bell. Tim jumped; he was thinking of a double whiskey at the tavern.

He picked up a pencil and began recording the message. It was from Winnipeg and in a strange hand. (Every telegrapher had a "signature" created by the manner and speed at which he sent his dots and dashes.) Tim jotted down:

LJ HAYS:
*MANITOBA* PIRATED FROM BERTH HERE EARLY THIS EVENING PD TJ SHORT MISSING PD MOST OF CREW MAROONED HERE PD WHAT

TO DO QUESTION MARK PLEASE RESPOND SOONEST PD END
/S/ ANDREWS

Tim stared at the message. So Hays had been right—Williams' people had seized the *Manitoba*!

But now he clicked his own key and sent:

WHO THE HELL ARE YOU QUESTION MARK
/S/ T. WOLFE

The response was immediate.

ANDREWS DASH PURSER OF *MANITOBA* PD CAN YOU INFORM HAYS QUESTION MARK GET INSTRUCTIONS QUESTION MARK

Tim sent back:

WILL TRY PD STAND FAST PD WILL GET BACK TO YOU AS SOON AS POSSIBLE PD END

Tim messaged St. Paul's station, where two 4-4-0 locomotives were berthed. He outlined the situation and ordered one to meet him at the Glyndon Station with men, guns and ammunition.

WE MAY BE AT WAR WITH THE PACIFIC NORTHERN

Tim concluded.

Then Tim locked up the station and rode to his farm, situated halfway to Glyndon. He would tell Rosie what had happened and where he was going, pick up his new hunting rifle and go on to Glyndon to meet the others. This time, he thought with satisfaction as he spurred his horse onward, he was on the right side!

He reined up when he saw the buggy parked outside his house. He didn't place it, wondering who might be paying a midnight visit to Rosie. Tim dismounted and walked the horse to the porch railing. He listened for sounds from within, but heard none. That, he thought, was also strange, for if Rosie had guests, surely they would be gabbing.

He started up the porch steps, but changed his mind and walked silently through the lush grass to the side of the house. He reached their bedroom window, which was covered with a thin cotton curtain, and stared inside.

Could he believe what he was seeing? He shook his head and rubbed his eyes, but the scene inside remained the same: Rosie, on the bed, tied and naked; on top of her, Governor Ben Williams, naked from the waist down looking to the side, where young Danielle stood, holding Rosie's big six-shooter in her little hands, pointing it straight at Ben's buttocks. The most bizarre scene Tim had ever seen in his life. Pulling himself away, Tim raced around the house, taking the four steps up to the porch in a single leap, reaching the bedroom in three additional running strides.

He took the heavy pistol from Danielle's trembling hands and pointed it at Williams' head.

"You son of a bitch!" Tim gritted through clenched teeth, a murderous look on his face.

"Tim, please take Danielle out, then untie me," Rosie pleaded through her tears. Tim didn't move.

"Tim! Please!" Rosie begged him.

"Go, Danielle," Tim blurted, "up to your room. Now!"

The little girl fled.

Williams remained where he had been when Tim entered the room—frozen in place on top of Rosie.

"Tim!" gasped Rosie. "Make him untie me—now!"

"I'll do it, Rosie. But first, I've got to settle up with the Governor." He advanced on Williams, whose eyes were glued to the gleaming barrel of the gun.

"Don't . . . don't be a fool, man!" Williams pleaded. "You kill me and they'll hang you from the nearest tree!"

Tim grabbed Ben around the throat and slowly lifted him off Rosie and to his feet. "Who, Governor? Who is there in this territory—or state—who would hang a man for killing the skunk who raped his woman? Nobody, that's who! And it's going to give me pleasure!"

"No, Tim! Damnit . . . for Christ's sake, would you please untie me right now?"

Tim blinked, then obeyed. "Untie her, Governor. Now!"

When she was free and had her robe on, she held the gun while Tim tied up the Governor. Then she told Tim all about Williams' plan—and the idea she had. "Take Williams over to the railhead, Tim, and maybe L.J. can use him to get whoever's pirated the *Manitoba*."

Tim was torn. One side of him wanted to dispatch Williams to his maker, for the Governor was the cause of all his troubles. But he recognized that what Rosie said was true—that Williams could be a valuable hostage and perhaps thwart the *Manitoba*'s new masters. Tim had sworn to help Hays.

"All right, Rosie," he finally agreed. "I'll take him to the railhead—though I'd rather cut out the bastard's black heart!"

He hoisted the trussed-up Williams as if he were a sack of potatoes, roughly threw him over his shoulder, and tossed him unceremoniously into the back of his buckboard. Moments later they were heading north to Glyndon to meet the train from St. Paul.

Shorty led the group of St. Paulers up to the outland side of the *Manitoba*, found no guards posted and climbed up on deck. Expecting no opposition at the railhead until he had announced himself, Jake Bronson had not bothered to post guards on the river side.

Shorty motioned for silence and the twelve dripping men stood in place, listening to the continuing long-range conversation between Bronson and Hays.

Now they split up with half of Shorty's men moving toward the ladders to the top deck, the others scaling the poles at midships. As they reached the top deck, Shorty heard Bronson's response to Hays' last declaration, "You'll not be tricking me, Hays. I'm as smart as you so don't think I'll believe that malarkey about a trap at Breckenridge—or any other place."

"Suit yourself, Jake, but you're not being smart at all. Maybe you think blood is thicker than water and the Governor'll protect you, but I can tell you your blood will spill nice and easy after you dock. Williams can't afford to have you alive to talk about him. Not you and not the rest of your men."

"You keep on talkin' like that and I'm goin' to have my men open up with this here toy of yours and fill you full of red-hot lead!"

Hays again tried to soothe Bronson's growing anger. "Come down and parley, Jake."

Suddenly the sounds of scuffling came from all over the ship—voices, curses, the sound of flesh striking flesh. Hays strained to see what was happening at both ends of the top deck, where the Gatlings were stationed—where Shorty's men and Andre Pelletier had leaped into action.

On the stern, Shorty's five brawny track layers made short work of the two Gatling gunners. The first went down from a fist filled with a railroad spike. The second backed away and begged for mercy before he was knocked over the side by a second St. Paul railroad man.

But Shorty and Andre were not as lucky up front. The first sounds from the stern came just as they were rushing the men at the prow Gatling and drew the attention of the gunners, who swung the weapon around squarely in the faces of their attackers.

Hearing the commotion outside, Thomas John Short left the safety of the locker and began climbing the ladder to the pilothouse, intent on taking the leader prisoner. He got only halfway up before Bronson caught him and knocked him to the deck with a quick downward swipe of the butt end of his six-gun.

Meanwhile, gleeful at having taken their objective and unaware that the party up front had failed, the railroaders commanding the stern gun fired off a few rounds into the air to mark their achievement.

Moments later, however, they realized they had taken only half the boat and began prying loose the bolts holding their two-wheeled Gatling battery to the deck.

Up front, Andre was held at bay by the men at the Gatling gun. He tensed as Bronson approached. If he could spring on Bronson and wrestle the big man to the deck, the Gatling would not be able to fire for fear of hitting the Governor's nephew. But a red-faced Bronson seemed to have sensed Andre's thoughts and skirted the prisoners widely, his six-gun pointed at them.

Andre swallowed hard. Bronson, Andre was now certain, would not hesitate to shoot if he were attacked.

He caught Shorty's eyes and tried to tell him he would rush Bronson by moving his own eyes once to the Governor's nephew. Shorty nodded almost imperceptibly.

For the first time in his life, Hays wished he carried a six-gun. The sight of Bronson pole-axing one of Hays' men on the ladder to the pilothouse, combined with the knowledge that some of his railroaders were now prisoners, made L.J. angry enough to kill. Bronson, red-faced and nearly out of control, stepped to the rail and pointed a finger at Hays.

"You've got one minute to order your men to surrender, Hays! Then I'm gonna have your men gunned down!"

With that, Jake backed away and had the prisoners shoved up against the rail, facing Hays. He saw that one of them, Andre, almost fell on his face.

"You can't win, Jake!" Hays called out. "Give it up right now and I'll pull my men off the ship so you can sail back to Winnipeg. Nobody's been hurt yet—let's keep it that way."

As Hays talked, he could see the men at the *Manitoba*'s stern working on the bolts holding the Gatling to the floor. He prayed they would loosen the gun and drag it to midships, where it could be trained on Bronson. Hays did not even consider ordering his men to surrender, for he doubted they would, no matter what he said.

Bronson shook a fist at Hays. "You gonna surrender, Hays? Last chance!"

"Don't be a fool, Jake! They wouldn't give up even if I told them to."

"All right, you bastard!" Bronson roared. "I'll show you I'm not bluffing. Just keep your eyes on this!" He turned to his two men at the Gatling. "Shoot them!" he ordered. "Then turn the gun on him!" He pointed down at Hays.

"Don't do it, you men!" Hays yelled, moving out into the river. "You'll hang if you do what that madman tells you!"

The men at the Gatling were uncertain, first swinging the gun toward Hays as he stepped into the river, then back again toward the prisoners. But they didn't fire.

"Shoot, you dumb bastards!" screamed Bronson. "Kill them!"

But the gunners only looked more uncertain.

And now Bronson went completely berserk. He shoved his six-shooter into his belt and crossed in front of the Gatling to get in behind it.

Andre and Shorty sprang as Bronson passed in front of the Gatling. But Bronson moved too fast, and was at the trigger of the Gatling before either of the prisoners could reach him.

The Gatling sprayed a rain of lead from its six revolving muzzles. One by one, Andre, then Shorty, then the others fell dead as Jake Bronson screamed insults, triggering the gun.

Hays was mesmerized by the horror he was seeing. He did not move or utter a sound as Bronson swiveled the Gatling around to bring it to bear on him.

At that precise moment, the railroaders at the stern had finished ripping up the Gatling from its mountings and wheeled it forward. They had reached midships when they heard the prow gun chattering as it mowed down Andre, Shorty and the others.

A moment later, as Bronson leveled his weapon at Hays, the St. Paulers began firing.

Jake Bronson died quickly, but horribly—cut to pieces by the St. Paulers' Gatling. The sight of Shorty and the others lying in pools of blood on the *Manitoba*'s deck incited their compatriots to a frenzy, and they continued firing their Gatling until they'd cut down every man of Bronson's force who did not dive overboard and swim for the other side of the river.

Bronson's shots toward Hays had gone wild and did not touch him, though they did manage to make a few dents in the iron sides of the 4-4-0 locomotive not far away.

Phil Crabtree came up to lead Hays away from the scene, but L.J., almost in a trance, would not go until he'd boarded the ship and seen what he knew was there—eight dead St. Paulers, including Andre and Shorty. L.J. walked over to the rail and vomited into the Red River.

Just then a train full of St. Paul railroaders from the St. Paul-Minneapolis area—every employee Hays had—came into view of the railhead. Tim Wolfe rode in the cab of the locomotive with Engineer Casey Parks and a tied-up Ben Williams.

When he saw the eerie moonlit scene at the railhead, Tim's mouth dropped open and all he could do was stare. As the train approached the track-layers' engine at the end of the track, Tim could smell the gunpowder of the *Manitoba*'s Gatlings.

"My God!" he exclaimed as he saw the carnage on the ship's deck at his left. "What in heaven's name has happened?"

Again, Tim was too late to help. These men died because of him, he thought. He was left no choice: kill the Governor, then himself.

Just as he set the barrel of the rifle against Ben's temple, Parks yanked it from his hands. Tim fell to his knees, and wept.

# Chapter 16

Jay Calhoun managed to stall the Canadian Pacific track layers some fifteen miles north of the border by sidetracking a shipment of rails, as he had promised Ben Williams, but Hays drove his crew north and reached the CPRR railhead a day earlier than his deadline.

The race was over! The St. Paul & Winnipeg Railroad was complete to Winnipeg.

But Hays was understandably sober-faced as his construction crew returned to Pembina afterward. It should have been a happy moment, but it could not be. The only ceremonies which marked the completion of the rails to Winnipeg were memorial services for Andre Pelletier, Shorty, and the other track layers who had given their lives to help Hays finish the road. During the ceremonies, Hays stood beside little Danielle, who had taken her father's death so very hard.

On the night of the massacre, Hays had returned with Tim to the farm. There, L.J. told Danielle what had happened. He told the girl everything, sparing himself not at all, admitting:

"I'm afraid your papa may have died because of a mistake I made. A mistake in judgment." The more he tried to explain why he'd done what he had done, the more he found himself growing guilty. They both cried. When finally he left her alone, Danielle was still crying. An hour later, though, when she came out of the bedroom, her eyes were red and puffy, but dry. She walked straight across the room to where Hays sat on the settee and stood facing him. Danielle took a deep breath, then began talking slowly.

"I've thought about what you told me, Mr. Hays. And I think you're wrong about it being your fault that my papa was killed. You did what you had to—just as he did what he had to. Papa didn't have to try to get on board the boat the way he did, and that makes me proud. It was the bravest thing he ever did and if my mama were here, she'd be proud, too.

"I think you're brave, too, Mr. Hays, 'cause you didn't have to be by the river, right in front of those terrible guns, tryin' to help my papa and the others. You blame yourself for not telling the men to surrender, but I think you were brave to do that, too. You knew somebody might get hurt; they all did. So I'm proud of you, too.

"I'm sorry my papa's not here anymore, 'cause he wanted to be part of your company. He told me after you hired him that you were a darn good railroad man, who was gonna be a great one. That you'd build yourself a railroad empire second to nobody's—and he was gonna help you do it!

"I wish he'd had the chance, but I sure don't blame you for taking it away." The little girl threw her arms around L.J. and sobbed some more.

Hays found himself fighting tears again—and losing.

In the weeks that followed, L.J. sparked a drive to have Ben Williams tried on murder charges in connection with the massacre on the *Manitoba*, as well as to have him impeached as Governor. He failed on both counts, as it turned out.

Though public opinion was in back of Hays, the courts declined to indict Williams because of a lack of evidence tying him to the *Manitoba* piracy. The court's refusal and Williams' political friends influenced the legislature to decline to impeach.

Tim wanted to prosecute the Governor for attempted rape, but Rosie would not agree to it. "It's not worth it," she told Tim, "for I'd be hurting you and the children with all the publicity."

There was a terse scene when Hays returned from Canada by the first St. Paul Railroad train to make the complete trip to St. Paul. Elizabeth, having been besieged by reporters after reports of the *Manitoba* massacre, drifted back to St. Paul to meet her husband at the St. Paul station. She made a fuss over him as he stepped down the steps of the caboose—flying into his arms and hugging him and kissing him as if she were truly glad to see him.

"Oh, L.J.," she gushed, "I'm so glad you're all right! They said you were almost killed! Is that true?"

Hays had vowed he would not speak of Elizabeth's unfaithfulness and now his resolve was stretched to its limit. "It is, but as you can see, Elizabeth, I am alive and well enough. The same, however, cannot be said for eight of my men. Thanks to our unworthy Governor—Mr. Williams—they are dead. All of them."

L.J.'s cynical tone made Elizabeth pause. She wondered if he knew about her affair with Williams. She decided not to touch his remark. "Oh, that is dreadful! How could anyone do such a thing?" And she went on, talking about the children, the press, traveling, ignoring altogether his allusion to the Governor's participation in the affair.

That night when Elizabeth came to his rooms in their mansion, she wore a filmy nightgown that left little to the imagination. But Hays turned her away and continued to resist the urge to reprimand her for her infidelity.

One Monday morning in mid-July, a visitor dropped by the St. Paul Railroad office. Lucille Morgan could not have looked more appealing as she sat next to Hays, listening to the rueful story behind the headlines she had read. She was dressing more conservatively these days, L.J. noted, but her figure remained perfect, and her face pretty enough to grace the cover of *Harper's Bazaar*, which it had done on two separate occasions in the past five years.

Hays' beard and mustache were thick and well groomed now, but he remained young looking. As she sat across from him, Lucille thought him more handsome, more wise and of course infinitely more successful.

When L.J. ended his story, Lucille said, "And what of the little girl, L. Jerome? Sweet little Danielle? What has become of her?"

"I wanted to bring her to St. Paul and raise her as my own, but Elizabeth . . . Well, we couldn't agree that it was the best thing for her."

Lucille made a face. "So Elizabeth wouldn't agree to raise her?"

Hays shook his head. "It wasn't her fault, Lucille. At first I thought it a fine idea, but then, well, Elizabeth and I are not precisely perfectly matched and . . . I just decided it would not be good for Danielle to be raised under such unhappy circumstances."

"You left her with Rosie Wolfe, then."

Hays nodded. "I know Danielle and Rosie like each other. She'll be a good mother to Danielle."

"That's important. I was raised without either parent, so I can tell you how difficult it is."

"I was, too, Lucille."

There was a moment's silence, strange in its intensity. L.J. knew a great deal about Lucille, he realized. Her father had been drowned in a boating accident in Newport and Lucille's mother had failed utterly in her duties. To that mother, a child was nothing more than a bauble to be displayed for guests and then ushered into hiding. In time, Lucille's mother had been totally taken up in a love affair. The child became a hindrance. Surrounded by extravagance and wealth, given her choice of nannies and governesses to satisfy her every whim, the child Lucille had been utterly alone.

L.J. knew. All too well, feeling her arms around him, he had learned of the yearning disguised behind her lovely coolness. He had wanted to rush in and fill that hollow in her life and yet he had not. Why?

In the silence that pursued them still, he wondered. And with the question came the terrible insecurity, the ache of his own failure. That hollowness, that sheltered area of longing was not just hers. It was his, too. Private, gnawing, womanish, the need for love threatened him with its potential for destruction. Now there was no question in his mind. He knew why he had turned away from Lucille to the tangible problems of steamships and locomotives, to situations he could solve with his mind. The simple fact was he did not have the resources of that certain strength to satisfy what she most needed.

Would he ever? He wondered still.

"If there's anything I can do, Lucille," he began. "Anything at all..."

He stopped, suddenly embarrassed.

To his infinite relief, she met his offer with a beautiful smile. "You're the sweetest, L. Jerome. I mean it, not because of the nice things you say, but because it's true. You haven't a mean bone in your body. Now tell me, would you take me to Breckenridge to see Danielle?"

"Why?" Then Hays frowned. "You mean to... I don't think Rosie would give her up."

"Are you that smart or am I that transparent?" Lucille demanded. "Yes, I think I can offer the child something she cannot get from Rosie Wolfe—not that Rosie wouldn't raise her well. It's just that... Didn't you say that she has three children of her own already?"

Hays chuckled. "But that doesn't mean they wouldn't get plenty of love and affection, Lucille."

"Oh, hell, L. Jerome! I'm sure Rosie wouldn't neglect Danielle. It's just that... Well, I'm all alone now—a divorced lady with few prospects. I've always wanted a child of my own, and I'm well able to care for her, to teach her, and to give her everything her heart desires, especially love."

L.J. took Lucille to Breckenridge that very day, unable to refuse her request. But it took her a full year to first convince Rosie that Danielle would be better off with her, and then the Minnesota courts, who had jurisdiction over her, since she was an orphan.

As for Danielle, the little tyke took to Lucille as a duck takes to water. But she was devoted to Rosie and refused to leave her at first.

Yet she did, and on the fateful day that Lucille and Danielle were set to depart by steamer from St.

# Railroad King

Paul, their destination first New Orleans, then points north by railroad, L.J. thought the little girl would have a change of heart, and make things quite difficult. Danielle clutched Hays tightly as they said good-by on the dock. "I'll miss you, Mr. Hays," she sniffled. "Will you write to me and tell me how your railroad's doing? I'll want to know just everything."

"If you'll stop calling me Mister, Danielle. Call me L.J. or something."

"What's your first name. Let me call you that."

Hays groaned. "You wouldn't want to do that—it's a silly name."

"Tell me."

"Lynne," he managed to utter softly. "Now there are only two of you who know what it is—you and Miss Lucille."

"I like it. Can I call you Uncle Lynne?"

Strangely, though he hated the name, he didn't mind it when Danielle called him by it.

When Lucille and her new charge had departed, L.J. returned to huddle with Phil Crabtree in his office. The PNRR was heading for the Pacific and L.J. wanted to do likewise. The only thing was, he needed a survey of the route he had in mind—along the 32nd parallel. If Hays built there, he would be laying track in the northernmost, coldest, most desolate stretch in the country.

And, of course, as always he needed capital. Lucille had promised to invest with him and that was a help. But he needed more. With the Red River now safely under his control and the railroad beginning to show a profit, L.J. was sure he could find others willing to invest in it—if he could devise a sane route through the Dakota and Montana Territories.

What fate would hold in store for Hays was a

slow and trouble-filled undertaking. There would be Indian trouble in the Black Hills of Dakota. A flock of settlers had invaded the territory in the wake of Custer's 1874 discovery of gold. And they would have to contend with Williams, who still controlled the Pacific Northern. But they would do it, for it was part of Hays' destiny.

On the day that Lucille Morgan and her charge Danielle arrived in New Orleans, L.J., Phil and a party of six surveyors headed by the brilliant Easterner Oscar Goodenough, left Crookston, crossed the Red River and headed west. Hays charged Goodenough to find the "straightest route, with the fewest grades and curves through the Rockies."

It would be a perilous journey indeed.

# AMERICAN EXPLORERS #2

They faced 900 miles of savage wilderness
where a young man chose between fortune and love.

## LEWIS & CLARK
# NORTHWEST GLORY

Set in the turbulent 1800s, this is the story of the Lewis and Clark expedition — and of the brave men and women who faced brutal hardship and fierce tests of will. They encountered an untamed wilderness, its savage mountain men, merciless fortune seekers and fiery Indian warriors. In the midst of this hostile land, two lovers are united in their undying passion. A truly incredible tale of love and adventure.

---

Please send me _____ copies of the second book in the AMERICAN EXPLORER series, *Lewis & Clark: NORTHWEST GLORY*. I am enclosing $3.00 per copy (includes 25¢ to cover postage and handling).

Please send check or money order (no cash or C.O.D.'s).

Name (please print) _____

Address _____ Apt. _____

City _____

State _____ Zip _____

*Send this coupon to:*
**MILES STANDISH PRESS**
37 West Avenue, Suite 305, Wayne, PA 19087
Please allow 6-8 weeks for delivery.
PA residents add 6% sales tax.

WR1